Lone Star Winter

Also by Diana Palmer

Dangerous
Heartless
Fearless
Her Kind of Hero
Nora
Big Sky Winter
Man of the Hour
Trilby
Lawman
Lacy
Hard to Handle
Heart of Winter
Outsider
Night Fever
Before Sunrise
Noelle
Lawless
Diamond Spur
The Texas Ranger
Lord of the Desert
The Cowboy and the Lady
Most Wanted
Fit for a King
Paper Rose
Rage of Passion
Once in Paris
After the Music
Roomful of Roses
Champagne Girl
Passion Flower
Diamond Girl
Friends and Lovers
Cattleman's Choice
Lady Love
The Rawhide Man

DIANA PALMER

Lone Star Winter

HQN™

HQN™

Recycling programs
for this product may
not exist in your area.

ISBN-13: 978-0-373-77496-8

LONE STAR WINTER

www.HQNBooks.com

Printed in U.S.A.

CONTENTS

THE WINTER SOLDIER

For J. Nelson

It was Monday, the worst day in the world to try to get a prescription filled. Behind the counter, the poor harassed male druggist was trying to field the telephone calls, fill prescriptions, answer questions from patrons and delegate duties to two assistants. It was always like this after the weekend, Cy Parks thought with resignation. Nobody wanted to bother the doctor on his days off, so they all waited until Monday to present their various complaints. Hence the rush on the Jacobsville Pharmacy. Michael, the pharmacist on duty, was smiling pleasantly despite the crush of customers, accustomed to the Monday madness.

That group putting off a visit to the doctor until

Monday included himself, Cy mused. His arm was throbbing from an encounter with one of his angry Santa Gertrudis bulls late on Friday afternoon. It was his left arm, too, the one that had been burned in the house fire back in Wyoming. The angry rip needed ten stitches, and Dr. "Copper" Coltrain had been irritated that Cy hadn't gone to the emergency room instead of letting it wait two days and risking gangrene. The sarcasm just washed right off; Coltrain could have saved his breath. Over the years, there had been so many wounds that Cy hardly felt pain anymore. With his shirt off, those wounds had been apparent to Coltrain, who wondered aloud where so many bullet wounds came from. Cy had simply looked at him, with those deep green eyes that could be as cold as Arctic air. Coltrain had given up.

Stitches in place, Coltrain had scribbled a prescription for a strong antibiotic and a painkiller and sent him on his way. Cy had given the prescription to the clerk ten minutes ago. He glanced around him at the prescription counter and thought he probably should have packed lunch and brought it with him.

He shifted from one booted foot to the other with noticeable impatience, his glittery green eyes sweeping the customers nearest the counter. They settled on a serene blond-haired woman studying him with evident amusement. He knew her. Most people in Jacobsville, Texas, did. She was Lisa Taylor Monroe. Her husband, Walt Monroe, an undercover narcotics officer with a federal agency, had recently been killed. He'd borrowed on his insurance policy, so there had been just enough money to bury him. At least Lisa had her small ranch, a legacy from her late father.

Cy's keen eyes studied her openly. She was sweet, but she'd never win any beauty contests. Her dark blond hair was always in a bun and she never put on makeup. She wore glasses over her brown eyes, plastic-framed ones, and her usual garb was jeans and a T-shirt when she was working around the ranch. Walt Monroe had loved the ranch, and during his infrequent visits home, he'd set out improving it. His ambitions had all but bankrupted it, so that Lisa was left after his death with a small savings account that probably wouldn't even pay the interest on the loans Walt had obtained.

Cy knew something about Lisa Monroe because she was his closest neighbor, along with Luke Craig, a rancher who was recently married to a public defender named Belinda Jessup. Mrs. Monroe there liked Charolais, he recalled. He wasn't any too fond of foreign cattle, having a purebred herd of Santa Gertrudis cattle, breeding bulls, which made him a profitable living. Almost as prosperous as his former sideline, he mused.

A good champion bull could pull upward of a million dollars on the market.

Lisa had no such livestock. Her Charolais cattle were steers, beef stock. She sold off her steer crop every fall, but it wouldn't do her much good now. She was too deeply in debt. Like most other people, he felt sorry for her. It was common gossip that she was pregnant, because in a small town like Jacobsville, everybody knew everything. She didn't look pregnant, but he'd overheard someone say that they could tell in days now, rather than the weeks such tests had once required. She must be just barely pregnant, he mused, because those tight jeans outlined a flat stomach and a figure that most women would covet.

But her situation was precarious. Pregnant, widowed and deeply in debt, she was likely to find herself homeless before much longer, when the bank was forced to foreclose on the property. Damned shame, he thought, when it had such potential for development.

She was clutching a boxed heating pad to her chest, waiting her turn in line at the second cash register at the pharmacy counter.

When Lisa was finally at the head of the line, she put down her heating pad on the counter and opened her purse.

"Another one, Lisa?" the young female clerk asked her with an odd smile.

She gave the other woman an irritated glance as she dug in her purse for her checkbook. "Don't you start, Bonnie," she muttered.

"How can I help it?" the clerk chuckled. "That's the third one this month. In fact, that's the last one we have in stock."

"I know that. You'd better order some more."

"You really need to do something about that dog," Bonnie suggested firmly.

"Hear, hear!" the other clerk, Joanne, seconded, peering at Lisa over her glasses.

"The puppy takes after his father," Lisa said defensively. He did, she mused. His father belonged to Tom Walker, and the mostly German shepherd dog, Moose, was a local legend. This pup was from the first litter he'd sired—without Tom's knowledge or permission. "But he's going to be a lot of protection, so I guess it's a trade-off. How much is this?"

Bonnie told her, waited while she wrote the check, accepted it and processed it. "Here you go," she told the customer. She glanced down at the other woman's flat stomach. "When are you due?"

"Eight months and two weeks," Lisa said quietly, wincing as she recalled that her husband, away from home and working undercover, had been killed the very night after she'd conceived, if Dr. Lou Coltrain had his numbers right. And when had Lou ever missed a due date? He was uncanny at predicting births.

"You've got that Mason man helping you with the ranch." Bonnie interrupted her thoughts. "You shouldn't need a dog with him there. Can't he protect you?"

"He only comes on the weekends," Lisa replied.

Bonnie frowned. "Luke Craig sent him out there, didn't he? But he said the man was supposed to spend every night in the bunkhouse!"

"He visits his girlfriend most nights," Lisa said irritably. "And better her than me! He doesn't bathe!"

Bonnie burst out laughing. "Well, there's one bright side to it. If he isn't staying nights, you only have to pay him for the weekends...Lisa," she added when she saw the guilty expression on the other woman's face, "you aren't still paying him for the whole week?"

Lisa flushed. "Don't," she said huskily.

"Sorry." Bonnie handed her a receipt. "It's just I hate the way you let people take advantage of you, that's all. There are so many rotten people in the world, and you're a walking, talking benevolence society."

"Rotten people aren't born, they're made," Lisa told her. "He isn't a bad man, he just didn't have a proper upbringing."

"Oh, good God!" Cy said harshly, glaring at her, having kept his mouth shut as long as possible without imploding. The woman's compassion hit him on a raw spot and made him furious.

Lisa's eyes were brown, big and wide and soft through the plastic frames of her glasses. "Excuse me?"

"Are you for real?" he asked curtly. "Listen, people dig their own graves and they climb into them. Nothing excuses cruelty."

"You tell her!" Bonnie said, agreeing.

Lisa recognized her taciturn neighbor from a previous encounter, long ago. He'd come right up to her when she'd been pitching hay over the fence to her cattle one day and told her outright that she should leave heavy work to her husband. Walt hadn't liked that comment, not at all. It had only been a few days after he'd let her do the same thing while he flirted with a pretty blond parcel delivery employee. Worse, Walt thought that Lisa had encouraged Cy's interference somehow and they'd had a fight—not the first in their very brief marriage. She didn't like the tall man and her expression told him so. "I wasn't talking to you," she pointed out. "You don't know anything about my business."

His eyebrows rose half an inch. "I know that you overpay the hired help." He looked pointedly at her flat belly. "And that you're the last person who should be looked upon as a walking benevolence society."

"Hear, hear!" Joanne said again from behind Bonnie.

Lisa glared at her. "You can be quiet," she said.

"Let your erstwhile employee go," he told her. "I'll send one of my men over to spend nights in the bunkhouse. Bonnie's right about one thing, you don't need to be by yourself after dark in such a remote place."

"I don't need your help," she said, glowering at him.

"Yes, you do. Your husband wouldn't have liked having you try to run that ranch alone," he added quietly, even though he didn't mean it, and he hoped that his distaste for the late Walt Monroe didn't show. He still recalled watching Lisa heft a huge bale of hay while her husband stood not ten paces away flirting with a pretty blond woman. It was a miracle she hadn't miscarried, the way she hefted heavy things around. He wondered if she even knew the chance she was taking…

She was looking at him with different eyes now. The concern touched her despite her hostility. She sighed. "I guess you're right," she said softly. "He wouldn't have."

He hated the way that softness made him feel. He'd lost so much. Everything. He wouldn't admit, even to himself, how it felt to have those dark eyes look at him with tenderness. He swallowed down the ache in his throat.

She let her gaze fall to his arm, the one that had just been stitched, and her soft gasp was audible. "You've been hurt!"

"Two prescriptions, Mr. Parks," Bonnie said with a grin, holding up a prescription sack. She bent to pick up the package, a strand of her short blond hair falling around her pretty bespectacled face. "And Dr. Coltrain said that if you don't take this pain medication, he'll have me flogged," she added impishly.

"We can't have that, I guess," Cy murmured dryly.

"Glad you agree." She accepted his credit card as Lisa turned to go.

"You drive into town?" Cy asked the widow.

"Uh, well, no, the car's got a broken water pump," she confessed. "I rode in with old Mr. Murdock."

"He'll be at the lodge meeting until midnight," he pointed out.

"Just until nine. I thought I'd go to the library and wait."

"You need your rest," Cy said curtly. "No sense in waiting until bedtime for a ride. I'll drive you home. It's on my way."

"Go with him," Bonnie said firmly as she waited for

Cy to put his credit card back into his wallet and sign the ticket. "Don't argue," she added when Lisa opened her mouth. "I'll phone the lodge and tell Mr. Murdock you got a ride."

"Were you ever in the army?" Cy asked the young woman with a rare twinkle in his green eyes.

She grinned. "Nope. But it's their loss."

"Amen," he said.

"Mr. Parks…" Lisa began, trying to escape.

Cy took her arm, nodded to Bonnie and herded Lisa out of the pharmacy onto the street where his big red Ford Expedition was parked. On the way they ran into the second pharmacist, a dark-eyed woman with equally dark hair.

"Hi, Nancy!" Lisa said with a grin.

Nancy gave a gamine smile. "Don't tell me, the line's two miles long already."

"Three. Want to go home with me?" Lisa asked.

Nancy sighed. "Don't I wish. See you!"

Nancy went on toward the pharmacy and Lisa turned back to let Cy open the door of the Expedition for her. "Imagine you with a red vehicle," she said dryly. "I would have expected black."

"It was the only one they had in stock and I was in a hurry. Here." He helped her up into the huge vehicle.

"Gosh," she murmured as he got in beside her, "you could kill an elephant with this thing."

"It's out of season for elephants." He scowled as she fumbled with the seat belt. "That's hard to buckle on the passenger side. Here, like this…" He leaned close to her and fastened it with finesse despite his damaged left hand and arm. It required a closeness he hadn't had with a woman since his wife and son died in the fire. He noticed that Lisa's eyes were a very soft dark brown and that her complexion was delicious. She had a firm, rounded little chin and a pretty mouth. Her ears were tiny. He wondered what that mass of dark gold hair looked like at night when she took the hairpins out, and his own curiosity made him angry. With compressed lips, he fastened the seat belt and moved away to buckle his own in place.

Lisa was relieved when he leaned back. He made her nervous when he was that close. Odd, that reaction, she thought, when she'd been married for two months. She should be used to men. Of course, her late husband hadn't been that interested in her body. He didn't seem to enjoy sleeping with her, and he was always in such a rush that she really didn't feel any of the things women were supposed to feel. She recalled that he'd married her on the rebound from the woman he really wanted, and the only thing about Lisa that really appealed to him had been her father's ranch. He'd had great ideas about starting an empire, but it was only a pipe dream. A dead dream, now. She stared out at the small town as they drove through it on the way out to their respective ranches.

"Do you have anyone managing the ranch for you?" he asked when they were on the lonely highway heading out of town.

"Can't afford anyone," she said wistfully. "Walt had big plans for the place, but there was never enough money to fulfill them. He borrowed on his salary and his life insurance policy to buy the steers, but he didn't look far enough ahead to see the drought coming. I guess he didn't realize that buying winter feed for those steers would put us in the hole." She shook her head. "I did so want his plans to work out," she said wistfully. "If they had, he was going to give up undercover work and come home to be a rancher." Her eyes were sad. "He was only thirty years old."

"Manuel Lopez is a vindictive drug lord," he murmured. "He doesn't stop at his victims, either. He likes to target whole families. Well, except for small children. If he has a virtue, that's the only one." He glanced at her. "All the more reason for you to be looked after at night. The dog is a good idea. Even a puppy will bark when someone comes up to the door."

"How do you know about Lopez?" she asked.

He laughed. It was the coldest sound Lisa had ever heard. "How do I know? He had his thugs set fire to my house in Wyoming. My wife and my five-year-old son died because of him." His eyes stared straight ahead. "And if it's the last thing I ever do, I'll see him pay for it."

"I had…no idea," she faltered. She winced at the look on his face. "I'm very sorry, Mr. Parks. I knew about the fire, but…" She averted her eyes to the dark landscape outside. "They told me that Walt only said two words before he died. He said, 'Get Lopez.' They will, you know," she added harshly. "They'll get him, no matter what it takes."

He glanced at her and smiled in spite of himself. "You're not quite the retiring miss that you seem to be, are you, Mrs. Monroe?"

"I'm pregnant," she told him flatly. "It makes me ill-tempered."

He slowed to make a turn. "Did you want a child so soon after your marriage?" he asked, knowing as everyone locally did that she'd only married two months ago.

"I love children," she said, smiling self-consciously. "I guess it's not the 'in' thing right now, but I've never had dreams of corporate leadership. I like the pace of life here in Jacobsville. Everybody knows everybody. There's precious little crime usually. I can trace my family back three generations here. My parents and my grandparents are buried in the town cemetery. I loved being a housewife, taking care of Walt and cooking and all the domestic things women aren't supposed to enjoy anymore." She glanced at him with a wicked little smile. "I was even a virgin when I married. When I rebel, I go the whole way!"

He chuckled. It was the first time in years that he'd felt like laughing. "You renegade."

"It runs in my family," she laughed. "Where are you from?"

He shifted uncomfortably. "Texas."

"But you lived in Wyoming," she pointed out.

"Because I thought it was the one place Lopez wouldn't bother me. What a fool I was," he added quietly. "If I'd come here in the first place, it might never have happened."

"Our police are good, but…"

He glanced at her. "Don't you know what I am? What I was?" he amended. "Eb Scott's whole career was in the Houston papers just after he sent two of Lopez's best men to prison for attempted murder. They mentioned that several of his old comrades live in Jacobsville now."

"I read the papers," she confessed. "But they didn't mention names, you know."

"Didn't they?" He maneuvered a turn at a stop sign. "Eb must have called in a marker, then."

She turned slightly toward him. "What were you?"

He didn't even glance at her. "If the papers didn't mention it, I won't."

"Were you one of those old comrades?" she persisted.

He hesitated, but only for a moment. She wasn't a gossip. There was no good reason for not telling her. "Yes," he said bluntly. "I was a mercenary. A professional soldier for hire to the highest bidder," he added bitterly.

"But with principles, right?" she persisted. "I mean, you didn't hire out to Lopez and help him run drugs."

"Certainly not!"

"I didn't think so." She leaned back against her seat, weary. "It must take a lot of courage to do that sort of work. I suppose it takes a certain kind of man, as well. But why did you do it when you had a wife and child?"

He hated that damned question. He hated the answer, too.

"Well?"

She wasn't going to quit until he told her. His hands tightened on the steering wheel. "Because I refused to give it up, and she got pregnant deliberately to get even with me." He didn't stop to think about the odd way he'd worded that, but Lisa noticed and wondered at it. "I curtailed my work, but I helped get the goods on Lopez before I hung it up entirely and started ranching full-time. I'd just come back from overseas when the fire was set. It was obvious afterward that I'd been careless and let one of Lopez's men track me back to Wyoming. I've had to live with it ever since."

She studied his lean, stark profile with quiet, curious eyes. "Was it the adrenaline rush you couldn't live without, or was it the confinement of marriage that you couldn't live with?"

His green eyes glittered dangerously. "You ask too damned many questions!"

She shrugged. "You started it. I had no idea that you were anything more than a rancher. Your foreman, Harley Fowler, likes to tell people that he's one of those dashing professional soldiers, you know. But he isn't."

The statement surprised him. "How do you know he isn't?" he asked.

"Because I asked him if he'd ever done the Fan Dance and he didn't know what I was talking about."

He stopped the truck in the middle of the road and just stared at her. "Who told you about that? Your husband?"

"He knew about the British Special Air Services, but mostly just what I told him—including that bit about the Fan Dance, one of their rigorous training tests." She smiled self-consciously. "I guess it sounds strange, but I love reading books about them. They're really something, like the French Foreign Legion, you know. A group of men so highly trained, so specialized, that they're the scourge of terrorists the world over. They go everywhere, covertly, to rescue hostages and gather intelligence about terrorist groups." She sighed and closed her eyes, oblivious to the expression of the man watching her. "I'd be scared to death to do anything like that, but I admire people who can. It's a way of testing yourself, isn't it, so that you know how you react under the most deadly pressure. Most of us never face physical violence. Those men have." Her eyes opened. "Men like you."

He felt his cheeks go hot. She was intriguing. He began to understand why Walt had married her. "How old are you?" he asked bluntly.

"Old enough to get pregnant," she told him pertly. "And that's all you're getting out of me."

His green eyes narrowed. She was very young, there

was no doubt about that. He didn't like the idea of her being in danger. He didn't like the idea of the man Luke Craig had sent over to look out for her, either. He was going to see about that.

"How old are you, if we're getting personal?" she asked.

"Older than you are," he returned mockingly.

She grimaced. "Well, you've got scars and lines in your face, and a little gray at your temples, but I doubt you're over thirty-five."

His eyebrows arched almost to his hairline.

"I'd like you to be my baby's godfather when he's born," she continued bluntly. "I think Walt would have liked that, too. He spoke very highly of you, although he didn't say much about your background. I was curious about that. Now I understand why he was so secretive."

"I've never been a godfather," he said curtly.

"That's okay. I've never been a mother." She frowned. "Come to think of it, the baby hasn't been a baby before, either." She looked down at her flat belly and smiled tenderly, tracing it. "We can all start even."

"Did you love your husband?"

She looked up at him. "Did you love your wife?" she countered instantly.

He didn't like looking at her belly, remembering.

He started down the road again, at a greater speed. "She said she loved me, when we married," he said evasively.

Poor woman, Lisa thought. And poor little boy, to die so young, and in such a horrible way. She wondered if the taciturn Mr. Parks had nightmares, and guessed that he did. His poor arm was proof that he'd tried to save his family. It must be terrible, to go on living, to be the only survivor of such a tragedy.

They pulled up in front of her dilapidated ranch house. The steps were flimsy and one of the boards was rotten. The house needed painting. The screens on the windows were torn, and the one on the screen door was half torn away. In the corral, he could hear a horse whinny. He hoped her fences were in better shape than the house.

He helped her down out of the truck and set her gently on her feet. She was rail-thin.

"Are you eating properly?" he asked abruptly as he studied her in the faint light from the porch, scowling.

"I said you could be the baby's godfather, not mine," she pointed out with an impish smile. "Thank you very much for the ride. Now go home, Mr. Parks."

"Don't I get to see this famous puppy?"

She grimaced as she walked gingerly up the steps,

past the rotten one, and put her key in the lock. "He stays on the screen porch out back, and even with papers down, I expect he's made a frightful mess… That's odd," she said when the door swung open without the key being turned in the lock. "I'm sure I locked this door before I… Where are you going?"

"Stay right there," he said shortly. He opened the truck, took out the .45 automatic he always carried and cocked it on his way back onto the porch.

Her face went pale. Reading about commandos was very different from the real thing when she saw the cold metal of the pistol in his hands and realized that he was probably quite proficient in its use. The thought chilled her. Like the sight of the gun.

He put her gently to one side. "I'm not going to shoot anybody unless I get shot at," he said reassuringly. "Stay there."

He left her on the porch and went carefully, quietly, through the house with the pistol raised at his ear, one finger on the trigger and his other hand, in spite of its injury, supporting the butt efficiently. He swept the house, room by room, closet by closet, until he got to the bedroom and heard a sound inside. It was only a sound, a faint whisper. There was a hint of light coming from under the door, which was just slightly ajar.

He kicked the door open, the pistol leveled the second he had a clear view of the bed.

The man's face was a study in shock when he saw the expression on Cy Parks's dark face and the glitter in his eyes. Bill Mason, Luke Craig's erstwhile cowboy-on-loan, was lying on the bed in his shorts with a beer bottle in one hand. When Cy burst in the door, he sat up starkly, his bloodshot eyes blinking as he swayed. He was just drunk enough not to realize how much trouble he was in.

"You're not Mrs. Monroe," he drawled loudly.

"And you're not Mr. Monroe. If you want to see daylight again, get the hell out of that bed and put your clothes on!"

"Okay. I mean yes, sir, Mr. Parks!"

The man tripped and fell, the beer bottle shattering on the floor as he sprawled nearby. "I broked it," he moaned as he dragged himself up holding on to the bedpost, "and it was my...my last one!"

"God help us! Hurry up!"

"Okay. Just let me find...my pants..." He hiccuped, tripped again and fell, moaning. "They must be here somewhere!"

Muttering darkly, Cy uncocked the pistol, put the safety on, and stuck it into the belt at his back. He went to find Lisa, who was standing impatiently on the porch.

"I saved you a shock," he told her.

"How big a shock?"

"The great unwashed would-be lover who was waiting for you, in your bed," he said, trying not to grin. It wasn't really funny.

"Oh, for heaven's sake, not again," she groaned.

"Again?"

She was made very uncomfortable by the look on his face. "Don't even think it!" she threatened angrily. "I'm not that desperate for a man, thank you very much. He gets drunk one night a week and sleeps it off in Walt's bed," she muttered, oblivious to both her phrasing and his surprised look. "I lock him in, so he can't cause me any trouble, and I let him out the next morning. He's got a drinking problem, but he won't get help."

"Does Luke Craig know that?"

"If he did, he'd fire him, and the poor man has no place to go," she began.

"He'll have a place to go tomorrow," he promised her with barely contained fury. "Why didn't you say something?"

"I didn't know you," she pointed out. "And Luke meant it as a kind gesture."

"Luke would eat him with barbecue sauce if he knew what he was doing over here!"

There was a muffled thud and then the tipsy man weaved toward the front door. "So sorry, Mrs. Monroe," Mason drawled, sweeping off his hat and almost going down with it as he bowed. "Very sorry. I'll be off, now." He hesitated at the top step with one foot in the air. "Where's my horse?" he asked blankly. "I left him out here somewhere."

"I'll send him to you. Go back to Craig's ranch."

"It's two miles!" the cowboy wailed. "I'll never make it!"

"Yes, you will. Get in the truck. And if you throw up in it, I'll shoot you!" Cy promised.

The cowboy didn't even question the threat. He tried to salute and almost fell down again. "Yes, sir, I'll get… get right in the truck, yes, sir, right now!"

He weaved to the passenger side, opened the door and pulled himself in, slamming the door behind him.

"I'd sleep on the sofa," Cy advised Lisa. "Until you can wash the sheets, at least."

"His girlfriend must be nuts. No woman in her right mind would sleep with him," she murmured darkly.

"I can see why. I'll send a man over to the bunkhouse. And he won't get drunk and wait for you in bed," he added.

She chuckled. "That would be appreciated." She hesitated. "Thanks for the ride home, Mr. Parks."

He hesitated, his narrow green eyes appraising her. She'd taken her husband's death pretty hard, and she had dark circles under those eyes. He hated leaving her alone. He had protective feelings for her that really disturbed him.

"I'll want to meet that pup when I come back again."

She managed a smile. "Okay."

"Go in and lock the door," he instructed.

She clutched her heating pad and her purse to her chest and glared at him, but he stared her down. *Oh, well,* she thought as she went inside, *some men just didn't know the meaning of diplomacy.* She'd have to make allowances for that little character flaw.

He waited until she got inside and locked the door before he climbed into his truck. He wondered why she'd said Walt's bed and not *their* bed. The question diverted him as he drove the intoxicated but quiet cowboy over to Luke Craig's house and showed him to Luke. The blond rancher cursed roundly, having closed the door so that his new wife, Belinda, wouldn't overhear.

"I'm very drunk," the cowboy said with a lopsided grin, swaying on the porch.

"He was stripped to his shorts, waiting for Lisa in her bed," Cy said, and he didn't grin. "I don't want this man sent over there again."

"He won't be. Good God, he's hidden it well, hasn't he?"

"I'm very drunk," the cowboy repeated, and the grin widened.

"Shut up," Cy told him. He turned back to Luke. "I'm sending one of my own men over to sleep in the bunkhouse. Can you handle him?"

"I'm *veerrryy* drunk," the cowboy interjected.

"Shut up!" chorused the two men.

Belinda Jessup Craig opened the front door and peered out at the tableau. "He's very drunk," she pointed out, and wondered why they looked so belligerent. "You'd better bring him inside, Luke. We can sober him up in the kitchen. You can't leave him stumbling around like that. I'll phone the Master's Inn and see if they've got room for him." She glanced at Cy's puzzled expression. "It's a halfway house for alcoholics. They offer treatment and continued support."

"She wants to save the world," Luke muttered, but he grinned at her.

"And he wants to control it," she shot back with a wink. "Care to come in for coffee, Mr. Parks?"

"No, thanks," he replied. "I have to get home."

"I'm sorry about the trouble," Luke said.

"Your heart was in the right place. She's special," he added in spite of himself.

Luke smiled slowly. "Yes. She is."

Cy cleared his throat. "Good night."

"Good night," Luke answered.

"Good night!" the cowboy echoed before Luke propelled him firmly into the house.

Chapter Two

Cy took his medicine and had the first good night's sleep he'd enjoyed in days. He'd sent a capable, older cowboy over to Lisa's ranch the night before to sleep in the bunkhouse and keep an eye on things. He'd also arranged covertly for sensitive listening equipment to be placed around her house, and for a man to monitor it full-time. He might be overly cautious, but he wasn't taking chances with a pregnant woman. He knew Manuel Lopez's thirst for revenge far too well. The drug lord had a nasty habit of targeting the families of people who opposed him. And Lopez might not know Lisa was pregnant. Cy wasn't willing to risk leaving Lisa out there alone.

The next day he drove over to Lisa's house and found her struggling with a cow in the barn, trying to pull a calf by hand. He couldn't believe she was actually doing that!

He'd barely turned off the engine before he was out of the big sports utility vehicle and towering over her in the barn. She looked up with a grimace on her face when she realized what a temper he was in.

"Don't you say a word, Cy Parks," she told him at once, wiping the sweat from her forehead. "There's nobody but me to do this, and the cow can't wait until one of my part-timers comes in from the lower pasture. They're dipping cattle..."

"So you're trying to do a job that you aren't half big enough to manage. Are you out of your mind?" he burst out. "You're pregnant, for God's sake!"

She was panting, sprawled between the cow's legs. She glared up at him and blew a stray strand of hair out of her eyes. "Listen, I can't afford to lose the cow or the calf..."

"Get up!" he said harshly.

She glared at him.

For all his raging temper, he reached down and lifted her tenderly to her feet, putting her firmly to one side. He got down on one knee beside the cow and looked at the situation grimly. "Have you got a calf-pull?"

She ground her teeth together. "No. It broke and I didn't know how to fix it."

He said a few words under his breath and went out to his truck, using the radio to call for help. Fortunately one of his men was barely two minutes away. Harley, his foreman, came roaring up beside Cy's truck, braked and jumped out with a length of rope.

"Good man, Harley," Cy said as he looped the rope around the calf's feet. "If we can't get him out ourselves, we can use the winch on my truck. Ready? Pull!"

They were bathed in sweat and cursing when they managed to get the calf halfway out.

"He's still alive," Cy said, grinning. "Okay, let's go again. Pull!"

Three more firm tugs and the calf slipped out. Cy cleared his nose and mouth and the little black-baldy bawled. The cow turned, gently licking away the slick birth membranes covering her calf.

"That was a near miss," Harley observed, grinning.

"Very near." Cy glowered at Lisa. "In more ways than one."

"Excuse me?" Harley asked.

"It was my cow," Lisa pointed out. "I thought I could do it by myself."

"Pregnant, and you think you're Samson," he said with biting sarcasm.

She put her hands on her hips and glared up at him. "Go away!"

"Gladly. When I've washed my hands."

"There's a pump over here," Harley reminded him, indicating it.

"You go ahead, son," Cy muttered, glancing at his stitched arm. "I've got a raw wound. I'll have to have antibacterial soap."

Harley didn't say anything, but his face was expressive. He thought his poor old crippled boss was a real basket case, barely fit to do most ranch work.

"Antibacterial soap, indeed. The germs would probably die of natural causes if they got in you!" Lisa muttered.

"At least my germs are intelligent! I wouldn't try pulling calves if I was pregnant!"

Lisa almost doubled over at the thought of a pregnant Cy Parks, which only served to make him angrier.

"I'll get back to your place and start the men culling cattle for the next sale, boss man. I can wash up there!" Harley called, and didn't wait for an answer. The amused expression on his face was eloquent—he wanted to get out of the line of fire!

"Craven coward," she muttered, staring after the

cloud of dust he and the truck vanished in. "Are all your men like that?"

He followed her into the kitchen. "He's not afraid of me," he said irritably. "He thinks I'm pitiable. In fact, he has delusions that he's soldier of fortune material since he spent two weeks having intense combat training with a weekend merk training school," he added with pure sarcasm. "Have you got a hand towel?"

She pulled one from a drawer while he lathered his arms, wincing a little as the water and soap stung the stitches.

"You don't want to get that infected," she said, studying the wound as she stood beside him with the towel.

"Thanks for the first-aid tip," he said with failing patience. "That's why I asked for antibacterial soap!" He took the towel she offered, but his eyes were on her flat belly even as he dried away the wetness. "You take chances," he said shortly. "Dangerous chances. A lot of women miscarry in the first trimester, even without doing stupid things like heavy lifting and trying to pull calves. You need to think before you act."

She studied his quiet, haunted face. Discussing pregnancy didn't seem to make him feel inhibited at all. "You must have been good to your wife while she was pregnant," she said gently.

"I wanted the baby," he replied. His face hardened. "She didn't. She didn't want a child until she was in her thirties, if then. But I wouldn't hear of her terminating the pregnancy," he added, and there was an odd, pained look in his eyes for an instant. "So she had the child, only to lose him in a much more horrible way. But despite everything, I wanted him from the time I knew he was on the way."

She felt his pain as if it were tangible. "I won't have anyone to share this with," she said, her voice husky with remembered loss and pain. "I was over the moon when they did the blood test and said I was pregnant. Walt wouldn't even talk about having children. He died the night after I conceived, but even if he'd lived long enough to know about the baby, he would have said it was too soon." She shrugged. "I guess it was."

She'd never told that to another soul. It embarrassed her that it had slipped out, but Cy seemed unshockable.

"Some men don't adjust well to children," he said simply. It went without saying that he wasn't one of them. He didn't know what else to say. He felt sorry for her. She obviously took pleasure in her pregnancy, and it was equally obvious that she loved children. He sat down at the table with her. Maybe she needed to get it out of her system. Evidently she could tell him things that she couldn't tell anyone else.

"Go on," he coaxed. "Get everything off your chest. I'm a clam. I don't tell anything I know, and I'm not judgmental."

"I think I sensed that." She sighed. "Want some coffee? I have to drink decaf, but I could make some."

"I hate decaf, but I'll drink it."

She smiled. She got up and filled the pot and the filter and started the coffeemaker while she got down white mugs. She glanced at him with pursed lips. "Black," she guessed.

He gave her an annoyed look. "Don't get conceited because you know how I take my coffee."

"I won't."

She poured the coffee into the cups and sat back down, watching as he cupped his left hand around it. "Does it still hurt?" she asked, referring to the burns on his hand.

"Not as much as it used to," he said flatly.

"You don't have anyone to talk to, either, do you?"

He shook his head. "I'm not much for bars, and the only friend I have is Eb. Now that he's married, we don't spend a lot of time together."

"It's worse when you hold things inside," she murmured absently, staring into her coffee. "Everybody thinks I had a fairy-tale marriage with a sexy man who loved danger and could have had any woman he wanted." She smiled wryly. "At first I thought so, too. He seemed like a dream come true. Boy, did my illusions leave skid marks taking off!"

"So did mine," he said flatly.

She leaned forward, feeling daring. "Yes, but I'll bet *you* weren't a virgin who thought people did it in the dark fully clothed!"

He burst out laughing. He hadn't felt like laughing since…he couldn't remember. Her eyes bubbled with joy; her laugh was infectious. She made him hungry, thirsty, desperate for the delight she engendered.

She grinned. "There. You look much less intimidating when you smile. And before you regret telling me secrets, I'd better mention that I've never told anybody what my best friend did on our senior trip to Florida. And I won't tell you now."

"Was it scandalous?"

"It was for Jacobsville." She chuckled.

"Didn't you do anything scandalous?"

"Not me," she popped back. "I'm the soul of propriety. My dad used to say that I was the suffering conscience of the world." Her eyes darkened. "He died of a stroke while he was using the tiller out in the garden. When he didn't come in for lunch, I knew something was wrong. I went out to find him." She moved her coffee cup on the table. "He was sitting against a tree with his thermos jug of coffee still in his hands, his eyes wide-open, stone dead." She shivered. "Mom had died when I was in sixth grade, of cancer. Dad loved her so much. He loved me, too." She lifted her sad eyes. "I suppose I'd rather have had him for a short time than not to have had him at all. Walter felt sorry for me and asked me to marry him, because I was so alone. He'd just lost the woman he loved and I think he wanted to marry me just to spite her. The ranch was a bonus. I was really infatuated with him at first, and he liked me and loved this ranch. I figured we had as good a chance of making a marriage work as people who were passionately in love." She sighed again. "Isn't hindsight wonderful?"

He leaned back in his chair and looked at her for a long time. "You're a tonic," he said abruptly. "You're astringent and sometimes you sting, but I like being around you."

"Thanks. I think," she added.

"Oh, it's a compliment," he murmured. "I wouldn't offer you anything except the truth."

"That really is a compliment."

"Glad you noticed."

"What happened to the drunk cowboy?" she asked.

"Luke's wife is getting him into a halfway house," he mused. "A real crusader, that lady. She is a bleeding heart."

"She likes lost causes," she countered. "I've heard a lot about her, and I like what I've heard. If I can get this ranch back on its feet, I'd like to help her."

"Another latent crusader," he teased.

"A lot of people need saving, and there aren't a lot of reformers around," she pointed out.

"True enough."

"Thanks for sending that other man over to keep a lookout. He's very nice. Did you know that he likes to do needlepoint?" she asked matter-of-factly.

He nodded. "Nels does some exhibition-quality handwork. Nobody teases him about it, either. At least, not since he knocked Sid Turpen into the water trough."

She chuckled. "He looked like that sort of man. I knit," she said. "Not very well, but it gives me something to do when I'm by myself."

"You're always by yourself," he said quietly. "Why don't you come home with me one or two evenings a week and we can watch television after I've finished with the books. I could come and fetch you."

Her heart jumped. She didn't need telling that he'd never made that invitation to anyone else. He was like a wounded wolf in his lair most of the time. "Wouldn't I be in the way?" she asked.

He shook his head. "I'm alone, too. You and the baby would be good company before and after he's born. You don't have a husband anymore. I don't have a family," he said bluntly. "I'd like to help you through the next few months. No strings," he added firmly. "And absolutely no ulterior motives. Just friendship."

She was touched. He made her feel welcome, warm and safe. She knew that a lot of people were intimidated by him, and that he was very standoffish. It was a huge compliment he was paying her. "Thanks," she said genuinely. "I'll take you up on that."

He sipped his coffee and put the cup down. "It might be good for both of us to spend less time alone with the past."

"Is that what you do, too, thinking about how it might have been, if…" She let the word trail away.

"If," he agreed, nodding. "If I'd smelled the smoke sooner, if I'd gone to bed earlier, if I'd realized that Lopez might send someone after me even from prison… and so forth."

"I kept thinking, what if I hadn't got pregnant so

soon after I married," she confessed. "But I'm not sorry I did, really," she added with a tiny smile. "I like it."

He searched her dark eyes for longer than he wanted to and dragged his attention away. All at once, he glanced at his watch and grimaced. "Good Lord, I almost forgot! I've got a meeting at the bank this morning that I can't miss—refinancing a loan so that I can replace my combine." He got to his feet. "No other problems except for drunk cowboys in your bed?" he asked whimsically.

She glared at him. "Don't look at me, I didn't put him there!"

His eyes roamed over her and he smiled slowly. "His loss."

"You get out of here, you fresh varmint," she said, rising. "And there's no use trying to seduce me, either. I'm immune."

"Really?" he asked with raised eyebrows and a twinkle in his green eyes. "Shall we test that theory?" He took a step in her direction.

She flushed and backed up a step. "You stop that," she muttered.

He chuckled as he reached for his hat. "Don't retreat. I'll keep to my side of the line in the sand. Keep that door locked," he added then, and not with a smile. "I'm having you watched, just in case Lopez does try something. But if you need me, I'll be as close as the telephone."

"I know that. Thank you."

"Your car has a busted water pump," he added, surprising her that he remembered. "I'll have one of my men come get it and overhaul it for you."

She was all but gasping. "But, you don't have to…!"

"I know I don't have to," he said, eyes flashing. "You can't be stuck out here without transportation, especially now."

She didn't want to accept what she knew was charity, but the temptation to have her little red car fixed and running again was too much. She couldn't afford an extra spark plug. "Thank you," she said a little stiffly. It hurt her pride to know that he was aware of her financial situation.

He searched her face quietly. "No need for thanks. I'll take care of you. And the baby."

She stared at him while confusing sensations washed over her like a gentle electric current. She'd never felt such a surge of emotion, with anyone.

"I don't have any ulterior motives, Lisa," he said, speaking her name for the first time. It sounded soft, mysterious, even beautiful in his deep, measured tones.

"Then thanks, for seeing about my car," she said gently. "And if you get sick, I'll take care of you. All right?"

His heart ran wild. He'd never had anybody offer to look after him. His wife hadn't been compassionate. It hit him right in the gut that Lisa thought of him with such kindness. He searched for an answer and couldn't find one.

"I'm sure you never get sick," she said quickly, a little intimidated by his scowl. "But just in case."

He nodded slowly.

She smiled, reassured.

He turned and went out the door, speechless for the first time in recent memory. He couldn't have managed a single word to save his life.

Lisa went onto the porch and watched him drive away with confused emotions. She shouldn't let things intensify. She was a recent widow and he hadn't been widowed all that long ago. People would gossip, if for no other reason than that Cy Parks was the town's hermit. On the other hand, she was lonely and a little afraid. She remembered what Walt had told her about Manuel Lopez and the men who worked for him in the narcotics underworld. She knew what they did to people who sold them out. A shiver ran down her spine. They'd killed Walt and they might not stop until they wiped out his whole family—that was the reputation that Lopez had. She wasn't going to put her baby at risk, regardless of what people thought. She touched her flat belly protectively.

She smiled. "I'm going to take such wonderful care of you."

The smile remained when she thought how Cy would care about the baby, too. He wasn't at all the sort of man he seemed on first acquaintance. But, then, who was? She went back inside to work in the kitchen, careful to make sure the doors were locked.

Cy used his cell phone to have a local wrecker service take Lisa's small car over to his ranch, where he had one of his two mechanics waiting to fix it. Harley was good with machinery, but he had the mechanic do the work instead. For reasons he didn't understand, he didn't like having his good-looking foreman Harley around Lisa.

He went to the meeting with his banker and then on to Ebenezer Scott's place, careful to phone ahead. There were men on the gate who didn't like unexpected company and might react instinctively.

Eb met him at the front door, more relaxed than Cy had seen him in years.

"How's it going?" he asked the newly married man.

Eb grinned. "Funny how nice a ball and chain can feel," was all he said, but his eyes were twinkling with delight. "How's it going on your end?"

"Let's go inside," Cy said. "I've found out a few things."

Eb took him into the kitchen and poured coffee into mugs. "Sally's teaching. I don't usually do more than grab a sandwich for lunch…"

Cy held up a hand. "I haven't got time, thanks. Listen, they've got the beehives on-site around that new warehouse on the land adjoining mine. There's a lot more activity there, panel trucks coming and going and deliveries after dark. I've spotted a number of unfamiliar faces. They don't look like beekeepers to me. Besides," he added curtly, "I saw a couple of Uzis."

"Automatic weapons at a honey plant," Eb murmured thoughtfully. "They must have armed, militant bees." He grinned at his own whimsy. "I'd hoped that Lopez might hesitate after his failed attempt on Sally's family." Sally, along with her aunt Jessica and Jessica's young son, Stevie, were targeted for vengeance by the drug lord. Luckily Lopez hadn't succeeded in his mission.

"We knew that Lopez had mentioned to one of his slimy followers that he needed a new distribution center. What better place than a little Texas town not far from the Gulf of Mexico, with no federal officers around?"

"He knows we're around," Cy pointed out.

"He only knows about me," came the reply. "Nobody locally knows about you. And he thinks I won't do anything because he's backed away from harming Sally's family. He figures the two guys who are taking the fall for him will keep the wolves from his door."

"I don't like it."

"Neither do I, but unless we can prove he's channeling drugs instead of honey through here, we can't do anything. Not anything legal," he added slowly.

"I'm not going up against Uncle Sam," Cy said firmly. "This isn't the old days. I don't fancy being an expatriated American."

Eb sighed. "We're older."

"Older and less reckless. Let Micah Steele go after him. He lives in Nassau and has connections everywhere. He wouldn't be afraid of getting kicked out of the States. He doesn't spend much time here anyway."

"His stepsister and his father live here," Eb pointed out. "He isn't going to want to put them in harm's way."

"From what I hear, his father hates him and his stepsister would walk blocks out of her way to avoid even passing him on the street," Cy said curtly. "Do you think he still cares about them?"

"Yes, I do. He came back with the express purpose of seeing his father and mending fences, but the old man refused to see him. It hurts him that his father won't even speak to him. And I've seen the way he looks at Callie, even if you haven't."

"Then why does he live in Nassau?"

Eb glanced around warily. "He's over here doing a job for me, so watch what you say," he cautioned. "I don't want him on the wrong side of me."

Cy leaned back in his chair and sipped coffee. "I suppose we all have our crosses to bear." He narrowed one eye at his oldest friend. "Do you think Lopez will make a try for Lisa?"

"It's possible," he said flatly. "Down in Mexico, a 'mule' crossed him. He killed the man's whole family except for one small child."

"That's what I thought. I sent Nels Coleman over to her ranch to stay nights in the bunkhouse. He used to work for the Treasury Department back in the late seventies."

"I know him. He's a good man."

"Yes, but not in Lopez's class. Your guys are."

Ebenezer nodded. "I have to have good people. The government and I are more than nodding acquaintances, and I run a high-tech operation here. I can't afford to let my guard down, especially now that I've got Sally to think of."

"It's been a long time since I've had to consider a woman," Cy replied, his green eyes quiet and thoughtful.

"Lisa Monroe is sweet," Ebenezer said. "She'll love that child to death."

"She's like that," Cy agreed, smiling. "I wish she wasn't so bullheaded. I went by to see her this morning and found her out in the barn, trying to pull a calf all by herself with her bare hands."

Ebenezer chuckled. "I won't turn your hair white by mentioning some of her other exploits, before she got pregnant."

"This isn't the first time she's done something outlandish?"

"Let's see." Ebenezer pursed his lips, recalling gossip. "There was the time she stood in the path of a bulldozer that was about to take down the huge live oak in the square that a peace treaty with the Comanche was signed under. Then she chained herself to a cage in the humane society when they were going to put down half a dozen dogs without licenses." He glanced at Cy. "The Tremayne brothers suddenly developed dog fever and between them, they adopted all six. Then there was the time she picketed the new chain restaurant because they refused to hire immigrants..."

"I get the idea," Cy murmured dryly.

"We were all surprised when she married Walt. He was a real man's man, but his job was like a religion to him. He didn't want anything to tie him down so that he couldn't advance in the agency. If he'd lived, that baby would have broken up the marriage for sure. Walt said often enough that he wasn't sure he ever wanted children." He shook his head. "He wasn't much of a husband to her, at that. Most of us felt that he married her on the rebound from that model who dropped him. He felt sorry for Lisa when her dad died and she was left all alone. Even after the wedding, he flirted with every pretty woman he saw. Lisa went all quiet and stopped staying home when he was around. He wasn't around much of that two months they were together, either. He volunteered for the undercover assignment the day they married. That shocked all of us, especially Lisa, and he got killed the same day he was introduced to Lopez."

"They knew who he was," Cy guessed.

"Exactly. And it was Walt's first undercover assignment, to boot. The only reason Rodrigo hasn't been discovered infiltrating Lopez's distribution network is that he's still a Mexican national and he has at least one cousin who's been with Lopez for years. The cousin would never sell him out."

"Lucky man," Cy remarked. "I hope we don't get him killed."

"So do I," Eb said with genuine concern. "Rodrigo's been in the business for a lot of years and he's the best undercover man I know. If anybody can help us put Lopez away for good, it's him. But meanwhile, we have to keep Lisa safe."

Cy went thoughtful. "She's a kind soul."

"Kind and naive," Eb replied. "People take advantage of her. That baby will wrap her right around its finger when it's born."

"I love kids," Cy said. "I miss mine."

"Lisa will love hers," came the quiet reply. "She'll need a friend, and not only because of Lopez. She can't run that ranch by herself. Walt was good with horses, and the men respected him. Lisa can't keep managing those two cowboys who work part-time for her, and she can't get a foreman because she hasn't enough capital to pay the going rate. Besides all that, she doesn't know beans about buying and selling cattle."

"Didn't her father teach her?"

"Not him," Ebenezer chuckled. "He didn't think women were smart enough to handle such things. He ran the ranch until the day he died. She was kept right out of it until then. Walt proposed to her at her father's funeral and married her shortly after."

"She loved her father, I gather."

"Of course she did, and he loved her. But he was a nineteenth-century man. He would have fit right in after the Civil War." He shook his head. "That ranch isn't solvent. Lisa's going to lose it eventually. She needs to go ahead and put it on the market and get the best price she can."

"I might see if she'll sell to me. I could rent her the house and have my own men work the ranch."

Ebenezer grinned. "Now, that's constructive thinking." He leaned forward, emptying his coffee cup. "As for those so-called beehives, I think we'd better send somebody over to have a quiet look after dark and see if there are really any bees in them."

"Good idea. Then we can start making plans if it looks like Lopez is sending drugs through here." Cy got to his feet. "Thanks for the coffee."

"Anytime. Watch your back."

Cy smiled. "I always do. See you."

When Cy got home, Harley was out in the front yard having an animated conversation with a foreigner in an expensive pickup truck. He turned as Cy drove up in front of the house. He cut off the engine and eyed the newcomer's vehicle with knowing eyes. Here was an opportunity not only to meet one of Lopez's executives, but to throw them off the track about him, as well.

"Hey, boss, this is Rico Montoya," he said with a grin. "He's our new neighbor with the honey export business. He just dropped by to say hello."

Sure he did, Cy thought, but he didn't reply. He got out of the utility vehicle slowly and deliberately favored his left arm as he moved to the pickup truck.

"Glad to meet you, Mr. Montoya," Cy said with a carefully neutral expression. "My men noticed the warehouse going up." He tried to look worried. "I don't really like bees close to my purebred Santa Gerts," he said without preamble. "I hope you're going to make sure there aren't any problems."

The man's eyebrows rose, surprised at Cy's lack of antagonism. Surely the rancher knew who he was and whose orders he was following. Or did he? His dark eyes narrowed thoughtfully. Parks was holding his crippled left arm in his right and he had the look of someone who'd seen one tragedy too many. Lopez had been worried about interference from this rancher, but Montoya was certain there wouldn't be any. This wasn't an adversary to worry about. This was a defeated man, despite his past. He relaxed and smiled at Cy. "You're very straightforward," he said with only a trace of an accent. He was wearing a silk suit and his thick hair was not only cut, but styled. There was a slight bulge under his jacket. "You have nothing to fear from our enterprise," he assured Cy. "We will be meticulous about our operation. Your cattle will be in no danger. I give you my word."

Cy stared quietly at the other man and nodded, as if convinced. Near him, Harley was gaping at the lack of antagonism that Mr. Parks showed to most visitors. It wasn't like him to favor that burned arm, either.

"I am very pleased to make your acquaintance, Mr. Parks," Montoya said with a grin. "I hope that we will be good neighbors."

"Thank you for taking the time to stop by and introduce yourself," Cy said with a noticeable lack of animation. He got a firmer grip on his injured arm. "We don't get many visitors."

"It was my pleasure. Good day, *señor*." Montoya smiled again, this time with faint contempt, and pulled his truck out of the driveway. Cy watched him go, arrow-straight, his mouth making a firm line in his lean, taut face.

"Mr. Parks, you are the oddest man I know," Harley said, shaking his head. "You weren't yourself at all."

Cy turned to him. "Who do you think that was?"

"Why, our new neighbor," Harley said carelessly.

"Nice of him to come over and say howdy," he added with a scowl. "Your arm bothering you?"

"Not in the least," Cy said, both hands on his lean hips as he studied the younger man. "What did you notice about our new hardworking neighbor?"

The question surprised Harley. "Well, he was Latin. He had a bit of an accent. And he was real pleasant…"

"He was wearing a silk suit and a Rolex watch," he said flatly. "The truck he was driving is next year's model, custom. He was wearing boots that cost more than my new yearling bull. And you think he makes that kind of money selling honey, do you?"

Harley's eyes widened. Once in a while, his boss threw him a curve. This was a damned big curve. He frowned. How had Cy noticed so much about a man he only saw for a minute or two when Harley, a trained commando he reminded himself, hadn't?

"That was one of Lopez's executives," Cy told the younger man flatly, nodding at his wide-eyed realization. "I want you to go work cattle over near that warehouse and take a pair of binoculars with you," Cy told his foreman. "Don't be obvious, but see who comes and goes for a few days."

"Sir?"

"You told Eb you wanted to help keep an eye on Lopez's operation. Here's your chance."

"Oh, I see, Mr. Scott told you to send me out there." Harley grinned from ear to ear. "Sure. I'll be glad to do it!"

"Just make sure you aren't caught spying," Cy told him flatly. "These people are killers. They won't hesitate if they think they're being watched deliberately."

"I can handle myself," Harley said with faint mockery.

"Yes, I know, you're professionally trained," Cy drawled.

The tone made Harley feel uncertain. But he put it down to jealousy and grinned. "I know how to watch people without getting noticed," he assured his boss. "Does Mr. Scott want tag numbers as well as descriptions of the people?"

"Yes, and pay attention to the trucks that come in."

"Okay."

Cy wanted to add more to those instructions, but he didn't want Harley to know everything. "Be sure you keep your mouth shut about this," he told Harley. "Eb won't like it if he thinks you're gossiping."

"I wouldn't want him mad at me!" Harley chuckled. "I'll keep quiet."

"See that you do."

Cy walked back to the house with a quick, sharp stride that reflected his anger. He'd just met a new link in Lopez's chain, probably one of his divisional managers. It would work to his advantage that he had just convinced the drug lord's associate that he was a crippled rancher with no interest in the bees except where his cattle were concerned.

Lopez thought he had it made with his "honey business" as a blind, here in little Jacobsville. But Cy was going to put a stick in his spokes, and the sooner, the better.

Harley drove the little red car with its new water pump back to Lisa Monroe early the next morning, with Cy following in his big utility vehicle.

Lisa was overjoyed at the way the engine sounded as Harley pulled up at the front porch and revved it before he turned it off.

"It hasn't ever sounded that good before!" she enthused. "Thank you, Harley!"

"You're very welcome, ma'am," he said, making her a mock bow with his hat held against his chest. "But I didn't fix it. I'm just delivering it."

She laughed and Cy glowered. She and Harley were close in age, or he missed his bet. The man, despite his bravado, was honest and hardworking and basically kind. Cy wondered how old Lisa was. Well, at least she was young enough to find Harley's company stimulating—probably much more stimulating than the company of an aging mercenary who was half-crippled and cynical....

"Won't you both come in for a cup of coffee?" she invited.

"I will," Cy told her. "Harley, go take a look around and see what needs doing. Then find Lisa's part-time help and get them on it."

"My pleasure, Mr. Parks," he said with a wicked grin and turned to follow the tersely given instructions.

Lisa gave Cy a speaking look.

"Go ahead," he invited. "Tell me that chores are getting done by people other than you. Tell me that the south pasture is being hayed before the predicted rains day after tomorrow. Tell me," he added mockingly, "that you've got your new calf crop vaccinated and tagged."

She got redder by the minute. She didn't want to tell him that she couldn't get the men to take her suggestions seriously. They were throwbacks to another age, most of them were twice her age, and the madder she got, the more indulgent they became. Once they threatened to quit, they had her over a barrel and she gave up. Hands were thin on the ground this time of year. She could barely afford to pay her employees as it was.

"Harley will get them moving," he told her.

Her lips compressed and her eyes sparked. She looked outraged.

"I know," he said helpfully. "It's a new age. Men and women are equals. You pay their wages and that means they need to do what you say."

She made a gesture of agreement, still without speaking.

"But if you want people to obey, you have to speak in firm tones and tell them who's the boss. And it helps," he added darkly, "if you hire people who aren't still living in the last ice age!"

"They were all I could find to work part-time," she muttered.

"Did you go over to the labor office and see who was available?" he asked.

The suggestion hadn't occurred to her. Probably she'd have found young, able-bodied help there. She could have kicked herself for being so blind.

"No," she confessed.

He smiled, and that wasn't a superior smile, either. "You aren't aggressive enough."

"I beg your pardon?"

"If you're going to hire that type of man, you have to have the whip hand. I'll teach you."

"If that means I'll end up being a local legend like you, I'm not sure I want to learn it," she replied with a twinkle in her dark eyes.

"Old lady Monroe," he recited, chuckling, "carries a shotgun and emasculates men in the barn."

She flushed. "Stop that."

"Isn't that a nicer image than sweet little Lisa who hasn't got the heart to fire a man just because he lies in wait in her bed dead drunk and stinking?"

"Cy!"

He grinned as she curled one hand into a fist. "Much better," he said. "Now hold that thought when you speak to your lazy hands next time. In fact, don't smile at them ever again. Be decisive when you speak, and don't ask, tell. You'll get better results."

She had to admit, she wasn't getting any results at all the way she was. On the other hand, she was still young, and feeling her way through leadership. She wasn't really a drill sergeant type, she had to admit, and the ranch was suffering because of it.

"I don't suppose you'd like a ranch?" she asked whimsically, and was startled when he replied immediately that he would.

"Oh." She stared at him, poleaxed.

"I'll give you the going market price. We'll get two appraisals and I'll match the highest one. You can rent the house from me and I'll manage the cattle. And the cowboys," he added wryly.

"It's not in very good shape," she said honestly, and pushed her glasses back up onto her nose.

"It will be. If you're willing, I'll have my attorney draw up the papers tomorrow."

"I'm very willing. I'll be happy to sign them. What about the appraisals?"

"I'll arrange for those. Nothing for you to worry about now."

"If only my father hadn't been such a throwback," she murmured, leading the way into the ramshackle house. "He thought a woman's place was in the kitchen, period. I'd much rather be working in the garden or doctoring cattle than cooking stuff."

"Can you cook?"

"Breads and meats and vegetables," she said. "Not with genius, but it's mostly edible."

She poured black coffee into a mug and handed it to him. When she sat down across the table from him, he noticed the dark, deep circles under her eyes.

"You aren't sleeping much, are you?" he asked.

She shrugged. "I'm still halfway in shock, I guess. Married and widowed and pregnant, and all in less than two months. That would be enough to unsettle most women."

"I imagine so." He sipped his coffee. She made the decaf strong and it tasted pretty good. He studied her narrowly. "You haven't had any more problems at night, have you?"

"None at all, thanks." She smiled. "And thank you for having my car fixed. I guess if people are going to own old cars, they need to be rich or know a lot about mechanics."

"They do," he agreed. "But I'll keep your little tin can on the road."

"It's not a tin can," she said. "It's a very nice little foreign car with an—" she searched for the right words "—eccentric personality."

"Runs when it feels like it," he translated.

She glared at him. "At least I don't have to have a ladder to get into it."

He smiled. "Remind me to have a step put on just for you."

She didn't reply, but that statement made her feel warm and safe. God knew why. She was certain he wasn't really going to modify his vehicle just for her. She'd only been in it once.

"Do you like opera?" he asked out of the blue.

She blinked. "Well, yes..."

"Turandot?"

"I like anything Puccini composed. Why?"

"It's playing in Houston. I thought we might go."

She pinched her jean-clad leg under the table to see if she was dreaming. It felt like it, but the pain was real. She smiled stupidly. "I'd really like that." Then her face fell. She moved restlessly and averted her eyes. "Better not, I guess."

"You don't have to wear an evening gown to the opera these days," he said, as if he'd actually read her mind. He smiled when her eyes came up abruptly to meet his. "I've seen students go in jeans. I imagine you have a Sunday dress somewhere."

"I do." She laughed nervously. "How did you know I was worried about clothes?"

"I read minds," he mused.

She sighed. "In that case, I'd love to go. Thank you."

He finished his coffee. "Friday night, then. I'll go round up Harley and see what he knows about your place." He got up, hesitating. "Listen, there are some things going on around here. I don't want to frighten you, but Lopez has men in and around town. I want you to keep your doors locked and be careful about strangers."

"I always am," she assured him.

"Do you keep a gun?"

She grinned. "No. I have Puppy Dog."

"Puppy Dog will get under a bed if there's trouble," he assured her flatly. "I've still got Nels staying in the bunkhouse at night, and he's armed. All you have to do is yell. He'll hear you. He's a very light sleeper."

"You can't be sure that Mr. Lopez means me harm."

"I'm not. But I'm a cautious man."

"All right," she said. "I'll keep both eyes out for trouble."

"I'll pick you up Friday night about five. Okay?"

She nodded. "I'll be ready." She went with him to the front door and stood behind the screened door to study him, frowning. "Cy, is it too soon for this?"

"Because you've been a widow such a short time?" He shook his head. "I know you miss Walt. I'm not offering anything heavy, just a trip to the opera. It's very unlikely that we'll see anybody who knows us in Houston."

"I guess you're right." She folded both arms around herself. "The walls are beginning to close in on me."

"I don't doubt it. A night at the opera isn't exactly a cause for gossip."

"Of course not." She smiled. "I'll see you Friday, then. And…thanks."

"I get lonely, too," he said with surprising candor. He gave her one last grin and walked out to find Harley.

His foreman was tight-lipped as he came striding out of the barn. When Harley forgot to be irritating, he was a cowboy and a half. Most of the men walked wide of him in a temper already. "The whole damned place is about to fall to pieces," he said without preamble. "The hay hasn't been cut, the corn hasn't been put in the silo, there are breaks in half the fences, the calves don't even have a brand.... What the hell kind of men did Mrs. Monroe hire?"

"Lazy ones, apparently," Cy said tightly. "Find them and put them all on notice. Lisa's selling me the place. We'll put on four new men to work this ranch and share chores with my own."

"That's a wise decision on her part," Harley said. "She doesn't seem to know much about the business end of cattle ranching."

"Her father thought women weren't smart enough to learn it," Cy mused.

"What an idiot," Harley replied. "My mother can brand cattle right along with the cowboys, and she keeps the books for Dad."

"A lot of women are big-time ranchers, too," Cy agreed. "But Lisa doesn't really have the knack, or the love, for it. Cattle ranching is hard work even if you do."

Harley nodded. "I'll put her part-timers on notice and get the boys over here with a tractor and a combine to hay those fields and harvest the corn."

"When you get that organized," Cy said, "I want to know what you saw over at the honey warehouse last night."

"Not much," Harley had to admit. "And I got challenged on your land by a man with a rifle. Good thing there was a cow down in the pasture for me to show him," he added with a grin. "I told him we had a problem with locoweed and offered to show him where it grew. He went back on his side of the fence and didn't say another word."

"That was a stroke of luck," Cy remarked. "Because we don't have any locoweed."

"We do now," Harley murmured. "I set out a couple of plants and netted them, just in case I get challenged again. Now that I have a legitimate reason to be out there, they won't pay much attention to me. And if they go looking for locoweed," he added with a mocking smile, "why, they'll find it, won't they?"

Cy smiled at the younger man. "You're a treasure, Harley."

"Glad you noticed, boss, and how about that raise?"

"Don't push your luck," came the dry reply. "I'll talk to you later."

"Sure thing."

Cy drove to the lawyer's office the next morning to discuss the land buy. Blake Kemp was tall, thirtyish, with a gray streak in his black, wavy hair, and pale blue eyes. He was the terror of the Jacobsville court circuit, although he looked mild-mannered and intelligent. Deceptive, Cy mused, studying him, because Kemp had a bite like a rattlesnake in court.

"I'm going to buy the Monroe place," Cy said without preamble. "Lisa can't run it alone, and she hasn't the capital to make improvements or even necessary maintenance."

"Good decision on her part," Blake told him. "And on yours. It's good land, and it adjoins your property." He pursed his chiseled lips. "Is that the only merger you're contemplating?"

Cy's eyes narrowed. "She's only been widowed two weeks," he pointed out.

Blake nodded. "I know that. But she's going to have a hard time paying rent. She doesn't even have a job anymore."

Cy studied him evenly.

"Well, I guess I could use a receptionist," he said. "Callie Kirby is my paralegal, and she can't really handle the research and the phones at the same time. Besides, Lisa worked for a colleague of mine last year. She knows her way around a law office."

"What happened to the brunette who works with Callie?" Cy asked.

"Gretchen's gone off to Morocco with a girlfriend from Houston," Blake said with a chuckle. "She spent the past few years nursing her mother through a fatal bout of cancer," he added solemnly. "And then the first man who took a shine to her insurance money broke her young heart. She needed a change of scene, and she said she doesn't want to work in a law office when she comes back. So there's a job available, if Lisa wants it."

"I'll tell her. Thanks."

He shrugged. "We all like Lisa. She's had a rough deal, one way or another."

"She has indeed. Now, about those appraisals…"

When Cy came to pick Lisa up for their trip to the opera, he was wearing a navy sports coat with dark slacks and a white shirt. His tie combined red and navy in a paisley print. He looked dignified and very handsome. Lisa was glad he hadn't worn a dinner jacket, because she had nothing that dressy in her small wardrobe. The best she could find was a simple gray jersey dress with long sleeves and a skirt that fell to her calves. She covered it with her one luxury, a light-weight black microfiber coat that was warm against the unseasonably cool autumn winds. Her hair was in a neat, complicated braid and she wore more makeup than usual to disguise her dark-circled eyes. She slept badly or not at all lately, and not completely because she missed Walt. She was having some discomfort that concerned her. She knew that pregnancies could fail in the early weeks, and it bothered her. She really needed to talk to her doctor when she went for the next visit. It might be nothing, but she didn't want to take any chances with her baby.

"Not bad at all," Cy mused, watching her pull on the coat over her clinging dress. She had a pretty figure.

"Thank you," she said, coloring a little. "You look nice, too."

"I talked to my attorney about the property," he said after he helped her into the utility vehicle and started the engine. "He's contacted two appraisal firms. They'll be out next week to see the ranch and give you an esti-mate."

That worried her. She hated seeing the family ranch

go out of the family, but what choice did she have? She smiled wanly. "Walt was planning a dynasty," she recalled. "He talked about all sorts of improvements we could make, but when I mentioned having kids to inherit it, he went cold as ice."

Cy glanced at her. "Not much point in working yourself to death just to have the empire go on the market the minute you're in the ground."

"That's what I thought." She turned her small purse over in her lap. "It's just as well that you'll have the ranch," she added. "You'll know how to make it prosper."

"You'll still be living there," he pointed out. "I'll be a damned good landlord, too."

"Oh, I know that." She stretched. "I'll still have to get a job, though. I'll want to put what I get for the ranch into a savings account, so the baby can go to college."

She surprised him constantly. He'd thought she might want to brighten up the house, even buy herself a decent car. But she was thinking ahead, to the day when her child would need to continue his education.

"Nothing for you?" he asked.

"I've got everything I really need," she said. "I don't have expensive tastes—even if Walt did. Besides, I've got a little nest egg left over from some cattle Walt sold off before he...before he died."

"I know of a job, if you want it."

He distracted her, which was what she supposed he'd intended. "Really?"

"Kemp needs a receptionist," he said. "Gretchen's gone off to Morocco and she isn't coming back to work for him. So now Callie Kirby's up to her ears in work. Kemp said you'd be welcome."

"What a nice man!" she exclaimed.

"Now there's a word that doesn't connect itself with Kemp." He gave a soft laugh. "Or didn't you know that people talk in whispers around him?"

"He doesn't seem that bad."

"He isn't, to people he likes." His eyes softened as they searched her averted face. "He'll like you, Lisa Monroe. You're good people."

"Thanks. So are you."

"Occasionally."

She glanced in his direction and smiled. "It's funny, isn't it, the way we get along? I was scared to death of you when you first moved here. You were so remote and difficult to talk to. People said you made rattle-snakes look companionable by comparison."

"I moved here not long after I buried my wife and

son," he replied, and memories clawed at his mind. "I hated the whole world."

"Why did you move here?" she asked curiously.

He wasn't surprised that she felt comfortable asking him questions. He wouldn't have tolerated it from anyone else. But Lisa, already, was under his thick skin. "I needed someone to talk to, I guess," he confessed. "Eb lived here, and he and I go back a long way. He'd never married, but he knew what it was to lose people. I could talk to him."

"You can talk to me, too," she pointed out. "I never tell what I know."

He smiled at her. "Who would you tell it to?" he drawled. "You don't have close friends, do you?"

She shrugged. "All my friends got married right out of high school. They've got kids of their own and, until fairly recently, I didn't even date much. I've been the odd one out most of my life. Other girls wanted to talk about boys, and I wanted to talk about organic gardening. I love growing things."

"We'll have to lay out a big garden spot for you next spring. You can grow all sorts of stuff."

"That would be nice. I've got a compost pile," she added brightly. "It's full of disgusting things that will produce terrific tomatoes next summer."

"I like cattle, but I'm not much of a gardener."

"It's a lot of work, but you get lovely things to eat, and they aren't poisoned by pesticides, either." She glanced out at the long, flat dark horizon. "I guess you aren't big on people who don't like to use chemicals."

"Haven't you heard?" he chuckled. "I go to cattlemen's association meetings with J. D. Langley and the Tremayne brothers."

"Oh, my," she said, because she'd heard about the uproar at some of those gatherings, where the Tremaynes had been in fistfights over pesticides and growth hormones. Their position against such things was legendary.

"I enjoy a good fight," he added. "I use bugs for pest control and organic fertilizer on my hay and corn and soybean crops." He glanced her way. "Guess where I get the fertilizer?"

"Recycled grass, huh?" she asked, and waited for him to get the point.

He threw back his head and roared. "That's one way of describing it."

"I have some of that, too, and I use it in my garden. I think it works even better than the chemical ones."

The subject of natural gardening and cattle raising supplied them with topics all the way to Houston, and Lisa thoroughly enjoyed herself. Here was a man who thought like she did. Walt had considered her organic approach akin to insanity.

The parking lot at the arts center was full. Cy managed to find one empty space about half a city block away.

"Now that's a full house," he remarked as he helped her down from the vehicle and repositioned her coat around her shoulders. "This thing sure is soft. Is it wool?" he asked, smoothing over it with his fingers.

"It's a microfiber," she told him. "It's very soft and warm. The nights are pretty chilly lately, especially for south Texas."

"The weather's crazy everywhere." He nudged a long, loose curl from her braided hair behind her ear, making her heart race with the almost sensual movement of his lean fingers. "I thought you might wear your hair loose."

"It's...difficult to keep in place when it's windy," she said, sounding and feeling breathless.

His fingers teased the curl and slowly dropped to her soft neck, tracing imaginary lines down it to her throat. He could feel her pulse go wild under his touch, hear the soft, broken whip of her breath at his chin. It had been far too long since he'd had anything warm and feminine this close to him. Restraints that had been kept in place with sheer will were crumbling just at the proximity. He moved a full step closer, so that her body was right up against him in the opening of her coat. His hands were both at the back of her neck now, caressing the silky skin below her nape.

"I haven't touched a woman since my wife died," he said in a faintly thick tone, his voice unusually deep in the silence. The distant sound of cars and horns and passing radios faded into the background.

She looked up, straight into his green eyes in the glow from a streetlight, and her heart raced. That look on his face was unfamiliar to her, despite her brief intimacy with her late husband. She had a feeling that Cy knew a lot more than her husband ever had about women.

Cy's thumbs edged around to tease up and down her long, strained neck. Her vulnerability made him feel taller, more masculine than ever. He wanted to protect her, care for her, watch over her. These were new feelings. Before, his relationships to women had been very physical. Lisa made him hungry in a different way.

She parted her lips to speak and he put a thumb gently over them.

"It's too soon," he said, anticipating her protest. "Of course it is. But I'm starving to death for a woman's soft mouth under my lips. Feel." He drew one of her hands to his shirt under the jacket and pressed it hard against the thunderous beat of his heart.

She was more confused than ever. This was totally unfamiliar territory. Walt had never said anything so blatantly vulnerable to her, not even when they were most intimate.

His free hand went around her waist and drew her slowly closer, pressing her to him as his body reacted powerfully to the touch of her soft warmth. He lifted an eyebrow and smiled wickedly at her frozen expression.

"Why, Mrs. Monroe, you're blushing," he chided softly.

"You wicked man…!"

His nose brushed lazily against hers in a tender nuzzling. "I've probably forgotten more about women than Walt ever knew in the first place," he said. "You don't act like a woman who's ever known satisfaction."

That was so close to the truth that it hurt. She stiffened.

He lifted his head and searched her eyes. His own narrowed. He moved her lazily against him and felt her breath catch, felt her hands cling to his lapels as if she were drowning.

"Oh…no," she choked as a surge of pure delight

worked its way up her spine. She hated herself. Her husband was only buried two weeks ago…!

While she was thinking of ways to escape, and fighting her own hunger, Cy backed her very gently against the big utility vehicle and edged one of her long legs out of his way to bring them into more intimate contact.

"This is the most glorious thing a man and a woman can do together," he murmured as his mouth lowered to hers. "He cheated you. I won't. Open your mouth."

Her lips parted on a shocked little gasp, and his mouth ground into them, parting them. He wasn't hesitant or tentative. He demanded, devoured. His mouth was a weapon, feinting, thrusting, biting, and all the while her body rippled with a thousand stings of new pleasure as she clung hard to his strength. Sensations she'd never known piled one upon the other until a hoarse moan tore out of her strained throat and went up into his mouth.

Another minute and he knew he wouldn't be able to pull back at all. He had her hips pinned with his, and his body ached for satisfaction.

With a rough curse he dragged his head up and moved away from her. She looked at him with dazed eyes in a flushed face, her mouth swollen from his kisses, her body shivering with new knowledge.

He drew himself up to his full height. His eyes glittered like green diamonds in a face like stone. He had to fight to get a normal breath of air into his lungs.

She tried to speak, but she couldn't manage even a whimper. Her body was still flying, soaring, trembling with little shivers of pleasure that made her knees weak.

He reached out and caught her small hand in one of his big ones, linking their fingers. "We'd better go inside," he said quietly.

"Yes." She let him pull her away from the truck and lead her toward the arts center. She was amazed that she could walk at all.

Turandot was beautiful. Lisa cried when the tenor sang "Nessun Dorma," one of her favorite arias. The sets were elegant, colorful, the Chinese costumes glittery and resembling fantasy more than reality. The dragon was a masterpiece of sound and fury and color. All in all, it was a magnificent production, and Puccini's glorious music brought it alive. Lisa had never seen an opera except on the public broadcasting television channel. She knew that she'd never forget this for as long as she lived, and every time she remembered it, she'd remember Cy sitting beside her in the dark.

Meanwhile, Cy was cursing himself silently for what had happened in the parking lot. It was months too soon for that. She was a pregnant, newly widowed woman and he'd let his emotions get out of control. His jaw tautened as he remembered the silky feel of her in his arms. He wanted to take care of her, and it looked as though she was going to need protection after all—from him.

Somehow he was going to have to get them back on a simple friendly footing. It wouldn't be easy. He had no idea how she felt about what had happened. She sat quietly beside him, obviously enjoying the opera. She even smiled at him from time to time. But if she was angry, it didn't show. He remembered her soft moan, her clinging arms. No, he thought, she'd gone in head-first, too, just as he had. But he had regrets and he suspected that she did, as well. He had to draw back before he put the delicate new feeling between them at risk. Lisa was off-limits in any physical way, and he was going to have to remember that.

Lisa saw his scowl and wondered if he had regrets about what had happened. Men got lonely, she knew, and he was a very masculine sort of man to whom women were no mystery. He was probably wondering how to tell her that it wasn't about her a few minutes ago, that any woman would have produced that reaction in a hungry man.

She would save him the trouble, she decided, the

minute they started home. He'd already done so much for her. She couldn't expect him to take over where Walt had left off; not that Walt had ever really felt passion for her. Walt had enjoyed her, she supposed, but there hadn't been any sizzling attraction between them. It shamed her to admit that what she'd felt in the parking lot with Cy had been infinitely more pleasurable than anything she'd ever done with her late husband. She didn't dare think about how it would be if they were truly intimate…

Her hand jerked in Cy's as the final curtain fell and the applause roared. She clapped automatically, but made sure that both her hands were tight on her purse when they started to leave.

"It's a beautiful opera," she remarked as he escorted her to the exit.

"Yes, it is," he agreed pleasantly. "I've seen it in a dozen different cities, but I still enjoy it."

"I guess you've been to the Metropolitan Opera in New York City?" she mused wistfully.

"Several times," he agreed.

She imagined him there, with some beautiful woman in an expensive evening gown and wrapped in furs. It wasn't far to imagine them going into a dark room together, where the coat and the evening gown were discarded. She swallowed hard and tried not to think about that.

He could feel tension radiating from her. She was clinging so hard to that tiny purse that she was leaving the indentations of her nails in the soft leather.

When they reached the Expedition, he opened the door for her, but held her back when she started to climb inside.

"I'm sorry about what happened earlier," he said gently. "I've made you uncomfortable."

Her wide eyes met his. "I thought I'd made you uncomfortable," she blurted out.

They stood just looking at each other until his lean face went harder than ever with the effort not to give in to the hunger she kindled in him.

"You poor man," she said huskily, wincing as she saw the pain in his eyes. "I know you're lonely, Cy, that you just needed someone to hold for a few minutes. It's all right. I didn't read anything into it."

His eyes closed on a wave of pain that hit him like a bat. She reached up and pulled his face down to her lips. She kissed him tenderly, kissed his eyes, his nose, his cheek, his chin, with brief undemanding little brushes of her mouth that comforted in the most exquisite way.

He took a ragged breath and his lean hands captured

her shoulders, tightening there when he lifted his face away from her warm mouth. "Don't do that," he said tersely.

"Why not?" she asked.

"I don't need comforting!" he said curtly.

She moved back a step. He looked as if she'd done something outrageous, when she'd only meant to be kind. It irritated her that he had to be antagonistic about it. "Oh, I see," she said, staring up at him. "Is this how it goes? 'Men are tough, little woman,'" she drawled, deepening her voice and her drawl, "'we can eat live snakes and chew through barbed wire. We don't want women fussin' over us!'" She grinned up at him deliberately.

He glared at her, his eyes glittering.

She raised her eyebrows. "Want me to apologize? Okay. I'm very sorry," she added.

His broad chest rose and fell heavily. "I want you to quit while you're ahead," he said in a tight voice.

She stared at him without guile. "I don't understand."

"Don't you?" His smile was full of mockery and he was seeing a succession of women from his wild days who liked to tease and run away, but not too far away. His lean hands tightened on her shoulders as his eyes slid down her body. "Your husband didn't tell you what teasing does to a man?"

"Teasing…?" Her eyes widened. "Was I?" she asked, and seemed not to know.

That fascinated expression was real. He did scowl then. "What you were doing…it arouses me," he said bluntly.

"You're kidding!"

He wanted to be angry. He couldn't manage it. She did look so surprised…. He dropped his hands, laughing in wholesale defeat. "Get in the damned truck."

He half lifted her in and closed the door on her barely formed question.

She was strapped in when he pulled himself up under the steering wheel, closed the door and reached for his seat belt.

"You were kidding," she persisted.

He looked right into her eyes. "I wasn't." He frowned quizzically. "Don't you know anything about men?"

"I was married for two months," she pointed out.

"To a eunuch, apparently," he said bluntly as he cranked the vehicle and pulled out of the parking lot and into traffic.

"I *am* pregnant," she stated haughtily.

He spared her an amused glance. "Pregnant and practically untouched," he replied.

She sighed, turning her attention to the city lights as he wound south through Houston to the long highway that would take them home to Jacobsville. "I guess it shows, huh?" she asked.

He didn't say anything for half a block or so. "Did you want him?"

"At first," she said. Her eyes sought his. "But not like I wanted you in the parking lot," she said honestly. "Not ever like that."

A flash of ruddy color touched his cheekbones. He was shocked at her honesty.

"Sorry, again," she murmured, looking away. "I guess I haven't learned restraint, either," she added.

He let out a long breath. "You take some getting used to," he remarked.

"Why?"

His eyes met hers briefly before they went back to the highway. Rain was beginning to mist the windshield. He turned on the wipers. "I don't expect honesty from a woman," he said curtly.

She frowned. "But surely your wife was honest."

"Why do you think so?"

"It's obvious that you loved your little boy," she began.

His laugh had the coldest ring to it that she'd ever

heard. "She wanted an abortion. I threatened to take away her credit cards and she gave in and had him."

"That must have been a difficult time for you," she said softly.

"It was." His jaw clenched. "She was surprised that I wanted her baby."

"Hers, and not yours?" she ventured.

"Hers by one of her lovers," he said bitterly. "She didn't really know which one."

There was an abrupt silence on the other side of the truck. He glanced at her frozen features with curiosity. "What sort of marriage do you think I had? I was a mercenary. The women you meet in that profession aren't the sort who sing in church choirs."

"How did you know I sang in the choir?" she asked, diverted.

He laughed, shaking his head. "I didn't, but it figures. You're her exact opposite."

She was still trying to understand what he was saying. "You didn't love her?"

"No, I didn't love her," he replied. "We were good together in bed and I was tired of living alone. So, I married her. I never expected it to last, but I wanted a child. God knows why, I assumed it was mine."

"Why did she marry you if it wasn't?"

"She liked having ten credit cards and driving a Jaguar," he said.

That produced another frown.

"I was rich, Lisa," he told her. "I still am."

She pulled her coat tighter around her and stared out the window, not speaking. She was shocked and more uncertain about him than ever. He was such a complex person, so multifaceted that just when she thought she was getting to know him, he became a stranger all over again.

"Now what is it?" he asked impatiently.

"I hope you don't think I agreed to come out with you…that I was eager to let you buy the ranch because…" She flushed and closed her mouth. She was so embarrassed that she wanted to go through the floor.

"If I'm rich, it's because I know pure gold when I see it," he said, casting her an amused glance. "Do you think I'll assume that you're a gold digger because you came out with me?"

"I kissed you back, too," she said worriedly.

He sighed with pure pleasure and relaxed into the seat, smiling to himself. "Yes, you did."

"But it was an accident," she persisted. "I didn't plan it…"

"That makes two of us." He pulled up at the last

streetlight before they left the city behind and turned to her. His eyes were narrow and very intent. "There are things in my past that are better left there. You'd never begin to understand the relationship I had with my wife, because you don't think in terms of material gain. When I was your age, you were the sort of woman I'd run from."

"Really? Why?" she asked.

He cocked an eyebrow and let his eyes run over her. "Because you told me once that you hadn't slept with Walt before you married him, Lisa," he drawled.

She glared at him. "I would have if I'd wanted to," she said mutinously.

"But you didn't."

She threw up her hands, almost making a basketball of her small purse. She retrieved it from the dash and plopped it back into her lap.

"You're the kind of woman that men marry," he continued, unabashed. "You like children and small animals and it would never occur to you to be cruel to anyone. If you'd gotten involved with me while I was still in my former line of work, you wouldn't have lasted a day with me."

"I don't suppose I would have," she had to agree. She looked through the windshield, wondering why it hurt so much to have him tell her that. Surely she hadn't been thinking in terms of the future just because of one passionate kiss? Of course, her whole body tensed remembering the pleasure of it, the exciting things he'd said...

"And you weren't Walt's usual date, either," he said surprisingly. "He liked experience."

She grimaced. "I found that out pretty quick. He said I was the most boring woman he'd ever gone to bed with. Except for our wedding night, and the night before he was killed, he slept in a separate bedroom."

No wonder she was the way she was, he mused as the light changed and he sent the big vehicle speeding forward. She probably felt like a total failure as a woman. The child must have been some sort of consolation, because she certainly wanted it.

"I'll bet you hate admitting that," he said.

"Yes, I do. I felt inadequate, dull, *boring*," she muttered. "He liked blondes, but not me."

"He liked that parcel service driver plenty," he recalled, his eyes narrowing. "You were pitching hay over the fence to the cows and he was flirting with her, right under your nose. I never wanted to hit a man more."

Her lips parted on a quick breath. "You saw... that?"

"I saw it," he said curtly. "That's why I stopped by

later and said something about the way you were pitching hay by yourself."

She shifted in the seat. "He said they were old friends," she replied. "I guess he really meant they were former lovers. He never treated me to that sort of charm and flirting. He really wanted Dad's ranch. It was a pity I went with the deal."

"It was his loss that he took you for granted," he corrected. "You're not inadequate. You proved that earlier tonight, in the parking lot."

She cleared her throat. "An incident best forgotten."

"Why?"

"Why?" She stared at him. "Walt's only been dead two weeks, that's why!"

He stopped at a four-way stop and turned in his seat on the deserted road to look at her. "Lisa," he said quietly, "it wouldn't have mattered even if he'd still been alive, and you know it. What happened was mutual and explosive."

"It was a fluke…"

His hand reached out and his fingers traced her lower lip. She couldn't even speak. "Would you like me to prove that it isn't?" he asked quietly. "There are plenty of dirt roads between here and home, and the seats recline all the way."

"Cy Parks!"

"Best of all," he mused, "we wouldn't even have to worry about pregnancy, would we?"

Her face was scarlet; she knew it was. He was making her breathless with that torturous brush of his fingers, and she was vulnerable. She'd never really known desire until tonight, and she wished she could turn the clock back a day. Life was difficult enough without this new complication.

He drew in a long breath and lifted his hand back to the steering wheel. "God knows I want to," he said shortly, "but you'd die of shock and never speak to me again afterward."

"I...certainly...would," she faltered, pushing her hair back unnecessarily just for something to do.

He shook his head. He'd known her such a short time, really, but she seemed to hold his attention even when he wasn't with her. Every future event he thought of these days, he considered her part in. It was disturbing to know that he considered her part of his life already.

She fiddled with the top button on her coat. Her eyes were restless, moving from the dark horizon to the occasional lighted window flashing past as the utility vehicle picked up speed. What he'd said disturbed her, mostly because she knew it was true. She'd have gone anywhere with him, done anything with him. It made her guilty because she should be mourning Walt.

"Don't brood," Cy told her. "You're safe. No more torrid interludes tonight, I promise."

She fought a smile and lost. "You're a terrible man."

"You have no idea how terrible." He paused to look both ways before he crossed a lonely intersection. "Harley's fired your part-time hired hands, by the way."

"He's what?"

"Calm down. They were being paid for work they didn't do. That's economically disastrous."

"But who'll get in the hay and brand the calves…?" she worried.

"You didn't hear the noise? Harley got the tractors out in your hay field early this morning. The haying's done. The corn crop is next. I'm hiring on four new men. Harley will supervise them, and your place will live up to its promise." He glanced at her. "You haven't decided not to sell it have you?"

"I can't afford to keep it," she confessed. "I'm glad you don't plan to build a subdivision on it or something. It's been in my family for a hundred years. Dad loved it with all his heart. I love it, too, but I have no idea how to make it pay. I'd like to see it prosper."

"I think I can promise you that it will."

She smiled, content with just being next to him. He turned on the radio and soft country music filled the cab. After a few minutes, her eyes slid shut as all the sleepless nights caught up with her.

She was vaguely aware of being gently shaken. She didn't want to be disturbed. She was warm and cozy and half-asleep.

"No," she murmured drowsily. "Go away."

"I have to," came a deep, amused voice at her ear. "Or we'll have a scandal we'll never live down. Come on, imp. Bedtime."

She felt herself tugged out of the seat and into a pair of warm, hard arms. She was floating, floating…

Cy didn't wake her again. He took off her shoes, tossed the cover over her, put her glasses on the bedside table and left her on the bed in her nice dress and coat. He didn't dare start removing things, considering his earlier passionate reaction to her. But he stood beside the bed, just watching her, enjoying the sight of her young face relaxed in sleep. He wondered how old she was. She never had told him.

He turned and went back out into the hall, pausing to check the lock on the back door in the kitchen before he went out the front one, locking it carefully behind him. He still wasn't convinced that Lopez wouldn't make a beeline for Lisa if he thought his men could get away with harming her. Cy was going to make sure that he didn't.

He stopped by the bunkhouse to have a word with Nels before he went home and climbed into his own bed. He stared at himself in the bedroom mirror, his eyes narrow and cynical as he studied his lean, scarred face and equally scarred body. He was only thirty-five, as Lisa had already guessed, but he looked older. His eyes held the expression of a man who'd lived with death and survived it. He was wounded inside and out by the long, lonely, terrible years of the past. Lisa soothed the part of him that still ached, but she aroused a physical need that he'd almost forgotten he had. She was a special woman, and she needed him. It was new to be needed on a personal level. He thought about the child she was carrying and wondered if it would be a boy or girl. She'd need someone to help her raise it. He wanted to do that. He had nobody, and neither did she. They could become a family—for the child's sake.

He turned off the lights and went to bed. But his dreams were restless and hot, and when he woke up the next morning, he felt as if he hadn't slept at all.

Harley got the calves branded and the corn in the silo in quick order.

"You've got a knack for inspiring cowboys to work, Harley," Cy told him one afternoon a few days later.

"I get out there and work with them, and make them ashamed of being lazy," Harley told him with a grin. "Most of them can't keep up with me."

"I noticed." Cy leaned back against the corral fence and stared at the younger man evenly, without blinking. "You were out near the warehouse last night. What did you see?"

"Three big trucks," Harley said solemnly. "One had some odd stuff on the back. Looked like oil drums lashed together."

That was disturbing. Cy knew that drug dealers threw portable bridges across rivers to let trucks full of their product drive to the other side. What Harvey was describing sounded like a makeshift pontoon bridge. Cy and the mercenaries he'd worked with had used them, too.

"Did you get a look at what was in the trucks?" he asked.

Harley shook his head. "The doors were closed and locked. I was afraid to risk trying to pick a lock, with all that hardware around. Those guys had Uzis."

"I know," Cy said without thinking.

Harley's eyebrows went up, and he grinned in a fairly

condescending way. "Do you now? Are you using Uzis to load cattle these days, boss?"

Cy realized what he'd said and chuckled. "I wasn't listening. Sorry."

"No problem. I noticed a couple of new faces over there," he added. "Tough-looking men, and they weren't wearing suits."

"Get back out there tonight," Cy told him. "And be very careful, Harley. I've got a bad feeling about this whole thing." He didn't add that he was worried about Lisa. He saw her every other day, and the paperwork had just been completed and signed, ready for the transfer of money and deeds. He wouldn't be surprised to learn that Lopez had an informant in town who'd tell him that. It might prompt the drug lord to hasty action, if he thought Lisa was selling the ranch in order to move away. He couldn't know that Cy planned to rent her the ranch house. He wouldn't like having to search for her.

Knowing that bothered him, and he mentioned it to Lisa when he stopped by to see her the next day. Harley had seen yet another unfamiliar face on the warehouse property, and he'd also seen flat after flat of jars being moved inside the structure. The drug dealers were getting ready to begin operations. Things would heat up very soon, or Cy missed his guess. He didn't want Lisa in the middle of it.

"Have you got family you could visit out of state?" he asked without preamble as he joined her in the living room, where she had gas logs burning in the fireplace.

She curled up on the sofa in her jeans and knit turtleneck white sweater and stared at him curiously. "I don't have family anywhere," she confessed. "Maybe a cousin or two up around Fort Worth, but I wouldn't know where to look for them."

He sighed heavily and leaned forward in the chair with his arms crossed over his knees. "All right," he said, seeming to come to a decision. "If you leave the house from now on, I want to know first. If you can't get me, you call Eb Scott."

"Why?"

He knew she was going to ask that. He didn't have a very logical reply. "I don't know what Lopez is up to," he said honestly. "He may have given up on ideas of targeting you. On the other hand, he may be lulling us into a false sense of security. I'd rather err on the side of caution."

"That suits me," she said agreeably.

"Do you have a phone by your bed?"

"Yes," she said. "It makes me feel more secure."

He stood up. "Don't forget to keep your doors locked, even in the daytime, when you're home alone."

"I'm not, much," she said without thinking. "Harley comes by every day to check on me, sometimes twice a day."

His eyes narrowed. He didn't like that, although he said, "Good for Harley."

She caught a nuance of something in his tone. "Do you mind?" she asked deliberately. He'd been remote and she'd hardly seen him since the night of the opera. She wondered if he'd been avoiding her, and she concluded that he was. His manner now was stand-offish and he seemed in a hurry to leave. She wanted to know if he was the least bit put out by Harley's attentiveness.

"It's your life," he said nonchalantly, tilting his wide-brimmed hat over one eye. "He's a steady young man with a good future."

He couldn't be thinking...or could he? She started to tell him that Harley was friendly, and that she had no romantic interest in him. But before she could, Cy was already on his way out the door.

She went after him, trying not to be undignified and run. She didn't catch up to him until he was going down the steps.

"When do we close on the sale?" she asked, having no other excuse for following him.

He turned at the door of the utility vehicle. "The first of next week, Kemp said. It will take that long to get the paperwork filed."

"Okay. You'll phone me?"

"I will. Or Kemp will."

That sounded less than friendly. She wrapped her arms around her chest and leaned against one of the posts that held up the long porch. "That's fine, then," she said with forced cheer. "Thanks."

He opened the door and hesitated. "Are you in a rush to close?"

She shrugged. "Not really. I just wanted to know when I'd need to start paying rent. I was going to go see Mr. Kemp next week about that job."

She thought he didn't want her around, and that was so far from the truth that it might as well have been in orbit. But he didn't want to rush her, frighten her. Hell, he didn't know what he wanted anymore.

"I'll see you Monday," he said, and got into the vehicle without another word. He didn't even look back as he drove away.

Lisa stared after him with her heart around her ankles. So much for her theory that he was attracted to her. She supposed that he'd had second thoughts. It might be just as well. He was mourning his son, whom he'd obviously loved even if it wasn't his own child, and she was a recent widow expecting a child of her own. She'd been spinning daydreams and it was time to stop and face reality. Cy wasn't her future even if she'd hoped he was hers. She turned and went back into the lonely house, pausing to close and lock the door behind her.

Chapter Five

The first time she heard the noise at the window, Lisa thought it was a squirrel. The old house seemed to attract them. They often scurried over the roof and came leaping down into the limbs of the big pecan trees that surrounded the porches. But she usually didn't hear them in the wee hours of the morning, and so loud that they woke her up. She tried to go back to sleep, but then the noise came again. This time it didn't sound like a squirrel. It sounded more like a window being forced open.

Lisa slipped out of bed in her sweatpants and white cotton top, hesitating at the door that led into the hall.

The noise had come from the room next door, the one Walt had occupied for most of their married life.

She heard a faint rubbing noise, like one a man might make climbing in a window. Her heart began racing and she dashed down the hall in her bare feet, down the wooden steps and into the kitchen. Her glasses were still in the nightstand drawer by her bed, and she could barely make out familiar objects in the dim light. She was headed for the back door when she was caught and lifted and a big, gentle hand was clapped over her mouth while she struggled pitifully in an embrace of steel.

"It's all right," Cy Parks whispered at her ear. "It's all right, we know there's someone trying to break in upstairs. Micah's rappeling from the roof down to the window of the room across the hall. He'll have him in a minute. Don't scream or you'll give him all the warning he needs to get away. Okay?"

She nodded.

He eased her back onto her feet, taking her soft weight against the black sweater he was wearing with black jeans, one lean arm holding her just under her breasts. She saw the glimmer of metal in his other black-gloved hand. Her frightened eyes drifted up to his face, and all she could see of it was his eyes. He was wearing some sort of black mask.

While she was studying him, she heard a loud thud, followed by a louder groan.

"All clear!" came a loud, deep voice from upstairs.

"Stay here." Cy let her go and went past her and up the staircase with an economy of motion that made her very glad she wasn't the enemy.

She leaned back against the counter and almost jumped out of her skin when the back door opened and Eb Scott came in pulling his mask off, grinning.

"Sorry," he said quickly. "But the man Cy had staying in the bunkhouse spotted two suspicious figures outside your window. Unless you're expecting Romeo, it's a bit late for social calls."

"I was asleep," she said, shaken. "I heard the noise and thought it was a squirrel. I was trying to get out the back door when Cy grabbed me." She whistled. "I thought my number was up."

"Good thing you slept light," Eb said solemnly. "We barely got here in time."

"Who is it, do you think?" she asked.

"One of Lopez's goons," Eb told her flatly. "And this definitely confirms our worst fears. Lopez is after you."

"But I didn't do anything!" she said, still shaken from the experience. "Why is he after me?" She brushed back the long, tangled curtain of hair from her flushed cheeks. She felt sick.

"He's going to set an example for anybody else who might consider trying to infiltrate his organization," Eb told her. "It doesn't matter what you did or didn't do. He doesn't care. Your husband betrayed him and he wants you to pay for it, too. He wants all the government agencies to know the price for selling him out—their lives and their families' lives."

The fear made a tight knot in the pit of her stomach. She sank down into one of the kitchen chairs with a protective hand over her belly. She felt twice her age.

She heard heavy footsteps on the staircase and out the front door before Cy came back into the room, tearing off his mask. He looked even more formidable than usual, and that said something about his present demeanor, Lisa thought.

"Micah's taking the guy over to the sheriff," he said. "He suddenly doesn't speak English, of course, and his friend lit a shuck while he was breaking into the house. We won't be able to prove a thing beyond the obvious."

"He'll be out on bond by tomorrow afternoon and out of the country an hour later," Ebenezer added.

Cy's expression was homicidal before he turned his glittery green eyes on Lisa. "You can't stay here a day longer," he said flatly. "Lopez doesn't make the same mistake twice. You've been put on notice. The next time, there won't be a near miss."

She ground her teeth together. "This is my ranch. I haven't sold it to you yet, and I'm staying here," she said furiously. "I'm not going to let some sleazy drug kingpin force me into hiding out like a scared kid!"

"Commendable courage," Cy remarked with a stoic expression. He reached into his belt and pulled out something dark. "Here."

He tossed her his automatic. She caught it and then dropped it with a gasp of pure horror.

"You'd better pick it up and learn to shoot straight and under fire," he said coldly. "You'd better learn to shoot to kill while you're at it. Because that—" he indicated the gun "—is the only way you'll survive if you insist on staying here alone. We were almost too late tonight. Next time, we might not be so lucky."

She glared at him, but she didn't argue. "I hate guns."

"Good God, so do I," Cy told her. "But when you get in a war, you don't throw potatoes at the enemy."

"Then what do I do?" she asked Cy.

Cy told her. "Go pack a bag. You're leaving."

"Leaving for where?" she demanded, standing up with both hands on her hips. "I told you already,

I've got no family, no close friends, and no place to go to!"

"Yes, you have. The Expedition's outside. I'll send Harley over in the morning to pick up your VW and bring it over, too."

Her dark eyes widened. It didn't help much, her glasses were upstairs on the bedside table and all she could see of Cy was a blur. "I can't go home with you. I've only been widowed a short time!"

"I've only been widowed three years," he reminded her. "So what?"

"I can stay with Callie Kirby!"

"Callie's apartment isn't big enough for Callie, much less Callie and you," he said. "I've got three bedrooms. You can even have a bathroom of your own."

She didn't want to give in. But the memory of someone trying to break in the house scared her. She knew that she couldn't shoot an intruder. That left her few options.

"When you make up your mind, I'll be in the truck," Cy told her.

He actually walked out the door. Eb followed him with an amused grin that he didn't let Lisa see.

Lisa glared after him, hesitant and bristling with hurt pride. But in the end, she went upstairs, changed into jeans and a shirt and packed a small bag. Ten minutes later, he opened the door of the utility vehicle so that she could climb in with her tote bag.

"If Harley so much as grins, I'll kick him in the shins," she said after she'd fumbled her seat belt together.

"So will I," Cy promised her.

She glanced at him from the warm folds of her flannel-lined denim jacket. "Would you have shot that man?"

"If there hadn't been another way to stop him, yes."

"I couldn't shoot anybody," she said.

"I know. That's why you have to stay with me until we get Lopez." He glanced at her. "It won't be so bad. I can cook."

"So can I."

"Good. Fair division of labor." He glanced at her with a faint smile. "When the baby comes, we'll take turns getting up for his meals."

She felt a warm glow wash over her. She smiled, too. "Oh, I wouldn't want to sleep if he was hungry," she mused dreamily. "I'd get up, too."

He remembered his wife complaining bitterly about lost sleep, making formula, giving bottles. She hated everything to do with the baby, and couldn't begin to understand his affection for the tiny little boy, who wasn't even...

He closed his mind to the anguish that memory fostered, and concentrated on his driving instead.

Apparently Cy's men were asleep in the bunkhouse, because the ranch house was quiet when they arrived. He helped Lisa out of the vehicle and carried her suitcase into the house.

"You'll probably like this room. It faces the rose garden," he added with a smile.

She looked around at the simple, old-fashioned room with its canopied double bed and gauzy white curtains and white furniture. "It's very pretty," she murmured.

"The house belonged to an elderly woman, who was the last living member of her family," he said. "She had to go into a nursing home. I learned the history of the house from her. It belonged to her father, who was one of the better known Texas Rangers. She raised two kids and three grandkids here. One of her grandsons was a congressman, and another worked for the U.S. Secret Service. She was very proud of them."

"Is she living in Jacobsville?"

He nodded. "I go to visit her every other week. You might like to go along occasionally. She's a walking history of Texas."

"I'd like that." She was studying him with open curiosity. He looked so different in that stark black outfit that she wondered if she would even have recognized him if she'd seen him on the street. Her husband had been in law enforcement, but even he hadn't looked as dangerous as Cy Parks in commando gear.

He lifted an eyebrow.

"Sorry," she murmured with a shy smile. "You look different, that's all."

"Think of it as a covert ops business suit," he mused. "The object is to blend in with the night."

"Oh, you did that very neatly," she agreed.

He chuckled. "Get some sleep. There won't be anybody to bother you here, and you can sleep as late as you like."

She grimaced. "What about Puppy Dog?"

"What?"

"Puppy Dog," she said. "He's all shut up on the back porch…"

"I'll fetch him at daybreak," he said. "But if he eats one of my chickens, he's dog bone stew. Got that?"

"You've got chickens?"

"Five," he said. "Rhode Island Reds. I like fresh eggs."

She smiled. "I like them, too."

"A woman after my own heart." He moved toward

the door. "The windows are electronically wired, by the way," he added with the doorknob in his hand. "If anyone tries to open them from the outside, they'll think we're being bombed."

"That's reassuring."

"So it is. Sleep tight."

"You, too."

He spared her a glance. "Don't get up until you want to. I'll haul Puppy Dog over here at daybreak."

"He likes to chew up things," she said worriedly.

"You shouldn't let him eat heating pads, while we're on the subject."

"He can reach the shelf I keep them on," she said. "I didn't realize it until I saw him jump up to pull it down. By then I'd lost two and I thought I'd left them on the sofa." She shook her head. "He's already very tall. His father, Moose, is almost five feet tall when he stands on his hind legs."

"He'll be good protection for you when he's trained."

"He seems to be training me," she said on a wistful breath.

"I'll take care of that. 'Night."

She smiled. "Thanks for rescuing me."

"I had good help," he told her.

She stood staring after him even when the door

closed. Her life had just gone up two notches on the complications scale. She forced herself not to think of how hungry he'd made her the night they'd gone to Houston to the opera, of how much she liked being close to him. He'd been very standoffish since, so it was obvious that he didn't like the small taste of her he'd had. She was safe with him. Safe, pregnant and a widow. She shouldn't be thinking about kissing Cy. The thought made her uncomfortable, but she slept soundly all night long.

Harley walked in the kitchen door with a wicker basket full of eggs and a disgusted look on his face. He stopped short when he saw Lisa, in jeans and a sweatshirt with her dark blond hair in an unruly bun, making coffee.

She gave him a challenging look back. "Where's Cy?" she asked.

"Gone to town to have his truck cleaned."

That sounded intriguing. "Does he do that a lot?"

"Only when dogs throw up in it."

"Oh, dear," she said.

"Seems your puppy doesn't like to go for rides," he murmured with a grin. He put the basket of eggs on the table. "He's out in the barn with the boss's collie."

"I didn't know Cy had a dog."

"He didn't know he had one, either, until it got run over week before last," he remarked. "He picked it up and took it to the vet. It was a stray that somebody had put out, half-starved, full of fleas, almost dead from lack of care. Amazing what some dog shampoo, flea medicine, regular meals and attention can do for a mangy old cur." He shook his head. "For a hard-nosed man, he sure has some soft spots. He'd never make a soldier, let me tell you." He held up a hand when she started to speak. "Don't tell him I said that," he added. "He pays me a good salary and he's a fine man to work for. He can't help it if he isn't exactly G.I. Joe. Considering what he's been through, I guess he's got some grit in him somewhere."

She almost bit her tongue through trying not to tell Harley what she knew about his soft-centered employer. But that was Cy's business, and she didn't want to get on his bad side when she'd only arrived.

"I rode over to your place with the boss and drove your little VW back with me. It's in the garage. None of my business, but are you staying awhile?" he asked curiously.

"I guess so," she sighed. She poured coffee into a cup. "A man broke into my house last night. Cy let me come over here."

"Broke into your house? Why?"

She grew pensive. "My husband was an undercover DEA agent," she told him. "He was infiltrating a drug lord's organization when he was exposed and executed. Apparently the drug lord likes to set examples, like wiping out whole families of people who oppose him. I'm on his list."

"Then you sure came to the right place," Harley said with a beaming grin. "As it happens, you'll be safer here than anywhere else in the county, except maybe with Ebenezer Scott." He seemed to stand two feet taller. "I was in the Army Rangers for two years and I've had commando training. Nobody can slip by me."

"I can't tell you how much better I feel, knowing that," she said, smiling pleasantly.

He almost blushed. "Good. Well, I'll get back to my chores. Glad you're okay, Miss…Mrs. Monroe," he corrected, tipping his hat on his way out.

"Thanks for bringing my car," she said.

"No problem." He shot a grin back at her as he left.

She sat down at the kitchen table beside the eggs and shook her head. He didn't have a clue what was going on. His life was apparently so dull that he couldn't live without the illusion of bravery. She wondered how he would respond to a real threat, and hoped she never had to find out. He seemed a nice sort of man, but she had a feeling that he wasn't quite as formidable as he made out.

Cy came in for lunch, helping himself to bread, mayonnaise and luncheon meat while Lisa poured iced tea into tall glasses.

"I can make sandwiches," she offered.

He gave her a grin. "I'm used to doing it myself. Want a couple?"

"Just one, thanks," she agreed and sat down at her place beside his at the small table. "I'm sorry about Puppy Dog messing up your truck."

His eyebrows lifted under disheveled black hair. "Who told you?"

"Harley." She gave him a gamine look. "He said that he'd be glad to protect me from potential attackers, seeing as how he's a trained commando."

Cy chuckled softly. "I was his age once. Seems like fifty years ago, now."

She put her elbows on the table and propped her chin on her hands, watching him make sandwiches. "Did you swagger, too?"

"Probably. At least, I did until I saw combat for the first time. Nobody tells you that people scream when they get shot. On television they just grunt or groan and hold the part that's been shot." He shook his head. "It's a lot more…vivid…in real life."

"Were you afraid, the first time?"

"I was afraid every time," he corrected with a level stare. "Only a fool pretends he isn't. You learn to face the fear and deal with it, just like everyone else does."

"It's difficult, isn't it?"

"Difficult to watch people die, yes," he told her. "Difficult to live with what you do, too. I remember a young boy in Africa who was fighting the rebels. He carried a carbine in his hands and ammunition belts that probably weighed more than he did, strapped around his chest. His name was Juba." He smiled as he worked. "He had a passion for chocolate bars. We always had a few in our packs, just a taste of something sweet to remind us of civilization. One day, Juba ran ahead of us into a building the rebels had just evacuated. We hadn't swept it for traps and he wouldn't stop when we tried to warn him. He broke a trip wire right in the doorway and blew himself up." His hand hesitated on the knife as he spread mayonnaise on the bread. His eyes were solemn and quiet. "He didn't die right away," he added grimly. "We gave him morphine from one of our medical kits. Then I sat under a silk cotton tree with him in my arms and talked to him until he died." His eyes fell back to his task. "He was eleven years old."

She winced. "That's very young to be fighting a war."

"He'd already lost his parents and two sisters in the cross fire," he recalled. "He was alone in the world, except for us. We'd thrown in with the government forces. They were overwhelmed by the rebels and advertised for mercenaries. My unit went in. I started with thirty men and came back with three." He passed her a plate with a sandwich on it and started making two more for himself. "The rebels took over the capital and formed a government of their own. It stood for two months before outside troops joined forces with the overthrown government, moved in and took back possession of their country. Before they did, ten thousand people were shot or blown up in the streets."

"I'm sure I wouldn't make a good soldier, even if Harley thinks he would," she remarked somberly.

"I wanted to make enough money to retire while I was still a young man," he mused. "I planned to come back home, buy a ranch, get married and settle down." He finished his own sandwiches and took a sip of his iced tea. "It almost worked. But along the way, I helped a government agency get hard evidence on that drug lord Lopez," he said, searching her eyes.

"As I mentioned a while back, he had my house in Wyoming set on fire. The hitch was, my son was supposed to be rescued before the incendiary device was placed. Lopez's henchman didn't think one kid more or less would matter." He traced an invisible pattern on his coffee mug. "The only consolation I had was that Lopez had the assassin eliminated for that slipup. He doesn't kill children."

"I'm so sorry," she murmured, watching him.

"So am I. But all the regrets in the world won't bring back that little boy."

His face was harder than rock. She sketched it with her eyes. "You can help me take care of my little boy."

He glanced at her. "What makes you think it's a little boy?"

"Wishful thinking, I guess. I love baseball and soccer and working around the ranch. I know girls can do those things, too, but I'd love a son."

"You'd love whatever you get," he chided.

"Yes. I would." She grimaced.

"What's the matter."

"I don't know." She laughed nervously. "I have these mild cramps sometimes. I read a book about being pregnant, and it said some women have fleeting cramps during early pregnancy."

He scowled. "That doesn't sound good."

She picked up her sandwich. "Maybe it's just nerves. It's been a rough few weeks."

"Sure it has. But if those cramps get any worse, you go see a doctor."

"I will."

After lunch, he took her out to the huge, airy barn to see Puppy Dog, who was comfortably contained in a huge stall with a drain in the concrete floor, and fresh wheat straw making a comfortable place for him to sleep.

"Hello, Puppy Dog," she said, going into the stall to pet the frisky, enormous puppy. "Did you miss me?" She glanced past him at the clean containers of dog food and water, and the dog toys liberally scattered along the wall. "Maybe not, considering all the toys."

"Dogs need something to play with. Keeps them active and healthy. I got half a dozen for Bob, too."

"Bob?"

He motioned to her. She gave Puppy Dog a last hug and went out of the stall. He whined for a minute and then went back to pick up a ball he liked.

In the stall next door was a huge white-and-tan collie with an intelligent face and soft brown eyes. There were still traces of malnutrition in the coat, but Bob was beginning to shape up into a beautiful animal.

"He's a doll," she said, smiling at him.

"*She's* a doll."

She hesitated. Turned. Raised her eyebrows.

"*She's* a doll," he repeated.

"Bob is not a female name…"

"If a boy can be named Sue, a girl dog can be named Bob."

"You listen to too many Johnny Cash songs," she accused with a chuckle.

"He's great, isn't he?" he asked. "'A Boy Named Sue' was great, but I loved everything he ever recorded."

"I have two of his albums myself," she confessed.

He grinned. "I knew you had good taste."

She liked the way his eyes twinkled when he smiled. He was something of a curiosity around town, because he had a reputation for being a hard case and unsociable. But here, on his home ground, he was relaxed, pleasant, even amusing. She wondered how many people ever got to see this side of him. Probably not many.

"What happened to that man who broke into my house?" she asked abruptly.

"Sheriff's got him locked up," he told her. "We left the crowbar right where it dropped. The man wasn't even wearing gloves. There are enough fingerprints on it to convict him. He'll make bond, of course, and then he'll go home."

"Home?"

He turned toward her. "A man wearing an Armani suit drove up here a few days ago and introduced himself as my new neighbor. There's a honey packing warehouse on my border. But it's not honey they're distributing, if you understand what I mean."

She stilled. "Drugs?"

"Raw cocaine," he replied. "Or, rather, cocaine paste. At least, that's what we suspect they're stockpiling in that warehouse."

"Here, in Jacobsville?" she gasped.

"Right here," he said.

"Then tell the sheriff and let him send some men out to arrest the owners!"

"They won't find cocaine if they do," he carelessly. "In fact, I'd bet my boots that they'll phone in a tip about themselves just to draw the law out there to check around. And while they're checking, all the honey in the jars will be real honey, and even a drug-sniffing dog won't find a trace of cocaine. Having searched the place once and found nothing, local law enforcement will logically hesitate before they go back out there a second time. At least, not without some concrete evidence of malfeasance. It's easy to get sued for harassment, and believe me, Lopez would howl at the idea of taking our sheriff to court over it."

"You sound very cynical," she told him.

"I know how these people operate. In my checkered past, I've dealt with drug dealers, gunrunners, diamond smugglers, hit men…"

Her eyes were growing wider by the second. "You outlaw, you."

"Count on it," he told her. "I did what the job called for. Wars make strange bedfellows. Got to have guns and ammunition, you know, not to mention explosives, communications equipment, medicines. You can't walk into the nearest superstore and buy those."

"You can buy guns," she began.

"Registered guns," he emphasized. "They're required by law to do a background check before they sell a gun, and there's a waiting period. If you know where to go, you can get everything from Uzis to C-4, and no waiting."

"I had no idea," she murmured, shaking her head.

"It's almost impossible to shut these drug cartels down. They are run on a corporate structure. In a sense, they're multinational corporations. They have a hierarchy, complete with divisional managers and regional distribution networks. When you understand the way they work, you also understand why it's such an uphill battle. You can't arrest every gang member in the country. That's what it would take to stop it. And even then," he added, "there would still be dealers. You know why? Because where there's demand, there's supply. As long as there are people willing to pay for illegal drugs, there will be people who sell them."

"That's very demoralizing," she pointed out.

"Of course it is. But you can't fight a war unless you know the enemy. Every time we shut down one of the cartels, we come one step closer to cutting off the supply. It's discouraging to see the statistics, but there are a lot of dedicated people trying to stop the drug trade. I like to think that one day, they'll succeed."

"I'd be very happy if they could put Mr. Lopez someplace where he can't shoot me," she told him.

He smiled. "At least," he said, "we've got *you* someplace where he can't. Now eat that sandwich. Waste not, want not."

She laughed softly and bit into the sandwich.

Lisa settled in at the ranch, much to the interest of Cy's cowboys, who walked around with stunned expressions every time they saw her. Most people around Jacobsville had the same attitude, because of Cy's remoteness. Of course, he had dropped the charges against Belinda Craig's rebellious young charge at her summer youth camp when the lad had been caught trespassing on his property. And he'd taken Candy Marshall, that nice young woman from the local cattlemen's association, out to the bar to look for Guy Fenton when he'd been drunk for the last time before he fell in love with Candy and married her. But other than those two incidents, he kept to himself and had little if anything to do with women. Now here was Lisa Monroe, a young widow alone and pregnant, living with him. It was delicious gossip.

As Cy had predicted, the man who was arrested for breaking into Lisa's house had skipped bond and left the country. That didn't let her out of the woods, though, he assured her. Lopez wouldn't stop until he accomplished whatever goal he'd set. Since it was common knowledge that Lisa was staying with Cy, the drug lord wouldn't have far to look to find her.

Also, as Cy had predicted, an anonymous tip led sheriff's deputies to the "honey warehouse" behind Cy's ranch. The flats of jars and the beehives Harley had watched them unload were searched and searched again, by deputies, DEA agents and drug-sniffing dogs. Predictably, they found nothing illegal and went away. It didn't take a genius to realize that it would be hard to get the law enforcement people out there again without vivid concrete evidence of illegal operation. Gossip was that the owners of the new "business" had already threatened a multimillion-dollar lawsuit against the various agencies for just setting foot on the property. Jacobsville was a small town in a small county and its sheriff's department already had such a tiny budget that they hadn't had a raise in two years. The county commissioners went pale at the thought of even a small lawsuit. Like it or not, the sheriff was constrained by politics and capital.

There was one encouraging new development. Rodrigo, the Mexican national who'd successfully infiltrated Lopez's distribution network, managed to get a brief message to Eb Scott, saying that a huge shipment of cocaine paste was scheduled to be shipped into the country soon through Mexico. He had few details as yet, but would keep his eyes and ears open and report anything pertaining to the shipment as soon as he heard it.

Lisa overheard Cy talking with Eb Scott on a shortwave radio—an odd way to communicate, she thought, when the telephone was right beside him.

When he gave his call sign and cut the unit off, she asked him about it.

"This—" he indicated the set "—has a scrambler. It's high-tech, not a conventional shortwave device."

She shook her head as she studied the array of electrical gadgets in the study where Cy did his bookwork. "I've never seen so many strange-looking things."

"Didn't Walt have equipment like this?" he asked curiously.

"If he did, he kept it someplace else." She sighed, thinking of Walt's horrible end and their very brief marriage. Absently her hand went to her belly.

"You were up walking the floor last night," he commented. "Why?"

She shifted. "I had some more cramps," she murmured. But she wasn't too concerned. When she called the doctor she was told it wasn't so unusual to have twinges now and again.

He scowled, watching her. "This isn't the first time you've had cramping. You need to call a doctor."

"I did, day before yesterday," she reminded him. "He said it's a fairly common complaint in early pregnancy, and as long as there's no bleeding there's no reason to worry. Actually I feel better than I have for weeks."

Cy managed not to say that she looked delectable, but she did. Her long, soft hair was loose around her shoulders and even with glasses on, she was pretty. He liked the little tip-tilted nose and the full, soft bow of a mouth. He liked the way she watched him, like a curious little bird, when he worked around the ranch. He especially liked the way she looked in cutoff jeans that showed the curves of her legs up to the thighs, and the way her knit blouse outlined her firm, small breasts. He remembered the feel of her in his arms, the softness of her young mouth, and his whole body clenched. She didn't know, couldn't know, what an ordeal it was for him to be in the same house with her and never touch her. But he didn't want her to feel threatened. She was at risk, and she had no place else to go.

She lifted both eyebrows when she saw that the dark scowl over his green eyes was getting more ominous by the minute. "What's wrong?" she asked.

"Don't go out in the yard like that," he said abruptly.

She looked down at herself and then back at him, puzzled. "I beg your pardon?"

"You heard me." He stood up, towering over her. That was a mistake because now he could see the upper curves of her breasts that her knit blouse left visible. "I don't want my men leering at you." Especially Harley, he thought angrily.

Her eyes kindled with humor. "You're leering at me right now," she pointed out, grinning because he obviously found her attractive. Her knees suddenly felt wobbly.

"I'm not leering. I'm noticing. But I've got some young men with bucking hormones and to them a woman in a steel drum would probably look sexy. Wear jeans and a blouse that buttons to your throat."

"Bucking hormones," she mused. "That's a new one."

"You aren't that naive," he grumbled. "You were married. You can tell when a man wants you."

Not really, she wanted to tell him. Walt had only slept with her twice, and apparently had to force himself both times. He wasn't really attracted to her physically, and the feeling had been mutual. It wasn't that way with Cy. She looked at him and her knees went weak.

"I'm not wearing a steel drum around the place to do housework," she informed him. "Hormones or no hormones. Heavens, I'm pregnant! Who's going to make a pass at a pregnant woman?"

"Any man under eighty who sees you dressed like that," Cy said flatly. "Up to and including me."

Her heart jumped into her throat as her eyes lifted to his and were captured. She felt the breath rush past her parted lips as the look intensified, making her feel odd in the strangest places, even more strongly than the night at the opera. She remembered the taste of his mouth on hers, and no matter how disloyal it might have been to her late husband, she wanted it again.

"Would you really?" she asked.

He looked uncomfortable. "We were talking about how you dressed. When you go outside around the men, don't wear shorts and low-cut blouses."

"Are you telling me that grown men can't control themselves and I have to go around in a coat all summer to keep from disturbing them?" she wanted to know. "That's not fair."

"Oh, hell, of course it's not fair! But men are going to look when there's something to see. All the legislation in the world won't kill a basic human instinct, and that one is hundreds of thousands of years old!"

Her eyes dropped to his hard mouth and she remembered, not for the first time, how delicious it felt when he kissed her. Then she felt guilty for even the thought. She was forgetting Walt, something that Cy hadn't. He hadn't touched her again since she moved in. He was respecting her husband's death. She was sorry about Walt, but when she got close to Cy, her emotions were all over the place.

"Harley seems to spend a lot of time in the house lately," he remarked unexpectedly.

"He gathers the eggs for me," she replied, fighting down the excitement she felt as his green gaze slid over her once again. "Ever since you found that chicken snake in the henhouse, I've been nervous about putting my hand in the nests."

"We moved the chicken snake into the barn," he reminded her.

"Well, it isn't in handcuffs or anything, now is it?" she demanded. "It can go wherever it wants to, and I've noticed that snakes seem to feel violent attractions to anyone who's scared of them."

"In that case, I don't suppose even the house is safe."

She immediately started looking around her feet and he burst out laughing.

"Never mind," he said on a sigh. "I guess Harley's better than a snake, at that."

"I know he isn't what he pretends to be," she replied with a smile. "But he's nice. Besides," she added with a calculating look that he missed, "isn't he helping to keep an eye on those people who set up the honey warehouse next door to you?"

He didn't like that, not one bit. Eb had agreed to let Harley spy on the drug dealers if he kept his mouth shut. Quite obviously he'd been bragging about his exploits to Lisa.

"Did he tell you that?" he asked quietly.

She didn't quite trust the look in his eyes. She didn't want to get Harley in trouble. On the other hand, she didn't like telling lies.

"He mentioned that he was watching them to make sure the bees didn't threaten your purebred cattle," she said, which was the truth. Or, at least, what Harley had told her.

"I see." He relaxed visibly and she knew she'd said

the right thing. She wondered why he was so concerned about bees, when plenty of people around Jacobsville kept them. Maybe he had a hidden fear of flying insects.

Cy's green eyes narrowed. Harley was young, in his late twenties, and despite his bravado, in peak physical condition. Cy was thirty-five and scarred, inside and out. Perhaps Lisa couldn't help liking the younger man. And he had been kind to her.

"If you'd rather I asked someone else to fetch the eggs, I can," she began, trying to find a way to erase that dark scowl on his lean face.

"Of course not," he said at once. "Why should I mind?"

He left her wondering about that, and she went back to what she'd been doing.

Two days later, Cy came into the kitchen and found Harley holding Lisa's hand in the living room.

Both of them turned and jerked at his sudden appearance. Harley's high cheekbones colored as Cy's green eyes glittered at him like a poisonous snake uncoiling.

"Hi, boss!" he said with forced enthusiasm. "I was, uh, just showing Lisa…Miss…Mrs. Monroe how to break a hold."

"Yes, he was," Lisa said quickly. She had on those same tight jeans and a yellow sweater with a vee neck that was much too low when she bent over. Cy's unsmiling scrutiny made her feel as if she'd just committed adultery. She'd put on the outfit deliberately, not for Harley, but for Cy. He hadn't been near her until now. Harley had.

"I'd better get back to the garage now, I guess," Harley said, still flushed. He was wearing a white T-shirt and jeans with a red rag sticking out of his back pocket. "I'm overhauling the cattle truck, boss."

"Good. Hadn't you better go do it?" Cy asked with a bite in his voice that he seldom used these days. He looked dangerous, something Harley noted with surprise.

"Sure thing!" Harley went through the kitchen and out the back door without another word.

"He really was showing me how to get out of a hold," she told Cy with her hands on her hips.

Cy moved toward her, too jealous to think properly. "Was he now? And you've learned the lesson? Show me. Let's see you get out of this hold!"

He had her around the waist and flush against every line of his lean, powerful body before she could speak. She opened her mouth to protest and his lips claimed hers, hungry and rough and demanding.

She wanted to fight. She really did. But the closeness of him, the warmth, the strength of him drained her of every semblance of protest. With a tiny little cry, she slid her arms under his and pushed as close as she could get, answering that hard kiss with all the pent-up longing of the weeks since he'd touched her. She felt a shudder go through him even as her own body rippled with passion.

He said something against her mouth that she didn't hear, didn't understand. Her mouth pushed up against his, answering the devouring fierceness of his hard lips. It wasn't a practiced sensuous kiss at all. It was flash-fire need, hunger, desire, out of control. It gave her an odd feeling of pride that she could throw him off balance. And as much as it shamed her to admit it even in the privacy of her mind, his jealousy of Harley made her even hungrier for him.

His body began to swell and old instincts jerked him out of her embrace. He stepped back, fighting the desire that tautened every muscle he had. The unexpected explosion left him shocked and uncertain.

They were both breathing unsteadily, staring at each other more like combatants than lovers.

"I don't like Harley touching you," he said bluntly, bristling with possessive instincts he hadn't known he had.

"I noticed." She sounded breathless.

His green eyes slid down her body and back up again with desire and possession equally mixed. "You're pregnant."

She nodded. Somewhere deep in her mind she wished it was Cy's baby. That was disloyal to Walt and she should be ashamed. Her hand went protectively to her waistline.

He muttered something under his breath and stepped back. "I shouldn't have touched you," he bit off. "God knows, I'm trying not to! I might manage it if you'd stop tempting me with tight jeans and shirts cut to the navel in front!"

So that was why he'd kept his distance. She was pregnant and he felt that he should be trying to take care of her, not make love to her. But he wanted her. She knew it in every cell of her body. It made her glow with new delight; with hope.

He got his breath back and glared at her. "Harley's fixing the truck. Make sure he stays out of here. If you don't tell him, I will, and I won't be diplomatic."

She wasn't offended by the possessive note in his deep voice. She liked it. "All right, Cy."

His eyes narrowed. Her compliance, unexpected, knocked the fire off his temper. "Stay inside and keep the doors locked."

"Okay."

"Don't assume that you're safe just because Harley's in the garage," he added tautly. "He isn't half as savvy as he thinks he is, and he's never dealt with men like Lopez."

"Okay," she repeated with a smile.

He drew in a heavy breath. "There's a loaded pistol in my middle desk drawer. Just in case."

"I'll remember."

Her mouth was swollen from the pressure of his, and it gave him a feeling of pride to see her disheveled and flustered because of him. He didn't smile, but his eyes did.

"Are you leaving?" she asked breathlessly.

"Yes." He dragged his eyes away from her to check his watch. "I've got to drive up to Kingsville to see a man about some new bulls."

She knew where he was going the minute he mentioned the town, and her soft sigh was all too audible. "I went on a tour of that ranch once, with Dad," she said. "It made our little operation look like a milkmaid enterprise. They had some beautiful breeding stock."

"I like Santa Gertrudis cattle," he said. "No better place to buy them than where the foundation herd originated." His eyes narrowed again as he studied her. "While I'm gone, don't go out of the house for any reason. Harley will have the house in sight all the time, and I've got surveillance equipment linked to Eb Scott's place. If anything happens that Harley can't handle, Eb can be here in five minutes. You aren't afraid by yourself?"

"By myself?" she exclaimed. "Cy, have you noticed those fifteen cowboys who work for you…?"

"Only six of them work here full-time. And none of them are around the ranch house for most of the day, except early in the morning and late in the afternoon," he told her. "Harley's working on one of the cattle trucks, which is the only reason that he'll be nearby. If you need him, push the intercom button and he'll come right up." He indicated the button next to the wall phone in the dining room. He hated having to tell her that. He hated the idea of Harley anywhere near her. "And keep all the doors locked."

"You're worried," she gathered.

"I've heard a few things. Yes, I'm worried. Humor me."

She shrugged and smiled up at him. "Okay, boss."

His eyebrow lifted and he smiled back. "Oh, that sounds sweet," he drawled. "Pity I know it's just lip service. You smile and nod your head when I tell you, for your own good, not to do something. And then you go right out and do it the minute my back's turned."

"It always worked with Dad," she mused. "It's a waste of time to argue with some men," she added.

He reached for his hat on the wall rack. "And some women," he countered. "Watch yourself."

"You do that, too," she returned smartly. "You're not on Lopez's good list, either."

He propped his hat on his head as the back door opened to admit Harley. He glanced at Lisa from under the wide brim. "Yes, but Lopez doesn't like to take unnecessary chances, and he's already had one bad brush with the law," he began as Harley's footsteps became audible behind him. "He won't come here unless he gets pretty desperate…"

"Because he knows I'm here, Mrs. Monroe," Harley interrupted with an irrepressible grin at his boss and their houseguest. "Nobody's going to lay a finger on you while I'm on the job."

"Of course," Lisa said and didn't dare look at Cy.

"I just came in to get a soft drink. It's thirsty work. You, uh, don't mind, boss?" he asked Cy warily.

"I don't mind," Cy lied. "But don't get careless," he told his young foreman, and with more than usual caution. "Lopez won't."

Harley dismissed Lopez and his entire organization with a flick of his hand. "All the same, he won't come around here."

Cy wanted to argue the point, but the younger man was in a concrete mind-set and he wouldn't listen to reason. He'd just have to hope that Harley wouldn't do something stupid.

"I'll be back late. Remember to keep the doors locked," he cautioned Lisa.

"You bet."

He left rather reluctantly. Harley got himself a cold drink out of the refrigerator and paused at the back door. Lisa went to the kitchen counter and got out a bowl and a knife and some potatoes and began peeling them for potato salad. "I wanted to make sure I hadn't got you in trouble," Harley said sheepishly. "Mr. Parks was pretty hot when he came in."

"It's all right," she assured him with a smile. "He's protective of me because of the baby," she added.

Harley grimaced. "I should have realized that. He isn't a man who has much to do with women, you see." He shrugged. It had seemed like violent jealousy to Harley, but now Mr. Parks's ill temper seemed justified. He wouldn't want anybody making passes at her when she was pregnant. Of course, he added silently as he looked at her, she did seem somewhat flustered and her mouth was swollen. He wondered…

"Don't you want that soft drink in a glass with

some ice?" she asked. His scrutiny was making her nervous.

"No, thanks, this is fine. Well, if you need me, just call, Mrs. Monroe. I'll be trying to find the oil leak in that engine."

He looked as if he'd found several, she mused, judging from all the black stains on his once-white sweatshirt. It never ceased to amaze her that Harley always found something white to put on when he was going to do a dirty job.

"I know where the intercom button is," she assured him. "But I don't think I'll need to use it."

"You never know. I'll lock the door as I go out. See you later."

"Sure."

He locked the door and moved slowly toward the garage. Lisa watched him walk back to the garage with a slight frown between her eyes. Cy was unusually worried about Lopez, and it made her uneasy. Surely the man wasn't going to risk having any more men picked up by the sheriff. After all, he'd lost two in the midnight raid on Lisa's house that had prompted Cy to bring her here to stay with him.

On the other hand, she had to admit, if the man based his reputation on keeping his word, he couldn't afford not to make good on a threat. But she was fairly certain that Lopez was long gone. Otherwise why would Cy have gone off in the first place?

Reassured, she went to the kitchen, put Lopez forcefully out of her thoughts and peeled the rest of the potatoes.

Harley finished most of his repairs on the truck and came back into the house for another drink, liberally stained with grease and a noticeable cut on the back of one lean hand. It was bleeding. There was even a little grease in his crew-cut sandy hair.

"Here," Lisa said at once, leading him to the kitchen sink. "Wash that with antibacterial soap while I find a bandage."

"It's nothing much, Mrs. Monroe," he protested, but very weakly.

She smiled to herself as she fetched adhesive bandages from the kitchen cabinet and began peeling one apart to cover the deep scratch after it was clean.

"I wish you'd been with us in Africa," he observed wryly, his blue eyes twinkling. "Several of us got banged up out in the bush."

"In the bush? With the lions?" she exclaimed.

He held out his dried hand for her to put on the bandage. "Didn't see any lions," he remarked. "But there were plenty of guerrillas. Not the furry kind, either." He sighed and smiled dreamily. "That's the life, Mrs.

Monroe, fighting for principles and a king's ransom in loot. When I get another two or three training courses under my belt, that's what I'm going to do—I'm going back to Africa to make my fortune."

"Or get yourself shot," she observed.

"Not a chance. I'm too handy with close quarter weapons." He looked as if he could strut sitting down as he said it. "My instructor said he'd never seen anybody who was such a natural in martial arts. And I can throw a knife, too."

"It wouldn't do you much good if the other guy had a gun, would it?" she asked innocently.

"It isn't so hard to disarm a man, if you know how," he said confidently. "They taught us a lot of tricks. I guarantee there isn't a man alive who could threaten me with a gun. I know my business."

Lisa almost winced at the certainty in his tone. He was young, probably not much older than she was, and she couldn't help thinking that a little knowledge could be a dangerous thing.

"Thanks for patching me up," he told her with a grin. "I found the leak. Now all I have to do is put all the parts back on the truck without having any left over."

She laughed as she put away the bandages. "I'd have bagsful left over," she mused. "I can cook and work horses and cattle, but I don't know a thing about engines."

"My dad's a mechanic," he told her. "He has his own garage. I grew up learning how to fix things. It comes in handy on a ranch this size, even though we have a full-time mechanic on the payroll." He shook his head. "It must cost a fortune to run a place like this. I guess Mr. Parks inherited his."

She went back to her potatoes, her head down as she asked, "You don't think he might have worked for it?"

"Not many professions that pay the kind of money he has, from what I've heard," he said. "Besides, he's not exactly a risk-taker. He doesn't do much of the heavy work around here and he really favors that left arm from time to time. I guess it still hurts him sometimes."

"I guess." She didn't add that he might change his mind about Cy if he ever saw him dressed in black and carrying an automatic weapon.

"Thanks for the first aid," he told her as he retrieved another soft drink from the refrigerator and closed it. "Better get back to work."

He went out and the door locked behind him. Lisa forced herself not to think about that hungry kiss she and Cy shared in the living room or if Cy was going to draw back into his shell again. He was a complex and attractive man, but she seemed to be off-limits. Pity. They had so much in common....

It was late afternoon when Lisa heard a truck pull up out by the barn. She was sure it was Cy. Without thinking, she got up from the kitchen table where she'd been rearranging a messy kitchen drawer and went right out the back door.

It wasn't Cy. It was three men, all foreign-looking. Harley saw them and came out of the garage, wiping his hands on a red work cloth.

"Can I help you boys?" he asked with faint menace.

"We are looking for Mr. Parks," the flashily dressed one said with an ear-to-ear grin.

"He's gone to Kingsville to look at bulls," Harley said obligingly. "I don't know when he'll be back."

"How convenient," the man drawled, and pulled an automatic weapon from under his jacket.

Harley froze in place and his jaw dropped.

Lisa realized the danger immediately. She closed and locked the back door and ran to Cy's study, locking herself inside. She grabbed the mic of the shortwave set, already positioned to the Scott ranch, and gave out a Mayday call.

"Stay in the house," Eb's calm but very hushed voice came over the air instantly. "Cy's on his way."

He left before she could ask what he meant. She didn't know whether to lock herself in and wait, or go to a window and try to see what had happened to poor Harley. She felt guilty that she hadn't been able to do anything for him, but she was one person against three men, one of whom was dangerously armed.

In the end, she grabbed the loaded pistol Cy had told her he kept in his center desk drawer and went cautiously down the hall. She peered out the curtain that covered the upper, glassed portion of the kitchen door. Harley was in the grip of a man at least his physical equal, a pistol at his throat. One of the other men was looming with that automatic weapon and she just glimpsed the third wandering into the garage, out of sight.

She ground her teeth together and held the huge .45

automatic pistol tighter, wondering what she should do. She'd never fired a pistol in her life, but if she had to use it, she thought she could. Shivering with nerves, her heart pounding, her mouth dry, she heard the sound of a truck approaching very fast. Cy's big red Expedition roared up in the yard. He was out of it seconds after the engine died.

But it wasn't the Cy she was used to seeing. He walked slowly toward the two visitors in plain sight, his tall figure bent slightly forward, and he was cradling his burned left arm in his right hand.

"You are Cy Parks," the man with the automatic weapon called in a cold tone.

"Yes," Cy replied quietly. He glanced at Harley, who was red-faced and nervous, held securely in the grip of the second man.

"We want the woman," the flashily dressed visitor continued. "You will bring her out to us. Now."

"She's a widow. She's pregnant," Cy began.

"This is nothing to us," the man replied. "We were told to bring the woman back. It will cost us our lives not to comply with the instructions we were given."

Cy sighed audibly. "I'll go get her," he said with resignation.

"Mr. Parks!" Harley burst out, horrified. "Man, you can't...you can't let them have Mrs. Monroe!"

"They'll shoot us if we don't, son," Cy told the other man in a subdued tone that matched his bent stance. As he spoke, he let go of his burned arm and let it dangle at his side. The right hand moved, just a fraction, but his limping posture had the full attention of the armed men. They didn't notice the movement under his long sleeve. "You might let poor old Harley go," he added. "He just works for me."

"Let a trained mercenary loose on the three of us?" The man laughed. "We heard him talking to the woman in the kitchen about his exploits in Africa."

Which meant, Cy deduced, that they had the house bugged. He'd have to do something about that, and quickly. He glanced at Harley and prayed that the younger man wouldn't panic and do something stupid.

"It was a lie. Honest!" Harley swallowed hard. "I'm not a merk. I'm just a simple, working cowboy…!"

"Why, of course he is. And do I look like any sort of threat to armed men?" Cy asked softly. "I mean, look at me. I'm just a poor cripple."

Harley grimaced. It hurt him to see poor old Mr. Parks grovel like that. If only he could get that pistol away from his throat. He might be able to do something to save Mrs. Monroe and his boss! His fears were still present but subsiding a little as he realized the danger his boss and Lisa were in. He had to conquer the fear. He knew what to do. Even if he'd had little training, he remembered the moves. And he'd been an army ranger when he was in the service, only a short time before he came to work for Cy Parks. He wasn't a coward. He could do what he needed to do, to protect Cy and Lisa. He could do it. His head lifted and new purpose narrowed his eyes as he watched the armed men.

The man with the automatic weapon shrugged. "I see that you are injured. But this man told the woman that he had commando training and would not hesitate to use it," he told Cy. "Am I to believe now that he is harmless?"

"No," Cy drawled. "It's more than enough if you believe I am," he said enigmatically and glanced at Harley. "You just stay put, Harley," he added in a tone that made Harley frown. "I'll just go get Mrs. Monroe..." His head turned abruptly to the left of the gunman and he pointed. "Good God, look at that!"

The man with the automatic weapon reacted predictably and was diverted for a few precious seconds. It was enough. Cy's hand moved so fast that his knife was in the man's shoulder before he could turn his head back, causing him to drop the automatic weapon as he groaned in shock and pain. Even as that knife hit the target, Cy whirled and sent a second knife slicing through the air. It hit the man holding the pistol at Harley's neck, pinning his forearm, pistol, sleeve and all, to the wood of the barn wall behind him. The man cried out and Harley ducked and got out of the way immediately.

Green eyes blazing, Cy rushed forward, aimed an explosive high kick at the first man's stomach, bringing him down instantly. He fell, trying to extricate the knife from his shoulder at the same time, with little success.

"There's…another man…in there!" Harley called urgently through his shock.

"There was." A deep chuckle accompanied the words. Eb Scott came out of the barn with a miserable-looking man in denims held at gunpoint. "He made a fatal error. Never turn your back to a dark corner. Nice timing, Cy."

Cy didn't answer. He jerked up the automatic weapon and spared a glance for the groaning man on the ground and the other one, pinned to the wall of the barn.

"I didn't want to do it like this," Cy said calmly, walking to the man his second knife had pinned to the barn wall. "But if you're going to set a trap, it's best done on your home ground and in your own time. Oh, shut up for God's sake," he growled at his victim as he jerked the knife out and wiped it on the man's shirt-sleeve. "You're barely nicked! When you get a Bowie knife sticking out of your arm, you can complain."

Harley was still staring at his boss with wide eyes. He hadn't said a single word. He felt his head to make sure it was where he'd left it.

"You all right, Harley?" Cy asked curtly.

"Shh...sure," he stammered.

"I'll just check on Lisa." Cy strode off toward the house.

Harley stared after his boss as if he'd never seen him before. "Did you see that?" Harley asked Eb Scott. "Did you see it? He had the second knife in the air even before the first one hit its target!"

"You said he was no threat!" the assailant with the formerly pinned forearm growled at the man in the suit. Both were holding their wounds.

"I thought he was crippled!" the flashily dressed man growled. The knife was still in his shoulder, and he didn't dare pull it out for fear it might hemorrhage at withdrawal.

"So did I," Harley murmured, but only Eb heard him.

"Cy's not quite what he seems," was all Eb had to say about it.

* * *

On the porch, Lisa had watched with surprise and disbelief as Cy easily took care of the two armed men, while Harley stood shell-shocked nearby. If she'd ever worried about him, her mind rested easier after she saw the ease with which he subdued the armed assailants. She watched him with covetous, protective eyes, almost limp with relief. She'd been so worried that he might die right in front of her eyes. She opened the door as Cy mounted the steps and rushed out to throw herself against his chest, oblivious to his shocked delight. She was still holding the gun in one hand.

He took it from her, keeping the other arm around her, and put the safety back on. "Were you going to come out shooting and rescue me?" he asked with a grin.

"If I got the chance, I was," she said huskily, clinging harder. "I certainly wasn't going to cower in the house and let them kill you."

His eyes were warm with affection as he lifted his dark head to search her flushed face. "Nice to know I can count on backup when I need it," he told her, tracing a soft pattern down her flushed cheek.

She smiled at him and only looked away when she heard sirens and saw two sheriff's cars pull up in the driveway with their lights flashing. "Speaking of backup," she gestured. "Did you plan this?"

He shrugged. "Eb planned it and convinced me to go along," he said quietly. "All those surveillance gadgets paid for themselves this afternoon. Eb was already in the barn when I left here. He waited to act after the guns were drawn because he didn't want to get Harley killed." He shook his head as he saw Harley standing morose and miserable against the barn with his arms folded while the deputies handcuffed the three men. Barely two minutes later, an ambulance joined the patrol cars. "What I didn't know was that Lopez had the house bugged," he added curtly. "When we get these guys in custody, I'm going to sweep the house and get rid of them."

"They can hear what we do in the house?" she asked worriedly.

He glanced down at her and knew she meant what they were doing in the living room before he left. He smiled slowly. "Not all of it," he murmured wickedly. "Probably they only had listening devices in the kitchen, since we spend so much time in there."

"Oh." She sighed with relief.

"I'd better go and have a word with the deputies," Cy told her. "You okay?"

She grinned. "Never better. Are you?"

"Can't hurt a weed," he replied, winked and walked back down the steps.

Eb and Cy explained what had happened to the deputies. Cy agreed to swear out a warrant so that the three men could be held. He was furious that Lopez had dared to send men onto his own place after Lisa. He wasn't ever going to get the chance to do that again. He swore it.

As the two wounded prisoners were being loaded up in the ambulance and the other one confined in the patrol car for the trip to jail, Cy joined Harley at the barn door.

"I'm all hot air," Harley said with cold self-contempt. He couldn't meet the older man's eyes. "All that damned bragging about what I could do, and how I could take care of everybody. And look at me! I was taken by surprise and overpowered by a man half my size. I'm a fraud, Mr. Parks. You ought to fire me on the spot."

Cy only smiled. Harley was showing the first signs of wisdom. And even if he'd been overpowered, he'd conquered whatever fears he had. Cy knew that the younger man's pride was in shreds at being surprised and captured. He'd been in similar situations himself. No need to rub it in, just because he'd overreacted at Harley holding Lisa's hand.

"If I fire you, who's going to gather Lisa's eggs every morning?" Cy asked.

Harley couldn't believe he'd actually heard that droll question. He forced his shamed eyes up, and found his boss's eyes twinkling.

"You don't want to fire me?" he asked.

"Not today," Cy replied. "Get back in there and finish getting that cattle truck fixed. We'll need it tomorrow to haul calves."

"It's finished," Harley said with a faint smile. "I was just putting it back together when those guys drove up and caught me off guard."

Harley still felt a little disoriented. Mr. Parks, on the other hand, didn't have a hair out of place and seemed supremely calm. Despite the cool weather, Harley felt perspiration on his forehead. He wiped his sweaty brow on his arm and let out a heavy breath. He even managed a grin. "I guess you learned how to throw a knife when you were in the military. You, uh, were in the military?"

"Somewhat."

"Well, it was amazing, what you did with those knives," Harley continued. "That's some aim you've got, Mr. Parks."

"I get in a little practice now and then."

Harley moved away from the barn. "You sure had

those guys foxed about how helpless you were," he said, chuckling. "They bought every word."

"To their cost," Cy said easily, without breaking stride. "You never underestimate an adversary, if you want to live."

"You've, uh, been in a few fights then?"

Cy's green eyes were enigmatic as he glanced back at the younger man. "Stop fishing, Harley. Get that truck running."

He turned again and started toward the house. Harley watched him go with raging curiosity. On an impulse he didn't even understand, Harley picked up the pistol his captor had dropped where it lay forgotten in the straw. He tossed it toward Cy Parks's back.

As if he sensed danger, Cy whirled immediately and caught the weapon in midair. He had it cocked and leveled at Harley's nose in the space between one heartbeat and the next. Harley stopped breathing as he looked down the barrel for seconds that seemed like hours.

Cy cursed harshly and lowered the gun. "If you ever do that again, so help me, I'll shoot you in the foot, Harley!" he growled, furious. He snapped on the safety and walked toward the sheriff's deputies to leave the weapon with them.

Harley let out the breath he'd been holding. He'd

served two years in the army himself, in the rangers. He didn't know a single man who could have done what Cy Parks just had. That was a sort of training that men only got in some elite fighting force, and it wasn't regular military. He forced himself to walk back to the garage without casting another glance at his enigmatic boss. He felt as if his legs had turned to rubber.

Lisa was uneasy all night. She kept hearing noises. She dreamed that Cy was in front of the man with the machine gun, but that he hadn't managed to throw those knives in time. She woke up crying, in a cold sweat.

The door opened, the light came on and Cy stood over her, dressed in pajama bottoms with his broad, hairy, scarred bare chest. His dark hair was tousled, his eyes narrow with concern.

"You screamed," he said.

She sat up in her sweatpants and pullover white cotton T-shirt and hugged her knees. She couldn't quite see him because her glasses were in the drawer of the bedside table. She could imagine how she looked with her eyes red and wet with tears and her long hair tangled all around her.

"Sorry if I woke you," she said miserably. "It's been a rough day."

"For me, too," he replied. "I'm sorry you ever got mixed up in this business."

"So am I, but there's not much we can do about that now." She pushed back her long, sweaty hair. "Now Lopez seems to be after you, too."

"No. He's after you. This was a test run, to see if he could get to you on my ranch."

"He didn't."

"No, he didn't."

"You think he'll try again."

"They say Lopez will follow a man to hell to get even with him," he said quietly. "I believe it."

"What am I going to do? I can't keep on staying here…"

"Why not?"

"Well…"

He came around the side of the bed. "Move over," he said, sitting down beside her on the bedspread. "Now listen. I've got a big house and plenty of room. As long as you're here, right here, I can protect you, and I will. You've got a baby coming and you need someone. There's no reason you can't stay."

She looked worried. She picked at the cover. "Cy, people are already talking about us…"

"They'll stop when we get married."

She didn't seem to breathe for a space of seconds. She

looked up at him with a curious mixture of shyness, excitement and pleasure. "Married."

"Married."

She picked at a fingernail while she turned the proposal over in her mind. She was barely widowed. Whatever would people think of her?

"We don't advertise what's going on in this town, but the people who count know that you're staying here because you're in danger," he said quietly. "As for all the rest, if we marry, no one will have any reason for talk. I'm not proposing for any hidden agenda," he added. "We'll have a marriage of convenience. Period."

That was vaguely disappointing, and she hoped she could keep him from seeing how it affected her.

"Okay," she said after a minute. "But you can kick me out when this Lopez thing is over," she added and managed a smile.

"Fair enough," he agreed, his face carefully schooled not to let any hint of emotion show through. "But only if you want to leave by then. I wouldn't make that offer to any other woman. I've had a bad time with marriage. If Lopez hadn't decided to target you, I wouldn't have proposed in the first place."

"I know that," she said.

"Not that you aren't attractive," he said unexpectedly. "I think you know that under different circumstances, you'd be first on the endangered list. I haven't made a secret of the way you affect me. But you're pregnant and a very recent widow. Under the circumstances, it would hardly be appropriate to take advantage of the situation."

He was talking in riddles and she was very puzzled by the look in his eyes when he spoke to her. Odd, how reluctant he sounded to have her leave. But surely he was marrying her for the reasons he'd mentioned. He'd been through his own time of pain. She knew that there must be times when he ached for the child who had died in such a terrible manner. But for whatever reason, he was offering Lisa a marriage of companion-ship, protection for her baby. She couldn't have turned it down to save her life. Living with him would be heaven, even if he kept her at arm's length.

"Are you sure it's the right thing to do?" she asked worriedly.

"Yes, I am," he said firmly. "And the sooner, the bet-ter."

She toyed with a fold of her sweatpants. "I might be in the way."

His chest rose and fell heavily. His eyes narrowed. He looked at her with such hunger that it was blatant when she met his eyes.

Involuntarily she let her knees down. The T-shirt was thin and his eyes went instantly to the thrust of her breasts against it. Her mauve nipples were very noticeable, making soft peaks under the fabric.

His breathing changed. Her own eyes went to that broad chest and she wondered how it would feel against her.

"Don't push your luck," he said in a husky tone. "It's been three years. More than that. I didn't want her after my son was born, and the feeling was mutual."

Her eyes lifted to his. "You want me."

He nodded, very slowly. His eyes went back to the T-shirt and her own roamed over his bare chest like seeking, exploring fingers. In the silence of the bedroom, the sound of their breathing was harsh and loud. She could hear her own heartbeat in her ears, see his at the base of his strong throat.

She shivered and his teeth clenched.

"That baby is just starting to develop," he said, almost choking on his own voice in a throat as dry as desert sand. "And you've had cramping. I won't risk it."

"I wasn't offering, really," she managed unsteadily. She bit her lower lip and frowned as she searched his lean, hard face. "I don't understand. I never…felt like this. I'm scared."

"Felt like what?" he asked, not at all embarrassed. "Tell me, Lisa."

She flushed. "I can't!" she bit off.

He took her by both arms and pulled her gently across him, so that her head lay in the crook of his powerful arm. His free hand went to her throat and caressed its way under her long, loosened dark blond hair. She relaxed against him helplessly, her breath coming in tiny little jerks as she looked up into his quiet, gentle eyes.

"Then I'll tell you," he said softly. "You want to pull the fabric out of the way and show yourself to me," he whispered. His thumb moved slowly over her parted lips. "You feel hot and swollen all over, and you aren't quite in control. That's what frightens you."

She shivered again. "It wasn't like this with Walt."

His big warm hand slid from her neck down to her collarbone and as he held her wide eyes, it moved blatantly over the hard peak of one small breast and pressed there.

She whimpered, closing her eyes with a faint shudder. Her hand pressed hard into his hair-roughened chest and she leaned her hot face against the cool, hard muscle of his upper arm.

His cheek lay gently against hers. He caressed her almost absently, with a slow, restrained tenderness that made her whole body tremble with passion.

Her nails bit into his chest as the hunger grew with every soft brush of his fingers.

She felt his mouth on her closed eyelids as his hand found the hem of the T-shirt and moved under it. She arched helplessly to the sensuous delight of that expert touch.

He smiled against her mouth as he kissed her very tenderly. All the while his hand explored the softness of her silky skin, arousing a need that made her moan helplessly.

She moved closer, her eyes opening, wide, dazed, soft as a doe's.

He slid the fabric under her chin and looked at the firmness of her young breasts while he traced them. Odd, he thought, that her breasts showed no evidence of a pregnancy that should be approaching its fifth week. He'd seen his wife's body, and he remembered the changes pregnancy made in it. He wondered if women differed in the physical signs.

"I'm very small," she whispered unsteadily.

"Do you think size matters?" he murmured with a wicked, soft smile.

"If it didn't, men wouldn't buy those picture magazines…"

He bent and brushed his mouth against hers. "The men who buy those magazines don't have real women to practice on."

"Is that why?" she asked, laughing breathlessly through her shyness.

"You're just right," he breathed, letting his fingers sketch her body. "And if you weren't five weeks pregnant, I'd do more than talk about it."

"Would you?"

He lifted his head and looked down at the soft thrust of her creamy pink breasts. His eyes narrowed as he imagined the feel of them under his mouth. He felt his body tense with desire. It made him ache.

"You want to put your mouth on me, don't you?" she asked daringly. "I…would let you."

"I know," he said in a choked tone. His eyes met hers. "And what do you think would happen then?"

Her face colored helplessly as images flashed through her whirling mind.

His eyes narrowed. "I haven't wanted a woman for a long time. I want you very badly. Don't make it hard for me to walk away."

She forced herself to breathe slowly, to deny the ache

inside her. She was suddenly ashamed of the way she'd
behaved, and she grimaced as she tugged her T-shirt
down and lifted herself out of his loosening arms.

"I'm sorry," she said without looking at him.

"No need to apologize." He got to his feet. His
arousal was noticeable but he didn't turn away. He
looked down at her with lingering traces of desire, and
she looked at him the same way.

"First, we get married," he said in a subdued tone
that didn't match his stormy eyes. "Then we talk to
your obstetrician. If it's safe, I'll make love to you. As-
suming that you want me to."

"I want you to," she said honestly, avoiding his prob-
ing gaze.

"That makes two of us."

She slipped back under the covers and only then
lifted her eyes back up to meet his. "I'm glad those
men didn't hurt you," she said.

"Harley took it hard," he replied.

"Of course he did. He's not so bad," she added with
a smile.

He didn't like hearing her say that. She was young
and she had all the normal urges. He wanted to marry
her right away, before Harley got to her. Maybe she'd

have felt the same desire for anyone who offered her tenderness. She'd barely been married and she hadn't wanted her husband. She was ripe for an affair. If it happened, it was going to be with him. He wasn't letting Harley near her.

"You look angry," she commented.

He forced a smile. "Frustrated," he said, deliberately letting his gaze slide over her.

"Oh."

"Your breasts aren't swollen," he remarked bluntly, "and your nipples aren't enlarged or dark. Has the doctor explained the normal changes pregnancy will make in them?"

"Well, yes," she said, fighting embarrassment. "I imagine I'm not far enough along for it to show much."

"That makes sense." He moved back to the door. "If you need me, sing out."

"Would you like musical comedy or grand opera?" she mused. "Because I can start right now and save you the trip back to your own bed."

He chuckled softly. "Not yet," he told her deliberately. "First the ring, then the doctor. First things first."

She sighed. "Okay. You're the boss."

"Yes, I am," he mused. "But that won't last much longer, I imagine," he murmured, and left her sitting there with puzzlement all over her face.

A week later, with Eb and Sally Scott for witnesses, Cyrus Jonathan Parks married Lisa Jane Taylor Monroe in a quiet civil service in front of a justice of the peace. She wore a simple beige dress and carried a small bouquet of orange autumn maple leaves and yellow chrysanthemums that seemed just right for an autumn wedding.

They'd discussed rings and chose simple gold wedding bands with no ornamentation, just right for a marriage of convenience.

Except that it was more than that. Lisa began to tremble every time she got within five feet of her handsome, taciturn new husband. He knew that she wanted him. He wanted her, too. But despite the flare of desire between them, all he'd really offered her was a refuge, not love eternal. He'd said quite bluntly that he wouldn't have married her at all unless she'd been in danger, and he didn't plan to stay married to her after Lopez was arrested or subdued. She had to remember that.

There was time for a small reception at the Jacobsville Methodist Church fellowship hall, where friends still suffering from belated shock at the sudden wedding of Jacobsville's most reclusive rancher had laden a table with delicious tidbits while cakes for both bride and groom graced a side table. Cy and Lisa were required to cut the bride's cake together and share the first piece. As she looked up into his eyes, the photographer Cy had hired took a photograph so revealing that when Lisa would see it a week later, she would be too embarrassed to show it to anyone. She'd looked like a woman absolutely besotted with the man beside her.

They went back to his ranch together after the reception, and she went inside quickly, to spare him the humiliation of not being able to carry her over the threshhold with his damaged arm. Incredibly, the well-meant action ignited an argument that had explosive consequences.

The front door slammed audibly as Lisa went down

the hall. He caught up with her in the bedroom she'd been occupying.

Green eyes blazing, he closed the door behind him. And locked it.

"Why didn't you paint a sign and have it hung on the front door?" he asked in a menacing tone. "We both know I have limited use of this," he extended his left arm. "But I could have carried you over the threshold. You aren't exactly a challenging weight!"

She just stared at him, stunned by the furious anger in his lean face. "I was only trying to spare your pride," she said tightly. "I never meant to insult you."

He threw off his jacket and tossed it onto a chair. His strong fingers went to his tie. That followed the jacket. He unbuttoned his shirt, all the while walking deliberately toward Lisa.

She'd never had cause to be afraid of him. She wasn't now, although her knees felt weak as water under her. He was devastatingly attractive to her, and if her heartbeat was shaking her, it wasn't out of fear. She wondered if he knew.

His hands caught her by the waist and brought her against him firmly. His glittery eyes searched her wide, surprised ones. His fingers contracted. He wasn't behaving rationally, and it wasn't much of a surprise. He'd gone without a woman for over three years and here was Lisa, his wife, who made him hungry as he'd never been hungry before. He thought briefly of the child she was carrying, and hesitated.

"Did you speak to the doctor about the baby…?"

"Since I haven't had any more cramps, he said it's all right," she said huskily, drowning in the strong arms enfolding her.

She was hardly aware of meeting him halfway when his head bent. He kissed her slowly, softly, and then with a hunger that made fires in her blood. She reached up on tiptoe to press hard against his strong body, clung as the kiss deepened and became slow and hungry, devouring her soft mouth.

Her submissive moan made him wild. He lifted her quite easily with his right arm, catching her neatly under her knees with the left one, and carried her to the bed with his mouth still demanding and rough on her eager lips.

It was broad daylight. The sun filtered in through the blinds, but she didn't feel inhibited by the light. Walt had always wanted the darkness, but Cy didn't seem to care at all. He caressed her out of her neat beige dress and the things under it, his mouth ardent and expert in a way she'd never experienced with her husband. Walt had always been in a hurry. Cy wasn't. Long before his shirt came off, she was twisting under him in a veritable orgy of pleasure, her nails biting into his shoulders, her gasps audible as each pleasure was eclipsed by a new one. It was like the night he'd proposed, but without his stoic restraint. He didn't seem to mind her knowing that he was desperate to have her, although he was patient and tender and restrained.

She wouldn't have believed that a man who'd gone without a woman for so long could be so patient. He acted as if he had all the time in the world. He laughed softly at her obvious desire, but he didn't satisfy it. His mouth worked its way lazily down her soft body to her breasts while she trembled in the wake of new and mysterious pleasures. She seemed to hang in midair as his mouth hovered over the hard peak of her breast. Then, tenderly, his mouth worked its way completely over it and began to suckle her, and she cried out in surprised ecstasy.

Her headlong response delighted him. She'd mentioned once that her husband hadn't been patient, and now he was willing to believe it. Despite her marriage and her pregnancy, she acted like a woman who'd never been intimate with anyone. Her ardent clinging, her soft cries of pleasure, her trembling made him feel more like a man than ever before. His own wife had hated this part of marriage, hated her child, hated him. In the old days, before his marriage, there had never been a shortage of women. But since he'd been widowed, there had been no one. Not until now. And this soft, eager woman beneath him was his wife. He groaned harshly against her breast as a wave of hot pleasure swept over him. His control was suddenly gone.

He wrestled the rest of his clothes off and jerked back the bedspread, moving Lisa onto the cool, crisp sheets. His body covered hers, feeling the heat and eagerness of it. He heard her faint gasp and felt the ripple of her soft body as she moved to accommodate him.

"Cy...!" she whispered, her nails gripping his upper arms.

His mouth closed her lips as he eased down. "Don't be afraid. I'll be careful with you," he whispered, reading the helpless fear in that soft exclamation. "Very, very careful. I won't hurt the baby."

That wasn't at all what she was thinking, to her shame, but she was too shy to tell him that she wasn't sure her slender body could adjust to his. He wasn't made like Walt, she could tell...

She gasped again as he moved lazily and a violent spasm of pleasure shook her entire body. Her nails bit into him and when he lifted his head to look at her, she knew her eyes must be like saucers. She was aware of her legs relaxing, her slender hips arching, her body trying to incite him to repeat that lazy movement of his body, to give her that shock of ecstasy again.

His soft, possessive eyes met hers. "Is this what you want me to do?" he whispered lazily, and he smiled as he moved and she tensed again, trembling.

She couldn't get the words out, but he didn't seem to need them. He shifted their positions and the next time he moved, she closed her eyes on a shuddering moan of exquisite pleasure. Never like this. She hadn't dreamed that a woman could feel such…!

He heard her voice, barely audible, pleading with him, sobbing at his throat. He was near the end of his endurance, but from the sound of her, he needn't be patient any longer. He caught her mouth firmly under his and moved deliberately, roughly, quickly, feeling her body take up the rhythm and echo it. The silken brush of her skin took the last of his control. He could feel her going up the spiral with him, he could hear the pleasure in her choked sobs, feel it in her cling-ing hands and arching body, in the grip of her long, elegant legs as they curled around his and tightened in spasms.

It was more than he'd hoped for. She fell with him into the white-hot heat of ecstasy, throbbed with him as reality became nothing more than a glimpse of light somewhere in the distance. He felt his body stiffen even as hers convulsed under the pressure of him. It was like being buried in warm, soft velvet…

"No!" she cried out as the pleasure fell away from her just as she'd grasped it. "No, no…!"

"What is it?" he asked huskily at her ear, his body shivering a little in the aftermath as he lay heavily above her. "Did I hurt you?"

"It didn't last," she sobbed, clinging. "I couldn't… make it last…!"

He understood at once. His mouth moved softly over her damp eyes, across her wet cheek and down to her parted lips where her breath came in husky little jerks. "Pleasure like that would be lethal in long doses," he whispered into her lips. He bit at her lower lip gently and then rubbed his mouth over it in soft little caresses.

She moved experimentally and felt the intimate pressure of him. Her eyes lifted to his, a little shy, and very soft.

His thumb brushed her lower lip while he searched her eyes in a silence so profound that she could hear their accelerated heartbeats.

"It was like making love to a virgin," he said in a deep, slow tone.

"It was like being one," she whispered honestly. Her fingers smoothed over the hard muscles in his upper arms. The one that had been damaged was only notice-able from the elbow to the hand, she observed. The rest of him, despite a few scars and depressions, was absolutely perfect.

He brushed back the loose strands of blond hair and, impulsively, took all the hairpins out to let it fall around her shoulders.

"That's better," he murmured, smiling.

They were still intimately joined, and her eyes searched over his lean, dark face with wonder.

His hips moved very sensuously and her whole body clenched visibly.

He reached to put the hairpins on the side table. He looked down into her eyes and moved again, with de-liberate sensuality, watching her lift toward him help-lessly.

He bent and put his mouth tenderly over hers, shift-ing onto his side with both lean hands on her hips as one long, powerful leg slid between both of hers. He felt her shiver as the pleasure began all over again. His last sane thought as she pressed into his body was that he hoped he had the stamina to survive what they were going to do to each other this time…

Much later, after a shower and a change of clothes, they had a small wedding supper of bacon and eggs and toast and coffee at the small kitchen table. Cy couldn't force himself to take his eyes off Lisa, and the attraction seemed to be mutual just at first. She couldn't stop touching him, even just to pass him the sugar or refill his cup. It was more than physical desire. It was a sort of intimacy he'd only seen in old movies. He'd had brief affairs, liaisons, even a wife. But with none of the other women had he felt this deep emotional bond.

His green gaze dropped to her belly and a surge of jealousy caught him unaware. She was carrying another man's child. When he'd first taken her in, protected her, it had been more out of pity and affection than anything else. But slowly desire and the need to possess had replaced his initial attraction, and jealousy had become a constant companion since he'd seen Harley holding her hand. But after what they'd shared in bed, he was unexpectedly jealous of her late husband and the baby, as well. He didn't understand his own riotous feelings. He was upset at the level of intimacy they'd attained and disturbed by the sense of possessiveness he felt for her. This hadn't been the plan at all. He'd married her to protect her and the baby from Lopez, not with any long-term relationship in mind. He'd proposed a marriage of convenience, which was interesting when he considered how quickly he'd maneuvered her into bed with the flimsiest of excuses.

Abstinence alone wouldn't have caused hunger that sweeping.

He didn't understand his sudden lack of restraint, and because he didn't, he was broody. At least he'd had the presence of mind to ask about the risk to the baby first. But that wasn't much comfort at the moment. He'd crossed the line, his own line, and he couldn't put her at risk again. He'd have to keep his uncontrollable urges to himself. As that thought persisted, he forced himself not to stare at Lisa. If he was going to practice restraint, he'd better get a head start, and right now.

She noticed the faint scowl on his heavy brow and looked at him quizzically as she sipped her second cup of coffee. "Is something wrong?" she asked.

He made a dismissing gesture with a movement of his shoulder. He smoothed his thumb absently over the fork he was holding. He seemed deep in thought and he was even more silent than normal.

She was getting more insecure by the minute. In bed, she'd felt as if she belonged to him completely, as if no two people on earth could have been any closer, any more intimate. Now, she was as far away from him as if they were still just neighbors. She wondered if she'd done something wrong. Maybe she'd been too…eager. She flushed, remembering her passionate, wanton behavior. He might be one of those men who didn't like aggressive women in bed. She swallowed the lump in her throat and averted her eyes from his taciturn expression. He hadn't complained, but he was very remote since they'd left the bedroom. She'd have to remember that he didn't like her undisciplined ardor, and not be so uninhibited again. Maybe if she could curtail her headlong response, it would ease the sudden tension between them.

She forced a smile to her face. "Would you like some more coffee?" she asked pleasantly.

He pushed his cup toward her to let her refill it, and finished the last of his eggs. He was furious at himself for the jealousy that had attacked him so unexpectedly. He'd married her to protect her from Lopez and help her take care of the child, and that was just what he was going to do. He'd be better off if he could keep in mind that passionate interludes in the bedroom weren't part of their deal, and stop trying to create new problems for himself and Lisa in the first days of their marriage. He'd broken faith with her by seducing her. Besides, he reminded himself, they still weren't out of the woods where Lopez was concerned. The man wouldn't stop just because Cy had married Lisa. In fact, he was willing to bet that the marriage would tempt Lopez to even further improvisation.

Meanwhile, he still had the problem of Lopez's warehouse behind his property. Since the blatant attack on Harley and Lisa, Cy had pulled Harley off the night surveillance, certain that Lopez's people would have night scopes now that would catch anyone spying on them. That excuse about locoweed worked once, but it wouldn't work again. Still, there was surveillance equipment that was undetectable by infrared glasses, and Cy initiated it. He hadn't shared it with Harley. The younger man hadn't quite recovered from the shock of seeing his supposedly crippled boss take down two professional assassins. He'd stopped asking questions, but he watched Cy from a safe distance and did nothing to upset him. He wouldn't even talk to Lisa unless Cy was around lately. It was almost comical.

She got up to put the dishes in the sink and he stacked his cup and saucer on his plate to simplify the chore for her. She smiled as she finished clearing the table and began to fill the sink with soapy warm water.

"I need to buy you a dishwasher," he said abruptly. "There wasn't much need for it when I lived alone, but we'll have dinner guests from time to time…"

"I don't mind washing dishes in the sink, Cy," she faltered, her wide dark eyes in their big lenses searching his.

He leaned against the counter, watching her deliberately, his face scowling and remote. "I wasn't as gentle as I should have been. Do you feel okay? Any queasiness or discomfort?" he asked bluntly.

"I feel great!" She smiled. "No cramping and I haven't had a hint of morning sickness since I've been pregnant."

Cy frowned. It had been a long time since his late wife had been pregnant, but he remembered everything he'd read on the subject. It was hard to overlook the lack of visible changes in Lisa's soft body, especially her breasts. He felt suddenly uneasy. Pregnancy tests weren't foolproof. Maybe she wasn't pregnant after all. But if she wasn't pregnant with her late husband's child, she could quite easily be pregnant with his right now. Especially, he thought ruefully, after his exhaustive lovemaking. He hadn't held anything back and he hadn't tried to protect her—useless when she was already pregnant, which he'd thought at the time. He'd proposed a temporary marriage to protect her. Making her pregnant with his own child wasn't part of the plan. He didn't want a binding relationship…did he?

She noticed his curious stare. "Why are you looking at me like that?" she asked uneasily.

"I like your hair loose around your shoulders," he said evasively.

"Do you?" She pushed the heavy fall of it back over

her shoulders with a tiny smile. "It's a nuisance to wash and dry."

"I had Harley bathe Puppy Dog, by the way," he mentioned, searching for a neutral subject.

"Did you? That was nice."

"Bob needed a bath, too," he said. He didn't add that putting Harley to work bathing dogs had made him feel pretty good. He was still brooding about the way Harley had tested his reflexes with the pistol. He hadn't wanted any of his men to know about his old life. That was wishful thinking, he supposed.

She hesitated, washing the same plate until it threatened to rub the pattern off.

"Speaking of Puppy Dog," he said, "didn't he stay in the house with you before you moved over here?"

"Yes," she agreed, "but he's big and clumsy, like his father, and you've got lots of breakable stuff. Anyway, he seems to like being out in the barn with Bob. It's almost as warm in there, with the doors closed, as it is in the house. And it's amazingly sanitary. For a barn."

"I like healthy stock. Sanitation is important." He glanced around the kitchen. "I thought I was a fairly decent housekeeper, but you've brightened the place up considerably."

"I like housework," she said absently. "I do know a

few things about the cattle business, but I enjoy cooking and cleaning and even ironing shirts." She fingered his. "I always thought I'd take to family life like a duck to water. I just never had the chance to prove it."

He scowled, thinking of the difference she'd made here. He'd gotten used to finding her in the kitchen or the living room when he came home every evening. He liked the little touches, the frilly curtains in the kitchen, the silk flowers on the table, the visible signs of her presence in his life. He thought about having her move back into her old house, and it was distasteful. He refused to pursue that line of thought.

His eyes went to her waistline and quickly away. She noticed and bit her lower lip while she finished washing utensils and put them in the other side of the sink to rinse.

"Does it bother you that I'm pregnant?" she blurted out.

He hesitated. He didn't know how to answer her. "The baby must be a comfort to you," he said slowly, "with your husband gone."

She didn't even feel as if she'd been married, she thought to herself. She'd slept with her husband exactly twice and the rest of the time he'd either been away from home or pretending that she wasn't there. He'd married her on the rebound.

He'd proposed to Lisa, having already confessed about the woman he'd loved leaving him. Lisa had no hope of marrying anyone else and she'd been very lonely since her father's death. A marriage of convenience wouldn't be so bad, she'd told herself. But Walt couldn't love her, and she couldn't love him. Now here she was in a second marriage of convenience with a man who didn't want her permanently any more than Walt had.

"I've always wanted children," she said noncommittally.

He was remembering the little boy who hadn't been his, and how painful it had been to lose him in such a violent manner. That led him to thoughts of Lopez and revenge.

Lisa saw the expression on his face and frowned. He hadn't wanted to harm her child, but it was obvious that he regretted their intimacy. She wished she could, but it had been the only time in her life she'd felt as if she belonged to someone.

"I'm sorry, by the way," she said quietly. "About not letting you carry me over the threshold," she added, avoiding his sudden intent gaze. "I really was trying to spare your pride."

He stared at her for a few seconds before he spoke. "There was some nerve damage and loss of muscle tissue to my arm after the fire," he said. "But I can do almost anything I could before. I don't advertise it," he added slowly. "It gives me a psychological advantage if people think I'm less capable than I am—especially since Eb's line of work became public knowledge."

"You don't want people to know what you did," she said with understanding. "Well, you may fool everyone else, but Harley goes out of his way not to upset you these days," she murmured.

"He's lucky I didn't shoot him," he muttered. His eyes narrowed. "Did you see it?"

She nodded.

"And you still didn't think I could carry you into the house."

She cleared her throat. "I was terribly shy of you, if you want the truth," she told him. "Walt was an ordinary man who never made me nervous. But my knees started shaking the minute I saw you. I didn't know what you'd expect of me. I was a little afraid of you."

"Why?"

Her shoulders rose and fell. "I haven't been completely honest with you about a few things. Not important things," she was quick to emphasize. "But I'd only been intimate with Walt twice and it was uncomfortable and quick and embarrassing. I…knew you were experienced, and that you'd expect more from a woman than Walt had. I thought I wouldn't be enough for you. If you meant us to have a real marriage, I mean, and not just one on paper."

So that was why. She hadn't been challenging him at all. She'd been afraid of the very thing her behavior precipitated.

"I'm sorry. I didn't understand," he added irritably.

"Not your fault. I sort of got carried away, too." She blushed.

A lot of things were becoming clear to him, predominantly her total lack of experience with intimacy. If she'd only slept with her husband twice and hadn't liked it, the past few hours must have shocked her speechless. Funny, most women weren't naive these days. His gaze darkened as he stared at her. She seemed mature sometimes. And then she'd throw him a curve, from out of nowhere. He couldn't fathom her.

"Are we going to sleep together at night?" she asked before her courage failed.

"No," he said flatly. "This afternoon should never have happened. I'm not going to put your baby at risk a second time."

She worked not to let her disappointment show. Now she was certain that she hadn't pleased him. She seemed to be an ongoing disappointment to men in bed, and she didn't know how to change it. "Okay," she said with forced carelessness.

He was glad she was taking it so calmly. She might not have loved her husband, but she genuinely wanted the baby and there was still a chance that she was pregnant, despite the lack of symptoms. He recalled now that some women did have cramping in the early stages, and it usually went away, just as hers had. And a lot of women never had morning sickness.

If she really was pregnant with Walt's child, he wasn't going to be the cause of her losing her baby. Nor was he going to touch her for the duration of their marriage of convenience. Once the threat of Lopez was removed, he was going to let her go back home and go to work for Kemp. They could have the marriage quietly annulled and it would be the best thing for both of them. He wasn't going to let himself love anyone ever again. He couldn't go through the hell of losing anyone else.

Lisa felt embarrassed, but she didn't let it show. It shouldn't have surprised her that she'd disappointed him in bed, considering the sophisticated women he'd probably attracted before his marriage. She was just a country woman with no experience, and thank God he didn't know her real age or he'd be doing more than clamming up when they talked. "I'll have supper when you come in," she said.

"I'll be late."

She nodded. "Okay."

He went to the door, hesitated, looked back and a flash of possessiveness showed in his green eyes as he stared at her. Her face colored and he forced himself to look away. She wasn't the first woman he'd taken to bed, and she wouldn't be the last. He had to stop seeing her as some sort of permanent fixture in his life. There was simply no future in it. He grabbed his hat off the rack, slanted it over one eye and walked out without another word.

Lisa went back to her dishes on shaky legs. She wondered if he had any idea what that smoldering look of his did to a woman.

Chapter Nine

Two more weeks passed with the occupants of the Parkses' house being polite to each other and not much more. Cy had swept the house for "bugs" the same day Lopez's men made their assault, making sure that he didn't miss any of Lopez's little listening devices. He had no idea how long the drug lord's men had been eavesdropping, but there hadn't been that many opportunities for them to get into the house. He didn't imagine it had been long.

He checked his surveillance tapes periodically as well, noting that the warehouse on the land behind his property had been joined by what looked like a small processing plant, supposedly for honey from the row upon row of beehives on the property. He saw nothing to indicate a drug presence, but Lopez had added several more men to the site, and there were several big eighteen-wheel trucks on the premises now. It looked very much as if Lopez planned to start shipping his product fairly soon.

Meanwhile, Cy had gone to see Eb Scott to check on Rodrigo's progress, and the status of the cocaine shipment he'd already reported.

"Narcs got it down in the Gulf," Eb murmured coolly. "The Coast Guard homed in on the boats that were carrying it and strafed them with gunfire. Needless to say, they gave themselves and their shipment up. The DEA made several arrests and confiscated enough cocaine paste to addict a small country."

"Damn," Cy murmured angrily. "So here we sit."

"Don't knock the confiscation," Eb mused. "I'd love to see them make that kind of haul on a daily basis."

"So would I, but I want to catch Lopez with his fingers in the cookie jar," the other man said. And soon, he could have added, because his hunger for his wife was growing less controllable by the day. He looked at her and ached. Anger made new lines in his lean face. "Meanwhile, he sits on the edge of my property like a volcano about to erupt and I can't do a damned thing about it. I suppose you know that the sheriff's department and the DEA were all over it because of an 'anonymous' tip."

"I know," Eb replied. "One of Lopez's men phoned in the tip, apparently, and then the man in charge of the honey operation threatened to sue everybody for harassment if they came out again and did any more searches." He shook his head. "You have to admire the plan, at least. It was a stroke of genius. Nobody's going to rush out there again to look around unless there's concrete evidence of drugs."

"And that," Cy agreed, "will be hard to come by now."

"Exactly." He leaned forward in his chair and studied Cy intently. "You look older."

Cy scowled. "That's what marriage does to a bachelor."

"It had the opposite effect on me," his friend replied. "I've had a streak of good luck since I married Sally."

"I noticed. Is Micah Steele still in town?" he asked abruptly.

"He's in and out. He had an assignment and he's due back next week. Had an apparently disastrous argument with his stepsister, Callie Kirby, over his father before he left."

"Callie isn't much for arguments," Cy pointed out. "If there was an argument, he started it."

"Could be."

"I wish we could nab Lopez and get Rodrigo out of there before he gets himself shot," Cy said, changing the subject. "He's good people. I don't want him killed on our account."

"Same here. He's been in the business at least as long as Dutch and J.D. and Laremos," he replied. "And they taught him everything he knows."

"They were the best."

"We weren't bad, either," Eb said on an amused laugh. "But I suppose we either settle down or die. Personally I consider marriage an adventure."

"Some do," he said without enthusiasm and changed the subject.

"Did you hear that Sally's aunt Jessica married Dallas and moved back to Houston with their son Stevie?" Eb asked unexpectedly. "Nobody was exactly surprised about it."

"At least she'll be looked after," Cy remarked.

"That's true." Eb frowned as he stared at his friend. "It's none of my business, but is it true that Lisa's pregnant?"

He was going to say yes, but Eb was watching him with the insight of years of friendship and he let his guard drop. "That's a good question," Cy replied, leaning forward. "I thought that she was, just after Walt was killed," he added. "But she had some symptoms I don't like and she doesn't show the normal signs of pregnancy." He grimaced. "We don't talk about it."

"She's young," Eb agreed. "I don't imagine she knows very much about pregnancy, since she was an only child more or less raised by her dad. He wasn't the sort to discuss intimate issues with her."

"She's young, you said," Cy returned quickly. "How young?"

"You mean to tell me that you're married to her and you don't know how old she is?"

"She hid the marriage license," he muttered. "Put her thumb over the birth date while I was signing it and confiscated it as soon as the JP signed it. Every time I've asked, she's changed the subject."

"I see."

"Well?" Cy prompted.

Eb grimaced. "She ought to tell you."

"Eb!"

The other man shifted restlessly. "She's twenty-one. Barely."

Cy's face went white. He leaned back in his chair as if he'd been shot. He took off his hat and wiped his sweaty brow on his sleeve. "Dear God!"

"That's legal age," Eb pointed out. "And you don't need me to tell you that she's amazingly mature for that age. Some women grow up quicker than others. She never really had a childhood. From what I've heard, from the age of six, she was riding horses in competitions and working around the ranch. For all that her dad wouldn't teach her management, there isn't much she doesn't know about the daily routine of ranch hands."

"Fourteen years my junior," Cy groaned. "I could never get her to tell me."

"Now you see why," his friend remarked. "You'd never have married her if you'd known."

"Of course I wouldn't have married her if I'd known, Lopez or no Lopez! I don't rob cradles!"

Eb chuckled. "She's no kid. Around Jacobsville we pay more attention to family than we do to age differences. Lisa comes from good people. So do you."

Cy had his face in his hands. "Walt wasn't even thirty," he remarked. "And damned Harley is barely twenty-eight. He's still in and out of the house all the time flirting with her when he doesn't think I see him. I caught him a couple of weeks ago showing her how to break handholds, right in my own living room."

"You know how to handle that," Eb said easily.

Green, glittery eyes came up to meet his. "I can't handle it. She's too damned young for me and I don't want to stay married to her!"

Eb's eyebrows went up at the vehemence of the statement. "What do you plan to do, then, kick her out and let Lopez…"

"Oh, for God's sake, you know I wouldn't do that! I just don't want her getting comfortable in my house," he added irritably. "I think she's still in shock at Walt's death and latching onto the first pair of comforting arms she can find."

"So that's it. And you don't want to take any chances until you know for sure."

Cy glared at him. "Don't psychoanalyze me!"

"Wasn't trying to," Eb said with a grin. "But she and Walt didn't marry for love eternal. He'd just lost Becky Wayne and his heart was broken. Everybody knew he married Lisa on the rebound. And she'd never been in love with anybody. She assumed it came naturally when you put on an engagement ring. That isn't the case."

"You ought to know," Cy said. "You got engaged to Maggie Barton, and I know for a fact you didn't love her."

"I was lonely," he said simply. "But until Sally stormed back into my life, I didn't know what love was. I do now."

Obviously. It was written all over him. Cy turned his eyes away.

Eb's expression became covertly amused. "If you don't want Lisa for keeps, you might let Harley get on the inside track. He's got potential..."

"Damn Harley!" Cy burst out, his eyes were blazing. "If he goes near her again, I'll feed him to my chickens!"

So much for Cy's true feelings, even if he wouldn't admit them. Eb chuckled. "I haven't forgotten what happened at your place when Lopez's men made a try for Lisa," Eb murmured. "Talk is that Harley's given up throwing pistols at you and he walks a mile around you lately."

"Some men have to learn the hard way that they aren't invulnerable. Harley got overconfident. It almost cost him his life. You know that the two assailants made bond and left the country?"

"I know. What was it, a million in bond, each?"

"Yep. Pocket change to Lopez, but the judge set bond as high as she could. I don't blame her."

"She's a good judge at that," Eb agreed.

Cy stood up, feeling shaky. "I've got to get back home. If you hear from Rodrigo, let me know. I'm still trying to keep an eye on the honey plant. Nothing's shown up so far."

"Wouldn't it be a hoot if Lopez had decided to turn

respectable and it's a real honey processing plant?" Eb mused.

"Sure, and pigs will fly."

"Not on my place, they won't," Eb said. He got up, too, and walked the other man to the front door. "But bullets may, before this mess is over," he added in a somber tone. "I don't like all this sudden quiet from Lopez's warehouse. They're up to something."

"That's exactly what I'm afraid of," Cy agreed, and he didn't smile.

As another week crawled by, Lisa could see that Cy was brooding about something. He continued to be standoffish and remote after their tempestuous afternoon in bed together, and he'd been somber and unapproachable altogether since he'd gone to see Eb Scott. But his eyes always seemed to be on her. She caught him watching her when she worked in the kitchen, when she washed clothes. He'd bought her a dishwasher, as he'd promised, and every sort of kitchen utensil and cookware any gourmet would have cherished. He surprised her with the romance novels she liked to read, and even scarce out-of-print editions of authors she enjoyed. He was forever buying toys for Puppy Dog and Bob, and coaxing Lisa into stores where he had accounts. She was spoiled constantly. But he never touched her.

One evening when they'd just finished watching the news, she cut off the television and followed him daringly into the office where he kept his computer and printer and fax-modem. He looked up from behind the massive oak desk with an expression of surprise.

"Can I come in?" she asked from the doorway.

He shrugged. "Help yourself."

That didn't sound welcoming, especially from a man to his new wife, but she smiled and walked up to the desk.

"Something bothering you?" he asked quietly.

"Yes."

"What?"

She stuck her hands into the pockets of her pretty embroidered purple apron. "I feel like an unwanted houseguest lately," she said flatly. "I want to know what I'm doing wrong."

He scowled and put down the pencil he was holding over a spreadsheet of figures. "You haven't done anything wrong, Lisa," he said.

"I must have. You can't seem to force yourself to come within five feet of me." Her voice sounded raw and she didn't quite meet his eyes.

He leaned back in the chair. A harsh sound came out

of his throat and his lips made a thin line as he studied her. "You didn't tell me you were just twenty-one."

She looked suddenly uncomfortable. "Does it matter?"

"Good God in heaven!" he exclaimed, explosively pushing himself up and out of his desk chair. "Of course it matters! You're still a kid and I'm thirty-five years old!"

She let out an expressive breath.

"You don't look your age," he muttered, walking away from her to stand in front of the dark window. The horizon was a faint silhouette in the distance, flat and cold-looking.

"That's what Walt used to say," she recalled. She leaned her hip against his desk and stared at his long back. "But I'm not as immature as you're making me out to be."

His shoulder moved jerkily. "If you were ten years older…"

"But I'm not. So what do you want to do about it?" she demanded, blowing a wisp of loose hair out of her mouth. "Do you want me to move back over to Dad's ranch and go to work for Mr. Kemp and pay rent? I'm willing."

He felt his heart stop. His expression was vulnerable for those few seconds, and he actually winced.

"Don't look so tormented. It won't cause any gossip if I go back home, wedding ring or no wedding ring. We can get an annulment."

"The gossips would have a field day over that!"

"I can't believe you care what people might say," she bit off. "I certainly don't."

"It isn't that." He rammed his hands into the pockets of his jeans and stared at her worriedly. "You've never been out of Jacobsville. You don't know beans about men." He drew in a slow breath. "You should have gone to college or at least seen a little more of the country and the world before you married."

"There was never enough money for travel," she said shortly. "My dad was a small rancher, not an aristocrat. If I went to college it would be to study veterinary medicine or animal husbandry, and I don't really see how I could do that with a baby on the way!"

He hesitated. Should he tell her what he suspected about the baby? It might be the best time to do it. But he couldn't think clearly. All he could think about was her age. He should have realized how young she was. He felt as if he'd taken unfair advantage of her, even if it had been the only way to protect her from Lopez. She had been married already, he reminded himself. It wasn't as if he'd snatched her from a cradle.

Her hand went to her waistline. "I'd much rather

have the baby than a degree, if you want the truth," she said.

His face hardened. He couldn't tell her. Not yet. For all he knew, she might truly have loved her late husband. What would it do to her if she wasn't pregnant? He turned back toward the desk. "I don't want you to move out. Lopez may be laying low, but I guarantee he hasn't gone away. I won't risk your life."

She stood glaring at him. "Fair enough. When he's finally caught, I'm out of here," she said flatly. "I am not living with a man who can't bring himself to touch me because I'm pregnant with another man's child!" she added, making a stab in the dark. It seemed to have paid off when he went rigid all over.

She turned and started out the door, sick at finally knowing the truth he hadn't wanted to tell her. It wasn't her age that bothered him, not really—it was Walt's baby!

"Damn it, that's not why!"

She whirled. "Then what is?"

He glared at her. She had a temper that easily matched his, despite her youth, and with her dark eyes flashing and her face flushed, she gave him a very inconvenient ache.

"It's strange that you don't have any pregnancy symptoms," he said flatly.

She didn't answer him for several tense seconds. "All right," she said finally. "I'll make an appointment first thing tomorrow."

"See that you do," he returned curtly.

She searched his drawn face, seeking answers to questions she didn't want to ask. "We were so close, the day we married," she said hesitantly. "You were… different. I thought you cared about me."

He managed a smile that mixed equal parts of self-contempt and mockery. "Didn't anyone ever tell you that men get sentimental after sex?"

She seemed to close up like a flower. She turned away from him without another word and left the room, quietly pulling the door closed behind her.

He ran an angry hand through his dark hair and cursed himself silently for that cruel remark. He'd never been so confused. He didn't know if she was carrying Walt's child or not. He didn't know how he really felt about her. He was sick at heart to realize how very young she was. On top of that, he was frustrated because Lopez wouldn't come out in the open and make a move. One thing he was sure about, though, was that Lisa had to be protected. He was going to take care of her the best he could. Then, when it was over, and she was safe, she could have a chance to decide whether or not she wanted to spend her life with a maimed ex-mercenary.

He wasn't going to continue to take advantage of her, even if it was killing him to stay out of her bed. If she wasn't pregnant, he wasn't going to take the slightest chance of making her that way. She was going to be completely free to decide her future. Even if it was with damned Harley.

Lisa went to the doctor and had the pregnancy test, and came back to the ranch looking more disturbed and worried than ever.

Cy was waiting for her in the living room. He stood up, his face strangely watchful. "Well?" he asked abruptly.

She moved restlessly, dropping her purse into a chair. She was wearing the same beige dress she'd worn the day they married, with a lightweight brown coat, and her hair was in a bun. She looked pale and quiet and not very happy.

"The test was positive," she said, avoiding his eyes. "He said pregnancy symptoms sometimes don't show up right away. He said there was nothing at all to worry about."

Cy didn't say anything. Apparently he'd been wrong right down the line. She was pregnant, and her child was Walt's. It was uncharitable of him to be disappointed about that, but he was.

She'd noted the expression that crossed his face and it wounded her. She knew that men were said to grow possessive once they'd been intimate with a woman, and it wasn't totally unexpected that he resented Walt's place in her life. It wouldn't be easy for a man to accept and raise a child that wasn't his.

"Are you sure you don't want me to leave?" she asked in a subdued tone.

"Of course not," he said automatically.

She lifted her eyes to his. "I won't get in your way."

"You aren't in my way."

She moved jerkily away. "Okay. Thanks."

She seemed to hesitate at the door, but only for a second. She went out, leaving Cy to watch her exit with a tangle of emotions.

He stopped by his office to check his messages before he retrieved his shepherd's jacket and slanted his hat across his green eyes. He went out by way of the kitchen so that he could tell Lisa where he was going.

Harley had just come in with the eggs, and he was leaning against the counter smiling at Lisa, who was smiling back. They were both so young...

"Sorry I didn't get them in first thing this morning,"

Harley was telling her, "but I had some work to do on the fence line."

"That's okay. I had an appointment in town," Lisa replied.

"I'll be late tonight," Cy said from the doorway. They both jumped, surprised by his sudden appearance. Harley cleared his throat, nodded at Lisa and went rushing down the steps toward the barn.

Cy didn't understand why until Lisa actually backed up against the sink.

"Now, what, for God's sake?" he demanded shortly.

"You ought to see your face in a mirror," she retorted.

His green eyes narrowed. "Harley spends too much time in here," he said flatly. "I don't like it."

Her eyebrows arched. "How would you know? You're never here!"

His lips made a thin line. He was bristling with unfamiliar emotions, the foremost of which was pure jealousy.

She glared up at him from her safe vantage point at the sink. "I didn't cheat on Walt and I won't cheat on you," she said coldly. "Just in case you wondered."

He glared back at her. His eyes, under the wide brim of the hat, glistened like green fire.

"I never should have agreed to come here," she said after a minute, her breath sighing out as she leaned back against the counter. "I've never been so miserable in my whole life."

That was worse than a slap in the face. His whole body tightened. "That makes two of us," he lied. "Don't worry. It won't be much longer before we'll have everything resolved. Once the sale of the ranch goes through, you'll have enough money to do what you please."

He turned and walked out. He didn't look back.

Lisa felt like breaking things. She was crazy about the stupid man, and he wouldn't give an inch. He didn't want her talking to Harley, he was resentful of her baby because it was Walt's, he alternately ignored and spoiled her. Now he'd offered to let her leave. She didn't want to. She'd grown used to living with him, even if it was like being alone most of the time. But he had said that she could go when things were resolved. Did that mean they were close to dealing with Lopez? She hoped so. The memory of the assault on her bedroom and then the attempted assault here still worried her. She felt safe with Cy, even with Harley. If she went home, she'd be watched, but she wouldn't feel safe.

Cy, driving toward town in his truck, was fuming. So she wanted to go home. Well, he'd see what he could do to hurry things up for her. First he went to Kemp's office and told him to push the paperwork through as fast as possible. Then he started toward Eb's place. There had to be some way to force Lopez to stick his neck in a noose.

But on the way, he decided to swing by the old Johnson house. It would be deserted now, of course, and there was only one other house on the stretch of outlying road. He didn't really know why it occurred to him to go that way. Maybe, he considered, his old instincts still worked at some level.

He pulled off the paved road and turned down the small county road that led to the Johnson place. He remembered Eb talking about the members of Lopez's cartel who had rented a house nearby and had accosted Sally Johnson before she'd married Eb. It was a crazy notion, and he needed his head read. All the same, he told himself, it never hurt to play a hunch.

He noticed the lack of traffic on the road, which was nothing unusual. This far out, there weren't a lot of people who opted for the badly kept county road instead of the newer highway that led to Victoria. The late autumn landscape was bleak and uninviting. All the leaves were off the trees now, and the last bunches of hay were cut and stacked in barns for winter forage. The weather had a nip in it. Nights were cold. He remembered winter nights when he and Eb were overseas, trudging through ice and snow. Life was much simpler here, if not overly comfortable.

He was watching the scenery, not paying a lot of attention to anything, when he noticed two huge tractor-trailer rigs parked near an old Victorian house. He didn't slow down or show any obvious interest in the once-deserted dwelling. But it was painfully clear why Lopez's "honey operation" was sitting still. He had a distribution center up and running already, only it wasn't behind Cy's property. The beehives were only a blind. Here was the real drug operation, complete with huge renovated barn and dangerous-looking employees sitting around the big rigs, which were backed up to the barn. Cy knew without looking that there would be locks on those barn doors and men with automatic weapons patrolling around it. He knew, too, that it wasn't hay that was being loaded into the trucks.

They'd been foxed. And now it was almost too late to close down the operation. He'd have bet money that this was Lopez's follow-up shipment to the one that had been confiscated down in the Gulf of Mexico. The odd-looking oil drums were scattered around, and had obviously been used to bridge rivers between Texas and the Gulf so that the men hauling the cocaine had been able to cross at places where the border patrol wouldn't be waiting for them.

He drove straight past the place without looking again. As he passed the deserted Johnson homestead, with its For Sale sign standing awry and uninviting, he knew that what they'd all dreaded was already taking place. Lopez was back in business, right here in Jacobsville. And if Cy and his friends were going to stop them, there wasn't much time to plan an assault.

At the end of the road, he turned back into the highway and burned rubber getting to Eb's place.

Chapter Ten

Eb was surprised by the news.

"Right under our damned noses," he exploded. "No wonder we couldn't find any evidence of drug smuggling at the honey warehouse. That was a blind, and we fell for it, just like raw recruits!"

"The question is, what do we do now?" Cy asked coldly. "And since Rodrigo didn't warn us about this, have they found him out and disposed of him?"

"I hope not," Eb said sincerely. "But I can't help thinking that he would have warned us if he'd been able to." He ran his hand through his hair. "Hell of a time to make this sort of discovery, when Lopez is ready to ship his new supply out to his distribution network."

"It gets worse. From what I saw, I'd say he's ready to go tonight."

"We'll have to go in now," Eb said at once. "Or we'll miss the chance. And we'll have to have help," he added. "I counted at least twelve men. Even with our experience, we won't be able to take that many men armed with machine guns."

"I know. But we can't do it without authorization, either," Cy returned. "We live here. I don't know about you, but I don't want to end up as an ex-patriated American."

"Neither do I." Eb's eyes narrowed. "There's another consideration, too. If Rodrigo's with them, still undercover, the feds won't know and they'll shoot him. We have to go in with them. I have a few contacts. I can call in favors."

"So can I," Cy agreed. "Let's compare notes. With a little luck, we may be able to bring down Lopez's local network and save Rodrigo all at once."

It was rushed and hectic to get the necessary people notified and in place, but they managed it, just. The sheriff pulled two deputies off patrol and called in two more special deputies. The DEA only had three men who could get to Jacobsville in time to assist with the surprise attack, but they were dispatched immediately.

Two of the best officers from the local police department, Palmer and Barrett, volunteered to go along with the sheriff's force to help. They might still be outnumbered, but hopefully it would be possible to take the drug dealers by surprise and close down their operation. Nobody wanted a drug cartel operating out of Jacobsville.

Cy was putting on his night gear when Lisa came into his room and gasped.

"Where are you going?" she exclaimed.

He turned, black face mask in hand, to study her. She was wearing sweats, yellow ones that made her blond hair look more blond. It was loose, around her shoulders, and she had that peculiar radiance that pregnancy bestowed on a woman's face.

"Lopez's goons are ready to haul their shipment out tonight. We're going to stop them," he said honestly.

Her worried eyes never left her taciturn husband, from his tall, powerful figure in black to his lean, scarred face and glittery green eyes. He was devastating to her, physically as well as mentally. He took her breath away. She hated knowing what he meant to do.

She went right up to him, her dark eyes looking even darker through the lenses of her glasses. "No," she said shortly. "No, you don't! There are plenty of people in law enforcement who do this for a living. I'm not letting you go after those drug dealers!"

He took her by both shoulders, pulled her against him, and bent and kissed the breath and the protest right out of her. His arms enfolded her, cradled her, while his hard mouth devoured her soft, parted lips. It was a long time before he lifted his dark head.

"If Lopez is allowed to set up an operation here, none of us will ever be safe again, especially you," he said quietly. "If we don't stop it now, we never will."

"You could be killed," she said miserably.

The worry on her face made him feel funny. He couldn't remember anyone caring if he lived or died, especially not his erstwhile wife who'd only wanted creature comforts. His welfare was of supreme unimportance to her. But Lisa was cut from another sort of cloth. She was brave and honest and loyal. He searched her face and realized with a start that he could give up anything, even his own life, easier than he could give up Lisa. She was too young for him, of course…

He kissed her again, long and hard, ignoring all the reasons why he should do his best to send her out the door and out of his life. For her own good, of course, he rationalized. Sadly, none of those reasons made any difference when he was within five feet of her. Her arms curled around him and she gave him back the kiss with every bit of strength in her body. It was like walking on hot coals. She couldn't get close enough.

She was breathless when he lifted his head, but the resolve was still there, in those narrow green eyes. "It amazes me," she whispered huskily, "what lengths you're willing to go to…in order to stay out of my bed."

He laughed despite the gravity of the situation. "Is that what you think?"

"Walt was my husband," she said quietly. "I was fond of him. I'm not sorry that I'll have his child, so that a part of him will live on. But you and I could have children of our own, as well. It isn't biology that makes a man a father, it's love. And you aren't ever going to convince me that you wouldn't love a baby, even if it wasn't yours genetically."

He sighed gently and smoothed back her disheveled hair. "I keep mixing you up with the past, when you're nothing like my late wife. I don't resent Walt's baby." He shrugged. "It's not the age difference, either, really. But you're young and I'm older than my years make me. Maybe you need someone closer to your own age."

"Someone like Harley?" she asked deliberately.

His face hardened and his eyes flashed dangerously. "*No!*"

Hope, almost deserted, began to twinkle in her eyes.

"That's what I thought you said." She pulled his head down and kissed him tenderly. "I know you can take care of yourself. I've seen you do it. But don't take chances. I want to be married a very long time."

"You do?" he murmured.

"Yes. I'm not going back to Dad's ranch. If you won't let me live in the house, I'll live in the barn with Puppy Dog and Bob and tell everybody in Jacobsville that you won't let me live with you…."

He was kissing her again. It was sweet and heady, and he didn't have time for it at all. He just couldn't seem to stop. He was starting to ache and that would never do.

"And I'm moving into your bedroom while you're gone," she added, her voice thready with passion. "So there."

"Maybe I can think up an objection before I come back," he murmured against her lips.

"You try to do that." She grinned.

He loosened her arms and put her gently away from him, his strong hands tight on her shoulders. "While I'm gone, stay in the house with the doors locked. I've got Nels on the front porch and Henry watching the back door. They're both armed. Stay away from the windows and don't answer the phone. You know where the spare pistol is," he added, and she nodded. "It's loaded."

She bit her lower lip, realizing from his demeanor how dangerous it would be for both of them. "Okay. I'll use it if I have to. But don't you let yourself get shot," she told him firmly.

"I know, come back with my shield or on it."

She smiled and nodded. "That's right. Because you're not a 'summer soldier' like Thomas Paine wrote about. You're a winter soldier, fighting through blizzards. But you have to come back to me in one piece."

"I'll do my best to oblige," he mused, smiling back. Her eyes were soft and dark. He almost got lost in them. His gloved hand came up to touch her flushed cheek. "What did I ever do in my life to deserve someone like you?" he asked in a breathlessly tender voice. He moved away from her before that softness captured him. "I'll be home when I can."

She put up a brave front. "Okay," she said, and without further protests.

He paused at the doorway for one long, last look at her. She was a hell of a woman. And he wasn't giving her up, whether or not it would have been for her own good. He read the same resolve in her own face. She didn't cry or complain or try to stop him. She stood there very bravely and kept smiling, even though her eyes were too bright to be normal. She was still standing there when he went out into the hall and disappeared.

Harley was sitting on the front porch with Nels, waiting for him with a lit cigarette and a scowl. He got to his feet when Cy came out the door dressed in black and wearing a face mask. Harley had on jeans and boots and a camo jacket left over from his army ranger days.

"You aren't leaving here without me," Harley said belligerently.

"Who says I'm leaving?"

"Don't insult me." Harley opened his jacket to disclose a .45 automatic. "I may not be a full-fledged merk, but I was a crack shot in the Rangers," he added. "And no matter how many men are going, I might still be useful."

That was much better than bragging that he had combat training, Cy supposed. He hesitated, but only for a minute.

"All right. Let's go. Nels, guard her with your life," he added to his man on the porch, who nodded solemnly.

Harley headed for the Expedition, but Cy shook his head. He indicated a black Bronco of questionable vintage, parked under a tree. There were two men already in it. Harley was shocked that he hadn't seen it at all until now.

He wasn't surprised to find Eb Scott in the front seat with an unfamiliar man much bigger than Eb or Cy, and both of the newcomers dressed similarly to Cy.

"Here," Eb said, handing a small container of black face paint to Harley. "You'll shine like a new moon without a mask."

Harley at least knew how to use camouflage paint. He wanted to ask half a dozen questions, the foremost of which was why his boss was going along on what was obviously a search and destroy mission. Then he remembered the way Cy had used that knife on the two intruders and the way he'd caught the pistol Harley had thrown at his retreating back. It had long since dawned on him that his boss hadn't always been a rancher.

"Stubbs and Kennedy are going to rendezvous with us at the old Johnson place," Eb said tautly. "We've got the sheriff's department out in force, too. You and Micah and I will set up a perimeter with the deputies and let the feds go in first."

"Who are Stubbs and Kennedy?" Harley asked.

"DEA," came the cold reply. "Walt Monroe was one of theirs. They get first crack at these mules."

Mules, Harley recalled, were the drug lords' transportation people. He handed the face paint back to Eb. "You said the old Johnson place," Harley began. "But the warehouse is right behind Mr. Parks's place."

"That was a damned blind," Cy said shortly. "To draw attention away from the real distribution point. I could kick myself for not realizing it sooner."

"No wonder we never saw any drugs changing hands," Harley realized.

"Listen," Eb said as he eased the Bronco off the main highway and down the back road that led first to the Johnson place and then to the rental house near it, "I want a promise from you, just on the off chance that Lopez is around. No storm trooper stuff."

"Mr. Scott, I wouldn't dream…!" Harley began.

"Not you," Eb said impatiently. "Him!"

He was staring in the rearview mirror straight at Cy, whose eyes were glittering.

"He set fire to my house," Cy said in a menacing tone, "killed my wife and my five-year-old son. If he's there, he's mine, and no power on earth will save him. Not even you."

"If you kill him, the DEA will string you up on the nearest courthouse lawn!"

"They're welcome," Cy returned grimly.

"And what about Lisa, when you're gone?" Micah

Steele interjected. "This isn't Africa. You're not on your own. You have to think about Lisa and her baby."

"Africa was a long time ago," Cy said irritably, noting Harley's intent stare.

"None of us have forgotten it," Micah persisted. "You walked right into a nest of snipers with machine guns firing. Your clothes were shot to pieces and you took ten hits in the body, and you kept right on going. You saved us from certain death. We won't forget how much we owe you. That's why we're not letting you near Lopez. If I have to knock you down and sit on you, I'll do it."

"They were lousy shots," Cy muttered.

"They were crack shots," Eb countered. "But you psyched them out by walking right into the gunfire. It won't work with Lopez's men. We have to let the DEA take point. We aren't even supposed to be in on this. I had to call in markers from all over Texas to get even this far. And to boot, I had to confess to Kennedy why we're here—to protect Rodrigo from everybody in case he's among these guys. Don't forget that we haven't heard a word from Rodrigo. He may also be with them and unable to get a message to us."

"They may have killed him already, too," Cy added.

"We won't know until we get there. Harley—" Eb glanced over the seat "—you stick close to Cy."

Harley was weighing the dangers of that position when Micah Steele began to chuckle. "That's all he'll be able to do, or don't you remember that it took Laremos and Brettman and Dutch all together to bring him down just after Juba was killed, and he went right after a company of crack government troops?"

Harley's gasp was audible. "Laremos and...!"

"Who do you think taught us all we know?" Eb mused. "Now put a sock in it, Harley. This is where things get dicey."

He pulled up at the old Johnson place and cut off the engine. He handed out high-tech night scopes and listening devices to Micah and Cy. Cy gave Harley a level stare.

"This isn't a weekend at a merk training school," he told the younger man in a firm tone. "If there's a fire-fight, you stay out of it. Eb and Micah and I are a team. We know to the last ditch how far we can trust each other and we work as a unit. You're the odd man out. That being the case, you could get somebody killed. You're backup, period. You don't shoot until and unless one of us tells you to."

Harley swallowed. He was getting the idea, and an odd sickness welled up in his stomach. He could hardly talk, because his mouth was so dry. "How will we know the bad guys from the good guys?"

"The DEA boys will have that imprinted on the back of their jackets in big letters. Palmer and Barrett from the police department and the deputies from the sheriff's department will all be in uniform. The bad guys will be trying to protect their product. This is important," he added intently. "If you should be captured, make damned sure that you're on the ground when we come in. Because if that happens, if we have to storm the house, the first thing we'll do is to take out everybody standing. Have you got that?"

"I've got it," Harley said. "But I'm not going to get myself captured."

The others synchronized watches, and piled out of the Bronco. With Eb in the lead, they made their way so stealthily that Harley felt like an elephant bringing up the rear. He realized at once that his so-called training session was nothing but a waste of money. And that his inexperience could prove deadly to his comrades.

Eb deployed Micah and Cy at the edge of the woods behind the barn. One of the feds motioned to them, and to the five sheriff's deputies. As he waved, four other men in DEA jackets split and went around both sides. Everybody hesitated.

Harley crouched with his heart beating him half to death. He'd been in the United States for his entire tour of duty with the Rangers, except for a brief stint in Bosnia, where he hadn't managed to get out of headquarters. He'd seen people who'd been in combat and he'd heard about it. But he had no practical experience, and now he felt like a high school freshman getting ready to give a book report in front of the whole class—on a book he hadn't read. His knees felt like rubber under him.

Time seemed to lengthen as the seconds ticked by. Then, quite suddenly, one of the government agents raised his arm high and brought it down.

"Move out!" Eb called to his team.

It was pandemonium. Lopez's men were in civilian clothing, not the black gear that Cy and the others were wearing. The sheriff's deputies and the police officers were in uniform, and the DEA boys had visible identification on their jackets. Everybody seemed to be firing at once.

Harley hesitated at the sharp firecracker pop of guns going off, the sound so ominous and deadly in real life, so unlike the enhanced gunfire used in movies and television. He got a grip on his nerve, clutched his pistol in both hands and moved out a few seconds in the general direction where Cy and Eb had just vanished.

He started to run, but he wasn't quick enough to get to cover. He ran right into the path of a submachine gun, and it wasn't held by one of his team. He stopped, his breath catching in his throat as he looked certain death in the face for the first time in his young life.

The small, dark man in jeans and checked shirt facing him ordered him in perfect English to drop his pistol. The leveled automatic weapon he was holding looked very professional. Harley's pride took a hard blow. He'd walked right into that by being careless and he steeled himself for what was coming. He knew that the man wouldn't hesitate to fire on him. With a muffled curse, he dropped his automatic to the ground.

"One less to worry about," the foreign man said with a vicious smile. *"Adios, señor…!"*

Harley heard the loud report as a shot was fired and he tensed, eyes closed, waiting for the pain to start. But the weapon spilled out of the other man's hands an instant before he crumpled and fell forward.

"Get the hell out of there, Harley!" Cy raged.

Harley's eyes opened to find his opponent lying very still on the ground, and Cy standing behind him. Cy picked up Harley's .45 and threw it to him.

"Get around in front of the barn. Hurry!" Cy told him. Harley felt shaky, but he caught the pistol and walked rapidly past the downed man. He glanced at him and had to fight the rise of bile in his throat. He'd never seen anyone like that…!

His heart was racing crazily, his mouth felt as if it had been filled with cotton. As he cleared the side of the building, he saw firefights. Some of the drug dealer's men were undercover, firing from behind the big transfer trucks. Others were in the barn. They were cornered, desperate, fighting for their lives if not their freedom.

The DEA guys moved in, motioning to their backup, their own weapons singing as they brought down man after man. Most of the wounds were nonlethal, but the noise from the men as they fell made Harley sick. Groans, screams…it wasn't like that in the movies. He watched the police officers, Palmer and Barrett, walk right into the gunfire and drop their opposition neatly and without killing them. He envied them their cool demeanor and courage. He reminded himself never to tick them off once this was all over!

His whole body seemed to vibrate as he followed his boss. What had he been thinking when he enrolled in that mercenary training school? It was all just a lot of baloney, which had made him overconfident and could have gotten him killed tonight. The comparison between himself and these professionals was embarrassing.

Cy went into the barn alone, but now Harley didn't hesitate. He took a sharp breath, ground his teeth together and went right in behind him, ready to back him up if he was needed. He fought the fear he felt and conquered it, shaky legs, shaky hands and all. He'd made a fool of himself once. He wasn't about to do it twice. He wasn't going to let Cy and the others down just because he had butterflies in his stomach. His lean jaw tautened with new resolve.

There was a man in an expensive suit with an automatic weapon firing from behind several bales of odd-looking hay in the barn. Harley noted that he was the man who'd come to Cy's ranch in the pickup truck to "introduce himself."

Cy's instincts were still honed to perfection. He pushed Harley to one side and stepped right into the foreign man's line of fire and raised his own weapon, taking careful aim. Not even the head of the other man was visible now as he crouched behind the bales.

"Drop the gun or I'll drop you, right through your damned product," Cy warned.

The foreign man hesitated, but Cy didn't. He fired. The bullet went right through the hay and into the man, who cried out, clutching his shoulder as his weapon fell.

"Same arm I got with the knife, wasn't it?" Cy asked coldly as he approached the man and dragged him to his feet. He pushed him back against one of the wooden posts that supported the hayloft and held his pistol right to the base of the man's neck. "Where's Lopez?"

The drug dealer swallowed. He saw his own death in Cy's masked face, in those terrible glittering green eyes.

Harley felt that familiar cold sickness in the pit of his stomach as the muzzle of Cy's .45 automatic pressed harder into the adversary's neck just for a few seconds. It wasn't a training exercise. The gun was real. So was the threat. He looked at his boss, at the man he thought he knew, and realized at once that Cy wasn't bluffing.

"Where's Lopez?" Cy repeated, and he pulled back the trigger deliberately.

"Please," the foreigner gasped, shivering. "Please! He is in Cancún!"

Cy stared at him for just an instant longer before he jerked the man around and sent him spinning away from the protection of the bales.

"Hey, Kennedy!" he called.

One of the DEA men came forward.

"Here's the site boss," Cy told him, pushing the injured man ahead. "I think you'll find him more than willing to talk. And if he isn't, just call me back," he added, watching the drug lord's man go even paler.

"I'll do that. Thanks," Kennedy said. "The sheriff's deputies and those police officers have most of them cuffed and ready to transport. We're going into the house. At least three of them managed to hole up in there. And there's a fourth man still missing. Watch your back."

"You do the same," Cy said. He glanced at Harley. "Let's check out the perimeter of the barn."

"Sure thing, boss," Harley drawled, but he was pale and somber and all traces of his former cockiness were gone. He held his pistol professionally and followed his boss out the door without a trace of hesitation. For the first time, Cy was really proud of him.

They trailed around back, watching as shadows merged with other shadows. There was a sudden crack of twigs and Harley spun around with his .45 leveled as another man carrying an automatic weapon stepped suddenly from behind one of the big trucks. His lean face was unmasked, and he was definitely foreign.

Harley fired, but Cy's hand shot out and knocked the barrel straight up.

"Good reflexes, Harley," Cy said, smiling, "but this guy's on our side. Hi, Rodrigo," he called to the unmasked newcomer. "Long time no see."

"*Muchas gracias* for the timely intervention," Rodrigo replied on a husky chuckle. He moved forward, his white teeth showing even in the darkness. "It would be a pity to have come this far and be shot by a comrade."

"No danger of that," Cy said with a smile as he clapped the other man on the shoulder. "We were afraid they'd killed you. How are you?"

"Disappointed," came the reply. "I had hoped to apprehend Lopez, but he remained in Cancún and refused to participate. Someone is feeding him information about the movement of the government agents. He knew you were coming tonight."

"Damn!" Cy burst out.

Eb Scott and Micah Steele, the taller man who'd accompanied them, came forward. "Rodrigo!" he greeted, shaking the other man's hand. "We thought you'd been killed when we didn't hear from you."

"Lopez was suspicious of me," he said simply. "I couldn't afford to do anything that might tip my hand." He waved his hand toward the barn. "As it is, he was warned in time to divert the cocaine shipment and substitute this for it," he added, indicating the neat bales. "This has a significant street value, of course, but it is hardly the haul we hoped for."

Harley was inspecting the "hay." He frowned as he sniffed a twig of it. "Hey! This is marijuana!"

"Bales of it," Cy agreed. "I noticed when we came in that the barn had a padlock on it."

"Now that's what I call keeping a low profile," Harley murmured dryly. "Locking a barn full of hay."

"It would have been coca paste, if Lopez hadn't been warned," Rodrigo told Cy. "What he'd set up behind your ranch was a small processing plant that would have turned coca paste into crack cocaine. If I'd had just another week…!"

Cy smiled. "We'd rather have you alive, Rodrigo. We aren't through yet."

"No, we aren't," Micah Steele said coldly. "I have a contact in Cancún who knows Lopez. He can get someone in the house."

"An inspired idea," Rodrigo said. "Just don't share it with your friends over there," he added bitterly. "They don't have much of a track record with infiltration. Someone else infiltrated Lopez's home once before and died for it."

"Excuse me?" Micah asked.

"They lost an agent who worked for Lopez as a housekeeper," Rodrigo said. "He pushed her off his yacht." His face tightened. "Then he took a fancy to my sister, who was singing in a night club. He assaulted her, and she committed suicide at his house by throwing herself…onto the rocks below."

Eb's eyes narrowed. He was remembering some of the crazy things Rodrigo had done before he took this assignment, behavior that had marked him as a madman. Now they made sense. "I'm sorry," Eb said simply.

"So was I." Rodrigo glanced at the government agents rounding up the stragglers. "I'd better get out of here before that guy with Kennedy recognizes me."

"Who, Cobb?" Eb asked, frowning.

Rodrigo nodded. "It was his office I ransacked," he murmured. "They say he'll follow you to hell if you cross him. I'm inclined to believe it."

Rodrigo murmured, "Well, whether or not Cobb recognizes me, I don't want to risk being apprehended while Lopez is still loose. I can't do any good in prison."

"You were never here," Eb replied, tongue-in-cheek.

"Absolutely," Cy agreed. "I haven't seen you in years."

Micah Steele lifted one huge hand to his eyes. "Forgot my glasses," he murmured. "I couldn't recognize my own brother without them."

"You don't wear glasses, and you don't have a brother," Cy reminded him.

Micah shrugged. "No wonder I couldn't recognize him." He grinned.

Harley listened to the byplay, wondering how these men could seem so calm and unconcerned after what they'd all been through. He was sick to his stomach and shaking inside. He was putting on a good enough front to fool everyone else apparently, though. That was some small compensation.

"Get going," Eb motioned to Rodrigo. "Kennedy's heading this way."

Rodrigo nodded. "I'll be around if you need me again."

"We'll remember," Cy said. "But it won't be infiltrating Lopez's gang next time."

"No, it damned sure won't," Micah Steele said with ice in his deep voice. "Next time, we'll go at him head-on, and he won't walk away."

"I will count the days." Rodrigo melted back into the darkness before Kennedy came around the barn and paused beside the small group.

"The four of you had better do a quick vanishing act," Kennedy told them. "Cobb's over there asking a

lot of questions about you guys, and he won't overlook
a breach of departmental procedure. Since he outranks
me, that wouldn't be good. As far as I'm concerned,
officially, you were special agents undercover and I
don't know who you are for your own protection. You
infiltrated Lopez's gang and took a powder the minute
the firefight was over. Since I never knew your names,
I couldn't confirm your involvement." He gave them a
big grin. "Unofficially, thanks for your help. At least
we've managed to shut down one of Lopez's little en-
terprises." His eyes narrowed. "The man you dropped
in the barn," Kennedy added, talking to Cy, "was the
one who popped a cap on Walt Monroe. We've been
hoping to happen onto him. Cobb says he'll go down
for murder one, and I guarantee he'll make it stick.
Monroe was one of his new recruits. He doesn't like
many people. He liked Walt."

"I'll pass that along to his widow," Cy said. "She'll
be glad."

He nodded. "Walt was a good man." He looked
around. "I only wish we'd had something really nasty to
pin on these guys. Distribution of cocaine would have
suited me better than distribution of marijuana."

"Yes," Cy agreed, "but even if this was small pick-
ings, it will hurt Lopez to have a hefty portion of his
transportation force out of action, not to mention the

lab he set up next to his beehives on my back property line. He's lost a big investment here tonight, in manpower, material and unrecoverable goods. He'll really be out for blood now. None of us will be safe until we get Lopez himself."

"Dream on," Kennedy said quietly. "He's more slippery than a greased python."

"Even pythons can be captured." Micah Steele's eyes glittered through his mask. "I've got a few friends in Nassau. We'll see what we can do about Lopez."

"I didn't hear you say that," Kennedy replied.

"Just as well," Micah chuckled. "Since I was never here."

"There's a lot of that going around," Kennedy murmured. "Get going before Cobb gets a good look at you. I'll take it from here."

Eb nodded and the others joined him for a quick jaunt back to the Johnson place where they'd left the truck.

Harley hadn't said a single word. Eb and Cy and Micah talked about Lopez and discussed options for getting to him. Harley sat and looked out the window.

It wasn't until Eb dropped the two men off at Cy Parks's ranch, several hundred yards from the house, that Cy was able to get a good look at his foreman.

Harley had the expression now, the one any combat

veteran would recognize immediately. The experience tonight had taken the edge off his youth, his impulsive nature, his bravado. He'd matured in one night, and he'd never be the same again.

"Now," Cy told him quietly, "look in a mirror. You'll see what was missing when you were talking about your 'exploits' on the mercenary training expedition. This is the real thing, Harley. Men don't fall and then get back up again. The blood is real. The screams are real. What you saw tonight is the face of war, and no amount of money or fame is worth what you have to pay for it in emotional capital."

Harley's head turned. He looked at his boss with new eyes. "You were one of them," he said. "That's what you did before you came here and started ranching."

"That's right," Cy said evenly. "I've killed men. I've watched men die. I've watched children die, fighting in wars not of their making. I did it for fame and glory and money. But nothing I have now is worth the price I paid for it." He hesitated. "Nothing," he added, "except that woman in my house right now. She's worth dying for."

Harley managed a wan smile. "I could have gotten you all killed tonight, because I didn't know what I was doing."

"But you didn't get us killed," Cy returned. "And

when the chips were down, you conquered your fear and kept going. That's the real definition of courage." He put a big, heavy hand on the other man's shoulder. "You have a way with ranch management, Harley. Believe me, it's a better path than hiring yourself out to whatever army needs foreign help. At the very least, you accumulate fewer bullet wounds."

Harley nodded. "So I saw. Good night, boss."

"Harley."

The younger man turned.

"I've never been prouder of you than I was tonight," Cy said quietly.

Harley tried to speak, couldn't, and settled for a jerky smile and a nod before he walked away.

Cy walked on toward the house, smiling faintly as he contemplated the movement of the curtains in the living-room window.

Before he even reached the porch, Lisa was out the front door and flying toward him. He caught her easily as she propelled herself from the second step. He folded her close, whirled her around and kissed her with his whole heart.

She held on to him for dear life, tears raining down her face as she thanked God that he'd come back to her in one piece.

"Can I keep you?" she whispered at his lips as he picked her up and carried her inside.

His heart jumped wildly. "Keep me?" he murmured, kicking the door shut with his foot. "Try to get rid of me…!"

She smiled under the fierce hunger of his mouth, savoring its coolness, its beloved contours, as he carried her into the bedroom and kicked that door shut, as well. She could feel the adrenaline surging through his powerful body even before she felt the aftereffects of passion in his hungry, devouring kisses. She had a feeling that it was going to be the most explosively sensual night of their married lives. And she was right.

Chapter Eleven

Two feverishly exciting hours later, Lisa lay trembling against the powerful body beside hers in the tangled covers of Cy's big bed. She stretched and moaned helplessly as the movement triggered delicious little aftershocks of pleasure.

"If you weren't already pregnant," he murmured huskily, "you would be, after that."

She lifted herself up and propped her forearms on his damp, hair-roughened, deeply scarred chest. She brushed her mouth against one of the scars lovingly. "I went back to the doctor again yesterday," she confessed.

"Why?" He was concerned now, his green eyes narrowing on her face.

She traced his hard mouth with her fingertips. "To have a sonogram to date the pregnancy and to have some blood work done." She looked straight into his eyes. "The baby is yours, Cy."

He shivered. She could feel the ripple of muscle go right down him. "What?" he asked.

"I'm only a few weeks along. That means the baby is yours—not Walt's." She slid down beside him and pillowed her cheek on his chest, letting one slender, pretty leg slide over his muscular, hairy one. "He told me he did some checking and the results from my first pregnancy test after Walt died were switched with someone else's. It was a mix-up at the lab. That explains why I haven't had any pregnancy symptoms until now."

He stroked her long hair absently. "I can't believe it."

"Me, either. But it makes sense. I didn't know, but before we married, Walt…had a vasectomy. I checked with his doctor to get information on Walt's RH factor."

Every tendon in his body pulled tight. He rolled over and looked down into her flushed face incredulously.

"He said he didn't want children," she confessed. "The doctor said that he wanted to make sure he didn't have any. The doctor wanted him to tell me. He never did."

He was speechless with wonder. His baby. She was carrying his baby. He thought of his late wife and the child she'd borne that belonged to another man. He'd married Lisa believing that she was pregnant with her dead husband's child. But here he was with a miracle. He was going to be a biological father, for the first time in his life. He felt moisture sting his eyes as his big, lean hand smoothed over her flat stomach gently.

The expression on his face made her feel warm inside, safe, cocooned. "No need to ask if you're pleased," she said in a tender, amused tone.

He laughed self-consciously. "Pleased? I'm ecstatic. I don't suppose my feet will touch the ground for weeks."

She smiled and pressed close. "Mine won't, either, and not only because of the baby."

"Why else, then?" he teased.

She sighed, drawing her fingers across his mouth. "Because you love me."

He didn't hesitate or deny it. He only smiled. "Sure of that, are you?"

"Yes."

"How?"

She linked her arms around his neck and pressed her mouth gently to his damp throat. "It shows, in so many ways. All the time."

His fingers tangled contentedly in her long hair. "Like what you feel about me shows," he murmured, holding her closer.

"Does it?"

"We nurture each other," he said softly. "I never realized married people could be close like this, tender like this, loving like this. I've been standing outside warm houses all my life, looking in, and now I'm right inside by the fireplace." His arms contracted. His face nuzzled gently against hers. "I love you with all that I am, all I ever will be. More than my life."

She moaned and pressed closer, shivering. "I love you more than my life, too," she breathed at his lips. "I'm going to give you a son, Cy."

"And a daughter," he whispered back, delighted. "And a few others, assorted."

She smiled against his mouth. "You'll be a wonderful daddy."

He kissed her with aching tenderness, almost overwhelmed with emotion. Out of such tragedy and anguish had come this woman, this angel, in his arms. He was still amazed that she could love him, want him, need him as she did, with his past, with his scarred body and scarred emotions. He'd never dared hope for so much in his life. He closed his eyes and thanked God for the biggest miracle he'd ever had.

"I'll take care of you as long as I live, Lisa."

"And I'll take care of you as long as I do," she murmured happily. "I hope we live a hundred years together."

He laughed softly and agreed, drowning in the warm delight of her body curled so close into his. It was unbearably sweet to love, to really love, and be loved in return.

Her leg moved sensuously against the inside of his and she felt his breath go jerky. She was more sure of herself now, eager for new lessons, new techniques, new adventures with this man, this winter soldier, she loved.

"Cy?" she whispered as her hand smoothed over his chest and then steadily down.

It was hard to talk. "What?" he managed in a husky tone.

"I want you to teach me."

"Teach you…what?" he bit off as her hand moved again.

"How to please you."

He would have answered her, if he'd been able. But his soft groan and the shivering of his powerful body as he eased over hers were more than enough to convince her that she was pleasing him already. She stretched like a contented cat under the warm, sinuous press of his lean hips and then moaned as the fever burned so high that she thought she might become ashes in his arms. Life had never been so sweet. And this was only the tip of the iceberg, the very beginning of their marriage. She pressed her mouth into his and held on tight, following him into the fire.

With Lopez's Jacobsville connection closed down, and all his local assets seized by the feds, it seemed a good guess that the drug lord would set up operations elsewhere. But he still had people, unknown people, acting as his eyes and ears. He also had someone inside the federal agency, Rodrigo had said, to tip him off about drug busts. Cy worried about who it was. Cy worried more about another possible attempt on Lisa, after the successful sneak attack on Lopez's shipment of marijuana.

Cy had gone to Eb's ranch at his friend's request to discuss future plans, and they were talking over cups of black coffee in the living room when Micah Steele came into the room. He was taller, bigger than both the other men. He had thick, straight, medium blond hair cut conventionally short. He was wearing a beige Armani suit that seemed perfect for his tall frame. It made his dark eyes look even darker. He wore a watch like Eb's on his left wrist and no other jewelry. Thirty-six years old, the former CIA agent spoke several languages fluently and had a temper that was explosive and quiet. Dutch van Meer used to say that Micah could get more results with a steady look than he could with a weapon.

"Why are you still in town?" Cy asked curiously.

"That's what I asked you over to tell you." Eb grimaced. "We've still got problems."

"When have we had anything else lately?" Cy said with resignation.

"The word is that Lopez's bosses in Colombia think he's slipping. First, he got arrested. Then he lost a shipment to the Coast Guard. We cost him a tidy sum in men and equipment here, not to mention marijuana. Yesterday, another group of his men were driving plastic bags of cocaine paste in several transfer trailer trucks bearing the logo of a grocery store chain. The DEA was tipped off, probably by Rodrigo, and the feds got all the trucks plus their cargo. The haul would have been worth millions, if not billions, in crack cocaine sales if it had been processed and put out on the streets. It's the largest confiscation by the DEA in years. Lopez's bosses are furious. They're ready to dump Lopez, and he's cut some sort of deal to keep his connection. The word is, he's making plans to eliminate the obstacles to his local smuggling traffic."

"That's no real surprise," Eb pointed out.

Micah's dark eyes narrowed. "No. But I didn't expect this quite so soon. He can't get to either of you without some difficulty, now that his operation here has been shut down. Any group of strangers in town would stick out like sore thumbs, and the local authorities are on alert. But one of my contacts said that Callie and my father might become targets, and that the last he heard, Lopez was going to call in a mechanic. One man, alone, might succeed where a larger group failed."

It went without saying that a "mechanic" meant a professional killer. "Why your family and not ours?" Cy asked.

Micah leaned against the mantel above the fireplace in Eb's study. He smiled mockingly, looking more elegant than a male model with his striking good looks. "You only helped shut down a small operation of Lopez's. But I tipped the DEA guys about the multimillion dollar cocaine shipment that was confiscated."

Cy whistled. "Did Rodrigo pass that tidbit along?"

"Not Rodrigo," came the reply. "It was a last act of defiance by his cousin, who," he added grimly, "is now dead. They pulled him out of a vat of industrial chemicals. They were only able to identify him by dental records."

"Any idea where Rodrigo is?" Eb wanted to know.

"Hiding out in Aruba, I gather from my sources. But he may not be safe, even so. Lopez has a long reach. He's got people everywhere."

"Plus an informant with the feds who's spilling the beans to Lopez about our government's attempts to bring him down," Cy added.

"That's how Lopez knew I blew the whistle on him. You'd better believe that Kennedy and Cobb are doing their best to find out who it is," Micah replied. "But I expect it's someone in a high position who's beyond suspicion. It won't be easy to ferret him out."

"He's risking a lot on Lopez's account, whoever he is," Eb mused.

"Lopez is paying him a million a tip," Micah interjected.

"Well, that would make it worth the risk for most people, I'm afraid," Eb said.

Micah dropped down into an easy chair and lit a cigar. Eb turned on the smokeless ashtray and handed it to him. Micah chuckled, taking it in one big hand.

"That will kill you," Eb said with a grin.

"In my line of work, bullets will probably get me long before smoking does. Besides, I don't expect to be here long." He checked the big watch on his wrist. "Callie gets off work in five minutes. I'm going to waylay her before she goes to pick up Dad at the senior citizen center."

His face changed when he mentioned his former stepsister. His dark eyes narrowed and his jaw went taut. He smoked absently, his mind obviously far away.

"If worse comes to worst, you could take her and your father down to Nassau with you and keep her out of Lopez's reach," Eb suggested.

Micah gave him a hellish glare. "Neither of them will talk to me right now, much less agree to go to Nassau. Haven't you heard?" he drawled. "I'm anybody's friend but theirs."

"You always start the fights," Eb pointed out. "You can't blame Callie for defending herself."

Micah took another draw from the cigar and thumped ashes in the ashtray. "I blame her for everything," he said icily. "If it hadn't been for her and her damned mother, my father would want to see me occasionally."

"Surely he doesn't still blame you for his divorce?" Cy remarked.

"He blames me for everything." He put out the cigar impatiently and turned the smokeless ashtray off. "I blame her mother."

"Whatever happened to her?" Eb asked.

"I have no idea," Micah said abruptly. "She dumped Callie and left town even before the divorce was final. She hired a lawyer to bring the papers to her in England so that she wouldn't have to see any of us again. Some mother."

"Callie never talks about her," Eb said thoughtfully. "It's not surprising. Her mother treated her like the hired help. Callie wasn't pretty enough or sophisticated enough to please her mama."

"There's nothing wrong with Callie," Micah replied absently. "She's naive, of course, but looks aren't that important. She's a good woman, in the true sense of the word. I should know," he added with a harsh laugh. "I've left a trail of the other kind behind me over the years."

"I won't argue with that," Eb had to agree. "They used to follow you around like flies after honey. Really beautiful women."

"Window dressing," Micah said carelessly. "Underneath they all had one thing in common—greed. Being rich and single has its drawbacks as well as its perks."

There was a brief silence while all of them recalled other times, other places.

"How's Lisa, by the way?" Micah asked. "Is the baby all right?"

"The test results got mixed when she had the first test, just after Walt was killed," Cy replied. He began to smile. "But she's pregnant now."

Eb scowled. "With Walt's baby. I know."

Cy shook his head. "Not Walt's baby. Mine." His eyes were brimming with pride, joy, delight. "Walt had a vasectomy before they married. He didn't want kids at all."

The other two men chuckled softly. "I thought you said she was too young for you," Eb said mischievously.

"I changed my mind. She's old for her age and I'm young for mine." He couldn't seem to stop smiling. "It's like a second chance. I never thought I'd get one."

"I'm glad for you," Eb said. "Glad for myself, too. We've made good marriages."

"I wish you could stop talking about it," Micah said disgustedly, glancing from one of them to the other. "I'll break out in hives any minute."

"Mr. Confirmed Bachelor," Eb said, jerking a thumb at the blond man.

"Napoleon before Waterloo," Cy agreed.

Micah got up out of his chair. "I'm going to see Callie. I brought Bojo over here with me, but he flew to Atlanta to see his brother. I guess it's just as well. If I had him tail her, he'd probably attract a little attention."

"Dressed in a long white silk robe and babushes on his feet? Who'd notice that in Jacobsville, Texas?" Eb asked dryly.

"He's Berber. The beard and mustache are traditional, like the accoutrements. He wouldn't blend, that's for sure," Micah said. He sighed. "I've had a hard time replacing Dallas since he got shot up and then left to marry Sally's aunt Jessica. Good men are really hard to find these days."

"They were just as hard to find back when we started out, too," Eb said. "Well, there's always Harley. He's hooked on adventure."

"No, he isn't," Cy said firmly. "He's the best foreman in two counties and I'm not recommending him for a target."

"He did pretty good that night," Eb said. "When the chips are down, he can keep his head."

"I want him to keep his head," Cy said. "That's the whole point of keeping him at home."

"How about Rodrigo?" Eb suggested.

Micah nodded slowly. "He could come to Nassau. He'd be safer there, with Bojo and me. I'll see if I can find him on my way home."

"Take care of yourself," Cy said.

Micah shook hands with him. "You do the same."

He left the two of them still talking about Rodrigo

and climbed into the racy black Porsche he drove. It was like him, power and grace conventionally packaged and deceptively straitlaced. Micah was a law unto himself.

Micah drove to the side street near Kemp's law office, where Callie's little yellow VW beetle was sitting. He liked the updated style of the body, and the color suited her. She was bright and sunny. Or she had been, until her mother ruined all their lives.

It was five o'clock on the dot, and he waited and watched the rearview. Sure enough, less than a minute later, Callie Kirby came out of the law office and went down the sidewalk toward her car, lost in thought as she dug in her purse for her car keys. It amazed him that everything didn't fall out on the pavement at her feet. He remembered Callie being all thumbs, a gangly teenager suffering from embarrassment, lack of social graces and a bubbly personality despite her drawbacks.

But this Callie had changed. She had pale blue eyes and an ordinary sort of face, but it had a gamine charm all its own. She wore her dark hair short. She was only medium height, a little thing compared to him. But for her size, she packed a wallop when she lost her temper. He was sorry they couldn't be friends. He didn't have many, and she would have had the distinction of being the only woman among them. His affairs had tarnished him in Callie's quiet eyes. She had no use for playboys. Especially Micah Steele. Like his father, she blamed him for the divorce and the anguish that came after it. She thought that he'd been having an affair with her mother. That was ironic, when her mother was the one woman on earth he'd ever considered totally repulsive.

Well, you couldn't go home again, they said. They were right. That door was closed forever. His father was old and weak and illness had taken much of the spirit out of him. He hated the separation between them. He loved his father. He was glad that Callie did, too, and that she took such good care of the old man. He thought about Lopez and the possibility of a hit man with those two gentle people as the targets, and his blood ran cold. He didn't want them to die for his actions. Lopez would know that, and it would please him. His teeth clenched as unwanted pictures of some nebulous tragedy began to take shape in his mind.

Callie came toward her car, noticed the low slung Porsche and stopped dead in her tracks, staring at it.

Micah climbed out of the car with his usual elegance of movement and went to join her beside her car.

"We need to talk."

She clutched her purse against her small breasts and

looked up at him with faint hauteur. Her heart was racing. He could see her blouse move jerkily above her breasts. He remembered vividly the feel of her in his arms that once…

"*We* never talk," she informed him. "You say what you want to, and then you walk away."

She had a point. He pulled the half-smoked cigar from its holder and lit it.

"That's illegal in the mall," she said with unholy glee. "Light up there, and they'll arrest you."

"You'd love that, wouldn't you?"

She wasn't going to be drawn into another verbal firefight with him. She straightened. "I'm tired and I still have to pick up Dad at the senior center. He stays with me now."

"I know." He hated the thought of Callie being his father's nurse and protector. It was one of many things he resented. "Have you heard from your mother?" he added mockingly.

She didn't flinch. But her eyelids did, just barely perceptibly. "I haven't heard from my mother since the divorce," she said calmly. "Have you?" she added with pure venom.

His dark eyes glittered at her.

She decided to cut her losses. "What do you want?" she asked bluntly.

Now that he had her attention, he didn't know how to put it. She had no idea what he did for a living. Even his father didn't know. He'd kept his profession secret from both of them. He'd inherited a large trust from his mother, which would never have been enough to furnish him with Porsches and Armani suits. They didn't seem to realize that, so he left them to draw their own conclusions. Now, with Lopez looming over him, his profession might get them both killed. He had to find a way to protect them. But how?

"I don't suppose you and Dad would like to come down to Nassau for a vacation?" he asked speculatively.

Her chin lifted proudly. "I'd rather holiday in hell," she said with a cold smile.

He let out a husky, hollow laugh. "That's what I thought."

"Your father is all right," she said, anticipating what she thought was wrong. "It was just a mild stroke."

"When did that happen?" he asked abruptly, with concern.

"No one called you?" She shifted her purse. "Sorry. We've all watched him carefully since that heart attack. It was two weeks ago, he lost the feeling on the left side of his face and couldn't move it. As I said, it was mild. It was a light stroke. But they were actually able to clean out the artery that was clogged and put a shunt in it. He's on blood thinners, and he has a good prognosis. You don't have to worry about him. I'm taking good care of him."

"On your salary," he said flatly, angered.

She stiffened. "I make a decent living and he's an economical guest. We struggle along together just fine. We don't need financial help," she added firmly. "In case you wondered," she added, reminding him that he'd accused her of being money-hungry just like her mother. It was one of many things he'd said to her that still hurt.

The words went right through him, but he hid his reaction. He wished he could forget the accusations he'd made, the hurtful things he'd said to her. But there was no going back. "Did you know your own father?" he asked, curious.

Her face grew taut. "I don't know who my father was. My mother's first husband was positive that it wasn't him. That's why he didn't press for custody when she divorced him."

She said it with savaged pride, and he was sorry he'd forced the admission from her. "So my father's standing in for him?" he probed gently.

"Jack Steele was kinder to me than anyone else ever

was," she said tightly. "It's no great burden to look after him. And you still haven't said why you're here."

He fingered the burning cigar and tried to find the words. "I've made an enemy," he said finally. "A very bad man to cross. I think he might target you and my father to get back at me."

Callie frowned. "Excuse me?"

His dark eyes met hers. "He's a drug lord. He heads one of the Colombian cartels. I just cost him several million dollars by tipping the DEA about a massive shipment of cocaine he sent over here."

Her blood ran cold. She worked in legal circles. She knew about drugs, not only their dangers, but also the penalties for using or selling them. She also knew about the Colombian cartels, because they were on the news most every night. They were graphic about how drug dealers got even with people who cost them money. She couldn't even shoot a gun, and Jack Steele, Micah's father, was practically an invalid despite his remarkable recovery. The two of them together would never be able to protect themselves from such an adversary, and she couldn't afford to hire a bodyguard.

She stared at Micah blankly. "Would he be that ruthless?" she had to ask.

"Yes."

Her chest rose and fell heavily. "Okay. What do we do?"

Straightforward. No accusations, no rage, no exaggerated fear. She simply asked, trusting that he'd know. And he did.

"I'm going to send someone over here to watch you and Dad," he replied. "Someone trustworthy."

"And what are you going to do?" she wanted to know.

"That's my business."

He looked, and sounded, harder than nails. She felt exposed, vulnerable. She was eighteen again, hearing him accuse her of setting him up with his father. He'd already been angry at her for what had happened when they'd been alone that last Christmas they'd all lived together. He'd given in to temptation and it had taken all his willpower to get away from her at all. He'd lectured her about being so free with her kisses, so wanton and forward. He'd left her in tears. It had only dawned on him much later that she'd had something alcoholic to drink. He'd walked out into the hall, where her mother had seen him in a state of unmistakable arousal and had made a blatant play for him, thinking *she'd* aroused him in her low-cut dress.

In the seconds it took his dimmed brain to react, his father had come out of the study and found him in the hall with Callie's mother, in a compromising position. Micah and his father had almost come to blows. Callie and her mother were summarily booted out the door and Micah had accused Callie of sending her father out there to catch him with his stepmother, out of revenge because he wouldn't kiss her. It had broken Callie's heart. Now, she withdrew from Micah Steele as if he were molten lava. She had no wish to repeat the lesson he'd taught her.

"Very well," she said demurely. "I'll look after Dad while you do…whatever you're going to do. I've got my grandfather's shotgun and some shells. I'll protect him at night."

He looked at her in a different way. "Can you shoot it?"

"If I have to," she replied. Her face was very pale, but she wasn't flinching. "Was there anything else?"

His dark eyes slid down her slender, graceful body and he remembered Callie in bathing suits, in flimsy gowns, in her one fancy dress at her birthday party— her eighteenth birthday party. She'd been wearing deep green velvet, cut low and sensuous, and he'd refused her invitation to attend the celebration. Like so many other things he'd said and done, he'd hurt her that day. She still looked impossibly young. She was barely twenty-two, and he was thirty-six, over a decade her senior.

He wanted to prolong the meeting. That was unlike him. He shrugged one shoulder indifferently instead. "Nothing important. Just watch your step. I'll make sure nobody gets close enough to hurt either of you."

She gave him one slow, eloquent look before she turned to her small car and unlocked it. She got in and drove off, without another word. And she didn't look back.

Chapter Twelve

Cy and Lisa were having a late supper at the kitchen table. They watched each other hungrily with every bite as they discussed the changes the baby would mean in their lives. They were delightful changes, and they spoke in low murmurs, smiling at each other between bites. The loud squeal of tires out front caught them unaware and made them tense. Surely it wasn't another attack by Lopez or his men…!

Cy was out of the chair and heading for the front door seconds later, his hand going automatically to the phone table drawer where the loaded .45 automatic was kept. He made a mental note to himself to keep his gun locked up once the baby arrived. He motioned

Lisa back and moved cautiously out onto the porch. Seconds later, he lowered the weapon. It was Micah Steele, but he was hardly recognizable.

His thick blond hair was disheveled, and he needed a shave. He looked as if he hadn't slept.

Cy didn't waste time asking questions. He caught the taller man by the arm and pulled him inside. "Coffee first. Then you can tell whatever you need to."

"I'll bring it to the study," Lisa offered.

Cy smiled at her and bent to kiss her cheek. "I'll bring it to the study," he corrected tenderly. "Growing mamas need their rest. Go watch TV."

"Okay." She kissed him back, sparing a curious and sympathetic glance for Micah, who nodded politely before he preceded Cy into the kitchen.

When Lisa was out of earshot, Cy poured coffee into two mugs and put them on the table.

"Would you rather talk in the study?" Cy asked him.

"This is fine." Micah cupped the mug in both hands and leaned over it in a slumped posture that said all too much about his mental condition.

Cy straddled a chair across from him. "Okay. What's wrong."

"Lopez has Callie," he said in a husky, tortured voice.

Cy sat stock-still. "When? And how?" he exploded.

"Yesterday, not five minutes after I spoke to her outside her office building," he said dully. "We had a brief conversation. I warned her that someone I knew might possibly target her or my father. She listened, but she didn't pay much attention. I told her I was going to have someone watch them for their own safety. But I'd barely gotten back to my motel when Eb phoned and said he'd had an urgent message from Rodrigo that Callie was going to be snatched. I phoned the adult day care where she leaves Dad every day and they said she hadn't picked him up." He looked absolutely devastated. "You can set your watch by Callie. She's always early, if she isn't right on time. I went looking for her, and I found her car about a block from the senior center on a side street. The driver's door was standing wide-open and her purse was still in it."

Cy cursed roundly. "Did you call the police?"

Micah shook his head. He ran a big hand through his hair restlessly. "I didn't know what to do." He looked at Cy in anguish. "Do you know what that snake will do to her? She's untouched, Cy. Absolutely untouched!"

He had a pretty good idea what Lopez would do, and it made him sick to consider it. Judging by Micah's behavior, his stepsister meant a lot more to him than he'd ever admitted; possibly, more than he'd realized himself.

"The first thing we do is call Chet Blake."

"A lot of good a local police chief is going to do us," Micah said miserably. "By now, Lopez has her out of the state, if not out of the country."

"Chet is a distant relation of our state attorney general, Simon Hart," Cy interrupted, "and he has a cousin who's a Texas Ranger. Lopez's men left some sort of trail, even if it's just a paper one. Chet has connections. He'll find out where Lopez has taken her. If she's in Mexico, we can contact the Mexican authorities and Interpol…"

Micah's steely glare interrupted him. "All I need to know is where she is," he said tautly. "Then I'll pack up Bojo and Rodrigo, and we'll play cowboys and drug dealers."

Cy wanted to try to reason with him, but the man was too far gone. He'd seen Micah in this mood before, and he knew there was nothing he could say or do to stop him. He spared a thought for Callie, who was probably terrified, not to mention Micah's father. The old man had already had a major heart attack and a stroke, and the news might easily be too much for him. Micah would have to make up a story and tell it to whoever was nursing him. He said as much.

"I've already taken care of that," Micah said heavily. "One of the freelance homebound nurses who sometimes visits him at the center went home with him. I've arranged for her to stay there until I come back—or until Callie does. I told her to say that Callie had an emergency out of town, a cousin in a car wreck. He doesn't know that she has no cousins. He'll believe it, and he won't have to be upset."

"Good thinking," Cy said. "What can I do?"

Micah finished his coffee. "You can keep an eye on Dad for me while I'm out of the country. You and Eb," he added. "If you don't mind."

"Certainly I don't mind," Cy told him. "We'll have somebody watch him constantly. I promise."

"Thanks," Micah said simply. He stood up. "I'll let you know when I've got her safe."

"If there's anything else you need, all you have to do is ask," Cy told him.

Micah smiled wanly. "Remember that old saying, that we don't appreciate what we've got until we lose it?"

"She'll be all right."

"I hope so. See you."

"Good luck."

Micah nodded and went out as quietly as he'd come in. Cy poured himself another cup of coffee, took out a glass and filled it with milk for Lisa before he closed up the kitchen and went to join her in the living room.

Her eyes lit up when he sat down on the sofa beside her, put the drinks down and slid his arm behind her to watch her knit.

"What was wrong with him?"

"Lopez got Callie," he said.

She grimaced and groaned. "Oh, poor Callie! Can he rescue her, do you think?"

"As soon as we find out where she is. I've got to make some phone calls in the study. Go on to bed when your program goes off. I'll be there in a little while."

She put her hand on his cheek and caressed it softly. "I love going to bed with you," she said softly.

He smiled at her, bending to kiss her lips tenderly. "I love doing everything with you," he said.

"Will it be enough for you, me and the baby?" she asked solemnly. "Will it make up for what you've lost?"

He drew her close and hugged her. "I'll always miss Alex," he replied, naming his five-year-old son who died in the Wyoming fire. "And I'll always blame myself for not being able to save him. But I love you, and I want our baby very much." He lifted his head and looked down into her dark eyes hungrily. "You'll be enough, Lisa."

She smiled again, and kissed him hungrily before he got up from the sofa. "I love you."

"I love you, too." He ruffled her long hair and grinned at her. "You've changed my whole life. I look forward to waking up every morning. I have such a pretty view in my bed."

She chuckled. "I have a very nice one of my own." She sobered. "Will Lopez hurt Callie?"

"I wish I knew. We'll do what we can to help Micah find her."

"Even when Lopez is not here, he's still here," she said. "One of these days, he's going to be called to account for all the evil things he's done."

"And he'll pay the price," Cy assured her.

He went to make his phone calls. He paused in the doorway to take one long look at his wife. Despite his sympathy for Micah Steele, he was grateful that he hadn't lost Lisa to Lopez's violence. His life was new again, fresh, full of promise and joy. After the storm, the rainbow. He smiled. The winter soldier had found a warm, loving home at last.

* * * * *

CATTLEMAN'S PRIDE

To Amy in Alabama

Chapter One

Libby Collins couldn't figure out why her stepmother, Janet, had called a real estate agent out to the house. Her father had only been dead for a few weeks. The funeral was so fresh in her mind that she cried herself to sleep at night. Her brother, Curt, was equally devastated. Riddle Collins had been a strong, happy, intelligent man who'd never had a serious illness. He had no history of heart trouble. So his death of a massive heart attack had been a real shock. In fact, the Collinses' nearest neighbor, rancher Jordan Powell, said it was suspicious. But then, Jordan thought everything was suspicious. He thought the government was building cloned soldiers in some underground lab.

Libby ran a small hand through her wavy black hair, her light green eyes scanning the horizon for a sight of her brother. But Curt was probably up to his ears in watching over the births of early spring cattle, far in the northern pasture of the Powell ranch. It was just barely April and the heifers, the two-year-old first-time mothers, were beginning to drop their calves right on schedule. There was little hope that Curt would show up before the real estate agent left.

Around the corner of the house, Libby heard the real estate agent speaking. She moved closer, careful to keep out of sight, to see what was going on. Her father had loved his small ranch, as his children did. It had been in their family almost as long as Jordan Powell's family had owned the Bar P.

"How long will it take to find a buyer?" Janet was asking.

"I can't really say, Mrs. Collins," the man replied. "But Jacobsville is growing by leaps and bounds. There are plenty of new families looking for reasonable housing. I think a subdivision here would be perfectly situated and I can guarantee you that any developer would pay top dollar for it."

Subdivision? Surely she must be hearing things!

But Janet's next statement put an end to any such suspicion. "I want to sell it as soon as possible," Janet continued firmly. "I have the insurance money in hand. As soon as this sale is made, I'm moving out of the country."

Another shattering revelation! Why was her stepmother in such a hurry? Her husband of barely nine months had just died, for heaven's sake!

"I'll do what I can, Mrs. Collins," the real estate agent assured her. "But you must understand that the housing market is depressed right now and I can't guarantee a sale—as much as I'd like to."

"Very well," Janet said curtly. "But keep me informed of your progress, please."

"Certainly."

Libby ran for it, careful not to let herself be seen. Her heart was beating her half to death. She'd wondered at Janet's lack of emotion when her father died. Now her mind was forming unpleasant associations.

She stood in the shadows of the front porch until she heard the real estate agent drive away. Janet left immediately thereafter in her Mercedes.

Libby's mind was whirling. She needed help. Fortunately, she knew exactly where to go to get it.

She walked down the road toward Jordan Powell's big Spanish-style ranch house. The only transportation Libby had was a pickup truck, which was in the shop today having a water pump replaced. It was a long walk to the Powell ranch, but Libby needed fortifying to tackle her stepmother. Jordan was just the person to put steel in her backbone.

It took ten minutes to walk to the paved driveway that led through white fences to the ranch house. But it took another ten minutes to walk from the end of the driveway to the house. On either side of the fence were dark red-coated Santa Gertrudis cattle, purebred seed stock, which were the only cattle Jordan kept. One of his bulls was worth over a million dollars. He had a whole separate division that involved artificial insemination and the care of a special unit where sperm were kept. Libby had been fascinated to know that a single straw of bull semen could sell for a thousand dollars, or much more if it came from a prize bull who was dead. Jordan sold those straws to cattle ranchers all over the world. He frequently had visitors from other countries who came to tour his mammoth cattle operation. Like the Tremayne brothers, Cy Parks, and a number of other local ranchers, he was heavily into organic ranching. He used no hormones or dangerous pesticides or unnecessary antibiotics on his seed stock, even though they were never sold for beef. The herd sires he kept on the ranch lived in a huge breeding barn—as luxurious as a modern hotel—that was on property just adjacent to the Collinses' land. It was so close that they could hear the bulls bellowing from time to time.

Jordan was a local success story, the sort men liked to tell their young sons about. He started out as a cowboy long before he ever had cattle of his own. He'd grown up the only child of a former debutante and a hobby farmer. His father had married the only child of wealthy parents, who cut her off immediately when she announced her marriage. They left her only the property that Jordan now owned. His father's drinking cost him almost everything. When he wasn't drinking, he made a modest living with a few head of cattle, but after the sudden death of Jordan's mother, he withdrew from the world. Jordan was left with a hard decision to make. He took a job as a ranch hand on Duke Wright's palatial ranch and in his free time he went the rounds of the professional rodeo circuit. He was a champion bull rider, with the belt buckles and the cash to prove it.

But instead of spending that cash on good times, he'd paid off the mortgage that his father had taken on the ranch. Over the years he'd added a purebred Santa Gertrudis bull and a barn, followed by purebred heifers. He'd studied genetics with the help of a nearby retired rancher and he'd learned how to buy straws of bull semen and have his heifers artificially inseminated. His breeding program gave him the opportunity to enter his progeny in competition, which he did. Awards starting coming his way and so did stud fees for his bull. It had been a long road to prosperity, but he'd managed it, despite having to cope with an alcoholic father who eventually got behind the wheel of a truck and plowed it into a telephone pole. Jordan was left alone in the world. Well, except for women. He sure seemed to have plenty of those, to hear her brother, Curt, talk.

Libby loved the big dusty-yellow adobe ranch house Jordan had built two years ago, with its graceful arches and black wrought-iron grillwork. There was a big fountain in the front courtyard, where Jordan kept goldfish and huge koi that came right up out of the water to look at visitors. It even had a pond heater, to keep the fish alive all winter. It was a dream of a place. It would have been just right for a family. But everybody said that Jordan Powell would never get married. He liked his freedom too much.

She went up to the front door and rang the doorbell. She knew how she must look in her mud-stained jeans and faded T-shirt, her boots caked in mud, like her denim jacket. She'd been helping the lone part-time worker on their small property pull a calf. It was a dirty business, something her pristine stepmother would never have done. Libby still missed her father. His unexpected death had been a horrible blow to Curt and Libby, who were only just getting used to Riddle Collins's new wife.

No sooner was Riddle buried than Janet fought to get her hands on the quarter-of-a-million-dollar insurance policy he'd left behind, of which she alone was listed as beneficiary. She'd started spending money the day the check had arrived, with no thought for unpaid bills and Riddle's children. They were healthy and able to work, she reasoned. Besides, they had a roof over their heads. Temporarily, at least. Janet's long talk with the real estate agent today was disquieting. Riddle's new will, which his children knew nothing about, had given Janet complete and sole ownership of the house as well as Riddle's comfortable but not excessive savings account. Or so Janet said. Curt was furious. Libby hadn't said anything. She missed her father so much. She felt as if she were still walking around in a daze and it was almost March. A windy, cold almost-March, at that, she thought, feeling the chill.

She was frowning when the door opened. She jumped involuntarily when instead of the maid, Jordan Powell himself opened it.

"What the hell do you want?" he asked coldly. "Your

brother's not here. He's supervising some new fencing up on the north property.

"Well?" he asked impatiently when she didn't speak immediately. "I've got things to do and I'm late already!"

He was so dashing, she thought privately. He was thirty-two, very tall, lean and muscular, with liquid black eyes and dark, wavy hair. He had a strong, masculine face that was dark from exposure to the sun and big ears and big feet. But he was handsome. Too handsome.

"Are you mute?" he persisted, scowling.

She shook her head, sighing. "I'm just speechless. You really are a dish, Jordan," she drawled.

"Will you please tell me what you want?" he grumbled. "And if it's a date, you can go right back home. I don't like being chased by women. I know you can't keep your eyes off me, but that's no excuse to come sashaying up to my front door looking for attention."

"Fat chance," she drawled, her green eyes twinkling up at him. "If I want a man, I'll try someone accessible, like a movie star or a billionaire...."

"I said I'm in a hurry," he prompted.

"Okay. If you don't want to talk to me..." she began.

He let out an impatient sigh. "Come in, then," he

muttered, looking past her. "Hurry, before you get trampled by the other hopeful women chasing me."

"That would be a short list," she told him as she went in and waited until he closed the door behind him. "You're famous for your bad manners. You aren't even housebroken."

"I beg your pardon?" he said curtly.

She grinned at him. "Your boots are full of red mud and so's that fabulously expensive wool rug you brought back from Morocco," she pointed out. "Amie's going to kill you when she sees that."

"My aunt only lives here when she hasn't got someplace else to go," he pointed out.

"Translated, that means that she's in hiding. Why are you mad at her this time?" she asked.

He gave her a long-suffering stare and sighed. "Well, she wanted to redo my bedroom. Put yellow curtains at the windows. With ruffles." He spat out the word. "She thinks it's too depressing because I like dark wood and beige curtains."

She lifted both eyebrows over laughing eyes. "You could paint the room red…."

He glared down at her. "I said women chased me, not that I brought them home in buckets," he replied.

"My mistake. Who was it last week, Senator Merrill's daughter, and before her, the current Miss Jacobs County…?"

"That wasn't my fault," he said haughtily. "She stood in the middle of the parking lot at that new Japanese place and refused to move unless I let her come home with me." Then he grinned.

She shook her head. "You're impossible."

"Come on, come on, what do you want?" He looked at his watch. "I've got to meet your brother at the old line cabin in thirty minutes to help look over those pregnant heifers." He lifted an eyebrow and his eyes began to shimmer. They ran up and down her slender figure. "Maybe I could do you justice in fifteen minutes…."

She struck a pose. "Nobody's sticking me in between roundup and supper," she informed him. "Besides, I'm abstaining indefinitely."

He put a hand over his heart. "As God is my witness, I never asked your brother to tell you that Bill Paine had a social disease…"

"I am not sweet on Bill Paine!" she retorted.

"You were going to Houston with him to a concert that wasn't being given that night and I knew that Bill had an apartment and a bad reputation with women," he replied with clenched lips. "So I just happened to mention to one of my cowhands, who was standing beside your brother, that Bill Paine had a social disease."

She was aghast, just standing there gaping at his insolence. Curt had been very angry about her accepting a date with rich, blond Bill, who was far above them in social rank. Bill had been a client of Blake Kemp's, where he noticed Libby and started flirting with her. After Curt had told her what he overheard about Bill, she'd cancelled the date. She was glad she did. Later she'd learned that Bill had made a bet with one of his pals that he could get Libby anytime he wanted her, despite her standoffish pose.

"Of course, I don't have any social diseases," Jordan said, his deep voice dropping an octave. He checked his watch again. "Now it's down to ten minutes, if we hurry."

She threw up her hands. "Listen, I can't possibly be seduced today, I've got to go to the grocery store. What I came to tell you is that Janet's selling the property to a developer. He wants to put a subdivision on it," she added miserably.

"A what?" he exploded. "A subdivision? Next door to my breeding barn?" His eyes began to burn. "Like hell she will!"

"Great. You want to stop her, too. Do you have some strong rope?"

"This is serious," he replied gravely. "What the hell is she doing, selling your home out from under you? Surely Riddle didn't leave her the works! What about you and Curt?"

"She says we're young and can support ourselves," she said, fighting back frustration and fury.

He didn't say anything. His silence was as eloquent as shouting. "She's not evicting you. You go talk to Kemp."

"I work for Mr. Kemp," she reminded him.

He frowned. "Which begs the question, why aren't you at work?"

She sighed. "Mr. Kemp's gone to a bar association conference in Florida," she explained. "He said I could have two vacation days while he's gone, since Mabel and Violet were going to be there in case the attorney covering his practice needed anything." She glowered at him. "I don't get much time off."

"Indeed you don't," he agreed. "Blake Kemp is a busy attorney, for a town the size of Jacobsville. You do a lot of legwork for him, don't you?"

She nodded. "It's part of a paralegal's job. I've learned a lot."

"Enough to tempt you to go to law school?"

She laughed. "No. Not that much. A history degree is

enough, not to mention the paralegal training. I've had all the education I want." She frowned thoughtfully. "You know, I did think about teaching adult education classes at night…."

"Your father was well-to-do," he pointed out. "He had coin collections worth half a million, didn't he?"

"We thought so, but we couldn't find them. I suppose he sold them to buy that Mercedes Janet is driving," she said somberly.

"He loved you and Curt."

She had to fight tears. "He wrote a new will just after he married her, leaving everything to her," she said simply. "She said she had it all in his safe-deposit box, along with the passbook to his big savings account, which her name was on as well as his. The way it was set up, that account belonged to her, so there was no legal problem with it," she had to admit. "Daddy didn't leave us a penny."

"There's something fishy going on here," he said, thinking out loud.

"It sounds like it, I guess. But Daddy gave everything to her. That was his decision to make, not ours. He was crazy about her."

Jordan looked murderous. "Has the will gone through probate yet?"

She shook her head. "She said she's given it to an attorney. It's pending."

"You know the law, even better than I do. This isn't right. You should get a lawyer," he repeated. "Get Kemp, in fact, and have him investigate her. There's something not right about this, Libby. Your father was the healthiest man I ever knew. He never had any symptoms of heart trouble."

"Well, I thought that, too, and so did Curt." She sighed, glancing down at the elegant blue-and-rose carpet, and her eyes grew misty. "He was really crazy about her, though. Maybe he just didn't think we'd need much. I know he loved us…." She choked back a sob. It was still fresh, the grief.

Jordan sighed and pulled her close against his tall, powerful body. His arms were warm and comforting as they enfolded her. "Why don't you just cry, Libby?" he asked gently. "It does help."

She sniffed into his shoulder. It smelled nice. His shirt had a pleasant detergent smell to it. "Do you ever cry?"

"Bite your tongue, woman," he said at her temple. "What would happen to the ranch if I sat down and bawled every time something went wrong? Tears won't come out of Persian carpet, you just ask my aunt!"

She laughed softly, even through the tears. He was a comforting sort of man and it was surprising, because he had a quick temper and an arrogance that put most people's backs up at first meeting.

"So that's why you yell at your cowboys? So you won't cry?"

"Works for me," he chuckled. He patted her shoulder. "Feel better?"

She nodded, smiling through tears. She wiped them away with a paper towel she'd tucked into her jeans. "Thanks."

"What are prospective lovers for?" he asked, smiling wickedly, and laughing out loud when she flushed.

"You stop corrupting me, you bad influence!"

"I said nothing corrupting, I just gave advance notice of bad intentions." He laughed at her expression. "At least it stopped the cascading waterfalls," he added, tongue in cheek, as he glanced at the tear tracks down her cheeks.

"Those weren't tears," she mumbled. "It was dew." She held up a hand. "I feel it falling again!"

"Talk to Kemp," he reiterated, not adding that he was going to do the same. "If she's got a new will and a codicil, signed, make her prove it. Don't let her shove you off your own land without a fight."

"I guess I could ask to see it," she agreed. Then she winced. "I hate arguments. I hate fights."

"I'll remember that the next time you come chasing after me," he promised.

She shook her head impotently, turning to go.

"Hey."

She glanced at him over her shoulder.

"Let me know what you find out," he said. "I'm in this, too. I can't manage a subdivision right near my barn. I can't have a lot of commotion around those beautiful Santa Gerts, it stresses them out too much. It would cost a fortune to tear down that barn and stick it closer to the house. A lawsuit would be cheaper."

"There's an idea," she said brightly. "Take her to court."

"For what, trying to sell property? That's rich."

"Just trying to help us both out," she said.

He glanced at his watch again. "Five minutes left and even I'm not that good," he added. "Pity. If you hadn't kept running your mouth, by now we could have…"

"You hush, Jordan Powell!" she shot at him. "Honestly, of all the blatant, arrogant, sex-crazed ranchers in Texas…!"

She was still mumbling as she went out the door. But when she was out of sight, she grinned. He was a tonic.

* * *

That night, Janet didn't say a word about any real estate deals. She ate a light supper that Libby had prepared, as usual without any compliments about it.

"When are you going back to work?" she asked Libby irritably, her dyed blond hair in an expensive hairdo, her trendy silk shell and embroidered jeans marking her new wealth. "It can't be good for you to lie around here all day."

Curt, who was almost the mirror image of his sister, except for his height and powerful frame, glared at the woman. "Excuse me, since when did you do any housework or cooking around here? Libby's done both since she turned thirteen!"

"Don't you speak to me that way," Janet said haughtily. "I can throw you out anytime I like. I own everything!"

"You don't own the property until that will goes through probate," Libby replied sweetly, shocked at her own boldness. She'd never talked that way to the woman before. "You can produce it, I hope, because you're going to have to. You don't get the property yet. Maybe not even later, if everything isn't in perfect order."

"You've been talking to that rancher again, haven't you?" Janet demanded. "That damned Powell man!

He's so suspicious about everything! Your father had a heart attack. He's dead. He left everything to me. What else do you want?" she raged, standing.

Libby stood, too, her face flushed. "Proof. I want proof. And you'd better have it before you start making any deals with developers about selling Daddy's land!"

Janet started. "De…developers?"

"I heard you this afternoon with that real estate agent," Libby said, with an apologetic glance at her brother, who looked shocked. She hadn't told him. "You're trying to sell our ranch and Daddy hasn't even been dead a month!"

Curt stood up. He looked even more formidable than Libby. "Before you make any attempt to sell this land, you're going to need a lawyer, Janet," he said in that slow, cold drawl that made cowhands move faster.

"How are you going to afford one, Curt, dear?" she asked sarcastically. "You just work for wages."

"Oh, Jordan will loan us the money," Libby said confidently.

Janet's haughty expression fluttered. She threw down her napkin. "You need cooking lessons," she said spitefully. "This food is terrible! I've got to make some phone calls."

She stormed out of the room.

Libby and Curt sat back down, both angry. Libby explained about the real estate agent's visit and what she'd overheard. Curt had only just come in when Libby had put the spaghetti and garlic bread on the table. It was Curt's favorite food and his sister made it very well, he thought, despite Janet's snippy comment.

"She's not selling this place while there's a breath left in my body," he told his sister. "Anyway, she can't do that until the will is probated. And she'd better have a legitimate will."

"Jordan said we needed to get Mr. Kemp to take a look at it," she said. "And I think we're going to need a handwriting expert to take a look, too."

He nodded.

"But what are we going to do about money to file suit?" she asked. "I was bluffing about Jordan loaning us the money. I don't know if he would."

"He's not going to want a subdivision on his doorstep, I'll tell you that," Curt said. "I'll talk to him."

"I already did," she said, surprising him. "He thinks there's something fishy going on, too."

"You can't get much past Jordan," he agreed. "I've been working myself to death trying not to think about losing Dad. I should have paid more attention to what was going on here."

"I've been grieving, too." She sighed and folded her

small hands on the tablecloth. "Isn't it amazing how snippy she is, now that Daddy's not here? She was all over us like poison ivy before he died."

"She married him for what he had, Libby," he said bitterly.

"She seemed to love him…."

"She came on to me the night they came back from that Cancún honeymoon," he said bitterly.

Libby whistled. Her brother was a very attractive man. Their father, a sweet and charming man, had been overweight and balding. She could understand why Janet might have preferred Curt to his father.

"I slapped her down hard and Dad never knew." He shook his head. "How could he marry something like that?"

"He was flattered by all the attention she gave him, I guess," Libby said miserably. "And now here we are. I'll bet she sweet-talked him into changing that will. He would have done anything for her, you know that— he was crazy in love with her. He might have actually written us out of it, Curt. We have to accept that."

"Not until they can prove to me that it wasn't forged," he said stubbornly. "I'm not giving up our inheritance without a fight. Neither are you," he asserted.

She sighed. "Okay, big brother. What do you want to do?"

"When do you go back to work?"

"Monday. Mr. Kemp's out of town."

"Okay. Monday, you make an appointment for both of us to sit down with him and hash this out."

She felt better already. "Okay," she said brightly. "I'll do that very thing. Maybe we do have a chance of keeping Daddy's ranch."

He nodded. "There's always hope." He leaned back in his chair. "So you went to see Jordan." He smiled indulgently. "I can remember a time not so long ago when you ran and hid from him."

"He always seemed to be yelling at somebody," she recalled. "I was intimidated by him. Especially when I graduated from high school. I had a sort of crush on him. I was scared to death he'd notice. Not that he was ever around here that much," she added, laughing. "He and Daddy had a fight a week over water rights."

"Dad usually lost, too," Curt recalled. He studied his sister with affection. "You know, I thought maybe Jordan was sweet on you himself—he's only eight years older than you."

"He's never been sweet on me!" she flashed at him, blushing furiously. "He's hardly even smiled at me, in all the years we've lived here, until the past few months! If anything, he usually treats me like a contagious virus!"

Curt only smiled. He looked very much like her, with the same dark wavy hair and the same green eyes. "He picks at you. Teases you. Makes you laugh. You do the same thing to him. People besides me have noticed. He bristles if anyone says anything unkind about you."

Her eyes widened. "Who's been saying unkind things about me?" she asked.

"That assistant store manager over at Lord's Department Store."

"Oh. Sherry King." She leaned back in her chair. "She can't help it, you know. She was crazy about Duke Wright and he wanted to take me to the Cattleman's Ball. I wouldn't go and he didn't ask anybody else. I feel sorry for her."

"Duke's not your sort of man," he replied. "He's a mixer. Nobody in Jacobsville has been in more brawls," he said, pausing. "Well, maybe Leo Hart has."

"Leo Hart got married, he won't be brawling out at Shea's Roadhouse and Bar anymore."

"Duke's not likely to get married again. His wife took their five-year-old son to New York City, where her new job is. He says she doesn't even look after the little boy. She's too busy trying to get a promotion. The child stays with her sister while she jets all over the world closing real estate deals."

"It's a new world," Libby pointed out. "Women are competing with men for the choice jobs now. They have to move around to get a promotion."

Curt's eyes narrowed. "Maybe they should get promotion before they get pregnant," he said impatiently.

She shrugged. "Accidents happen."

"No child of mine is ever going to be an accident," Curt said firmly.

"Nice to be so superior," she teased, eyes twinkling. "Never to make mistakes…"

He swiped at her with a napkin. "You don't even stick your toes in the water, so don't lecture me about drowning."

She chuckled. "I'm sensible, I am," she retorted. "None of this angst for me. I'll just do my routine job and keep my nose out of emotional entanglements."

He studied her curiously. "You go through life avoiding any sort of risk, don't you, honey?" he mused.

She moved one shoulder restlessly. "Daddy and Mama fought all the time, remember?" she said. "I swore I'd never get myself into a fix like that. She told me that she and Daddy were so happy when they first met, when they first married. Then, six months later, she was pregnant with you and they couldn't manage one pleasant meal together without shouting." She shook her head. "That means you can't trust emotions.

It's better to use your brain when you think about marrying somebody. Love is…sticky," she concluded. "And it causes insanity, I'm sure of it."

"Why don't you ask Kemp if that's why he's stayed single so long? He's in his middle thirties, isn't he, and never even been engaged."

"Who'd put up with him?" she asked honestly. "Now there's a mixer for you," she said enthusiastically. "He actually threw another lawyer out the front door and onto the sidewalk last month. Good thing there was a welcome mat there, it sort of broke the guy's fall."

"What did he want?" Curt asked.

She shook her head. "I have no idea. But I don't expect him to be a repeat client."

Curt chuckled. "I see what you mean."

Libby went to bed early that night, without another word to Janet. She knew that anything she said would be too much. But she did miss her father and she couldn't believe that he wouldn't have mentioned Libby and Curt in his will. He did love them. She knew he did.

She thought about Jordan Powell, too, and about Curt's remark that he thought Jordan was sweet on her. She tingled all over at the thought. But that wasn't going to happen, she assured herself. Jordan was gorgeous and he could have his pick of pretty women. Libby Collins would be his last resort. The world wasn't ending yet, so she was out of the running.

She rolled over, closed her eyes, and went to sleep.

Chapter Two

Janet wasn't at breakfast the next morning. Her new gold Mercedes was gone and she hadn't left a note. Libby saw it as a bad omen.

The weekend passed with nothing remarkable except for Janet's continued absence. The truck was ready Saturday and Curt picked it up in town, catching a lift with one of Jordan's cowboys. It wasn't as luxurious as a Mercedes, but it had a good engine and it was handy for hauling things like salt blocks and bales of hay. Libby tried to picture hauling hay in Janet's Mercedes and almost went hysterical with laughter.

Libby went back to work at Blake Kemp's office early Monday morning, dropped off by Curt on his way to the feed store for Jordan. She felt as if she hadn't really had a vacation at all.

Violet Hardy, Mr. Kemp's secretary, who was dark-haired, blue-eyed, pretty and somewhat overweight, smiled at her as she came in the door. "Hi! Did you have a nice vacation?"

"I spent it working," Libby confessed. "How did things go here?"

Violet groaned. "Don't even ask."

"That bad, huh?" Libby remarked.

Mabel, the blonde grandmother who worked at reception, turned in her chair after transferring a call into Mr. Kemp's office. "Bad isn't the word, Libby," she said in a whisper, glancing down the hall to make sure the doors were all closed. "That lawyer Mr. Kemp got to fill in for him got two cases confused and sent the clients to the wrong courtrooms in different counties."

"Yes—" Violet nodded "—and one of them came in here and tried to punch Mr. Kemp."

Libby pursed her lips. "No. Did he have insurance?"

All three women chuckled.

"For an attorney who handles so many assault cases," Violet whispered, "he doesn't practice what he preaches. Mr. Kemp punched the guy back and they wound up out on the street. Our police chief, Cash Grier, broke it up and almost arrested Mr. Kemp."

"What about the other guy? Didn't he start it?" Libby exclaimed.

"The other guy was Duke Wright," Violet confessed, watching Libby color. "And Chief Grier said that instead of blaming Mr. Kemp for handling Mrs. Wright's divorce, he should thank him for not bankrupting Mr. Wright in the process!"

"Then what?" Libby asked.

All three women glanced quickly down the hall.

"Mr. Wright threw a punch at Chief Grier."

"Well, that was smart thinking. Duke's in the hospital, then?" Libby asked facetiously.

"Nope," Violet said, her blue eyes twinkling. "But he was in jail briefly until he made bail." She shook her head. "I don't expect he'll try that twice."

"Crime has fallen about fifty percent since we got Cash Grier as chief," Violet sighed, smiling.

"And Judd Dunn as assistant chief," Libby reminded her.

"Poor Mr. Wright," Mabel said. "He does have the worst luck. Remember that Jack Clark who worked for him, who was convicted of murdering that woman in Victoria? Mr. Wright sure hated the publicity. It came just when he was trying to get custody of his son."

"Mr. Wright would have a lot less trouble if he didn't spend so much time out looking for it," came a deep, gruff voice from behind them.

They all jumped. Blake Kemp was standing just at the entrance to the hallway with a brief in one hand and a coffee cup in the other. He was as much a dish as Jordan Powell. He had wavy dark hair and blue eyes and the most placid, friendly face—until he got in front of a jury. Nobody wanted to be across the courtroom from Kemp when a trial began. There was some yellow and purple discoloration on one high cheekbone, where a fist had apparently landed a blow. Duke Wright, Libby theorized silently.

"Libby, before you do anything else, would you make a pot of coffee, please?" he asked in a long-suffering tone. He impaled a wincing Violet with his pale blue eyes. "I don't give a damn what some study says is best for me, I want caffeine. C-A-F-F-E-I-N-E," he added, spelling it letter by letter for Violet's benefit.

Violet lifted her chin and her own blue eyes glared right back at him. "Mr. Kemp, if you drank less of it, you might not be so bad-tempered. I mean, really, that's the second person you've thrown out of our office in a month! Chief Grier said that was a new city record…."

Kemp's eyes were blazing now, narrow and intent.

"Miss Hardy, do you want to still be employed here tomorrow?"

Violet looked as if she was giving that question a lot of deliberation. "But, sir…" she began.

"I like caffeine. I'm not giving it up," Kemp said curtly. "You don't change my routine in this office. Is that clear?"

"But, Mr. Kemp—!" she argued.

"I don't remember suggesting anything so personal to you, Miss Hardy," he shot back, clearly angry. "I could, however," he added, and his cold blue eyes made insinuations about her figure, which was at least two dress sizes beyond what it should have been.

All three women gasped at the outrageous insinuation and then glared at their boss.

Violet flushed and stood up, as angry as he was, but not intimidated one bit by the stare. "My…my father always said that a woman should look like a woman and not a skeleton encased in skin. I may be a little overweight, Mr. Kemp, but at least I'm doing something about it!"

He glanced pointedly at a cake in a box on her desk.

She colored. "I live out near the Hart Ranch. I promised Tess Hart I'd pick that up at the bakery for her before I came to work and drop it by her house when

I go home for lunch. It's for a charity tea party this afternoon." She was fuming. "I do not eat cake! Not anymore."

He stared at her until she went red and sat back down. She averted her eyes and went back to work. Her hands on the computer keyboard were trembling.

"You fire me if you want to, Mr. Kemp, but nothing I said to you was as mean as what you were insinuating to me with that look," Violet choked. "I know I weigh too much. You don't have to rub it in. I was only trying to help you."

Mabel and Libby were still glaring at him. He shifted uncomfortably and put the brief down on Violet's desk with a slap. "There are six spelling errors in that. You'll have to redo it. You can buzz me when the coffee's ready," he added shortly. He turned on his heel and took his coffee cup back into his office. As an afterthought, he slammed the door.

"Oh, and like anybody short of a druggist could read those chicken scratches on paper that you call handwriting!" Violet muttered, staring daggers after him.

Libby let out the breath she'd been holding and gaped at sweet, biddable Violet, who'd never talked back to Mr. Kemp in the eight months she'd worked for him. So did Mabel.

"Well, it's about time!" Mabel said, laughing delightedly. "Good for you, Violet. It's no good, letting a man walk all over you, no matter how crazy you are about him!"

"Hush!" Violet exclaimed, glancing quickly down the hall. "He'll hear you!"

"He doesn't know," Libby said comfortingly, putting an arm around Violet. "And we'll never tell. I'm proud of you, Violet."

"Me, too," Mabel grinned.

Violet sighed. "I guess he'll fire me. It might not be a bad thing. I spend too much time trying to take care of him and he hates it." Her blue eyes were wistful under their long, thick lashes. "You know, I've lost fifteen pounds," she murmured. "And I'm down a dress size."

"A new diet?" Libby asked absently as she checked her "in" tray.

"A new gym, just for women," Violet confessed with a grin. "I love it!"

Libby looked at the other woman with admiration. "You're really serious about this, aren't you?"

Violet's shoulder moved gently. She was wearing a purple dress with a high collar and lots of frills on the bodice and a very straight skirt that clung to her hips. It was the worst sort of dress for a woman who had a big bust and wide hips, but nobody had the heart to tell Violet. "I had to do something. I mean, look at me! I'm so big!"

"You're not that big. But I think it's great that you're trying so hard, Violet," Libby said gently. "And to keep you on track, Mabel and I are giving up dessert when you eat lunch with us."

"I have to go home and see about Mother most every day at lunchtime," Violet confessed. "She hates that. She said I was wasting my whole life worrying about her, when I should be out having fun. But she's already had two light strokes in the past year since Daddy died. I can't leave her alone."

"Honey, people like you are why there's a heaven," Mabel murmured softly. "You're one in a million."

Violet waved her away. "Everybody's got problems," she laughed. "For all we know, Mr. Kemp has much bigger ones than we do. He's such a good person. When Mother had that last stroke, the bad one, he even drove me to the hospital after I got the call."

"He is a good person," Libby agreed. "But so are you."

"You'd better make that coffee, I guess," Violet said wistfully. "I really thought I could make it half and half and he wouldn't be able to taste the difference. He's so uptight lately. He's always in a hurry, always under pressure. He drinks caffeine like water and it's so bad for his heart. I know about hearts. My dad died of a heart attack last year. I was just trying to help."

"It's hard to help a rattlesnake across the road, Violet," Mabel said, tongue in cheek.

Libby was curious about the coincidence of Violet's father dying of a heart attack, like her father, such a short time ago. "Violet could find one nice thing to say about a serial killer," Libby agreed affectionately. "Even worse, she could find one nice thing to say about my stepmother."

"Ouch," Mabel groaned. "Now there's a hard case if I ever saw one." She shook her head. "People in Branntville are still talking about her and old man Darby."

Libby, who'd just finished filling the coffeepot, started it brewing and turned jerkily. "Excuse me?"

"Didn't I ever tell you?" Mabel asked absently. "Just a sec. Good morning, Kemp Law Offices," she said. "Yes, sir, I'll connect you." She started to push the intercom button when she saw with shock that it was already depressed. The light was on the switch. She and Libby, who'd also seen it, exchanged agonized glances. Quickly, without telling Violet, she pushed it off and then on again. "Mr. Kemp, it's Mrs. Lawson for you on line two." She waited, hung up, and swung her chair around. She didn't dare tell poor Violet that

Mr. Kemp had probably heard every single word she'd said about him.

"Your stepmother, Janet," Mabel told Libby, "was working at a nursing home over in Branntville. She sweet-talked an old man who was a patient there into leaving everything he had to her." She shook her head. "They said that Janet didn't even give him a proper funeral. She had him cremated and put in an urn and there was a graveside service. They said she bought a designer suit to wear to it."

Libby was getting cold chills. There were too many similarities there to be a coincidence. Janet had wanted to have Riddle Collins cremated, too, but Curt and Libby had talked to the funeral director and threatened a lawsuit if he complied with Janet's request. They went home and told Janet the same thing and also insisted on a church funeral at the Presbyterian church where Riddle had been a member since childhood. Janet had been furious, but in the end, she reluctantly agreed.

Violet wasn't saying anything, but she had a funny look on her face and she seemed pale. She turned away before the others saw. But Libby's expression was thought-provoking.

"You're thinking something. What?" Mabel asked Libby.

Fortunately, the phone rang again while Libby was deciding if it was wise to share her thoughts.

Violet got up from her desk and went close to Libby. "She wanted to cremate your father, too, didn't she?"

Libby nodded.

"You should go talk to Mr. Kemp."

Libby smiled. "You know, Violet, I think you're right." She hugged the other girl and went back to Mabel. "When he gets off the phone, I need to talk to him."

Mabel grinned. "Now you're talking." She checked the board. "He's free. Just a sec." She pushed a button. "Mr. Kemp, Libby needs to speak to you, if it's convenient."

"Send her in, Mrs. Jones."

"Good luck," Mabel said, crossing her fingers.

Libby grinned back.

"Come in," Kemp said, opening the door for Libby and closing it behind her. "Have a seat. I don't need ESP to know what's on your mind. I had a call from Jordan Powell at home last night."

Her eyebrows arched. "Well, he jumped the gun!"

"He's concerned. Probably with good reason," he added. "I went ahead on my own and had a private detective I know run a check on Janet's background. This isn't the first time she's become a widow."

"I know," Libby said. "Mabel says an elderly man in a nursing home left her everything he had. She had him sent off to be cremated immediately after they got him to the funeral home."

He nodded. "And I understand from Don Hedgely at our funeral home here that she tried to have the same thing done with your father, but you and your brother threatened a lawsuit."

"We did," Libby said. "Daddy didn't believe in cremation. He would have been horrified."

Kemp leaned back in his desk chair and crossed his long legs, with his hands behind his head. He pursed his lips and narrowed his blue eyes, deep in thought. "There's another thing," he said. "Janet was fired from that nursing home for being too friendly with their wealthiest patients. One of whom—the one you know about—was an elderly widower with no children. He died of suspicious causes and left her his estate."

Libby folded her arms. She felt chilled all over now. "Wasn't it enough for her?" she wondered out loud.

"Actually, it took the entire estate to settle his gambling debts," he murmured. "Apparently, he liked the horses a little too much."

"Then there was our father." She anticipated his next thought.

He shook his head. "That was after Mr. Hardy in San Antonio."

Libby actually gasped. It couldn't be!

Kemp leaned forward quickly. "Do you think Violet is happy having to live in a rented firetrap with her invalid mother? Her parents were wealthy. But a waitress at Mr. Hardy's favorite restaurant apparently began a hot affair with him and talked him into making her a loan of a quarter of a million dollars to save her parents from bankruptcy and her father from suicide. He gave her a check and had a heart attack before he could stop payment on it—which he planned to do. He told his wife and begged forgiveness of her and his daughter before he died." His eyes narrowed. "He died shortly after he was seen with a pretty blonde at a San Antonio motel downtown."

"You think it was Janet? That it wasn't a heart attack at all—that she killed him?"

"I think there are too many coincidences for comfort in her past," Kemp said flatly. "But the one eyewitness who saw her with Hardy at that motel was unable to pick her out of a lineup. She'd had her hair color changed just the day before the lineup. She remained a brunette for about a week and then changed back to blond."

Libby's face tightened. "She might have killed my father," she bit off.

"That is a possibility," Kemp agreed. "It's early days yet, Libby. I can't promise you anything. But if she's guilty and I can get her on a witness stand, in a court of law, I can break her," he said with frightening confidence. "She'll tell me everything she knows."

She swallowed. "I don't want her to get away with it," she began. "But Curt and I work for wages…"

He flapped his hand in her direction. "Every lawyer takes a pro bono case occasionally. I haven't done it in months. You and Curt can be my public service for the year," he added, and he actually smiled. It made him look younger, much less dangerous than he really was.

"I don't know what to say," she said, shaking her head in disbelief.

He leaned forward. "Say you'll be careful," he replied. "I can't find any suspicion that she ever helped a young person have a heart attack, but I don't doubt for a minute that she knows how. I'm working with Micah Steele on that aspect of it. There isn't much he doesn't know about the darker side of medicine, even if he is a doctor. And what he doesn't know about black ops and untimely death, Cash Grier does."

"I thought Daddy died of a heart condition nobody knew he had." She took a deep breath. "When I tell Curt, he'll go crazy."

"Let me tell him," Kemp said quietly. "It will be easier."

"Okay."

"Meanwhile, you have to go back home and pretend that nothing's wrong, that your stepmother is innocent of any foul play. That's imperative. If you give her a reason to think she's being suspected of anything, she'll bolt, and we may never find her."

"We'd get our place back without a fight," Libby commented wistfully.

"And a woman who may have murdered your father, among others, would go free," Kemp replied. "Is that really what you want?"

Libby shook her head. "Of course not. I'll do whatever you say."

"We'll be working in the background. The most important thing is to keep the pressure on, a little at a time, so that she doesn't get suspicious. Tell her you've spoken to an attorney about the will, but nothing more."

"Okay," she agreed.

He got up. "And don't tell Violet I said anything to you about her father," he added. His broad shoulders moved restlessly under his expensive beige suit, as if he were carrying some difficult burden. "She's... sensitive."

What a surprising comment from such an insensitive man, she thought, but she didn't dare say it. She only smiled. "Certainly."

She was reaching for the doorknob when he called her back. "Yes, sir?"

"When you make another pot of coffee," he said hesitantly, "I guess we could use some of that half and half."

Her dropped jaw told its own story.

"She means well," he said abruptly, and turned back to his desk. "But for now, I want it strong and black and straight up. Call me when it's made and I'll bring my cup."

"It should be ready right now," she faltered. Even in modern times, few bosses went to get their own coffee. But Mr. Kemp was something of a puzzle. Perhaps, Libby thought wickedly as she followed him down the hall, even to himself.

He glanced at Violet strangely, but he didn't make any more comments. Violet sat with her eyes glued to her computer screen until he poured his coffee and went back to his office.

Libby wanted so badly to say something to her, but she didn't know what. In the end, she just smiled and made a list of the legal precedents she would have to look up for Mr. Kemp at the law library in the county courthouse. Thank God, she thought, for computers.

She was on her way home in the pickup truck after a long day when she saw Jordan on horseback, watching several men drive the pregnant heifers into pastures close to the barn. He had a lot of money invested in those purebred calves and he wasn't risking them to predators or difficult births. He looked so good on horseback, she thought dreamily. He was arrow-straight and his head, covered by that wide-brimmed creamy Stetson he favored, was tilted in a way that was particularly his. She could have picked him out of any crowd at a distance just by the way he carried himself.

He turned his head when he heard the truck coming down the long dirt road and he motioned Libby over to the side.

She parked the truck, cut off the engine, and stood on the running board to talk to him over the top of the old vehicle. "I wish I had a camera," she called. "Mama Powell, protecting his babies…"

"You watch it!" he retorted, shaking a finger at her.

She laughed. "What are you going to do, jump the fence and run me down?"

"Poor old George here couldn't jump a fence. He's twenty-four," he added, patting the old horse's withers. "He hates his corral. I thought I'd give him a change of scenery, since I wasn't going far."

"Everything gets old, I guess. Most everything, anyway," she added with a faraway, wistful look in her eyes. She had an elderly horse of her own, that she might yet have to give away because it was hard to feed and keep him on her salary.

He dismounted and left George's reins on the ground to jump the fence and talk to her. "Did you see Kemp?" he asked.

"Yes. He said you phoned him."

"I asked a few questions and got some uncomfortable answers," he said, coming around the truck to stand beside her. His big lean hands went to her waist and he lifted her down close to him. Too close. She could smell his shaving lotion and feel the heat off his body under the Western cut long-sleeved shirt. In her simple, jacketed suit, she felt overly dressed.

"You don't look too bad when you fix up," he commented, approving her light makeup and the gray suit that made her eyes look greener than they were.

"You don't look too bad when you don't," she replied. "What uncomfortable answers are you getting?"

His eyes were solemn. "I think you can guess. I don't like the idea of you and Curt alone in that house with her."

"We have a shotgun somewhere. I'll make a point of buying some shells for it."

He shook her by the waist gently. "I'm not teasing. Can you lock your bedroom door? Can Curt?"

"It's an old house, Jordan," she faltered. "None of the bedroom doors have locks."

"Tell Curt I said to get bolts and put them on. Do it when she's not home. In the meantime, put a chair under the doorknob."

"But why?" she asked uncertainly.

He drew a long breath. His eyes went to her soft bow of a mouth and he studied it for several seconds before he spoke. "There's one very simple way to cause a heart attack. You can do it with a hypodermic syringe filled with nothing but air."

She couldn't speak for a moment. "Could they...tell that if they did an autopsy on my father?"

"I'm not a forensic specialist, despite the fact that

there are half a dozen shows on TV that can teach you how to think you are. I'll ask somebody who knows," he added.

She hated the thought of disinterring her father. But it would be terrible if he'd met with foul play and it never came out.

He tilted her face up to his narrow dark eyes. "You're worrying. Don't. I'm as close as your phone, night or day."

She smiled gently. "Thanks, Jordan."

His thumbs moved on her waist while he looked down at her. His face hardened. His eyes were suddenly on her soft mouth, with real hunger.

The world stopped. It seemed like that. She met his searching gaze and couldn't breathe. Her body felt achy. Hungry. Feverish. She swallowed, hoping it didn't show.

"If you play your cards right, I might let you kiss me," he murmured.

Her heart skipped. "Excuse me?"

One big shoulder lifted and fell. "Where else are you going to get any practical experience?" he asked. "Duke Wright is a candidate for the local nursing home, after all…"

"He's thirty-six!" she exclaimed. "That isn't old!"

"I'm thirty-two," he pointed out. "I have all my own

teeth." He grinned to display them. "And I can still outrun at least two of my horses."

"That's an incentive to kiss you?" she asked blankly.

"Think of the advantages if you kiss me during a stampede," he pointed out.

She laughed. He was a case. Her eyes adored him. "I'll keep you in mind," she promised. "But you mustn't get your hopes up. This town is full of lonely bachelors who can't get women to kiss them. You'll have to take a number and wait."

"Wait until what?" he asked, tweaking her waist with his thumbs.

"I don't know. Christmas? I could kiss you as part of your present."

His eyebrows arched. "What's the other part?"

"It's not Christmas. Listen, I have to get home and make supper."

"I'll send Curt on down," he said.

She was seeing a new pattern. "To make sure I'm not left alone with Janet, is that right?"

"For my peace of mind," he corrected. "I've gotten…used to you," he added slowly. "As a neighbor," he added deliberately. "Think how hard it would be to break in another one, at my age."

"You just said you weren't old," she reminded him.

"Maybe I am, just a little," he confessed. He drew her up until she was standing completely against him, so close that she could feel the hard press of his muscular legs against her own. "Come on," he taunted, bending his head with a mischievous little smile. "You know you're dying to kiss me."

"I am?" she whispered dreamily as she studied the long, wide, firm curve of his lips.

"Desperately."

She felt his nose brushing against hers. Somewhere, a horse was neighing. A jet flew over. The wind ruffled leaves in a small tree nearby. She was deaf to any sound other than the throb of her own heartbeat. There was nothing in the world except Jordan's mouth, a scant inch from her own. He'd never kissed her. She wanted him to. She ached for him to.

His hands tightened on her waist, lifting her closer. "Come on, chicken. Give it all you've got."

Her hands were flat against his chest, feeling the warm muscles under his cotton shirt. She tasted his breath. Her arms slid up to his shoulders. He had her hypnotized. She wanted nothing more than to drown in him.

"That's it," he whispered.

She closed her eyes and lifted up on her tiptoes as

she felt the slow, soft press of her own lips against his for the first time.

Her knees were weak. She didn't think they were going to support her. And still Jordan didn't move, didn't respond.

Frustrated, she tried to lift up higher, her arms circled his neck and pulled, trying to make his mouth firm and deepen above hers. But she couldn't budge him.

"Oh, you arro…!"

It was the opening he'd been waiting for. His mouth crushed down against her open lips and his arms contracted hungrily. Libby moaned sharply at the rush of sensation it caused in her body. It had never been like this in her life. She was burning alive. She ached. She longed. She couldn't get close enough….

"Hey, Jordan!"

The distant shout broke the spell. Jordan jerked his head around to see one of his men waving a wide-brimmed hat and gesturing toward a pickup truck that was driving right out into the pasture where Jordan was putting those pregnant heifers.

"It's the feed supplement I ordered," he murmured, letting her go slowly. "Damn his timing."

He didn't smile when he said that. She couldn't manage even a word.

He touched her softly swollen mouth with his fingertips. "Maybe you could take me on a date and we could get lost on some deserted country road," he suggested.

She took a breath and shook her head to clear it. "I do not seduce men in parked cars," she pointed out.

He snapped his fingers. "Damn!"

"He's waving at you again," she noted, looking over his shoulder.

"All right, I'll go to work. But I'll send Curt on home." He touched her cheek. "Be careful, okay?"

She managed a weak smile. "Okay."

He turned and vaulted the fence, mounting George with the ease of years of practice as a horseman. "See you."

She nodded and watched him ride away. Her life had just changed course, in the most unexpected way.

Chapter Three

But all Jordan's worry—and Libby's unease—was for nothing. When she got home, Janet's Mercedes was gone. There was a terse little note on the hall table that read, Gone to Houston shopping, back tomorrow.

Even as she was reading it, Curt came in the back door, bareheaded and sweaty.

"She's gone?" he asked.

She nodded. "Left a note. She's gone to Houston and won't be back until tomorrow."

"Great. It'll give me time to put locks on the bedroom doors," he said.

She sighed. "Jordan's been talking to you, hasn't he?" she asked.

"Yes, and he's been kissing you, apparently," he

murmured, grinning. "Old Harry had to yell himself hoarse to get Jordan's attention when they brought those feed supplements out."

She flushed. She couldn't think of a single defense. But she hadn't heard Harry yelling, except one time. No wonder people were talking.

"Interested in you, is he?" Curt asked softly.

"He wanted me to ask him out on a date and get him lost on a dirt road," she said.

"And you said…?"

She moved restively. "I said that I didn't seduce men in parked cars on deserted roads, of course," she assured him.

He looked solemn. "Sis, we've never really talked about Jordan…."

"And we really don't need to, now," she interrupted. "I'm a big girl and I know all about Jordan. He's only teasing. I'm older and he's doing it in a different way, that's all."

Curt wasn't smiling. "He isn't."

She cleared her throat. "Well, it doesn't matter. He's not a marrying man and I'm not a frivolous woman. Besides, his tastes run to beauty queens and state senators' daughters."

He hesitated.

She smiled before he could say anything else. "Let

it drop. We've got enough on our minds now without adding more to them. Let's rush to the hardware store and buy locks before she gets back."

He shrugged and let it go. There would be another time to discuss Jordan Powell.

When Libby got home from work Tuesday evening she was still reeling from the shocking news that a fed-up Violet had quit her job and gone to work for Duke Wright. Blake Kemp had not taken the news well. Her mood lifted when she found Jordan's big burgundy double-cabbed pickup truck sitting in her front yard. He was sitting on the side of the truck bed, whittling a piece of wood with a pocket knife, his broad-brimmed hat pushed way back on his head. He looked up at her approach and jumped down to meet her.

"You're late," he complained.

She got out of her car, grabbing her purse on the way. "I had to stay late and type up some notes for Mr. Kemp."

He scowled. "That's Violet's job."

"Violet's leaving," she said on a sigh. "She's going to work for Duke Wright."

"But she's crazy for Kemp, isn't she?" Jordan wondered.

She scowled at him. "You aren't supposed to know that," she pointed out.

"Everybody knows that." He looked around the yard. "Janet hasn't shown up. Curt said she'd gone to Houston."

"That's what the note said," she agreed, walking beside him to the front porch. "Curt put the locks on last night."

"I know. I asked him."

She unlocked the door and pushed it open. "Want some coffee?"

"I'd love some. Eggs? Bacon? Cinnamon toast?" he added.

"Oh, I see," she mused with a grin. "Amie's gone and you're starving, huh?"

He shrugged nonchalantly. "She didn't have to leave. I only yelled a little."

"You shouldn't scare her. She's old."

"Dirt's old. Amie's a spring chicken." He chuckled. "Anyway, she was shopping for antique furniture on the Internet and she found a side table she couldn't live without in San Antonio. She drove up to look at it. She said she'd see me in a couple of days."

"And you're starving."

"You make the nicest scrambled eggs, Libby," he

coaxed. "Nice crisp bacon. Delicious cinnamon toast. Strong coffee."

"It isn't the time of day for breakfast."

"No law that you can't have breakfast for supper," he pointed out.

She sighed. "I was planning a beef casserole."

"It won't go with scrambled eggs."

She put her hands on her hips and gave him a considering look. "You really are a pain, Jordan."

He moved a step closer and caught her by the waist with two big lean hands. "If you want me to marry you, you have to prove that you're a good cook."

"Marry...?"

Before she could get another word out, his mouth crushed down over her parted lips. He kissed her slowly, tenderly, his big hands steely at her waist, as if he were keeping them there by sheer will when he wanted to pull her body much closer to his own.

Her hands rested on his clean shirt while she tried to decide if he was kidding. He had to be. Certainly he didn't want to marry anybody. He'd said so often enough.

He lifted his head scant inches. "Stop doing that."

She blinked. "Doing what?"

"Thinking. You can't kiss a man and do analytical formulae in your head at the same time."

"You said you'd never marry anybody…."

His eyes were oddly solemn. "Maybe I changed my mind."

Before she could answer him, he bent his head and kissed her again. This time it wasn't a soft, teasing sample of a kiss. It was bold, brash, invasive and possessive. He enveloped her in his hard arms and crushed her down the length of his powerful body. She felt a husky groan go into her mouth as he grew more insistent.

Against her hips, she felt the sudden hardness of his body. As if he realized that and didn't like having her feel it, he moved away a breath. Slowly, he lifted his hard mouth from her swollen lips and looked down at her quietly, curiously.

"This is getting to be a habit," she said breathlessly. Her body was throbbing, like her heart. She wondered if he could hear it.

His dark eyes fell to the soft, quick pulsing of her heart, visible where her loose blouse bounced in time with it. Beneath it, two hard little peaks were blatant. He saw them and his eyes began to glitter.

"Don't look at me like that," she whispered gruffly.

His eyes shot up to catch hers. "You want me," he said curtly. "I can see it. Feel it."

Her breath was audible. "You conceited…!"

His hands caught her hips and pushed them against his own. "It's mutual."

"I noticed!" she burst out, jerking away from him, red-faced.

"Don't be such a child," he chided, but gently. "You're old enough to know what desire feels like."

Her face grew redder. "I will not be seduced by you in my own kitchen over scrambled eggs!"

His eyebrows arched. "You're making them, then?" he asked brightly.

"Oh!" She pushed away from him. "You just won't take no for an answer!"

He smiled speculatively. "You can put butter on that," he agreed. His eyes went up and down her slender figure while she walked through to the kitchen, leaving her purse on the hall table as she went. "Not going to change before you start cooking?" he drawled, following her in. "I don't mind helping."

She shot him a dark glare.

He held up both hands. "Just offering to be helpful, that's all."

She laughed helplessly. "I can dress myself, thanks."

"I was offering to help you undress," he pointed out.

She had to fight down another blush. She was a

modern, independent woman. It was just that the thought of Jordan's dark eyes on her naked body had an odd, pleasurable effect on her. Especially after that bone-shaking kiss.

"You shouldn't go around kissing women like that unless you mean business," she pointed out as she got out a big iron skillet to cook the bacon in.

"What makes you think I didn't mean it?" he probed, straddling a kitchen chair to watch her work.

"You? Mr. I'll-Never-Marry?"

"I didn't say that. I said I didn't want to get married."

"Well, what's the difference?" she asked, exasperated.

His dark eyes slid down to her breasts with a boldness that made her uncomfortable. "There's always the one woman you can't walk away from."

"There's no such woman in your life."

"Think so?" He frowned. "What are you doing with that?" he asked as she put the skillet on the burner.

"You're the one who wanted bacon!" she exclaimed.

"Bacon, yes, not liquid fat!" He got up from the chair, pulled a couple of paper towels from the roll and pulled a plate from the cabinet. "Don't you know how to cook bacon?"

He proceeded to show her, layering several strips of bacon on a paper-towel coated plate and putting another paper towel on top of it.

She was watching with growing amusement. "And it's going to cook like that," she agreed. "Uh-huh."

"It goes in the microwave," he said with exaggerated patience. "You cook it for…"

"What's wrong?"

He was looking around, frowning, with the plate in one big hand. He opened cupboards and checked in the china cabinet. "All right, I'll bite. Where is it?"

"Where is what?"

"Your microwave oven!"

She sighed. "Jordan, we don't have a microwave oven."

"You're kidding." He scowled at her. "Everybody's got a microwave oven!"

"We haven't got one."

He studied her kitchen and slowly he put the plate back on the counter with a frown. The stove was at least ten years old. It was one of the old-fashioned ones that still had knobs instead of buttons. She didn't even have a dishwasher. Everything in the kitchen was old, like the cast-iron skillet she used for most every meal.

"I didn't realize how hard things were for you and

Curt," he said after a minute. "I thought your father had all kinds of money."

"He did, until he married Janet," she replied. "She wanted to eat out all the time. The stove was worn-out and so was the dishwasher. He was going to replace them, but she had him buy her a diamond ring she wanted, instead."

He scowled angrily. "I'm sorry. I'm really sorry."

His apology was unexpected and very touching. "It's all right," she said gently. "I'm used to doing things the hard way. Really I am."

He moved close, framing her oval face in his big warm hands. "You never complain."

She smiled. "Why should I? I'm healthy and strong and able to do anything that needs doing around here."

"You make me ashamed, Libby," he said softly. He bent and kissed her with aching tenderness.

"Why?" she whispered at his firm mouth.

"I'm not really sure. Do that again."

He nibbled her upper lip, coaxing her body to lean heavily against his. "This is even better than dessert," he murmured as he deepened the pressure of his mouth. "Come here!"

He lifted her against him and kissed her hungrily, until her mouth felt faintly bruised from the slow, insistent pressure. It was like flying. She loved kissing Jordan. She hoped he was never going to stop!

But all at once, he did, with a jerky breath. "This won't do," he murmured a little huskily. "Curt will be home any minute. I don't want him to find us on the kitchen table."

Her mouth flew open. "Jordan!"

He shrugged and looked sheepish. "It was heading that way. Here." He handed her the plate of bacon. "I guess you'd better fry it. I don't think it's going to cook by itself."

She smiled up at him. "I'll drain it on paper towels and get rid of some of the grease after it's cooked."

"Why are you throwing those away?" he asked when she put the bacon on to fry and threw away the paper towels it had laid on.

"Bacteria," she told him. "You never put meat back on a plate where it's been lying, raw."

"They teach you that in school these days, I guess?"

She nodded. "And lots of other stuff."

"Like how to use a prophylactic...?" he probed wickedly.

She flushed. "They did not! And I'll wash your mouth out with soap if you say that again!" she threatened.

"Never mind. I'll teach you how to use it, when the time comes," he added outrageously.

"I am not using a prophylactic!"

"You want kids right away, then?" he persisted.

"I am not having sex with you on my kitchen table!"

There was a sudden stunned silence. Jordan was staring over her shoulder and his expression was priceless. Grimacing, she turned to find her older brother standing there with his mouth open.

"Oh, shut your mouth, Curt," she grumbled. "It was a hypothetical discussion!"

"Except for the part about the prophylactic," Jordan said with a howling mad grin. "Did you know that they don't teach people how to use them in school?"

Curt lost it. He almost doubled over laughing.

Libby threw a dish towel at him. "Both of you, out of my kitchen! I'll call you when it's ready. Go on, out!"

They left the room obediently, still laughing.

Libby shook her head and started turning the bacon.

"Hasn't Janet even phoned to say if she was coming back today?" Jordan asked the two siblings when they were seated at the kitchen table having supper.

"There wasn't anything on the answering machine,"

Libby said. "I checked it while the bacon was cooking. Maybe she thinks we're on to something and she's running for it."

"No, I don't think so," Curt replied at once. "She's not about to leave this property to us. Not considering what it would be worth to a developer."

"I agree," Jordan said. "I've given Kemp the phone number of a private detective I know in San Antonio," he added. "He's going to look into the case for me."

"We'll pay you back," Curt promised, and Libby nodded.

"Let's cross our bridges one at a time," Jordan replied. "First order of business is to see if we can find any proof that she's committed a crime in the past."

"Mabel said she was suspected in a death at a nursing home in Branntville," she volunteered.

"So Kemp told me," Jordan said. "This is good bacon," he added.

"Thanks," she said with a smile.

"Violet's father was another one of her victims," Libby added.

Jordan nodded while Curt scowled curiously at both of them. "But they can't prove that. Not unless there's enough evidence to order an exhumation. And, considering the physical condition of Violet's mother," he added, "I'm afraid she'd never be able to agree to it. The shock would probably kill her mother."

Libby sighed. "Poor Violet. She's had such a hard life. And now to have to change jobs…"

"She works for Kemp, doesn't she?" Curt asked.

"She did. She quit today," Libby replied. "She's going to work for Duke Wright."

"Oh, Sherry King's going to love that," Curt chuckled.

"She doesn't own Duke," Libby said. "He doesn't even like her."

"She's very possessive about men she wants."

"More power to her if she can put a net over him and lock him in her closet."

Jordan chuckled. "He's not keen on the thought of a second wife."

"He's still trying to get custody of his son, isn't he?" Curt asked. "Poor guy."

"He won't be the first man who lost a woman to a career," Jordan reminded him. "Although it's usually the other way around." He glanced at Libby. "Just for the record, I think you're more important than a new bull, no matter what his ancestry is."

"Gee, thanks," she replied, tongue in cheek.

"It never hurts to clear up these little details before they become issues," he said wryly. "On the other hand, it would be nice if you'd tell me if you have plans to go to law school and move to a big city to practice law?"

"Not me, thanks," she replied. "I'm very happy where I am."

"You don't know any other life except this one," he persisted. "What if you regret not spreading your wings further on down the road?"

"We can't see into the future, Jordan," she replied thoughtfully. "But I don't like cities, although I'm sure they're exciting for some people. I don't like parties or business and I wouldn't trade jobs with Kemp for anything on earth. I'm happy looking up case precedents and researching options. I wouldn't like having to stand up in a courtroom and argue a case."

"You don't know that," he mused, and a shadow crossed his face. "What if you got a taste of it one day and couldn't live without it, but it was too late?"

"Too late?"

"What if you had kids and a husband?" he prompted.

"You're thinking about Duke Wright," she said slowly.

He drew in a hard breath, aware that Curt was watching him curiously. "Yes," he told her. "Duke's wife was a secretary. She took night courses to get her law degree and then got pregnant just before she started practice. While Duke was giving bottles and changing diapers, she was climbing the ladder at a prestigious San Antonio law firm, living there during the week and coming home on weekends. Then they offered her a job in New York City."

Libby couldn't quite figure out the look on his face. He was taking it all quite seriously and she'd thought he was teasing.

"So you see," he continued, "she didn't know she wanted a career until it was too late. Now she's making a six-figure annual income and their little boy's in her way. She doesn't want to give him up, but she doesn't have time to take care of him properly. And Duke's caught in the middle."

"I hadn't realized it was that bad," she confessed. "Poor Duke."

"He had a choice," he told her. "He married her thinking she wanted what he did, a nice home and a comfortable living, and kids." He drew a breath. "But she was very young," he added, his eyes studying her covertly. "Maybe she didn't really know what she wanted. Then."

"I suppose some women don't," she replied. "It's a new world. Maybe it took her a long time to realize the opportunities and then it was too late to go back."

He lowered his eyes to his boots. "That's very possible."

"But it's Duke's problem," she added, smiling. "Want some pie? I've got a cherry one that I made yesterday in the refrigerator."

He shook his head. "Thanks. But I won't stay." He got to his feet. "I'll tell Kemp to let you know what the private detective finds out. Meanwhile," he added, glancing at Curt, "not a word to Janet. Okay?"

They both nodded.

"Thanks, Jordan," Curt added.

"What are neighbors for?" he replied, and he chuckled. But his eyes didn't quite meet Libby's.

"Jordan was acting very oddly tonight, wasn't he?" Libby asked her brother after they'd washed the dishes and put them away.

"He's a man with a lot on his mind," he replied. "Calhoun Ballenger's making a very powerful bid for that senate seat that old man Merrill's had for so many years. They say old man Merrill's worried and so's his daughter, Julie. You remember, she's been pursuing Jordan lately."

"But he and Calhoun have been friendly for years," she said.

"So they have. There's more. Old man Merrill got

pulled over for drunk driving by a couple of our local cops. Now Merrill's pulling strings at city hall to try and make the officers withdraw the charges. Merrill doesn't have a lot of capital. Jordan does."

"Surely you don't think Jordan would go against Cash Grier, even for Julie?" she wondered, concerned.

He started to speak and then thought better of it. "I'm not sure I really know," he said.

She rubbed at a clean plate thoughtfully. "Do you suppose he's serious about her? She and her father are very big socially and they have a house here that they stay in from time to time. She has a college degree. In fact, they say she may try her hand at politics. He was talking about marriage and children to us—like he was serious about it." She frowned. "Does that kind of woman settle down? Or was that what he meant, when he said some women don't know what they want until they find it?"

"I don't know that he's got marriage on his mind," Curt replied slowly. "But he's spent a good deal of time with Julie and the senator just lately."

That hurt. She bit her lower lip, hard, and forced her mind away from the heat and power of Jordan's kisses. "We've got a problem of our own. What are we going to do about Janet?"

"Kemp's working on that, isn't he? And Jordan's

private detective will be working with him. They'll turn up something. She isn't going to put us out on the street, Libby," he said gently. "I promise you she isn't."

She smiled up at him. "You're sort of nice, for a brother."

He grinned. "Glad you noticed!"

She didn't sleep all night, though, wondering about Jordan's odd remarks and the way he'd looked at her when he asked if she had ambitions toward law practice. She really didn't, but he seemed to think she was too young to know her own mind.

Well, it wasn't really anything to worry about, she assured herself. Jordan had no idea of marrying her, regardless of her ambition or lack thereof. But Curt had said he was seeing a lot of Julie Merrill. For some unfathomable reason, the thought made her sad.

Chapter Four

It was late afternoon before Janet came back, looking out of sorts. She threw herself onto the sofa in the living room and lit a cigarette.

"You'll stink up the place," Libby muttered, hunting for an ashtray. She put it on the table.

"Well, then, you'll have to invest in some more air freshener, won't you, darling?" the older woman asked coldly.

Libby stared at her angrily. "Where have you been for three days?"

Janet avoided looking at her. "I had some business to settle."

"It had better not have been any sales concerning this property," Libby told her firmly.

"And who's going to stop me?" the other woman demanded hotly.

"Mr. Kemp."

Janet crushed out the cigarette and got to her feet. "Let him try. You try, too! I own everything here and I'm not letting you take it away from me! No matter what I have to do," she added darkly. "I earned what I'm getting, putting up with your father handling me like a live doll. The repulsive old fool made my skin crawl!"

"My father loved you," Libby bit off, furious that the awful woman could make such a remark about her father, the kindest man she'd ever known.

"He loved showing me off, you mean," Janet muttered. "If he'd really loved me, he'd have given me the things I asked him for. But he was so cheap! Well, I'm not being cheated out of what's mine," she added, with a cold glare at Libby. "Not by you or your brother. I have a lawyer, too, now."

Libby felt sick. But she managed a calm smile. "We have locks on our bedroom doors, by the way," she said out of the blue. "And Mr. Kemp is having a private detective check you out."

Janet looked shocked. "W-what?"

"Violet who works in my office thinks you might have known her father— Mr. Hardy from San Antonio?"

she added deliberately. "He had a heart attack, just like Daddy…?"

Janet actually went pale. She jumped to her feet as if she'd been stung.

"Where are you going?" Libby asked seconds later, when the older woman rushed from the room.

Janet went into her bedroom and slammed the door. The sound of objects bouncing off walls followed in a furious staccato.

Libby bit her lip. She'd been warned not to do anything to make Janet panic and make a run for it, but the woman had pricked her temper. She wished she hadn't opened her mouth.

With dark thoughts, she finished baking a ham and made potato salad to go with it, along with homemade rolls. It gave her something to do besides worry.

But when Curt came home to eat, he was met by Janet with a suitcase, going out the door.

"Where are you off to?" he asked her coolly.

She threw a furious glance at the kitchen. "Anywhere I don't have to put up with your sister!" she snarled. "I'll get a motel room in town. You'll be hearing from my attorney in a day or so."

Curt's eyebrows lifted. "Funny. I was just about to tell you the same thing. I had a phone call from Kemp while I was at work. His private investigator has turned up some very interesting information about your former employment at a nursing home in Branntville…?"

Janet brushed by him in a mad rush toward her Mercedes. She threw her case in and jumped in behind it, spraying dirt as she spun out of the driveway.

"Well, that's clinched it," Curt mused as he joined his troubled sister in the kitchen. "She won't be back, or I'll miss my bet."

"I don't think it was a good idea to run her off," she commented as she set the table. "I'd already opened my big mouth and mentioned the locks on our bedroom doors and Violet's father to her."

"It's okay," Curt said gently. "I'm doing what Kemp told me to. I put her on the run."

"Mr. Kemp said to do that?"

He nodded, tossing his hat onto a side table and pulling out a chair. "Any coffee going? We've been mucking out line cabins all day. I'm beat!"

"Mucking out line cabins, not stables?"

"The river ran out of its banks right into that cabin on the north border," he said heavily. "We've been shoveling mud all afternoon. Crazy, isn't it? We had drought for four years, now it's floods. God must really be mad at somebody!"

"Don't look at me, I haven't done a single thing out of line."

He smiled. "When have you ever?" He studied her as she put food on the table. "Jordan says he's taking you out to a movie next week…watch it!"

Her hands almost let go of the potato salad bowl. She caught it and put it down carefully, gaping at her brother. "Jordan's taking me to a movie?"

"It's what usually happens when men start kissing women," he said philosophically, leaning back in his chair with a wicked grin. "They get addicted."

"How did you know he was kissing me last night?"

He grinned wickedly. "I didn't."

She cleared her throat and turned away, reddening as she remembered the passionate kiss she and Jordan had shared before the supper he'd coaxed her to cook for him. She hadn't slept well all night thinking about it. Or about what Curt had said, that Jordan was spending a lot of time with Julie Merrill. But he couldn't be interested in the woman, if he wanted to take Libby out!

"You never got addicted to any women," she pointed out.

He shrugged. "My day will come. It just hasn't yet."

"What were you telling Janet about a private investigator and the nursing home?"

"Oh, yes." He waited until she sat down and they said grace before he continued, while piling ham on his plate. "I'm not sure how much Kemp told you already but it seems that Janet has changed her legal identity since she worked in the nursing home. Also her hair color. She was under suspicion for the death of that elderly patient who liked to play the horses. She was making off with his bank account when it seems she was paid a visit by a gentleman representing a rather shadowy figure who was owed a great deal of money by the deceased. She left everything and ran for her life." He smiled complacently. "You see, there were more debts than money left in the elderly gentleman's entire estate!"

Libby was listening intently.

"There's more." He took a bite of ham. "This is nice!" he exclaimed when he tasted it.

"Isn't it?" She smiled. "I got it from Duke Wright. He's sidelining into a pork products shop and he's marketing on the Internet. He's doing organic bacon and ham."

"Smart guy."

She nodded. "There's more, you said?"

"Yes. They've just managed to convince Violet's mother that her husband might have been murdered. She's agreed to an exhumation."

"But they said the shock might be fatal!"

"Mrs. Hardy loved her husband. She never believed it was a heart attack. He'd had an echocardiogram that was misread, leading to a heart catheterization. They found nothing that would indicate grounds for a heart attack."

"Poor Violet," Libby said sadly. "It's going to be hard on her, too." She glanced up at her brother. "I still can't believe she quit and is going to work for Duke Wright."

"I know," he said. "She was crazy about Kemp!"

She nodded sadly. "Serves him right. He's been unpleasant to her lately. Violet's tired of eating her heart out for him. And who knows. It might prompt Mr. Kemp to do some soul-searching."

"More than likely he'll just hire somebody else and forget all about her. If he wanted to be married, he could be," he added.

"He doesn't date anybody, does he?" she asked curiously.

He shook his head. "But he's not gay."

"I never thought he was. I just wondered why he keeps so much to himself."

"Maybe he's like a lot of other bachelors in Jacobsville, he's got a secret past that he doesn't want to share!"

"We're running out of bachelors," she retorted. "The Hart boys were the last to go and nobody ever thought they'd end up with families."

"Biscuits were their downfall," he pointed out.

"Jordan doesn't like biscuits," she mused. "I did ask, you know."

He chuckled. "Jordan doesn't have a weakness and he's never lacked dates when he wanted them." He eyed her over his coffee cup. "But he may be at the end of his own rope."

"Don't look at me," she said, having spent too much time lately thinking about Jordan's intentions toward her. "I may be the flavor of the week, but Jordan isn't going to want to marry down, if you see what I mean."

His eyes narrowed. "We may not be high society, but our people go back a long way in Jacobs County."

"That doesn't put us in monied circles, either," she reminded him. Her eyes were dreamy and faraway. "He's got a big, fancy house and he likes to keep company with high society. Maybe that's why he's been taking Senator Merrill's daughter around. It gets him into places he was never invited to before. We'd never fit. Especially me," she added in a more wistful tone than she realized.

"That wouldn't matter."

She smiled sadly. "It would and you know it. He'll need a wife who can entertain and throw parties, arrange sales, things like that. Most of all, he'll want a woman who's beautiful and intelligent, someone he'll be proud to show off. He might take me to a movie. But believe me, he won't take me to a minister."

"You're sure of that?"

She looked up at him. "You said it yourself—Jordan has been spending a lot of time with the state senator's daughter. He's running for reelection and the latest polls say that Calhoun Ballenger is almost tied with him. He needs all the support he can get, financial and otherwise. I think Jordan's going to help him, because of Julie."

"Then why is he kissing you?"

"To make her jealous?" she pondered. "Maybe to convince himself that he's still attractive to women. But it's not serious. Not with him." She looked up. "And I don't have affairs, whether it's politically correct or not."

He sighed. "I suppose we all have our pipe dreams."

"What's yours, while we're on the subject?"

He smiled. "I'd like to start a ranch supply company. The last one left belonged to Ted Regan's father-in-law. When he died, the store went bust, and then his daughter Corrie married Ted Regan and didn't need to make her own living. The hardware store can order most supplies, but not cattle feed or horse feed. Stuff like that."

She hadn't realized her brother had such ambitions. "If we weren't in such a financial mess, I'd be more than willing to cosign a loan with the house as collateral."

He stared at her intently. "You'd do that for me?"

"Of course. You're my brother. I love you."

He reached out and caught her hand. "I love you, too, sis."

"Pipe dreams are nice. Don't you give yours up. Eventually we'll settle this inheritance question and we might have a little capital to work with." She studied him with pride. "I think you'd make a great success of it. You've kept us solvent, up until Janet's unexpected arrival."

"She'll be out for blood. I should probably call Kemp and update him on what's happened."

"That might not be a bad idea. Maybe we should get a dog," she added slowly.

"Bad idea. We can hardly afford to feed old Bailey, your horse. We'd have to buy food for a dog, too, and it would break us."

She saw his eyes twinkle and she burst out laughing, too.

* * *

Janet's attorney never showed up and two days later, Janet vanished, leaving a trail of charges to the Collinses for everything from clothes to the motel bill.

"You won't have to pay that," Kemp told Libby when he'd related the latest news to her. "I've already alerted the merchants that she had no authority to charge anything to you or Curt, or the estate."

"Thanks," she said with relief. "What do we do now?"

"I've got the state police out looking for her," he replied, his hands deep in his slacks' pockets. "On suspicion of murder. You won't like what's coming next."

"What?"

"I want to have your father exhumed."

She ground her teeth together. "I was afraid of that."

"We'll be discreet. But we need to have the crime lab check for trace evidence of poisoning. You see, we know what killed the old man at the nursing home where she worked. I believe she did kill him. Poisoners tend to stick to the same routine."

"Poor Daddy," she said, feeling sick. Now she wondered if they might have saved him, if they'd only realized sooner that Janet was dangerous.

"Don't play mind games with yourself, Libby," Kemp said quietly. "It does no good."

"What a terrible way to go."

"The poison she used was quick," he replied. "Some can cause symptoms for months and the victim dies a painfully slow death. That wasn't the case here. It's the only good news I have for you, I'm afraid. But after they autopsy Mr. Hardy, there may be more forensic evidence to make a case against her. We've found a source for the poison."

"But the doctor said that Daddy died of a heart attack," she began.

"He might have," Kemp had to admit. "But he could as easily have died of poison or an air embolism."

"Jordan mentioned that," she recalled.

He smiled secretively. "Jordan doesn't miss a trick."

"But Janet's gone. What if they discover that Daddy's death was foul play and then they can't find her?" Libby pointed out. "She's gotten away with it at least two times, by being cagey."

"Every criminal eventually makes a mistake," he said absently. "She'll make one. Mark my words."

She only nodded. She glanced at Violet's empty desk and winced.

"I have an ad in the paper for a new secretary," he

said coldly. "Meanwhile, Mabel's going to do double duty," he added, nodding toward Mabel, who was on the phone taking notes.

"It's going to be lonely without her," she said without thinking.

Kemp actually ground his teeth, turned on his heel and went back into his office. As an afterthought, he slammed the door.

Libby lost it. She laughed helplessly. Mabel, off the phone now and aware of Kemp's shocking attitude, laughed, too.

"It won't last long," Mabel whispered. "Violet was the only secretary he's ever had who could make and break appointments without hurting people's feelings. She was the fastest typist, too. He's not going to find somebody to replace her overnight."

Libby agreed silently. But it promised to be an interesting working environment for the foreseeable future.

Libby didn't even notice there was a message on the answering machine until after supper, when she'd had a lonely sandwich after Curt had phoned and said he was eating pizza with the other cowboys over at the Regan place for their weekly card game.

Curious, Libby punched the answer key and listened to the message. In a silken tone, the caller identified himself as an attorney named Smith and said that Mrs. Collins had hired him to do the probate on her late husband's will. He added that the children of Riddle Collins would have two weeks to vacate the premises.

Libby went through the roof. Her hands trembled as she tried to call Kemp and failing to reach him, she punched in Jordan's number.

It took a long time for him to answer the phone and when he finally did, there was conversation and music in the background.

"Yes?" he asked curtly.

Libby faltered. "Am I interrupting? I can call you another time..."

"Libby?" His voice softened. "Wait a minute." She heard muffled conversation, an angry reply, and the sound of a door closing. "Okay," he said. "What's wrong?"

"I can't get Mr. Kemp," she began urgently, "and Janet's attorney just called and said we had two weeks to get out of the house before they did the probate!"

"Libby," he said softly, "just sit down and use your mind. Think. When has anybody ever been asked to vacate a house just so that probate papers could be filed?"

She took a deep breath and then another. Her hands

were still cold and trembling but she was beginning to remember bits and pieces of court documents. She was a paralegal. For God's sake, she knew about probate!

She sighed heavily. "Thanks. I just lost it. I was so shocked and so scared!"

"Is Curt there?"

"No, he went to his weekly card game with the cowboys over at Ted Regan's ranch," she said.

"I'm sorry I can't come over and talk to you. I'm having a fundraising party for Senator Merrill tonight."

Merrill. His daughter Julie was the socialite. She was beautiful and rich and…socially acceptable. Certainly, she'd be at the party, too.

"Libby?" he prompted, when she didn't answer him.

"That's…that's okay, Jordan, I don't need company, honest," she said at once. "I just lost my mind for a minute. I'm sorry I bothered you. Really!"

"You don't have to apologize," he said, as if her statement unsettled him.

"I'll hang up now. Thanks, Jordan!"

He was still talking when she put the receiver down, very quickly, and put the answering machine back on. If he called back, she wasn't answering him. Janet's vicious tactics had unsettled her. She knew Janet had gotten someone to make that phone call deliberately, to upset Riddle's children.

It was her way of getting even, no doubt, for what Libby and Curt had said to her. She wondered if there was any way they could trace a call off an answering machine? A flash of inspiration hit her. Before Jordan would have time to call and foul the connection, she jerked up the phone and pressed the *69 keys. It gave her the number of the party who'd just phoned and she wrote it down at once, delighted to see that it was not a local number. She'd give it to Kemp the next morning and let his private investigator look into it.

Feeling more confident, she went back to the kitchen and finished washing up the few dishes. She couldn't forget Jordan's deep voice on the phone and the sound of a woman's voice arguing angrily when he went into another room to talk to Libby. It must be that senator's daughter. Obviously she felt possessive of Jordan and was wary of any potential rival. But Libby was no rival, she told herself. Jordan had just kissed her. That was all.

If only she could forget how it had felt. Then she remembered something else: Jordan's odd statements about Duke Wright's wife, and how young she was, and how she didn't quite know she wanted a career until she was already married and pregnant. He'd given Libby an odd, searching look when he said that.

The senator's daughter, Julie Merrill, was twenty-six, she recalled, with a degree in political science. Obviously she already knew what she wanted. She wanted Jordan. She was at his house tonight, probably hostessing the party there. Libby looked down at her worn jeans and faded blouse and then around her at the shabby but useful furniture in the old house. She laughed mirthlessly. What in the world would Jordan want with her, anyway? She'd been daydreaming. She'd better wake up, before she had her heart torn out.

She didn't phone Jordan again and he didn't call her back. She did give the telephone number of the so-called attorney to Mr. Kemp, who passed it along to his investigator.

Several days later, he paused by Libby's desk while she was writing up a precedent for a libel case, and he looked smug.

"That was quick thinking on your part," he remarked with a smile. "We traced the number to San Antonio. The man isn't an attorney, though. He's a waiter in a high-class restaurant who thinks Janet is his meal ticket to the easy life. We, uh, disabused him of the idea and told him one of her possible futures. We understand that he quit his job and left town on the next bus to make sure he wasn't involved in anything she did."

She laughed softly. "Thank goodness! Then Curt and I don't have to move!"

Kemp glared at her. "As if I'd stand by and let any so-called attorney toss you out of your home!"

"Thanks, boss," she said with genuine gratitude.

He shrugged. "Paralegals are thin on the ground," he said with twinkling blue-gray eyes.

"Callie Kirby and I are the only ones that I know of in town right now," she agreed.

"And Callie's got a child," he said, nodding. "I don't think Micah's going to want her to come back to work until their kids are in school."

"I expect not. She's got Micah's father to help take care of, too," she added, "after his latest stroke."

"People die," he said, and his eyes seemed distant and troubled.

"Mabel called in sick," she said reluctantly. "She's got some sort of stomach virus."

"They go around every spring," he agreed with a sigh. "Can you handle everything, or do you want to get a temp? If you do, call the agency. Ask if they've got somebody who can type."

She gave him her most innocent look. "Of course I

can do the work of three women, sir, and even make coffee…"

He laughed. "Call the agency."

"Yes, sir."

He glowered. "It's Violet's fault," he muttered, turning. "I'll bet she's cursed us. We'll have sick help from now on."

"I'm sure she'd never do that, Mr. Kemp," she assured him. "She's a nice person."

"Imagine taking offense at a look and throwing in the towel. Hell, I look at people all the time and they don't quit!"

She cleared her throat and nodded toward the door, which was just opening.

A lovely young woman with a briefcase and long blond hair came in. "I'm Julie Merrill," she said with a haughty smile. "Senator Merrill's daughter? You advertised for a secretary, I believe."

Libby could not believe her eyes. Jordan's latest love and she turned up here looking for work! Of all the horrible bad luck…

Kemp stared at the young woman without speaking.

"Oh, not me!" Julie laughed, clearing her throat. "Heavens, I don't need a job! No, it's my friend Lydia.

She's just out of secretarial school and she can't find anything suitable."

"Can she type?"

"Yes! Sixty words a minute. And she can take short-hand, if you don't dictate too fast."

"Can she speak?"

Julie blinked. "I beg your pardon?"

Kemp gave her a scrutiny that would have stopped traffic. His eyes became a wintry blue, which Libby knew from experience meant that his temper was just beginning to kindle.

"I don't give jobs through third persons, Miss Merrill, and I don't give a damn who your father is," he said with a cool smile.

She colored hotly and gaped at him. "I...I...just thought...I mean, I could ask...!"

"Tell your friend she can come in and fill out an application, but not to expect much," he added shortly. "I have no respect for a woman who has to be helped into a job through favoritism. And in case it's escaped your attention," he added, moving a step closer to her, "nobody works for me unless they're qualified."

Julie shot a cold glare at Libby, who was watching intently. "I guess you think she's qualified," she said angrily.

"I have a diploma as a trained paralegal," Libby

replied coolly. "It's on the wall behind you, at my desk."

Kemp only smiled. It wasn't a nice smile.

Julie set her teeth together so hard that they almost clicked. "I don't think Lydia would like this job, anyway!"

Kemp's right eyebrow arched. "Was there anything else, Miss Merrill?"

She turned, jerking open the door. "My father will not be happy when I tell him how you've spoken to me."

"By all means, tell him, with my blessing," Kemp said. "One of his faults is a shameful lack of discipline with his children. I understand you've recently expressed interest in running for public office in Jacobs County, Miss Merrill. Let me give you a piece of advice. Don't."

Her mouth fell open. "How dare you...!"

"It's your father's money, of course. If he wants to throw it away, that's his concern."

"I could win an election!"

Kemp smiled. "Perhaps you could. But not in Jacobs County," he said pleasantly. His eyes narrowed and became cold and his voice grew deceptively soft. "Closet skeletons become visible baggage in an election. And no one here has forgotten your high-school party. Especially not the Culbertsons."

Julie's face went pale. Her fingers on the briefcase tightened until the knuckles showed. She actually looked frightened.

"That was…a terrible accident."

"Shannon Culbertson is still dead."

Julie's lower lip trembled. She turned and went out the door so quickly that she forgot to close it.

Kemp did it for her, his face cold and hard, full of repressed fury.

Libby wondered what was going on, but she didn't dare ask.

Later, of course, when Curt got home from work, she couldn't resist asking the question.

He scowled. "What the hell did Julie want in Kemp's office? Lydia doesn't need a job, she already has a job—a good one—at the courthouse over in Bexar County!"

"She said Lydia wanted to work for Mr. Kemp, but she was giving me the evil eye for all she was worth."

"She wants Jordan. You're in the way."

"Sure I am," she laughed coldly. "What about that girl, Shannon Culbertson?"

Curt hesitated. "That was eight years ago."

"What happened?"

"Somebody put something in her drink—which she wasn't supposed to have had in the first place. It was a forerunner of the date-rape drug. She had a hidden heart condition. It killed her."

"Who did it?"

"Nobody knows, but Julie tried to cover it up, to save her father's senate seat. Kemp dug out the truth and gave it to the newspapers." He shook his head. "A vindictive man, Kemp."

"Why?" she asked.

"They say Kemp was in love with the girl. He never got over it."

"But Julie's father won the election," she pointed out.

"Only because the leading lights of the town supported him and contributed to his reelection campaign. Most of those old-timers are dead or in nursing homes and the gossip around town is that Senator Merrill is already over his ears in debt from his campaign. Besides which, he's up against formidable opposition for the first time in recent years."

Chapter Five

So that was Kemp's secret, Libby thought. A lost love. "Yes, I know," she said. "Calhoun Ballenger has really shaken up the district politically. A lot of people think he's going to win the nomination right out from under Merrill."

"I'm almost sure he will," Curt replied. "The powers that be in the county have changed over the past few years. The Harts have come up in the world. So have the Tremaynes, the Ballengers, Ted Regan, and a few other families. The power structure now isn't in the hands of the old elite. If you don't believe that, notice what's going on at city hall. Chief Grier is making a record number of drug busts and I don't need to remind you that Senator Merrill was arrested for drunk driving."

"That never was in the paper, you know," she said with a wry smile.

"The publisher is one of his cronies—he refused to run the story. But Merrill's up to his ears in legal trouble. So he's trying to get the mayor and two councilmen who owe him favors to fire the two police officers who made the arrest and discredit them. The primary election is the first week of May, you know."

"Poor police," she murmured.

"Mark my words, they'll never lose their jobs. Grier has contacts everywhere and despite his personal problems, he's not going to let his officers go down without a fight. I'd bet everything I have on him."

She grinned. "I like him."

Curt chuckled. "I like him, too."

"Mr. Kemp said they traced the lawyer's call to San Antonio," she added, and told him what was said. "Why would she want us out of the house?"

"Maybe she thinks there's something in it that she hasn't gotten yet," he mused. "Dad's coin collection, for instance."

"I haven't seen that in months," she said.

"Neither have I. She probably sold it already," he said with cold disgust. "But Janet's going to hang herself before she quits." He gave his sister a sad look. "I'm sorry about the exhumation. But we really need to know the truth about how Dad died."

"I know," she replied. The pain was still fresh and she had to fight tears. She managed a smile for him. "Daddy wouldn't mind."

"No. I don't think he would."

"I wish we'd paid more attention to what was going on."

"He thought he loved her, Libby," he said. "Maybe he did. He wouldn't have listened to us, no matter what we said, if it was something bad about her. You know how he was."

"Loving her blindly may have cost him his life."

"Try to remember that he died happy. He didn't know what Janet was. He didn't know that she was cheating him."

"It doesn't help much."

He nodded. "Nothing will bring him back. But maybe we can save somebody else's father. That would make it all worthwhile."

"Yes," she agreed. "It would."

That evening while they were watching television, a truck drove up. A minute later, there was a hard knock on the door.

"I've got it," Curt said, leaving Libby with her embroidery.

There were muffled voices and then heavy footsteps coming into the room.

Jordan stared at Libby curiously. "Julie came to your office today," he said.

"She was looking for a job for her friend Lydia," Libby said in a matter-of-fact tone.

"That's not what she said," Jordan replied tersely. "She told me that you treated her so rudely that Kemp made her leave the office."

Libby lifted both eyebrows. "Wow. Imagine that."

"I'm not joking with you, Libby," Jordan said, and his tone chilled. "That was a petty thing to do."

"It would have been," she agreed, growing angry herself, "if I'd done it. She came into the office in a temper, glared at me, made some rude remarks to Mr. Kemp and got herself thrown out."

"That's not what she told me," he repeated.

Libby got to her feet, motioning to Curt, who was about to protest on her behalf. "I don't need help, Curt. Stay out of it, that's a nice brother." She moved closer to Jordan. "Miss Merrill insinuated that Mr. Kemp had better offer Lydia a job because of her father's position in the community. And he reminded her about her high-school graduation party where a girl died."

"He what?" he exploded.

"Mr. Kemp doesn't take threats lying down," she said, uneasy because of Jordan's overt hostility. "Miss Merrill was very haughty and very rude. And neither of us can understand why she'd try to get Lydia a job at Kemp's office, because she's already got one in San Antonio!"

Jordan didn't say anything. He just stood there, silent.

"She was with you when I phoned your house, I guess, and she got the idea that I was chasing you," she said, gratified by the sudden blinking of his eyelids. "You can tell her, for me," she added with saccharine sweetness, "that I would not have you on a hot dog bun with uptown relish. If she thinks I'm the competition, all she has to do is look where I live." Her face tautened. "Go ahead, Jordan, look around you. I'm not even in your league, whatever your high-class girlfriend thinks. You're a kind neighbor whom I asked for advice and that's all you ever were. Period," she lied, trying to save face.

He still wasn't moving or speaking. But his eyes were taking on a nasty glitter. Beside his lean hips, one of his hands was clenched until the knuckles went white. "Ever?" he prodded, his tone insinuating things.

She knew what he meant. She swallowed hard,

trying not to remember the heat and power of the kisses they'd shared. Obviously, they'd meant nothing to him!

"Ever," she repeated. "I certainly wasn't trying to tie you down, Jordan. I'm not at all sure that I want to spend the rest of my life in Jacobsville working for a lawyer, anyway," she added deliberately, but without looking at him. "I've thought about that a lot, about what you said. Maybe I do have ambitions."

He didn't speak for several seconds. His eyes became narrow and cold.

"If you'd like to show your Julie that I'm no competition, you can bring her down here and show her how we live," she offered with a smile. "That would really open her eyes, wouldn't it?"

"Libby," Curt warned. "Don't talk like that."

"How should I talk?" she demanded, her throat tightening. "Our father is dead and it looks like our stepmother killed him right under our noses! She's trying to take away everything we have, getting her friends to call and threaten and harass us, and now here's Jordan's Goody-two-shoes girlfriend making me out to be a man-stealer, or somebody. How the hell should I talk?"

Jordan let out a long breath. "I thought you knew what you wanted," he said after a minute.

"I'm young. Like you said," she said cynically. "Sorry I ever asked you for help, Jordan, and made your girlfriend mad. You can bet I'll never make that mistake twice."

She turned and went into the kitchen and slammed the door behind her. She was learning really bad habits from Mr. Kemp, she decided, as she wiped tears away with a paper towel.

She heard the door open behind her and close again, firmly. It was Curt, she supposed, coming to check on her.

"I guess I handled that badly," she said, choking on tears. "Has he gone?"

Big, warm hands caught her shoulders and turned her around. Jordan's eyes glittered down into hers. "No, he hasn't gone," he bit off.

He looked ferocious like that. She should have been intimidated, but she wasn't. He was handsome, even bristling with temper.

"I've said all I have to say," she began.

"Well, I haven't," he shot back, goaded. "I've never looked down on you for what you've got and you know it."

"Julie Merrill does," she muttered.

His hands tightened and relaxed. He looked vaguely embarrassed. His dark eyes slid past her to the worn calendar on the wall. "You know how I grew up," he said heavily. "We had nothing. I was never invited to parties. My parents were glorified servants in the eyes of the town's social set."

She drew in a short breath. "And now Julie's opening the doors and inviting you in and you like it."

He seemed shocked by the statement. His eyes dropped to meet hers. "Maybe."

"Can't you see why?" she asked quietly. "You're rich now. You made something out of nothing. You have confidence, and power, and you know how to behave in company. But there's more to it than that, where the Merrills are concerned."

"That's not your business," he said shortly.

She smiled sadly. "They need financial backing. Their old friends aren't as wealthy as they used to be. Calhoun Ballenger has the support of the newer wealthy people in Jacobsville and they don't deal in 'good old boy' politics."

"In other words, Julie only wants me for money to run her father's reelection campaign."

"You know better than that," she replied, searching his hard face hungrily. "You're handsome and sexy. Women adore you."

One eyebrow lifted. "Even you?"

She wanted to deny it, but she couldn't. "Even me,"

she confessed. "But I'm no more in your class, really, than you're in Julie's. They're old money. It doesn't really matter to them how rich you get, you'll never be one of them."

His eyes narrowed angrily. "I am one of them," he retorted. "I'm hobnobbing with New York society, with Kentucky Thoroughbred breeders, with presidential staff members—even with Hollywood producers and actors!"

"You could do that on your own," she said. "You don't need the Merrills to make you socially acceptable. And in case you've forgotten, Christabel and Judd Dunn have been hobnobbing with Hollywood people for a year. They're not rich. Not really."

He was losing the argument and he didn't like it. He glared down at her with more riotous feelings than he'd entertained in years. "Julie wants to marry me," he said, producing the flat statement like a weapon.

She managed not to react to the retort, barely. Her heart was sinking like lead in her chest as she pictured Julie in a designer wedding gown flashing diamonds like pennies on her way to the altar.

"She doesn't want a career," he added, smiling coldly.

Neither did Libby, really. She liked having a job, but she also liked living in Jacobsville and working around the ranch. She'd have liked being Jordan's wife more than anything else she could think of. But that wasn't going to happen. He didn't want her.

She tried to pull away from Jordan's strong hands, but he wasn't budging.

"Let me go," she muttered. "I'm sure Julie wouldn't like this!"

"Wouldn't like what?" he drawled. "Being in my arms, or having you in them?"

"Are you having fun?" she challenged.

"Not yet," he murmured, dropping his gaze to her full lips. "But I expect to be pretty soon…"

"You can't…!"

But he could. And he was. She felt the warm, soft, coaxing pressure of his hard mouth before she could finish the protest. Her eyes closed. She was aware of his size and strength, of the warmth of his powerful body against hers. She could feel his heartbeat, feel the rough sigh of his breath as he deepened the kiss.

He hadn't really meant to do this. He'd meant it as a punishment, for the things she'd said to him. But when he had her so close that he could feel her heart beating like a wild thing against him, nothing else seemed to matter except pleasing her, as she was pleasing him.

He drew her up closer, so that he could feel the soft, warm imprint of her body on the length of his. He traced her soft mouth with his lips, with the tip of his tongue. He felt her stiffen and then lift up to him. He gathered her completely against him and forgot Julie, forgot the argument, forgot everything.

She felt the sudden ardor of his embrace grow unmanageable in a space of seconds. His mouth was insistent on hers, demanding. His hands had gone to her hips. They were pressing her against the sudden rigidity of his powerful body. Even as she registered his urgent hunger for her, she felt one of his big, lean hands seeking between them for the soft, rounded curve of her breast...

She pulled away from him abruptly, her mouth swollen, her eyes wild. "N-no," she choked.

He tried to pull her back into his arms. "Why not?" he murmured, his eyes on her mouth.

"Curt," she whispered.

"Curt." He spoke the name as if he didn't recognize it. He blinked. He took a deep breath and suddenly realized where they were and what he'd been doing.

He drew in a harsh, deep breath.

"You have to go home," she said huskily.

He stood up straight and stared down his nose at her. "If you will keep throwing yourself into my arms, what do you expect?" he asked outrageously.

She gaped at him.

"It's no use trying to look innocent," he added as he moved back another step. "And don't start taking off your blouse, it won't work."

"I am not…!" she choked, crossing her arms quickly.

He made a rough sound in his throat. "A likely story. Don't follow me home, either, because I lock my doors at night."

She wanted to react to that teasing banter that she'd enjoyed so much before, but she couldn't forget that he'd taken Julie's side against her.

She stared at him coldly. "I won't follow you home. Not while you're spending all your free time defending Julie Merrill, when I'm the one who was insulted."

He froze over. "The way Julie tells it, you started on her first."

"And you believe her, of course. She's beautiful and rich and sophisticated."

"Something no man in his right mind could accuse you of," he shot back. With a cold glare, he turned and went out the door.

He didn't pause to speak to Curt, who was just coming in the front door. He shot him a look bare of courtesy and stormed outside. He was boiling over with emotion, the strongest of which was frustrated desire.

* * *

Libby didn't explain anything to her brother, but she knew he wasn't blind or stupid. He didn't ask questions, either. He just hugged her and smiled.

She went to bed feeling totally at sea. How could an argument lead to something so tempestuous that she'd almost passed out at Jordan's feet? And if he really wanted Julie, then how could he kiss Libby with such frustrated desire? And why had he started another fight before he left?

She was still trying to figure out why she hadn't slapped his arrogant face when she fell asleep.

The tension between Jordan and his neighbors was suddenly visible even to onlookers. He never set foot on their place. When he had a barbecue for his ranch hands in April, to celebrate the impressive calf sale he'd held, Curt wasn't invited. When Libby had a small birthday party to mark her twenty-fourth birthday, Jordan wasn't on the guest list. Jacobsville being the small town it was, people noticed.

"Have you and Jordan had some sort of falling out?" Mr. Kemp asked while his new secretary, a sweet little brunette fresh out of high school named Jessie, was out to lunch.

Libby looked up at him with wide-eyed innocence. "Falling out?"

"Julie Merrill has been telling people that she and Jordan have marriage plans," he said. "I don't believe it. Her father's in financial hot water and Jordan's rich. Old man Merrill is going to need a lot of support in today's political climate. He made some bad calls on the budget and education and the voters are out to get him."

"So I've heard. They say Calhoun Ballenger's just pulled ahead in the polls."

"He'll win," Kemp replied. "It's no contest. Regardless of Jordan's backing."

"Mr. Kemp, would they really use what happened at Julie's party as a weapon against her father?" she asked carefully.

"Of course they would!" he said shortly. "Even in Jacobs County, dirty laundry has a value. There are other skeletons in that closet, too. Plenty of them. Merrill has already lost the election. His way of doing business, under the table, is obsolete. He's trying to make Cash Grier fire those arresting officers and swear they lied. It won't happen. He and his daughter just don't know it and she refuses to face defeat."

"She's at Jordan's house every day now," she said on

a sigh that was more wistful than she knew. "She's very beautiful."

"She's a tarantula," Kemp said coldly. "She's got her finger in a pie I can't tell you about, but it's about to hit the tabloids. When it does, her father can kiss his career goodbye."

"Sir?"

He lifted both eyebrows. "Can you keep a secret?"

"If I can't, why am I working for you?" she asked pertly.

"Those two officers Grier's backing, who caught the senator driving drunk—" he said. "They've also been investigating a house out on the Victoria road where drugs are bought and sold. That's the real reason they're facing dismissal. Merrill's nephew is our mayor."

"And he's in it up to his neck, I guess?" she fished.

He nodded. "The nephew and Miss Merrill herself. That's where her new Porsche came from."

Libby whistled. "But if Jordan's connected with her..." she said worriedly.

"That's right," he replied. "He'll be right in hot water with her, even though he's not doing anything illegal. Mud not only sticks, it rubs off."

She chewed her lower lip. "You couldn't warn him, I guess?"

He shook his head. "We aren't speaking."

She stared at him. "But you're friends."

"Not anymore. You see, he thinks I took your side unjustly against Miss Merrill."

She frowned. "I'm sorry."

He chuckled. "It will all blow over in a few weeks. You'll see."

She wasn't so confident. She didn't think it would and she hated the thought of seeing Jordan connected with such an unsavory business.

She walked down to Barbara's Café for lunch and ran right into Julie Merrill and Jordan Powell, who were waiting in line together.

"Oh, look, it's the little secretary," Julie drawled when she saw Libby in line behind them. "Still telling lies about me, Miss Collins?" she asked with a laugh.

Jordan was looking at Libby with an expression that was hard to classify.

Libby ignored her, turning instead to speak to one of the girls from the county clerk's office, who was in line behind her.

"Don't you turn your back on me, you little creep!" Julie raged, attracting attention as she walked right up to Libby. Her eyes were glazed, furious. "You told Jordan that I tried to throw my weight around in Kemp's office and it was a lie! You were just trying to make yourself look good, weren't you?"

Libby felt sick at her stomach. She was no good at dealing with angry people, despite the fact that she had to watch Kemp's secretaries do it every day. She wasn't really afraid of the other girl, but she was keenly aware of their differences on the social ladder. Julie was rich and well-known and sophisticated. Libby was little more than a rancher's daughter turned legal apprentice.

"Jordan can't stand you, in case you wondered, so it's no use calling him up all the time for help, and standing at his door trying to make him notice you!" Julie continued haughtily. "He wouldn't demean himself by going out with a dirty little nobody like you!"

Libby pulled herself up and stared at the older girl, keenly aware of curious eyes watching and people listening in the crowded lunch traffic. "Jordan is our neighbor, Miss Merrill," she said in a strained tone. Her legs were shaking, but she didn't let it show. "Nothing more. I don't want Jordan."

"Good. I'm glad you realize that Jordan's nothing more than a neighbor, because you're a nuisance! No man in his right mind would look at you twice!"

"Oh, I don't know about that," Harley Fowler said suddenly, moving up the line to look down at Julie Merrill with cold eyes. "I'd say her manners are a damned sight better than yours and your mouth wouldn't get you into any decent man's house in Jacobsville!"

Julie's mouth fell open.

"I wouldn't have her on toast!" one of the Tremaynes' cowboys ventured from his table.

"Hey, Julie, how about a dime bag?" some anonymous voice called. "I need a fix!"

Julie went pale. "Who said that?" she demanded shakily.

"Julie, let's go," Jordan said curtly, taking her by the arm.

"I'm hungry!" she protested, fighting his hold.

Libby didn't look up as he passed her with Julie firmly at his side. He didn't look at her, either, and his face was white with rage.

As she went out the door, there was a skirl of belligerent applause from the patrons of the café. Julie made a rude gesture toward them, which was followed by equally rude laughter.

"Isn't she a pain?" The girl from the clerk's office laughed. "Honestly, Libby, you were such a lady! I'd have laid a chair across her thick skull!"

"Me, too," said another girl. "Nobody can stand her. She thinks she's such a debutante."

Libby listened to the talk with a raging heartbeat.

She was sick to her stomach from the unexpected confrontation and glad that Jordan had gotten the girl out of the room before things got ugly. But it ruined her lunch. It ruined her whole day.

It didn't occur to Libby that Jordan would be upset about the things that Julie had said in the café, especially since he hadn't said a word to Libby at the time. But he actually came by Kemp's office the next day, hat in hand, to apologize for Julie's behavior.

He looked disappointed when Kemp was sitting perched on the edge of Libby's desk, as if he'd hoped to find her alone. But he recovered quickly.

He gave Kemp a quick glare, his gaze returning at once to Libby. "I wanted to apologize for Julie," he said curtly. "She's sorry she caused a scene yesterday. She's been upset about her father facing drunk-driving charges."

"I don't receive absentee apologies," Libby said coldly. "And you'll never convince me that she would apologize."

Kemp's eyebrows collided. "What's that?"

"Julie made some harsh remarks about me in Barbara's Café yesterday," Libby told him, "in front of half the town."

"Why didn't you come and get me?" Kemp asked.

"I'd have settled her hash for her," he added, with a dangerous look at Jordan.

"Harley Fowler defended me," Libby said with a quiet smile. "So did several other gentlemen in the crowd," she added deliberately.

"She's not as bad as you think she is," Jordan said grimly.

"The hell she's not," Kemp replied softly. He got up. "I know things about her that you're going to wish you did and very soon. Libby, don't be long. We've got a case first thing tomorrow. I'll need those notes," he added, nodding toward the computer screen. He went to his office and closed the door.

"What was Kemp talking about?" Jordan asked Libby curiously.

"I could tell you, but you wouldn't believe me," she said sadly, remembering how warm their relationship had been before Julie Merrill clouded the horizon.

He drew in a long breath and moved a little closer, pushing his hat back over his dark hair. He looked down at her with barely contained hunger. Mabel was busy in the back with the photocopier and the girl who was filling in for Violet had gone to a dental appointment. Mr. Kemp was shut up in his office. Libby kept hoping the phone would ring, or someone would come in the front door and save her from Jordan. It was all she could do not to throw herself into his arms, even after the fights they'd had. She couldn't stop being attracted to him.

"Look," he said quietly, "I'm not trying to make an enemy of you. I like Julie. Her father is a good man and he's had some hard knocks lately. They really need my help, Libby. They haven't got anybody else."

She could just imagine Julie crying prettily, lavishing praise on Jordan for being so useful, dressing up in her best—which was considerably better than Libby's best—and making a play for him. She might be snippy and aggressive toward other women, but Julie Merrill was a practiced seducer. She knew how to wind men around her finger. She was young and beautiful and cultured and rich. She knew tricks that most men— even Jordan—wouldn't be able to resist.

"Why are you so attracted to her?" Libby wondered aloud.

Jordan gave her an enigmatic look. "She's mature," he said without thinking. "She knows exactly what she wants and she goes after it wholeheartedly. Besides that, she's a woman who could have anybody."

"And she wants you," she said for him.

He shrugged. "Yes. She does."

She studied his lean, hard face, surprising a curious

rigidity there before he concealed it. "I suppose you're flattered," she murmured.

"She draws every man's eye when she walks into a room," he said slowly. "She can play the piano like a professional. She speaks three languages. She's been around the world several times. She's dated some of the most famous actors in Hollywood. She's even been presented to the queen in England." He sighed. "Most men would have a hard time turning up their noses at a woman like that."

"In other words, she's like a trophy."

He studied her arrogantly. "You could say that. But there's something more, too. She needs me. She said everyone in town had turned their backs on her father. Calhoun Ballenger is drawing financial support from some of the richest families in town, the same people who promised Senator Merrill their support and then withdrew it. Julie was in tears when she told me how he'd been sold out by his best friends. Until I came along, he actually considered dropping out of the race."

And pigs fly, Libby thought privately, but she didn't say it. The Merrills were dangling their celebrity in front of Jordan, a man who'd been shut out of high society even though he was now filthy rich. They were offering him entry into a closed community. All that and beautiful Julie, as well.

"Did you hear what she said to me in Barbara's Café?" she wondered aloud.

"What do you mean?" he asked curiously.

"You stood there and let her attack me, without saying a word."

He scowled. "I was talking to Brad Henry while we stood in line, about a bull he wanted to sell. I didn't realize what was going on until Julie raised her voice. By then, Harley Fowler and several other men were making catcalls at her. I thought the best thing to do would be to get her outside before things escalated."

"Did you hear her accuse me of chasing you? Did you hear her warn me off you?"

He cocked his head. "I heard that part," he admitted. "She's very possessive and more jealous of me than I realized. But I didn't like having her insult you, if that's what you mean," he said quietly. "I told her so later. She said she'd apologize, but I thought it might come easier from me. She's insecure, Libby. You wouldn't think so, but she really takes things to heart."

A revelation a minute, Libby was thinking. Jordan actually believed what he was saying. Julie had really done a job on him.

"She said that you wouldn't waste your time on a nobody like me," she persisted.

"Women say things they don't mean all the time." He shrugged it off. "You take things to heart, too, Libby," he added gently. "You're still very young."

"You keep saying that," she replied, exasperated. "How old do I have to be for you to think of me as an adult?"

He moved closer, one lean hand going to her slender throat, slowly caressing it. "I've thought of you like that for a long time," he said deeply. "But you're an addiction I can't afford. You said it yourself—you're ambitious. You won't be satisfied in a small town. Like the old-timers used to say, you want to go and see the elephant."

She was caught in his dark eyes, spellbound. She'd said that, yes, because of the way he'd behaved about Julie's insults. She'd wanted to sting him. But she didn't mean it. She wasn't ambitious. All she wanted was Jordan. Her eyes were lost in his.

"The elephant?" she parroted, her gaze on his hard mouth.

"You want to see the world," he translated. But he was moving closer as he said it and his head was bending, even against his will. This was stupid. He couldn't afford to let himself be drawn into this sweet trap.

Libby wanted a career. She was young and ambitious. He'd go in headfirst and she'd take off and leave him, just as Duke Wright's young wife had left him in search of fame and fortune. He'd deliberately drawn back from Libby and let himself be vamped by Julie Merrill, to show this little firecracker that he hadn't been serious about those kisses they'd exchanged. He wasn't going to risk his heart on a gamble this big. Libby was in love with love. She was attracted to him. But that wasn't love. She was too young to know the difference. He wasn't. He'd grabbed at Julie the way a drowning man reaches for a life jacket. Libby didn't know that. He couldn't admit it.

While he was thinking, he was parting her lips with his. He forgot where they were, who they were. He forgot the arguments and all the reasons he shouldn't do this.

"Libby," he growled against her soft lips.

She barely heard him. Her blood was singing in her veins like a throbbing chorus. Her arms went around his neck in a stranglehold. She pushed up against him, forcing into his mouth in urgency.

His arms swallowed her up whole. The kiss was slow, deep, hungry. It was invasive. Her whole body began to throb with delight. It began to swell. Their earlier kisses had been almost chaste. These were erotic. They were…narcotic.

A soft little cry of pleasure went from her mouth into his and managed to penetrate the fog of desire she was drowning him in.

He jerked back from her as if he'd been stung. He fought to keep his inner turmoil from showing, his weakness from being visible to her. His big hands caught her waist and pushed her firmly away.

"I know," she said breathlessly. "You think I've had snakebite on my lip and you were only trying to draw out the poison."

He burst out laughing in spite of himself.

She swallowed hard and backed away another step. "Just think how Julie Merrill would react if she saw you kissing me."

That wiped the smile off his face. "That wasn't a kiss," he said.

"No kidding?" She touched her swollen mouth ironically. "I'll bet Julie could even give you lessons."

"Don't talk about her like that," he warned.

"You think she's honest and forthright, because you are," she said, a little breathless. "You're forgetting that her father is a career politician. They both know how to bend the truth without breaking it, how to influence public opinion."

"Politics is a science," he retorted.

"It can be a horrible corruption, as well," she reminded him. "Calhoun Ballenger has taken a lot of heat from them, even a sexual harassment charge that had no basis in fact. Fortunately, people around here know better, and it backfired. It only made Senator Merrill look bad."

His eyes began to glitter. "That wasn't fiction. The woman swore it happened."

"She was one of Julie's cousins," she said with disgust.

He looked as if he hadn't known that. He scowled, but he didn't answer her.

"Julie thinks my brother and I are so far beneath her that we aren't even worth mentioning," she continued, folding her arms over her chest. "She chooses her friends by their social status and bank accounts. Curt and I are losers in her book and she doesn't think we're fit to associate with you. She'll find a way to push you right out of our lives."

"I don't have social status, but I'm welcome in their home," he said flatly.

"There's an election coming up, they don't have enough money to win it, but you do. They'll take your money and make you feel like an equal until you're not needed anymore. Then you'll be out on your ear.

You don't come from old money, Jordan, even if you're rich now..."

"You don't know a damned thing about what I come from," he snapped.

The furious statement caught her off guard. She knew Jordan had made his own fortune, but he never spoke about his childhood. His mother worked as a housekeeper. Everybody knew it. He sounded as if he couldn't bear to admit his people were only laborers.

"I didn't mean to be insulting," she began slowly.

"Hell! You're doing your best to turn me against Julie. She said you would," he added. "She said something else, too—that you're involved with Harley Fowler."

She refused to react to that. "Harley's sweet. He defended me when Julie was insulting me."

That was a sore spot, because Jordan hadn't really heard what Julie was saying until it was too late. He didn't like Harley, anyway.

"Harley's a nobody."

"Just like me," she retorted. "I'd much rather have Harley than you, Jordan," she added. "He may be just a working stiff, but he's got more class than you'll ever have, even if you hang out with the Merrills for the next fifty years!"

That did it. He gave her a furious glare, spit out

a word that would have insulted Satan himself and marched right out the door.

"And stay out!" she called after it slammed.

Kemp stuck his head out of his office door and stared at her. "Are you that same shy, introverted girl who came to work here last year?"

She grinned at him through her heartbreak. "You're rubbing off on me, Mr. Kemp," she remarked.

He laughed curtly and went back into his office.

Later, Libby was miserable. They'd exhumed her father's body and taken it up to the state crime lab in Austin for tests.

Curt was furious when she told him that Jordan had been to her office to apologize for the Merrill girl.

"As if she'd ever apologize to the likes of us," he said angrily. "And Jordan just stood by and let her insult you in the café without saying a word!"

She gaped at him. "How did you know that?"

"Harley Fowler came by where I was working this morning to tell me about it. He figured, rightly, that you'd try to keep it to yourself." He sank down into a chair. "I gave Jordan notice this afternoon. In two weeks, I'm out of there."

She grimaced. "But, Curt, where will you go?"

"Right over to Duke Wright's place," he replied with

a smile. "I already lined up a job and I'll get a raise, to boot."

"That's great," she said, and meant it.

"We'll be fine. Don't worry about it." He sighed. "It's so much lately, isn't it, sis? But we'll survive. We will!"

"I know that, Curt. I'm not worried."

But she was. She hated being enemies with Jordan, who was basically a kind and generous man. She was furious with the Merrills for coming between them for such a selfish reason. They only wanted Jordan's money for the old man's reelection campaign. They didn't care about Jordan. But perhaps he was flattered to be included in such high society, to be asked to hang out with their friends and acquaintances.

But Libby knew something about the people the Merrills associated with that, perhaps, Jordan didn't. Many of them were addicts, either to liquor or drugs. They did nothing for the community; only for themselves. They wanted to know the right people, be seen in the right places, have money that showed when people looked. But to Libby, who loved her little house and little ranch, it seemed terribly artificial.

She didn't have much but she was happy with her life. She enjoyed planting things and watching them grow. She liked teaching Vacation Bible School in the summer and working in the church nursery with little children. She liked cooking food to carry to bereaved families when relatives died. She liked helping out with church bazaars, donating time to the local soup kitchen. She didn't put on airs, but people seemed to like her just the way she was.

Certainly Harley Fowler did. He'd come over to see her the day after Julie's attack in the café, to make sure she was all right. He'd asked her out to eat the following Saturday night.

"Only to Shea's," he chuckled. "I just paid off a new transmission for my truck and I'm broke."

She'd grinned at him. "That's okay. I'm broke, too!"

He shook his head, his eyes sparkling as he looked down at her with appreciation. "Libby, you're my kind of people."

"Thanks, Harley."

"Say, can you dance?"

She blinked. "Well, I can do a two-step."

"That's good enough." He chuckled. "I've been taking these dance courses on the side."

"I know. I heard about the famous waltz with Janie Brewster at the Cattleman's Ball last year."

He smiled sheepishly. "Well, now I'm working on

the jitterbug and I hear that Shea's live band can play that sort of thing."

"You can teach me to jitterbug, Harley," she agreed at once. "I'd love to go dancing with you."

He looked odd. "Really?"

She nodded and smiled. "Really."

"Then I'll see you Saturday about six. We can eat there, too."

"Suits me. I'll leave supper for Curt in the refrigerator. That was really nice of you to go to bat for him with your boss, Harley," she added seriously. "Thanks."

He shrugged. "Mr. Parks wasn't too pleased with the way Powell's sucking up to the Merrills, either," he said. "He knows things about them."

"So do I," she replied. "But Jordan doesn't take well-meant advice."

"His problem," Harley said sharply.

She nodded. "Yes, Harley. It's his problem. I'll see you Saturday!" she added, laughing.

When she told Curt about the upcoming date, he seemed pleased. "It's about time you went out and had some fun for a change."

"I like Harley a lot," she told her brother.

He searched her eyes knowingly. "But he's not Jordan."

She turned away. "Jordan made his choice. I'm making mine." She smiled philosophically. "I dare say we'll both be happy!"

Chapter Six

Libby and Harley raised eyebrows at Shea's Roadhouse and Bar with their impromptu rendition of the jitterbug. It was a full house, too, on a Saturday night. At least two of the Tremayne brothers were there with their wives, and Calhoun Ballenger and his wife, Abby, were sitting at a table nearby with Leo Hart and his wife, Janie.

"I'm absolutely sure that Calhoun's going to win the state senate seat," Harley said in Libby's ear when they were seated again, drinking iced tea and eating hamburgers. "It looks like he's going to get some support from the Harts."

"Is Mr. Parks in his corner, too?" she asked.

He nodded. "All the way. The political landscape has been changing steadily for the past few years, but old man Merrill just keeps going with his old agenda. He hasn't got a clue what the voters want anymore. And, more important, he doesn't control them through his powerful friends."

"You'd think his daughter would be forward thinking," she pointed out.

He didn't say anything. But his face was eloquent.

"Somebody said she was thinking of running for public office in Jacobsville," she began.

"No name identification," Harley said at once. "You have to have it to win an office. Without it, all the money in the world won't get you elected."

"You seem to know something about politics," she commented.

He averted his eyes. "Do I?" he mused.

Harley never talked about his family, or his past. He'd shown up at Cy Parks's place one day and proved himself to be an exceptional cowboy, but nobody knew much about him. He'd gone on a gigantic drug bust with Jacobsville's ex-mercenaries and he had a reputation for being a tough customer. But he was as mysterious in his way as the town's police chief, Cash Grier.

"Wouldn't you just know they'd show up and spoil

everything?" Harley said suddenly, glaring toward the door.

Sure enough, there was Jordan Powell in an expensive Western-cut sports coat and Stetson and boots, escorting pretty Julie Merrill in a blue silk dress that looked simple and probably cost the earth.

"Doesn't she look expensive?" Harley mused.

"She probably is," Libby said, trying not to look and sound as hurt as she really was. It killed her to see Jordan there with that terrible woman.

"She's going to find out, pretty soon, that she's the equivalent of three-day-old fish with this crowd," Harley predicted coolly, watching her stick her nose up at the Ballengers as she passed them.

"I just hope she doesn't drag Jordan down with her," Libby said softly. "He started out like us, Harley," she added. "He was just a working cowboy with ambition."

Jordan seated Julie and shot a cool glance in Harley and Libby's direction, without even acknowledging them. He sat down, placing his Stetson on a vacant chair and motioned a waiter.

"Did you want something stronger to drink?" Harley asked her.

She grinned at him. "I don't have a head for liquor, Harley. I'd rather stick to iced tea, if you don't mind."

"So would I," he confided, motioning for a waiter.

The waiter, with a fine sense of irony, walked right past Jordan to take Harley's order. Julie Merrill was sputtering like a stepped-on garden hose.

"Two more iced teas, Charlie," Harley told the waiter. "And thanks for giving us preference."

"Oh, I know who the best people are, Harley," the boy said with a wicked grin. And he walked right past Jordan and Julie again, without even looking at them. A minute later, Jordan got up and stalked over to the counter to order their drinks.

"He'll smolder for the rest of the night over that," Harley mused. "So will she, unless I miss my guess. Isn't it amazing," he added thoughtfully, "that a man with as much sense as Jordan Powell can't see right through that debutante?"

"How is it that you can?" Libby asked him curiously.

He shrugged. "I know politicians all too well," he said, and for a moment, his expression was distant. "Old man Merrill has been hitting the bottle pretty hard lately," he said. "It isn't going to sit well with his constituents that he got pulled over and charged with drunk driving by Jacobsville's finest."

"Do you think they'll convict him?" she wondered aloud.

"You can bet money on it," Harley replied. "The world has shifted ten degrees. Local politicians don't meet in parked cars and make policy anymore. The sunshine laws mean that the media get wind of anything crooked and they report it. Senator Merrill has been living in the past. He's going to get a hell of a wake-up call at the primary election, when Calhoun Ballenger knocks him off the Democratic ballot as a contender."

"Mr. Ballenger looks like a gentleman," Libby commented, noticing the closeness of Calhoun and his brunette wife, Abby. "He and his wife have been married a long time, haven't they?"

"Years," Harley said. "He and Justin are honest and hardworking men. They came up from nothing, too, although Justin's wife, Shelby, was a Jacobs before she married him," he reminded her. "A direct descendant of Big John Jacobs. But don't you think either of the Ballenger brothers would have been taken in by Julie Merrill, even when they were still single."

She paused to thank the waiter, who brought their two glasses of tall, cold iced tea. Jordan was still waiting for his order at the counter, while Julie glared at Libby and Harley.

"She's not quite normal, is she?" Libby said quietly. "I mean, that outburst in Barbara's Café was so… violent."

"People on drugs usually are violent," Harley replied. "And irrational." He looked right into Libby's eyes. "She's involved in some pretty nasty stuff, Libby. I can't tell you what I know, but Jordan is damaging himself just by being seen in public with her. The campaigns will get hot and heavy later this month and some dirty linen is about to be exposed to God and the general public."

Libby was concerned. "Jordan's a good man," she said quietly, her eyes going like homing pigeons to his lean, handsome face.

He caught her looking at him and glared. Julie, seeing his attention diverted, looked, too.

Once he returned to the table Julie leaned over and whispered something to Jordan that made him give Libby a killing glare before he started ignoring her completely.

"Watch your back," Harley told Libby as he sipped his iced tea. "She considers you a danger to her plans with Jordan. She'll sell you down the river if she can."

She sighed miserably. "First my stepmother, now Julie," she murmured. "I feel like I've got a target painted on my forehead."

"We all have bad times," Harley told her gently, and slid a big hand over one of hers where it lay on the table. "We get through them."

"You, too?" she wondered aloud.

"Yeah. Me, too," he replied, and he smiled at her.

Neither of them saw the furious look on Jordan Powell's face, or the calculating look on Julie's.

The following week, when Libby went to Barbara's Café for lunch, she walked right into Jordan Powell on the sidewalk. He was alone, as she was, and his expression made her feel cold all over.

"What's this about you going up to San Antonio for the night with Harley last Wednesday?" he asked bluntly.

Libby couldn't even formulate a reply for the shock. She'd driven Curt over to Duke Wright's place early Wednesday afternoon and from there she'd driven up to San Antonio to obtain some legal documents from the county clerk's office for Mr. Kemp. She hadn't even seen Harley there.

"I thought you were pure as the driven snow," Jordan continued icily. His dark eyes narrowed on her shocked face. "You put on a good act, don't you, Libby? I don't need to be a mind reader to know why, either. I'm rich and you and your brother are about to lose your ranch."

"Janet hasn't started probate yet," she faltered.

"That's not what I hear."

"I don't care what you hear," she told him flatly. "Neither Curt nor I care very much what you think, either, Jordan. But you're going to run into serious problems if you hang out with Julie Merrill until her father loses the election."

He glared down at her. "He isn't going to lose," he assured her.

She hated seeing him be so stubborn, especially when she had at least some idea of what Julie was going to drag him down into. She moved a step closer, her green eyes soft and beseeching. "Jordan, you're an intelligent man," she began slowly. "Surely you can see what Julie wants you for…"

A worldly look narrowed his eyes as they searched over her figure without any reaction at all. "Julie wants me, all right," he replied, coolly. "That's what's driving you to make these wild comments, isn't it? You're jealous because I'm spending so much time with her."

She didn't dare let on what she was feeling. She forced a careless smile. "Am I? You think I don't know when a man is teasing me?"

"You know more than I ever gave you credit for

and that's the truth," he said flatly. "You and Harley Fowler." He made it sound like an insult.

"Harley is a fine man," she said, defending him.

"Obviously you think so, or you wouldn't be shacking up with him," he accused. "Does your brother know?"

"I'm a big girl now," she said, furious at the insinuation.

"Both of you had better remember that I make a bad enemy," he told her. "Whatever happens with your ranch, I don't want to have a subdivision full of people on my border."

He didn't know that Libby and Curt had already discussed how they were going to manage without their father's life insurance policy to pay the mortgage payments that were still owed. Riddle had taken out a mortgage on the ranch to buy Janet's Mercedes. Janet had waltzed off with the money and the private detective Jordan had recommended to Mr. Kemp had drawn a blank when he tried to dig into Janet's past. The will hadn't been probated, either, so there was no way Riddle Collins's children could claim any of their inheritance with which to pay bills or make that huge mortgage payment. They'd had to let their only helper—their part-time cowboy—go, for lack of funds to pay him. They only had one horse left and they'd had to sell off most of their cattle. The only money coming in right now was what Curt and Libby earned in their respective jobs, and it wasn't much.

Of course, Libby wasn't going to share that information with a hostile Jordan Powell. Things were so bad that she and Curt might have to move off the ranch anyway because they couldn't make that mortgage payment at the end of the month. It was over eight hundred dollars. Their collective take-home pay wouldn't amount to that much and there were still other bills owing. Janet had run up huge bills while Riddle was still alive.

Jordan felt sick at what he was saying to Libby. He was jealous of Harley Fowler, furiously jealous. He couldn't bear the thought of Libby in bed with the other man. She wasn't even denying what Julie had assured him had happened between them. Libby, in Harley's arms, kissing him with such hunger that his toes tingled. Libby, loving Harley…

Jordan ached to have her for himself. He dreamed of her every night. But Libby was with Harley now. He'd lost his chance. He couldn't bear it!

"Is Harley going to loan you enough money to keep the ranch going until Janet's found?" he wondered aloud. He smiled coldly. "He hasn't got two dimes to rub together, from what I hear."

Libby remembered the mortgage payments she couldn't make. Once, she might have bent her pride enough to ask Jordan to loan it to her. Not anymore. Not after what he'd said to her.

She lifted her chin. "That's not your business, Jordan," she said proudly.

"Don't expect me to lend it to you," he said for spite.

"Jordan, I wouldn't ask you for a loan if the house burned down," she assured him, unflinching. "Now, if you'll excuse me, I'm using up my lunch hour."

She started to go around him, but he caught her arm and marched her down the little alley between her office and the town square. It was an alcove, away from traffic, with no prying eyes.

While she was wondering what was on his mind, he backed her up against the cold brick and brought his mouth down on her lips.

She pushed at his chest, but he only gave her his weight, pressing her harder into the wall. His own body was almost as hard, especially when his hips shifted suddenly, and lowered squarely against her own. She shivered at the slow caress of his hands on her rib cage while the kiss went on and on. She couldn't breathe. She didn't want to breathe. Her body ached for something more than this warm, heady torment.

She moaned huskily under the hard, furious press of his mouth.

He lifted his head a bare inch and looked into her wide green eyes with possession and desire. It never stopped. He couldn't get within arm's length of her without giving in to temptation. Did she realize? No. She had no idea. She thought it was a punishment for her harsh words. It was more. It was anguish.

"You still want me," he ground out. "Do you think I don't know?"

"What?" she murmured, her eyes on his mouth. She could barely think at all. She felt his body so close that when he breathed, her chest deflated. Her breasts ached at the warm pressure of his broad chest. It was heaven to be so close to him. And she didn't dare let it show.

"Are you trying to prove something?" she murmured, forcing her hands to push instead of pull at his shoulders.

"Only that Harley isn't in my league," he said in a husky, arrogant tone, as he bent again and forced her mouth open under the slow, exquisite skill of his kisses. "In fact," he bit off against her lips, "neither are you, cupcake."

She wanted to come back with some snappy reply. She really did. But the sensations he was arousing were hypnotic, drugging. She felt him move one long, powerful jean-clad leg in between both of hers. It was broad daylight, in the middle of town. He was making love to her against a wall. And she didn't care.

She moved against him, her lips welcoming, her hands spreading, caressing, against his rib cage, his chest. There was no tomorrow. There was only Jordan, wanting her.

Her body throbbed in time with her frantic heartbeat. She was hot all over, swelling, aching. She wanted relief. Anything…!

Voices coming close pushed them apart when she would have said that nothing could. Jordan stepped back, his face a rigid mask. She looked up at him, her crushed mouth red from the ardent pressure, her eyes soft and misty and dazed.

Her pocketbook was on the ground. He reached down and handed it back to her, watching as she put the strap over her shoulder and stared up at him, still bemused.

She wanted to tell him that Harley was a better lover, to make some flip remark that would sting him. But she couldn't.

He was in pretty much the same shape. He hated the very thought of Harley. But even through the jealousy, he realized that Libby's responses weren't those of any experienced woman. When Julie kissed him, it was with her whole body. She was more than willing to do anything he liked. But he couldn't take Julie to bed because he didn't want her that way. It was a source of irritation and amazement to him. And to Julie, who made sarcastic remarks about his prowess.

It wasn't a lack of ability. It was just a lack of desire. But he raged with it when he looked at Libby. He'd never wanted a woman to the point of madness until now and she was the one woman he couldn't have.

"Women and their damned ambitions," he said under his breath. "Damn Harley. And damn you, Libby!"

"Damn you, too, Jordan," she said breathlessly. "And don't expect me to drag you into any more alleys and make love to you, if that's going to be your attitude!"

She turned and walked away before he had time to realize what she'd said. He had to bite back a laugh. This was no laughing matter. He had to get a grip on himself before Libby realized what was wrong with him.

After their disturbing encounter, she wondered if she and Curt wouldn't do better to just move off their property and live somewhere else. In fact, she told herself, that might not be a bad idea.

Mr. Kemp didn't agree.

"You have to maintain a presence on the property," he told Libby firmly. "If you move out, Janet might use that against you in court."

"You don't understand," she groaned. "Jordan is driving me crazy. And every time I look out the window, Julie's speeding down the road to Jordan's house."

"Jordan's being conned," he ventured.

"I know that, but he won't listen," Libby said, sitting down heavily behind her desk. "Julie's got him convinced that I'm running wild with Harley Fowler."

"That woman is big trouble," he said. "I'd give a lot to see her forced to admit what she did to the Culbertson girl at that party."

"You think it was her?" she asked, shocked.

He shrugged. "Nobody else had a motive," he said, his eyes narrow and cold. "Shannon Culbertson was running against her for class president and Julie wanted to win. I don't think she planned to kill her. She was going to set her up with one of the boys she was dating and ruin Shannon's reputation. But it backfired. At least, that's my theory. If this gets out it's going to disgrace her father even further."

"Isn't he already disgraced enough because of the drunk-driving charges?" she asked.

"He and his cronies at city hall are trying desperately to get those charges dropped, before they get into some newspaper whose publisher doesn't owe him a favor," Kemp replied, perching on the edge of her desk. "There's a disciplinary hearing at city hall next month for the officers involved. Grier says the council is going to try to have the police officers fired."

She smiled. "I can just see Chief Grier letting that happen."

Kemp chuckled. "I think the city council is going to be in for a big surprise. Our former police chief, Chet Blake, never would buck the council, or stand up for any officer who did something politically incorrect with the city fathers. Grier isn't like his cousin."

"What if they fire him, too?" she asked.

He stood up. "If they even try, there will be a recall of the city council and the mayor," Kemp said simply. "I can almost guarantee it. A lot of people locally are fed up with city management. Solid waste is backing up, there's no provision for water conservation, the fire department hasn't got one piece of modern equipment, and we're losing revenue hand over fist because nobody wants to mention raising taxes."

"I didn't realize that."

"Grier did." He smiled to himself. "He's going to shake up this town. It won't be a bad thing, either."

"Do you think he'll stay?"

Kemp nodded. "He's put down deep roots already,

although I don't think he realizes how deep they go just yet."

Like everyone else in Jacobsville, Libby knew what was going on in Cash Grier's private life. After all, it had been in most of the tabloids. Exactly what the situation was between him and his houseguest, Tippy Moore, was anybody's guess. The couple were equally tight-lipped in public.

"Could I ask you to do something for me, sir?" she asked suddenly.

"Of course."

"Could you find out if they've learned anything about...Daddy at the state crime lab and how much longer it's going to be before they have a report?" she asked.

He frowned. "Good Lord, I didn't realize how long it had been since the exhumation," he said. "Certainly. I'll get right on it, in fact."

"Thanks," she said.

He shrugged. "No problem." He got to his feet and hesitated. "Have you talked to Violet lately?" he asked reluctantly.

"She's lost weight and she's having her hair frosted," she began.

His lips made a thin line. "I don't want to know

about her appearance. I only wondered how she likes her new job."

"A lot," she replied. She pursed her lips. "In fact, she and my brother are going out on a date Saturday night."

"Your brother knows her?" he asked.

She nodded. "He's working for Duke Wright, too…"

"Since when?" he exclaimed. "He was Jordan's right-hand man!"

She averted her eyes. "Not anymore. Jordan said some pretty bad things about me and Curt quit."

Kemp cursed. "I don't understand how a man who was so concerned for both of you has suddenly become an enemy. However," he added, "I imagine Julie Merrill has something to do with his change of heart."

"He's crazy about her, from what we hear."

"He's crazy, all right," he said, turning back toward his office. "He'll go right down the tubes with her and her father if he isn't careful."

"I tried to tell him. He accused me of being jealous."

He glanced back at her. "And you aren't?" he probed softly.

Her face closed up. "What good would it do, Mr. Kemp? Either people like you or they don't."

Kemp had thought, privately, that it was more than liking on Jordan's part. But apparently, he'd been wrong right down the line.

"Bring your pad, if you don't mind, Libby," he said. "I want you to look up a case for me at the courthouse law library."

"Yes, sir," she said, picking up her pad. It was always better to stay busy. That way she didn't have so much time to think.

She was walking into the courthouse when she met Calhoun Ballenger coming out of it. He stopped and grinned at her.

"Just the woman I was looking for," he said. "On the assumption that I win this primary election for the Democratic candidate, how would you like to join my campaign staff in your spare time?"

She caught her breath. "Mr. Ballenger, I'm very flattered!"

"Duke Wright tells me that you have some formidable language skills," he continued. "Not that my secretaries don't, but they've got their hands full right now trying to get people to go to the polls and vote for me in May. I need someone to write publicity for me. Are you interested?"

"You bet!" she said at once.

"Great! Come by the ranch Saturday about one. I've invited a few other people, as well."

"Not…the Merrills or Jordan Powell?" she asked worriedly.

He glowered at her. "I do not invite the political competition to staff meetings," he said with mock hauteur. He grinned. "Besides, Jordan and I aren't speaking."

"That's a relief," she said honestly.

"You're on the wrong side of him, too, I gather?"

She nodded. "Me and half the town."

"More than half, if I read the situation right," he said with a sigh. "A handful of very prominent Democrats have changed sides and they're now promoting me." He smiled. "More for our side."

She smiled back. "Exactly! Well, then, I'll see you Saturday."

"I've already invited your boss and Duke Wright, but Duke won't come," he added heavily. "I invited Grier, and Duke's still browned off about the altercation he had with our police chief."

"He shouldn't have swung on him," she pointed out.

"I'm sure he knows that now," he agreed, his eyes twinkling. "See you."

She gave him a wave and walked into the courthouse

lobby. Jordan Powell was standing there with a receipt for his automobile tag and glaring daggers at Libby.

"You're on a friendly basis with Calhoun Ballenger, I gather?" he asked.

"I'm going to work on his campaign staff," she replied with a haughty smile.

"He's going to lose," he told her firmly. "He doesn't have name identification."

She smiled at him. "He hasn't been arrested for drunk driving, to my knowledge," she pointed out.

His eyes flashed fire. "That's a frame," he returned. "Grier's officers planted evidence against him."

She glared back. "Chief Grier is honest and open-handed," she told him. "And his officers would never be asked to do any such thing!"

"They'll be out of work after that hearing," he predicted.

"You swallow everything Julie tells you, don't you, Jordan?" she asked quietly. "Maybe you should take a look at the makeup of our city council. Those were people who once owned big businesses in Jacobsville and had tons of money. But their companies are all going downhill and they're short of ready cash. They aren't the people who have the power today. And if you think Chief Grier is going to stand by and let them railroad his employees, you're way off base."

Jordan didn't reply at once. He stared at Libby until her face colored.

"I never thought you'd go against me, after all I've done for you and Curt," he said.

She was thinking the same thing. It made her ashamed to recall how he'd tried to help them both when Janet was first under suspicion of murder and fraud. But he'd behaved differently since he'd gotten mixed up with Senator Merrill's daughter. He'd changed, drastically.

"You have done a lot for us," she had to agree. "We'll always be grateful for it. But you took sides against us first, Jordan. You stood by with your mouth closed in Barbara's Café and let Julie humiliate me."

Jordan's eyes flashed. It almost looked like guilt. "You had enough support."

"Yes, from Harley Fowler. At least someone spoke up for me."

He looked ice-cold. "You were rude to Julie first, in your own office."

"Why don't you ask Mr. Kemp who started it?" she replied.

"Kemp hates her," he said bluntly. "He'd back your story. I'm working for Senator Merrill and I'm going to get him reelected. You just side with the troublemakers and do what you please. But don't expect me to come around with my hat in my hand."

"I never did, Jordan," she said calmly. "I'm just a nobody around Jacobsville and I'm very aware of it. I'm not sophisticated or polished or rich, and I have no manners. On the other hand, I have no aspirations to high society, in case you wondered."

"Good thing. You'd never fit in," he bit off.

She smiled sadly. "And you think you will?" she challenged softly. "You may have better table manners than I do—and more money—but your father was poor. None of your new high-class friends is ever going to forget that. Even if you do."

He said something nasty. She colored a little, but she didn't back down.

"Don't worry, I know my place, Mr. Powell," she replied, just to irritate him. "I'm a minor problem that you've put out beside the road. I won't forget."

She was making him feel small. He didn't like it.

"Thank you for being there when we needed you most," she added quietly. "We aren't going to sell our land to developers."

"If you ever get title to it," he said coldly.

She shrugged. "That's out of our hands."

"Kemp will do what he can for you," he said, feeling guilty, because he knew that she and Curt had no money for attorneys. He'd heard that Janet was still missing and that Kemp's private detective had drawn a blank when he looked into her past. Libby and Curt must be worried sick about money.

"Yes, Mr. Kemp will do what he can for us." She studied his face, so hard and uncompromising, and wondered what had happened to make them so distant after the heated promises of those kisses they'd exchanged only weeks before.

"Curt likes working for Wright, I suppose?" he asked reluctantly.

She nodded. "He's very happy there."

"Julie had a cousin who trains horses. He's won trophies in steeplechase competition. He's working in Curt's place now, with my two new Thoroughbreds."

"I suppose Julie wants to keep it all in the family," she replied.

He glared down at her. "Keep all what in the family?"

"Your money, Jordan," she said sweetly.

"You wouldn't have turned it down, if I'd given you the chance," he accused sarcastically. "You were laying it on thick."

"Who was kissing whom in the alley?" she returned huskily.

He didn't like remembering that. He jerked his

wide-brimmed hat down over his eyes. "A moment of weakness. Shouldn't have happened. I'm not free anymore."

Insinuating that he and Julie were much more than friends, Libby thought correctly. She looked past Jordan to Julie, who was just coming out of the courthouse looking elegant and cold as ice. She saw Libby standing with Jordan and her lips collided furiously.

"Jordan! Let's go!" she called to him angrily.

"I was only passing the time of day with him, Julie," Libby told the older woman with a vacant smile.

"You keep your sticky hands to yourself, you little liar," Julie told her as she passed on the steps. "Jordan is mine!"

"No doubt you mean his money is yours, right?" Libby ventured.

Julie drew back her hand and slapped Libby across the cheek as hard as she could. "Damn you!" she raged.

Libby was shocked at the unexpected physical reply, but she didn't retaliate. She just stood there, straight and dignified, with as much pride as she could muster. Around the two women, several citizens stopped and looked on with keen disapproval.

One of them was Officer Dana Hall, one of the two

police officers who had arrested Senator Merrill for drunk driving.

She walked right up to Libby. "That was assault, Miss Collins," she told Libby. "If you want to press charges, I can arrest Miss Merrill on the spot."

"Arrest!" Julie exploded. "You can't arrest me!"

"I most certainly can," Officer Hall replied. "Miss Collins, do you want to press charges?"

Libby stared at Julie Merrill with cold pleasure, wondering how it would look on the front page of Jacobsville's newspaper.

"Wouldn't that put another kink in your father's reelection campaign?" Libby ventured softly.

Julie looked past Libby and suddenly burst into tears. She threw herself into Jordan Powell's arms. "Oh, Jordan, she's going to have me arrested!"

"No, she's not," Jordan said curtly. He glanced at Libby. "She wouldn't dare."

Libby cocked her head. "I wouldn't?" She glared at him. "Look at my cheek, Jordan."

It was red. There was a very obvious handprint on it.

"She insulted me," Julie wailed. "I had every right to hit her back!"

"She never struck you, Miss Merrill," Officer Hall

replied coldly. "Striking another person is against the law, regardless of the provocation."

"I never meant to do it!" Julie wailed. She was sobbing, but there wasn't a speck of moisture under her eyes. "Please, Jordan, don't let them put me in jail!"

Libby and Officer Hall exchanged disgusted looks.

"Men are so damned gullible," Libby remarked with a glare at Jordan, who looked outraged. "All right, Julie, have it your way. But you'd better learn to produce tears as well as broken sobs if you want to convince another woman that you're crying."

"Jordan, could we go now?" Julie sobbed. "I'm just sick…!"

"Not half as sick as you'll be when your father loses the election, Julie," Libby drawled sweetly, and walked up the steps with Officer Hall at her side. She didn't even look at Jordan as she went into the courthouse.

Calhoun Ballenger's meeting with his volunteer staff was a cheerful riot of surprises. Libby found herself working with women she'd known only by name a few months earlier. Now she was suddenly in the cream of society, but with women who didn't snub her or look down their noses at her social position.

Libby was delighted to find herself working with Violet, who'd come straight from her job at Duke Wright's ranch for the meeting.

"This is great!" Violet exclaimed, hugging Libby. "I've missed working with you!"

"I've missed you, too, Violet," Libby assured her. She shook her head as she looked at the other woman. "You look great!"

Violet grinned. She'd dropped at least two dress sizes. She was well-rounded, but no longer obese even to the most critical eye. She'd had her brown hair frosted and it was waving around her face and shoulders. She was wearing a low-cut dress that emphasized the size of her pretty breasts, and her small waist and voluptuous hips, along with high heels that arched her small feet nicely.

"I've worked hard at the gym," Violet confessed. She was still laughing when her eyes collided with Blake Kemp's across the room. The expression left her face. She averted her eyes quickly. "Excuse me, won't you, Libby? I came with Curt. You, uh, don't mind, do you?" she added worriedly.

"Don't be silly," Libby said with a genuine smile. "Curt's nice. So are you. I think you'd make a lovely couple…"

"Still happy with Duke Wright, Miss Hardy?" came a cold, biting comment from Libby's back.

Blake Kemp moved into view, his pale eyes expressive on Violet's pretty figure and the changes in the way she dressed.

"I'm…very happy with him, Mr. Kemp," Violet said, clasping her hands together tightly. "If you'll excuse me…"

"You've lost weight," Kemp said gruffly.

Violet's eyes widened. "And you actually noticed?"

The muscles in his face tautened. "You look… nice."

Violet's jaw dropped. She was literally at a loss for words. Her eyes lifted to Kemp's and they stood staring at each other for longer than was polite, neither speaking or moving.

Kemp shifted restlessly on his long legs. "How's your mother?"

Violet swallowed hard. "She's not doing very well, I'm afraid. You know…about the exhumation?"

Kemp nodded. "They're still in the process of evaluating Curt and Libby's father's remains, as well, at the crime lab. So far, they have nothing to report."

Violet looked beside him at Libby and winced. "I didn't know, Libby. I'm so sorry."

"So am I, for you," Libby replied. "We didn't want to do it, but we had to know for sure."

"Will they really be able to tell anything, after all this time?" Violet asked Kemp, and she actually moved a step closer to him.

He seemed to catch his breath. He was looking at her oddly. "I assume so." His voice was deeper, too. Involuntarily, his lean fingers reached out and touched Violet's long hair. "I like the frosting," he said reluctantly. "It makes your eyes look…bluer."

"Does it?" Violet asked, but her eyes were staring into his as if she'd found treasure there.

With an amused smile, Libby excused herself and joined her brother, who was talking to the police chief.

Cash Grier noticed her approach and smiled. He looked older somehow and there were new lines around his dark eyes.

"Hi, Chief," she greeted him. "How's it going?"

"Don't ask," Curt chuckled. "He's in the middle of a controversy."

"So are we," Libby replied. "We're on the wrong side of the election and Jordan Powell is furious at us."

"We're on the right side," Cash said carelessly. "The city fathers are in for a rude awakening." He leaned down. "I have friends in high places." He paused. "I also have friends in low places." He grinned.

Libby and Curt burst out laughing, because they recognized the lines from a country song they'd all loved.

Calhoun Ballenger joined them, clapping Cash on the back affectionately. "Thanks for coming," he said. "Even if it is putting another nail in your coffin with the mayor."

"The mayor can kiss my…" Cash glanced at Libby and grinned. "Never mind."

They all laughed.

"She's lived with me all her life," Curt remarked. "She's practically unshockable."

"How's Tippy?" Calhoun asked.

Cash smiled. "Doing better, thanks. She'd have come, too, but she's still having a bad time."

"No wonder," Calhoun replied, recalling the ordeal Tippy had been through in the hands of kidnappers. It had been in all the tabloids. "Good thing they caught the culprits who kidnapped her."

"Isn't it?" Cash said, not giving away that he'd caught them, with the help of an old colleague. "Nice turnout, Calhoun," he added, looking around them. "I thought you invited Judd."

"I did," Calhoun said at once, "but the twins have a cold."

"Damn!" Cash grimaced. "I told Judd that he and Crissy needed to stop running that air conditioner all night!"

"It wasn't that," Calhoun confided. "They went to the Coltrains' birthday party for their son—his second birthday—and that's where they got the colds."

Cash sighed. "Poor babies."

"He's their godfather," Calhoun told Libby and Curt. "But he thinks Jessamina belongs to him."

"She does," Cash replied haughtily.

Nobody mentioned what the tabloids had said—
that Tippy had been pregnant with Cash's child a few
weeks earlier and lost it just before her ordeal with the
kidnapping.

Libby diplomatically changed the subject. "Mr. Kemp
said that you can put up campaign posters in our office
windows," she told Calhoun, "and Barbara's willing
to let you put up as many as you like in her café," she
added with a grin. "She said she's never going to forgive
Julie Merrill for making a scene there."

Calhoun chuckled. "I've had that sort of offer all
week," he replied. "Nobody wants Senator Merrill back
in office, but the city fathers have thrown their support behind him and he thinks he's unbeatable. What
we really need is a change in city government, as well.
We're on our second mayor in eight months and this
one is afraid of his own shadow."

"He's also Senator Merrill's nephew," Curt added.

"Which is why he's trying to make my officers
back down on those DWI charges," Cash Grier
interposed.

"I'd like to see it. Carlos Garcia wouldn't back down
from anybody," Calhoun mused. "Or Officer Dana Hall,
either."

"Ms. Hall came to my assistance at the courthouse
this week," Libby volunteered. "Julie Merrill slapped

me. Officer Hall was more than willing to arrest her, if I'd agreed to press charges."

"Good for Dana," Cash returned. "You be careful, Ms. Collins," he added firmly. "That woman has poor impulse control. I wouldn't put it past her to try and run somebody down."

"Neither would I," Curt added worriedly. "She's already told Jordan some furious lies about us and he believes her."

"She can be very convincing," Libby said, not wanting to verbally attack Jordan even now.

"It may get worse now, with all of you backing me," Calhoun told the small group. "I won't have any hard feelings if you want to withdraw your support."

"Do I look like the sort of man who backs away from trouble?" Cash asked lazily, with a grin.

"Speaking of Duke Wright," Libby murmured dryly, "he's throwing his support to Mr. Ballenger, too. But he had, uh, reservations about coming to the meeting."

Cash chuckled. "I don't hold grudges."

"Yes, but he does," Calhoun said on a chuckle. "He'll get over it. He's got some personal problems right now."

"Don't we all?" Cash replied wistfully, and his dark eyes were troubled.

Libby and Curt didn't add their two cents' worth, but they exchanged quiet looks.

The campaign was winding down for the primary, but all the polls gave Calhoun a huge lead over Merrill. Printed materials were ordered, along with buttons, pencils, bumper stickers and key chains. There was enough promotional matter to blanket the town and in the days that followed, Calhoun's supporters did exactly that in Jacobs County and the surrounding area in the state senatorial district that Merrill represented.

Julie Merrill was acting as her father's campaign manager and she was coordinating efforts for promotion with a group of teenagers she'd hired. Some of them were delinquents and there was a rash of vandalisms pertaining to the destruction of Calhoun's campaign posters.

Cash Grier, predictably, went after the culprits and rounded them up. He got one to talk and the newspapers revealed that Miss Merrill had paid the young man to destroy Calhoun's campaign literature. Julie denied it. But the vandalism stopped.

Meanwhile, acting mayor Ben Brady was mounting a fervent defense for Senator Merrill on the drunk-driving charges and trying to make things hot for the two officers. He ordered them suspended and tried to get the city council to back him up.

Cash got wind of it and phoned Simon Hart, the state's attorney general. Simon phoned the city attorney and they had a long talk. Soon afterward, the officers were notified that they could stay on the job until the hearing the following month.

Meanwhile, the state crime lab revealed the results of its report to Blake Kemp. He walked up to Libby's desk while she was on the phone and waited impatiently for her to hang up.

"They can't find any evidence of foul play, Libby," he said at once.

"And if there was any, they would?" she asked quickly.

He nodded. "I'm almost certain of it. The crime lab verified our medical examiner's diagnosis of myocardial infarction. So Janet's off the hook for that one, at least."

Libby sat back with a long sigh and closed her eyes. "Thank God. I couldn't have lived with it if she'd poisoned Daddy and we never knew."

He nodded. "On the other hand, they hit pay dirt with Violet's father," he added.

She sat up straight. "Poison?"

"Yes," he said heavily. "I'm not going to phone her.

I'm going over to Duke Wright's place to tell her in person. Then I'll take her home to talk to her mother. She'll need someone with her."

Yes, she would, and Libby was secretly relieved that Kemp was going to be the person. Violet would need a shoulder to cry on.

"I'll phone Curt and tell him," she said.

"Libby, give me half an hour first," he asked quietly. "I don't want him to tell Violet."

She wondered why, but she wasn't going to pry. "Okay."

He managed a brief smile. "Thanks."

"What about Janet?" she wondered miserably. "They still haven't found her."

"They will. Now all we need is a witness who can place her with Mr. Hardy the night of his death, and we can have her arrested and charged with murder," he replied.

"Chance would be a fine thing, Mr. Kemp," she said heavily.

"Don't give up hope," he instructed. "She's not going to get away with your inheritance. I promise."

She managed a smile. "Thanks."

But she wasn't really convinced. She went home that afternoon feeling lost and alone. She'd told Curt the good news after Violet had gone home with Kemp. Curt had been as relieved as she had, but there was still the problem of probate. Everything was in Janet's name, as their father had instructed. Janet had the insurance money. Nobody could do anything with the estate until the will was probated and Janet had to sign the papers for that. It was a financial nightmare.

There was a message on the answering machine when Libby got home. She pushed the Play button and her heart sank right to her ankles.

"This is the loan officer at Jacobsville Savings and Loan," came the pleasant voice. "We just wanted to remind you that your loan payment was due three days ago. Please call us if there's a problem." The caller gave her name and position and her telephone number. The line went dead.

Libby sat down beside the phone and just stared at it. Curt had told her already that they weren't going to be able to make the payment. Jordan had assured her that he wasn't going to loan her the money to pay it. There was nobody else they would feel comfortable asking. She put her face in her hands and let the tears fall. The financial establishment would repossess the ranch. It wouldn't matter where Janet was or what state the probate action was in. They were going to lose their home.

* * *

She went out to the barn and ran the currycomb over Bailey, her father's horse. He was the last horse they had.

The barn leaked. It was starting to rain and Libby felt raindrops falling on her shoulder through a rip in the tin roof from a small tornado that had torn through a month earlier. The straw on the floor of the barn needed changing, but the hay crop had drowned in the flooding. They'd have to buy some. Libby looked down at her worn jeans, at the small hand resting on them. The tiger's eye ring her father had given her looked ominous in the darkened barn. She sighed and turned back to the horse.

"Bailey, I don't know what we're going to do," she told the old horse, who neighed as if he were answering her.

The sound of a vehicle pulling up in the yard diverted her. She looked down the long aisle of the barn to see Jordan's pickup truck sitting at the entrance. Her heart skipped as he got out and came striding through the dirty straw, his cotton shirt speckled with raindrops that had escaped the wide brim of his white straw hat.

"What do you want?" she asked, trying to ignore him to finish her grooming job on the horse.

"My two new Thoroughbreds are missing."

She turned, the currycomb suspended in her small hand. "And you think we took them?" she asked incredulously. "You honestly think we'd steal from you, even if we were starving?"

He averted his face, as if the question had wounded him.

"Please leave," she said through her teeth.

He rammed his hands into his pockets and moved a step closer, looking past her to Bailey. "That horse is useless for ranch work. He's all of twenty."

"He's my horse," she replied. "I'm not getting rid of him, whatever happens."

She felt his lean, powerful body at her back. "Libby," he began. "About that bank loan…"

"Curt and I are managing just fine, thanks," she said without turning.

His big, strong hands came down heavily on her shoulders, making her jump. "The bank president is a good friend of the Merrills."

She pulled away from him and looked up, her unspoken fears in her green eyes. "They can't do anything to us without Janet," she told him. "She has legal power of attorney."

"Damn it, I know that!" he muttered. "But it's not

going to stop the bank from foreclosing, don't you see? You can't make the loan payment!"

"What business is that of yours?" she asked bitterly.

He drew in a slow breath. "I can talk to the president of the Jacobsville Merchant Bank for you," he said. "He might be willing to work out something for the land. You and Curt can't work it, anyway, and you don't have the capital to invest in it. The best you could do is sell off your remaining cattle and give it up."

She couldn't even manage words. She had no options at all and he had to know it. She could almost hate him.

"We can't sell anything," she said harshly. "I told you, Janet has power of attorney. And she was named in Daddy's will as the sole holder of the property. We can't even sell a stick of furniture. We're going to have to watch the bank foreclose, Jordan, because Janet has our hands tied. We're going to lose everything Daddy worked for, all his life…"

Her lower lip trembled. She couldn't even finish the sentence.

Jordan stepped forward and wrapped her up tight in his arms, holding her while she cried. "Damn, what a mess!"

She beat a small fist against his massive chest. "Why?" she moaned. "Why?"

His arms tightened. "I don't know, baby," he whispered at her ear, his voice deep and soothing. "I wish I did."

She nuzzled closer, drowning in the pleasure of being close to him. It had been so long since he'd held her.

His chest rose and fell heavily. "Kemp's detective hasn't tracked her down yet?"

"Not yet. But she didn't...kill Daddy. The autopsy showed that he died of a heart attack."

"That's something, I guess," he murmured.

"But Violet's daddy was poisoned," she added quietly, her eyes open as they stared past Jordan's broad chest toward his truck parked at the front of the barn. "So they'll still get her for murder, if they can ever find her."

"Poor Violet," he said.

"Yes."

His hand smoothed her hair. It tangled in the wavy soft strands. "You smell of roses, Libby," he murmured deeply, and the pressure of his arms changed in some subtle way.

She could feel the sudden tautness of his lean body against her, the increasing warmth of his embrace.

But he'd taken Julie's side against her and she wasn't comfortable being in his arms anymore.

She tried to pull away, but he wouldn't let her.

"Don't fight me," he said gruffly. "You know you don't want to."

"I don't?"

He lifted his head and looked down into her misty and wet green eyes. His voice was deep with feeling. "You haven't stopped wanting me."

"I want hot chocolate, too, Jordan, but it still gives me migraine, so I don't drink it," she said emphatically.

His dark eyebrows lifted. "That's cute. You think you convinced me?"

"Sure," she lied.

He laughed mirthlessly, letting his dark eyes fall to her lips. "Let's see."

He bent, drawing his lips slowly, tenderly, across her mouth in a teasing impression of a kiss. He was lazy and gentle and after a few seconds of imitating a plank of wood, her traitorous body betrayed her.

She relaxed into the heat of his body with a shaky little sigh and found herself enveloped in his arms. He kissed her again, hungrily this time, without the tenderness of that first brief exchange.

She moaned and tried to protest the sudden crush of his lean hand at the base of her spine, rubbing her body against him. But he didn't give her enough breath or strength to protest and the next thing she knew, she was on her back in a stall of fresh hay and his body was completely covering hers.

"No, Jordan," she protested weakly.

"Yes," he groaned. His long leg slid lazily against hers, and between them, while his big, warm hands smoothed blatantly over her rib cage, his thumbs sliding boldly right over her breasts. "Don't think," he whispered against her parted lips. "Just give in. I won't hurt you."

"I know that," she whispered. "But…"

He nibbled on her lower lip. His thumbs edged out gently and found her nipples. They moved lazily, back and forth, coaxing the tips into hard little nubs. She shivered with unexpected pleasure.

He lifted his head and looked into her eyes while he did it again. If she was used to this sort of love play, it certainly didn't show. She was pliable, yielded, absolutely fascinated with what he was doing to her body. She liked it.

That was all he needed to know. His leg became insistent between hers, coaxing them to move apart, to admit the slow, exquisite imprint of his hips between her long legs. It was like that day in the alley beyond her office, when she hadn't cared if all of

Jacobsville walked by while he was pressing her aching body against the brick wall. She was drowning in pleasure.

Surely, she thought blindly, it couldn't be wrong to give in to something so sweet! His hands on her body were producing undreamed of sensations. He was giving her pleasure in hot, sweeping waves. He touched her and she ached for more. He kissed her and she lifted against him to find his mouth and coax it into ardor. One of her legs curled helplessly around his powerful thigh and she moaned when he accepted the silent invitation and moved into near intimacy with her.

He was aroused. He was powerful. She felt the hard thrust of him against her body and she wanted to rip off her clothes and invite his hands, his eyes, his body, into complete surrender with her. She wanted to feel the ecstasy she knew he could give her. He was skilled, masterful. He knew what she needed, what she wanted. He could give her pleasure beyond bearing, she knew it.

His lean hands moved under her blouse, searching for closeness, unfastening buttons, invading lace. She felt his fingers brush tenderly, lovingly, over her bare breasts in an intimacy she'd never shared with anyone.

Her dreams of him had been this explicit, but she'd never thought she would live them in such urgent passion. As he touched her, she arched to help him, moved to encourage him. Her mouth opened wide under his. She felt his tongue suddenly thrust into it with violent need.

She moaned loudly, her fingertips gripping the hard muscle of his upper arms as he thrust her blouse and bra up to her throat and bent at once to put his mouth on her breasts.

The warm, moist contact was shattering. She stiffened with the shock of pleasure it produced. He tasted her in a hot, feverish silence, broken only by his urgent breathing and the rough sigh of her own voice in his ear.

"Yes," he groaned, opening his mouth. "Yes, Libby. Here. Right here. You and me. I can give you more pleasure than damned Harley ever dreamed of giving you!"

Harley. Harley. She felt her body growing cold. "Harley?" she whispered.

He lifted his head and looked down at her breasts with grinding urgency. "He's had you."

"He has not!" she exclaimed, shocked.

He scowled, in limbo, caught between his insane

need to possess her and his jealousy of the other man.

She took advantage of his indecision by jerking out of his arms and pulling her blouse down as she dragged herself out of the stall. She groped for fastenings while she flushed with embarrassment at what she'd just let him do to her.

She looked devastated. Her hair was full of straw, like her clothes. Her green eyes were wild, her face flushed, her mouth swollen.

He got to his feet, still in the grip of passion, and started toward her. His hat was off. His hair was wild, from her searching fingers, and his shirt was half-open over hair-matted muscle.

"Come back here," he said huskily, moving forward.

"No!" she said firmly, shivering. "I'm not standing in for Julie Merrill!"

The words stopped him in his tracks. He hesitated, his brows meeting over turbulent dark eyes.

"Remember Julie? Your girlfriend?" she persisted shakily. Throwing his lover in his face was a way to cover her hurt for the insinuation he'd made about her and Harley. "What in the world would she think if she could see you now?"

He straightened, but with an effort. His body was

raging. He wanted Libby. He'd never wanted anyone, anything, as much as he wanted her.

"Julie has nothing to do with this," he ground out. "I want you!"

"For how long, Jordan?" she asked bitingly. "Ten minutes? Thirty?"

He blinked. His mind wasn't working.

"I am nobody's one-night stand," she flashed at him. "Not even yours!"

He took a deep breath, then another one. He stared at her blankly while he tried to stop thinking about how sweet it was to feel her body under his hands.

"I want you to leave, now," she repeated, folding her arms over her loose bra. She could feel the swollen contours of her breasts and remembered with pure shame how it felt to have him touching and kissing them.

"That isn't what you wanted five minutes ago," he reminded her flatly.

She closed her eyes. "I'm grass-green and stupid," she said curtly. "It wouldn't be the first time an experienced man seduced an innocent girl."

"Don't make stupid jokes," he said icily. "You're no innocent."

"You believe what you like about me, Jordan, it

doesn't matter anymore," she interrupted him. "I've got work to do. Why don't you go home?"

He glared at her, frustrated desire riding him hard. He cursed himself for ruining everything by bringing up Harley Fowler. "You're a hard woman, Libby," he said. "Harder than I ever realized."

"Goodbye, Jordan," she said, and she turned away to pick up the curry comb she'd dropped.

He gave her a furious glare and stormed out of the barn to his truck. Bailey jumped as Jordan slammed the door and left skid marks getting out of the driveway. She relaxed then, grateful that she'd managed to save herself from that masterful seduction. She'd had a close call. She had to make sure that Jordan never got so close to her again. She couldn't trust him. Not now.

Janet was still in hiding before the primary election and probate hadn't begun. But plenty had changed in Jacobsville. Libby and Curt had been forced to move out of the farmhouse where they'd grown up, because the bank had foreclosed.

They hadn't said a word to Jordan about it. Curt moved into the bunkhouse at the Wright ranch where he worked. Libby moved into a boardinghouse where two other Jacobsville career women lived.

Bailey would have had to be boarded and Libby didn't have the money. But she worked out a deal with a dude ranch nearby. Bailey would be used for trail rides for people who were nervous of horses and Libby would help on the weekends. It wasn't the ideal solution, but it was the only one she had. It was a wrench to give up Bailey, even though it wasn't going to be forever.

Jordan and Julie Merrill were apparently engaged. Or so Julie was saying, and she was wearing a huge diamond on her ring finger. Her father was using every dirty trick in the book to gain his party's candidacy.

Julie Merrill was vehemently outspoken about some unnamed dirty tactics being used against her father in the primary election campaign, and she went on television to make accusations against Calhoun Ballenger.

The next morning, Blake Kemp had her served as the defendant in a defamation lawsuit.

"They're not going to win this case," Julie raged at Jordan. "I want you to get me the best attorney in Austin! We're going to put Calhoun Ballenger right in the gutter where he belongs, along with all these jump-up nouveau riche that think they own our county!"

Jordan, who was one of those jump-ups, gave her a curious look. "Excuse me?" he asked coolly.

"Well, I'm not standing by while Ballenger talks my father's constituents into deserting him!"

"You're the one who's been making allegations, Julie," Jordan said quietly. "To anyone who was willing to listen."

She waved that away. "You have to do that to win elections."

"I'm not going to be party to anything dishonest," Jordan said through his teeth.

Julie backed down. She curled against him and sighed. "Okay. I'll tone it down, for your sake. But you aren't going to let Calhoun Ballenger sue me, are you?"

Jordan didn't know what he was going to do. He felt uneasy at Julie's temperament and her tactics. He'd taken her side against Kemp when she told him that one of the boys at her graduation party had put something in the Culbertson girl's drink and she couldn't turn him in. She'd cried about Libby Collins making horrible statements against her. But Libby had never done such a thing before.

He'd liked being Julie's escort, being accepted by the social crowd she ran around with. But it was getting old and he was beginning to believe that Julie was only playing up to him for money to put into her father's campaign. Libby had tried to warn him and he'd jumped down her throat. He felt guilty about that, too. He felt guilty about a lot of things lately.

"Listen," he said. "I think you need to step back and take a good look at what you're doing. Calhoun Ballenger isn't some minor citizen. He and his brother own a feedlot that's nationally known. Besides that, he has the support of most of the people in Jacobsville with money."

"My father has the support of the social set," she began.

"Yes, but Julie, they're the old elite. The demographics have changed in Jacobs County in the past ten years. Look around you. The Harts are a political family from the roots up. Their brother is the state attorney general and he's already casting a serious eye on what's going on in the Jacobsville city council, about those police officers the mayor's trying to suspend."

"They can't do anything about that," she argued.

"Julie, the Harts are related to Chief Grier," he said shortly.

She hesitated. For the first time, she looked uncertain.

"Not only that, they're related to the governor and the vice president. And while it isn't well-known locally, Grier's people are very wealthy."

She sat down. She ran a hand through her blond hair. "Why didn't you say this before?"

"I tried to," he pointed out. "You refused to listen."

"But Daddy can't possibly lose the election," she said with a child's understanding of things. "He's been state senator from this district for years and years."

"And now the voters are looking for some new blood," he told her. "Not only in local government, but in state and national government. You and your father don't really move with the times, Julie."

"Surely, you don't think Calhoun can beat Daddy?" she asked huskily.

"I think he's going to," he replied honestly, ramming his hands into his pockets. "He's way ahead of your father in the polls. You know that. You and your father have made some bad enemies trying to have those police officers fired. You've gotten on the wrong side of not only Cash Grier, but the Harts, as well. There will be repercussions. I've already heard talk of a complete recall of the mayor and the city council."

"But the mayor is Daddy's nephew. How could they...?"

"Don't you know anything about small towns?" he ground out. "Julie, you've spent too much time in Austin with your father and not enough around here where the elections are decided."

"This is just a hick town," she said, surprised. "Why should I care what goes on here?"

Jordan's face hardened. "Because Jacobs County is the biggest county in your father's district. He can't get reelected without it. You've damaged his campaign by the way you've behaved to Libby Collins."

"That nobody?" she scoffed.

"Her father is a direct descendant of old John Jacobs," he pointed out. "They may not have money and they may not be socially acceptable to you and your father, but the Collinses are highly respected here. The reason Calhoun's got such support is because you've tried to hurt Libby."

"But that's absurd!"

"She's a good person," he said, averting his eyes as he recalled his unworthy treatment of her—and of Curt—on Julie's behalf. "She's had some hard knocks recently."

"So have I," Julie said hotly. "Most notably, having a lawsuit filed against me for defamation of character by that lawyer Kemp!" She turned to him. "Are you going to get me a lawyer, or do I have to find my own?"

Jordan was cutting his losses while there was still time. He felt like ten kinds of fool for the way he'd behaved in the past few weeks. "I think you'd better do that yourself," he replied. "I'm not going against Calhoun Ballenger."

She scoffed. "You'll never get that Collins woman to like you again, no matter what you do," she said haughtily. "Or didn't you know that she and her brother have forfeited the ranch to the bank?"

He was speechless. "They've what?"

"Nobody would loan them the money they needed to save it," she said with a cold smile. "So the bank president foreclosed. Daddy had a long talk with him."

He looked furious. His big fists clenched at his hips. "That was low, Julie."

"When you want to win, sometimes you have to fight dirty," she said simply. "You belong to me. I'm not letting some nobody of a little dirt rancher take you away from me. We need you."

"I don't belong to you," he returned, scooping up his hat. "In fact, I've never felt dirtier than I do right now."

She gaped at him. "I beg your pardon! You can't talk to me like that!"

"I just did." He started toward the door.

"You're no loss, Jordan," she yelled after him. "We needed your money, but I never wanted you! You're one of those jump-ups with no decent background. I'm sorry I ever invited you here the first time. I'm ashamed that I told my friends I liked you!"

"That makes two of us," he murmured icily, and he went out the door without a backward glance.

Kemp was going over some notes with Libby when Jordan Powell walked into the office without bothering to knock.

"I'd like to talk to Libby for a minute," he said solemnly, hat in hand.

Libby stared at him blankly. "I can't think what you have to say," she replied. "I'm very busy."

"She is," Kemp replied. "I'm due in court in thirty minutes."

"Then I'll come back in thirty minutes," Jordan replied.

"Feel free, but I won't be here. I have nothing to say to you, Jordan," she told him bluntly. "You turned your back on me when I needed you the most. I don't need you now. I never will again."

"Listen," he began impatiently.

"No." She turned back to Kemp. "What were you saying, boss?"

Kemp hesitated. He could see the pain in Jordan's face and he had some idea that Jordan had just found out the truth about Julie Merrill. He checked his watch. "Listen, I can read your writing. Just give me the pad and I'll get to the courthouse. It's okay," he added when she looked as if he were deserting her to the enemy. "Really."

She bit her lower lip hard. "Okay."

"Thanks," Jordan said stiffly, as Kemp got up from the desk.

"You owe me one," he replied, as he passed the taciturn rancher on the way out the door.

Minutes later, Mabel went into Kemp's office to put some notes on his desk, leaving Jordan and Libby alone.

"I've made some bad mistakes," he began stiffly. He hated apologies. Usually, he found ways not to make them. But he'd hurt Libby too badly not to try.

She was staring at her keyboard, trying not to listen.

"You have to understand what it's been like for me," he said hesitantly. He sat down in a chair next to her desk, with his wide-brimmed hat in his hands. "My people were like yours, poor. My mother had money, but her people disinherited her when she married my dad. I never had two nickels to rub together. I was that Powell kid, whose father worked for wages, whose mother was reduced to working as a housekeeper." He stared at the floor with his pride aching. "I wanted to be somebody, Libby. That's all I ever wanted. Just to have respect from the people who mattered in this town." He shrugged. "I thought going around with Julie would give me that."

"I don't suppose you noticed that her father belongs

to a group of respectable people who no longer have any power around here," she said stiffly.

He sighed. "No, I didn't. I had my head turned. She was beautiful and rich and cultured, and she came at me like a hurricane. I was in over my head before I knew it."

Libby, who wasn't beautiful or rich or cultured, felt her heart breaking. She knew all this, but it hurt to hear him admit it. Because it meant that those hungry, sweet kisses she'd shared with him meant nothing at all. He wanted Julie.

"I've broken it off with her," he said bluntly.

Libby didn't say anything.

"Did you hear me?" he asked impatiently.

She looked up at him with disillusioned eyes. "You believed her. She said I was shacking up with Harley Fowler. She said I attacked her in this office and hurt her feelings. You believed all that, even though you knew me. And when she attacked me in Barbara's Café and on the courthouse steps, you didn't say a thing."

He winced.

"Words don't mean anything, Powell," she said bitterly. "You can sit there and apologize and try to smooth over what you did for the rest of your life, but I won't listen. When I needed you, you turned your back on me."

He drew in a long breath. "I guess I did."

"I can understand that you were flattered by her attention," she said. "But Curt and I have lost everything we had. Our father is dead and we don't even have a home anymore."

He moved his hat in his hands. "You could move in with me."

She laughed bitterly. "Thanks."

"No, listen," he said earnestly, leaning forward.

She held up a hand. "Don't. I've had all the hard knocks I can handle. I don't want anything from you, Jordan. Not anything at all."

He wanted to bite something. He felt furious at his own stupidity, at his blind allegiance to Julie Merrill and her father, at his naivete in letting them use him. He felt even worse about the way he'd turned on Libby. But he was afraid of what he'd felt for her, afraid of her youth, her changeability. Now he only felt like a fool.

"Thanks for the offer and the apology," she added heavily. "Now, if you'll excuse me, I have to get back to work."

She turned on the computer, brought up her work screen and shut Jordan out of her sight and mind.

He got up slowly and moved toward the door. He hesitated at it, glancing back at her. "What about the autopsy?" he asked suddenly.

She swallowed hard. "Daddy died of a heart attack, just like the doctors said," she replied.

He sighed. "And Violet's father?"

"Was poisoned," she replied.

"Riddle had a lucky escape," he commented. "So did you and Curt."

She didn't look at him. "I just hope they can find her, before she kills some other poor old man."

He nodded. After a minute, he gave her one last soulful glance and went out the door.

Life went on as usual. Calhoun's campaign staff cranked up the heat. Libby spent her free time helping to make up flyers and make telephone calls, offering to drive voters to the polls during the primary election if they didn't have a way to get to the polls.

"You know, I really think Calhoun's going to win," Curt told Libby while they were having a quick lunch together on Saturday, after she got off from work.

She smiled. "So do I. He's got all kinds of support."

He picked at his potato chips. "Heard from Jordan?"

She stiffened. "He came by the office to apologize a few days ago."

He drew in a long breath. "Rumor is that Julie Merrill's courting Duke Wright now."

"Good luck to her. He's still in love with his wife. And he's not quite as gullible as Jordan."

"Jordan wasn't so gullible," he defended his former boss. "When a woman that pretty turns up the heat, most normal men will follow her anywhere."

She lifted both eyebrows. "Even you?"

He grinned. "I'm not normal. I'm a cowboy."

She chuckled and sipped her iced tea. "They're still looking for Janet. I've had an idea," she said.

"Shoot."

"What if we advertise our property for sale in all the regional newspapers?"

"Whoa," he said. "We can't sell it. We don't have power of attorney and the will's not even in probate yet."

"She's a suspected murderess," she reminded him. "Felons can't inherit, did you know? If she's tried and convicted, we might be able to get her to return everything she got from Daddy's estate."

He frowned, thinking hard. "Do you remember Dad telling us about a new will he'd made?"

She blinked. "No."

"Maybe you weren't there. It was when he was in the hospital, just before he died. He could hardly talk for the pain and he was gasping for breath. But he said there was a will. He said he put it in his safest place."

He frowned heavily. "I never thought about that until just now, but what if he meant a new will, Libby?"

"It wouldn't have been legal if it wasn't witnessed," she said sadly. "He might have written something down and she found it and threw it out. I doubt it would stand up in court."

"No. He went to San Antonio without Janet, about two days before he had the heart attack," he persisted.

"Who did he know in San Antonio?" she wondered aloud.

"Why don't you ask Mr. Kemp to see if his private detective could snoop around?" he queried softly.

She pursed her lips. "It would be a long shot. And we couldn't afford to pay him...."

"Dad had a coin collection that was worth half a million dollars, Libby," Curt said. "It's never turned up. I can't find any record that he ever sold it, either."

Her lips fell open. In the agony of the past few months, that had never occurred to her. "I assumed Janet cashed it in...."

"She had the insurance money," he reminded her, "and the property—or so she assumed. But when we were sorting out Dad's personal belongings, that case he kept the coins in was missing. What if—" he added eagerly "—he took it to San Antonio and left it with someone, along with an altered will?"

She was trying to think. It wasn't easy. If they had those coins, if nothing else, they could make the loan payment.

"I can ask Mr. Kemp if he'll look into it," she said. "He can take the money out of my salary."

"I can contribute some of mine," Curt added.

She felt lighter than she had in weeks. "I'll go ask him right now!"

"Finish your sandwich first," he coaxed. "You've lost weight, baby sister."

She grimaced. "I've been depressed since we had to leave home."

"Yeah. Me, too."

She smiled at him. "But things are looking up!"

She found Kemp just about to leave for the day. She stopped him at the door and told him what she and Curt had been discussing.

He closed the door behind them, picked up the phone, and dialed a number. Libby listened while he outlined the case to someone, most likely the private detective he'd hired to look for Janet.

"That's right," he told the man. "One more thing, there's a substantial coin collection missing, as well. I'll ask." He put his hand over the receiver and asked

Libby for a description of it, which he gave to the man. He added a few more comments and hung up, smiling.

"Considering the age of those coins and their value, it wouldn't be hard to trace them if they'd been sold. Good work, Libby!"

"Thank my brother," she replied, smiling. "He remembered it."

"You would have, too, I expect, in time," he said in a kindly tone. "Want me to have a talk with the bank president?" he added. "I think he might be more amenable to letting you and Curt back on the property with this new angle in mind. It might be to his advantage," he added in a satisfied tone.

"You mean, if we turn out to have that much money of our own, free and clear, it would make him very uncomfortable if we put it in the Jacobsville Municipal Bank and not his?"

"Exactly."

Her eyes blazed. "Which is exactly where we will put it, if we get it," she added.

He chuckled. "No need to tell him that just yet."

Her eyebrows lifted. "Mr. Kemp, you have a devious mind."

He smiled. "What else is new?"

* * *

Libby was furious at herself for not thinking of her father's impressive coin collection until now. She'd watched those coins come in the mail for years without really noticing them. But now they were important. They meant the difference between losing their home and getting it back again.

She sat on pins and needles over the weekend, until Kemp heard from the private detective the following Monday afternoon.

He buzzed Libby and told her to come into the office.

He was smiling when she got there. "We found them," he said, chuckling when she made a whoop loud enough to bring Mabel down the hall.

"It's okay," Libby told her coworker, "I've just had some good news for a change!"

Mabel grinned and went back to work.

Libby sat down in the chair in front of Kemp's big desk, smiling and leaning forward.

"Your father left the coins with a dealer who locked them in his safe. He was told not to let Janet have them under any circumstances," he added gently. "Besides that, there was a will. He's got that, too. It's not a self-made will, either. It was done by a lawyer in the dealer's office and witnessed by two people who work for him."

Libby's eyes filled with tears. "Daddy knew! He knew she was trying to cut us out of the will!"

"He must have," he conceded. "Apparently she'd made some comments about what she was going to do when he died. And she'd been harassing him about his health, making remarks about his heart being weak, as well." His jaw clenched. "Whatever the cause, he changed the will in your favor—yours and Curt's. This will is going to stand up in a court of law and it changes the entire financial situation. You and Curt can go home and I'll get the will into probate immediately."

"But the insurance..."

He nodded. "She was the beneficiary for one of his insurance policies." He smiled at her surprise. "There's another one, a half-a-million-dollar policy, that he left with the same dealer who has the will. You and Curt are co-beneficiaries."

"He didn't contact us!" she exclaimed suddenly.

"Yes, and that's the interesting part," he said. "He tried to contact you and Janet told him that you and Curt were out of the country on an extended vacation. She planned to go and talk to him the very day you made the remarks about Violet's father and having locks put on your bedroom doors. She ran for her life before she had time to try to get to the rest of your inheritance." He chuckled. "Maybe she had some idea of what the seller was guarding and decided that the insurance policy would hold her for a while without risking arrest."

"Oh, thank God," she whispered, shivering with delight. "Thank God! We can go home!"

"Apparently," he agreed, smiling. "I'm going to drive up to San Antonio today and get those documents and the coin collection."

She was suddenly concerned. "But what if Janet hears about it? She had that friend in San Antonio who called and tried to get us off the property…" She stopped abruptly. "That's why they were trying to get us out of the house! They knew about the coin collection!" She sat back heavily. "But they could be dangerous…."

"Cash Grier is going with me."

She pursed her lips amusedly. "Okay."

He chuckled. "Nobody is going to try to attack me with Grier in the car. Even if he isn't armed."

"Good point," she agreed.

"So call your brother and tell him the news," he said. "And stop worrying. You're going to land on your feet, Libby."

"How's Violet?" she asked without thinking.

He stood up, his hands deep in his pockets. "She and her mother are distraught, as you might imagine. They never realized that Mr. Hardy had been the victim of foul play. I've tried to keep it out of the papers, but when Janet's caught, it's going to be difficult."

"Is there anything I can do?"

He smiled. "Take them a pizza and let Violet talk to you about it," he suggested. "She misses working here."

"I miss her, too."

He shifted, averting his gaze. "I offered to let her come back to work here."

"You did?" she asked, enthused.

"She's going to think about it," he added. "You might, uh, tell her how shorthanded we are here, and that the temporary woman we got had to quit. Maybe she'll feel sorry for us and come back."

She smiled. "I'll do my best."

He looked odd. "Thanks," he said stiffly.

Chapter Nine

The very next day, Kemp came into the office grinning like a lottery winner. He was carrying a cardboard box, in which was a mahogany box full of rare gold coins, an insurance policy, a few personal items that had belonged to Riddle Collins and a fully executed new will.

Libby had to sit down when Kemp presented her with the hard evidence of her father's love for herself and Curt.

"The will is legal," he told her. "I'm going to take it right to the courthouse and file it. It will supersede the will that Janet probably still has in her possession. You should take the coins to the bank and put them in a safe-deposit box until you're ready to dispose of them. The dealer said he'll buy them from you at market value anytime you're ready to sell them."

"But I'll have to use them as collateral for a loan to make the loan payment…"

"Actually, no, you won't," Kemp said with a smile, drawing two green-covered passbooks out of the box and handing them to her.

"What are these?" she asked blankly.

"Your father had two other bank accounts, both in San Antonio." He smiled warmly. "There's more than enough there to pay off the mortgage completely so that the ranch is free and clear. You'll still have a small fortune left over. You and your brother are going to be rich, Libby. Congratulations."

She cried a little, both for her father's loving care of them even after death and for having come so close to losing everything.

She pulled a tissue out of the pocket of her slacks and wiped her red eyes. "I'll take these to the Jacobsville Municipal Bank right now," she said firmly, "and have the money transferred here from San Antonio. Then I'll have them issue a cashier's check to pay off the other bank," she added with glee.

"Good girl. You can phone the insurance company

about the death benefit, too. How does it feel, not to have to worry about money?"

She chuckled. "Very good." She eyed him curiously. "Does this mean you're firing me?"

"Well, Libby, you won't really need to work for a living anymore," he began slowly.

"But I love my job!" she exclaimed, and had the pleasure of watching his high cheekbones go ruddy. "Can't I stay?"

He drew in a long breath. "I'd be delighted if you would," he confessed. "I can't seem to keep a paralegal these days."

She smiled, remembering that Callie Kirby had been one, until she'd married Micah Steele. There had been two others after her, but neither had stayed long.

"Then it's settled. I have to go and call Curt!"

"Go to the bank first, Libby," he instructed with a grin. "And I'll get to the courthouse. Mabel, we're going to be out of the office for thirty minutes!"

"Okay, boss!"

They went down the hall together and they stopped dead.

Violet was back at her desk, across from a grinning Mabel, looking radiant. "You said I could come back," she told Kemp at once, looking pretty and uncertain at the same time.

He drew in a sharp breath and his eyes lingered on her. "I certainly did," he agreed. "Are you staying?"

She nodded.

"How about making a fresh pot of coffee?" he asked.

"Regular?" she asked.

He averted his gaze to the door. "Half and half," he murmured. "Caffeine isn't good for me."

He went out the door, leaving Violet's jaw dropped.

"I told you he missed you," Libby whispered as she followed Kemp out the door and onto the sidewalk.

Libby and Curt were able to go home the next morning. But their arrival was bittersweet. The house had been ransacked in their absence.

"We'd better call the sheriff's office," Curt said angrily, when they'd ascertained that the disorder was thorough. "We'll need to have a report filed on this for insurance purposes."

"Do we even have insurance?"

He nodded. "Dad had a homeowner's policy. I've been keeping up the payments, remember?"

She righted a chair that had been turned over next to the desk her father had used in his study. The filing cabinet had been emptied onto the floor, along with a lot of other documents pertaining to the ranch's business.

"They were looking for that coin collection," Curt guessed as he picked up the phone. "I'll bet anything Janet knew about it. She must be running short of cash already!"

"Thank God Mr. Kemp was able to track it down," she said.

"Sheriff's department?" Curt said into the telephone receiver. "I need you to send someone out to the Collins ranch. That's right, it's just past Jordan Powell's place. We've had a burglary. Yes. Okay. Thanks!" He hung up. "I talked to Hayes. He's going to come himself, along with his investigator."

"I thought he was overseas with his army unit in Iraq," she commented.

"He's back." He glanced at her amusedly. "You used to have a case on him, just before you went nuts over Jordan Powell."

She hated hearing Jordan's name mentioned. "Hayes is nice."

"So he is." He toyed with the telephone cord. "Libby, Jordan's having some bad times lately. His association with the Merrills has made him enemies."

"That was his choice," she reminded her brother.

"He was good to us, when Dad died."

She knew that. It didn't help. Her memories of Jordan's betrayal were too fresh. "Think I should do anything before they get here?"

"Make coffee," he suggested dryly. "Hayes's investigator is Mack Hughes, and he lives on caffeine."

"I'll do that."

Sheriff Hayes Carson pulled up at the front steps in his car, a brightly polished black vehicle with all sorts of antennae sticking out of it. The investigator, Mack Hughes, pulled up beside it in his black SUV with a deck of lights on the roof.

"Thanks for coming so quickly," Curt said, shaking hands with both men. "You remember my sister, Libby."

"Hello, Elizabeth," Hayes said with a grin, having always used her real first name instead of the nickname most people called her by. He was dashing, with blond hair and dark eyes, tall and muscular and big. He was in his mid-thirties; one tough customer, too. He and Cash Grier often went head-to-head in disputes, although they were good colleagues when there was an emergency.

"Hi, Hayes," she replied with a smile. "Hello, Mack."

Mack, tall and dark, nodded politely. "Let's see what you've got."

They ushered the law enforcement officers inside and stood back while they went about searching for clues.

"Any idea who the perpetrators were?" Hayes murmured while Mack looked around.

"Someone connected to our stepmother, most likely," Libby commented. "Dad had a very expensive coin collection and some secret bank accounts that even we didn't know about. If that's what they were looking for, they're out of luck. Mr. Kemp tracked them to San Antonio. Everything's in the bank now and a new will we recovered is in the proper hands."

Hayes whistled softly. "Lucky for you."

There was a sudden commotion in the front yard, made by a truck skidding to a stop between the two law-enforcement vehicles. A dusty, tired Jordan Powell came up the steps, taking them two at a time, and stopped abruptly in the living room.

"What's happened?" he asked at once, his eyes homing to Libby with dark concern.

"The house was ransacked," Hayes told him. "Have you seen anything suspicious?"

"No. But I'll ask my men," Jordan assured them. He looked at Libby for a long time. "You okay?"

"Curt and I are fine, thanks," she said in a polite but reserved tone.

Jordan looked around at the jumble of furniture and paper on the floor, along with lamps and broken pieces of ceramic items that had been on the mantel over the fireplace.

"This wasn't necessary," Jordan said grimly. "Even if they were looking for something, they didn't have to break everything in the house."

"It was malicious, all right," Hayes agreed. He moved just in front of Libby. "I heard from Grier that you've had two confrontations with Julie Merrill, one of them physically violent. She's also been implicated in acts of vandalism. I want to know if you think she might have had any part in this."

Libby glanced at Jordan apprehensively.

"It could be a possibility," Jordan said, to her dismay. "She was jealous of Libby and I've just broken with Julie and her father. She didn't take it well."

"I'll add her to the list of suspects," Hayes said quietly. "But I have to tell you, she isn't going to like being accused."

"I don't care," Curt replied, answering for himself as well as Libby. "Nobody has a right to do something like this."

"Boss!" Mack called from the back porch. "Could you ask the Collinses to come out here, please?"

Curt stood aside to let Libby go first. On the small back stoop, Mack was squatting down, looking at a big red gas can. "This yours?" he asked Curt.

Curt frowned. "We don't have one that big," he replied. "Ours is locked up in the outbuilding next to the barn."

Mack and Hayes exchanged curious looks.

"There's an insurance policy on the house," Libby remarked worriedly. "It's got Janet, our stepmother, listed as beneficiary."

"That narrows down the suspects," Hayes remarked.

"Surely she wouldn't…" Libby began.

"You've made a lot of trouble for her," Jordan said grimly. "And now she's missed out on two savings accounts and a will that she didn't even know existed."

"How did you know that?" Libby asked belligerently.

"My cousin owns the Municipal Bank," Jordan said nonchalantly.

"He had no business telling you anything!" Libby protested.

"He didn't, exactly," Jordan confessed. "I heard him

talking to one of his clerks about opening the new account for you and setting up a safe-deposit box."

"Eavesdropping should be against the law," she muttered.

"I'll make a note of it," Hayes said with a grin.

She grinned back. "Thanks, Hayes."

He told Mack to start marking evidence to be collected. "We'll see if we can lift any latent prints," he told the small group. "If it was Janet, or someone she hired, they'll probably have been wearing gloves. If it was Julie Merrill, we might get lucky."

"I hope we can connect somebody to it," Libby said wearily, looking around. "If for no other reason than to make them pay to help have this mess cleaned up!"

"I'll take care of that," Jordan said at once, and reached for his cell phone.

"We don't need—!" Libby began hotly.

But Jordan wasn't listening. He was talking to Amie at his ranch, instructing her to phone two housekeepers she knew who helped her with heavy tasks and send them over to the Collins place.

"You might as well give up," Hayes remarked dryly. "Once Jordan gets the bit between his teeth, it would take a shotgun to stop him. You know that."

She sighed angrily. "Yes. I know."

Hayes pushed his wide-brimmed hat back off his

forehead and smiled down at Libby. "Are you doing anything Saturday night?" he asked. "They're having a campaign rally for Calhoun's supporters at Shea's."

"I know, I'm one of them," she replied, smiling. "Are you going to be there?"

He shrugged. "I might as well. Somebody'll have a beer too many and pick a fight, I don't doubt. Tiny the bouncer will have his hands full."

"Great!" she said enthusiastically.

Jordan was eavesdropping and not liking what he heard. He wanted to tell Hayes to back off. He wanted to tell Libby what he felt. But he couldn't get the words out.

"If you two are moving back in," Hayes added, "I think we'd better have somebody around overnight. I've got two volunteer deputies in the Sheriff's Posse who would be willing, I expect, if you'll keep them in coffee."

She smiled. "I'd be delighted. Thanks, Hayes. It would make me feel secure. We've got a shotgun, but I don't even know where it is."

"You could both stay with me until Hayes gets a handle on who did this," Jordan volunteered.

"No, thanks," Libby said quietly, trying not to re-member that Jordan had already asked her to do that.

No matter how she felt about the big idiot, she wasn't going to step into Julie Merrill's place.

"This is our home," Curt added.

Jordan drew in a long, sad breath. "Okay. But if you need help…"

"We'll call Hayes, thanks," Libby said, turning back to the sheriff. "I need to tidy up the kitchen. Is it all right?"

Hayes went with her into the small room and looked around. There wasn't much damage in there and nothing was broken. "It looks okay. Go ahead, Libby. I'll see you Saturday, then?"

She grinned up at him. "Of course."

He grinned back and then rejoined the men in the living room. "I'm going to talk to my volunteers," he told Curt. "I'll be in touch."

"Thanks a lot, Hayes," Curt replied.

"Just doing my job. See you, Jordan."

"Yeah." Jordan didn't offer to shake hands. He glared after the other man as he went out the front door.

"I can clean my own house," Libby began impatiently.

Jordan met her eyes evenly. "I've made a lot of mistakes. I've done a lot of damage. I know I can't make it up to you in one fell swoop, but let me do what I can to make amends. Will you?"

Libby looked at her brother, who shrugged and walked away, leaving her to deal with Jordan alone.

"Some help you are," Libby muttered at his retreating back.

"I don't like the idea of that gas can," Jordan said, ignoring her statement. "You can't stay awake twenty-four hours a day. If Janet is really desperate enough to set fire to the house trying to get her hands on the insurance money, neither you nor Curt is going to be safe here."

"Hayes is getting us some protection," she replied coolly.

"I know that. But even deputies have to use the bathroom occasionally," he said flatly. "Why won't you come home with me?"

She lifted her chin. "This is my place, mine and Curt's. We're not running anymore."

He sighed. "I admire your courage, Libby. But it's misplaced this time."

She turned away. "I've got a lot to do, Jordan. Thanks anyway."

He caught her small waist from behind and held her just in front of him. His warm breath stirred the hair at the back of her head. "I was afraid."

"Of…what?" she asked, startled.

His big hands contracted. "You're very young, even

for a woman your age," he said stiffly. "Young women are constantly changing."

She turned in his hold, curious. She looked up at him without understanding. "What has that got to do with anything?"

He reached out and traced her mouth with his thumb. He looked unusually solemn. "You really don't know, do you?" he asked quietly. "That's part of the problem."

"You aren't making any sense."

"I am. You're just not hearing what I'm saying." He bent and kissed her softly beside her ear, drawing away almost at once. "Never mind. You'll figure it out one day. Meanwhile, I'm going to do a better job of looking after you."

"I can—"

He interrupted at once. "If you say 'look after myself,' so help me, I'll…!"

She glared at him.

He glared back.

"You're up against someone formidable, whoever it is," he continued. "I'm not letting anything happen to you, Libby."

"Fat lot you cared before," she muttered.

He sighed heavily. "Yes, I know. I'll eat crow without catsup if it will help you trust me again."

"Julie's very pretty," she said reluctantly.

"She isn't a patch on you, butterfly," he said quietly.

She hesitated. But she wasn't giving in easily. He'd hurt her. No way was she going to run headfirst into his arms the first time he opened them.

She watched him suspiciously.

His broad chest rose and fell. "Okay. We'll do it your way. I'll see you at Shea's."

"You're the enemy," she pointed out. "You're not on Calhoun's team."

He shrugged. "A man can change sides, can't he?" he mused. "Meanwhile, if you need me, I'll be at the house. If you call, I'll come running."

She nodded slowly. "All right."

He smiled at her.

Curt came back in. He was as cool to Jordan as his sister. The older man shrugged and left without another word.

"Now he's changed sides again," Libby told Curt when Jordan was gone.

"Jordan's feeling his age, Libby," Curt told her. "And some comments were made by his cowboys about that kiss they saw."

Her eyebrows arched. "What?"

He sighed. "I never had the heart to tell you. But one of the older hands said Jordan was trying to rob the cradle. It enraged Jordan. But it made him think, too. He knows how sheltered you've been. I think he was trying to protect you."

"From what?"

"Maybe from a relationship he didn't think you were ready for," he replied. "Julie was handy, he'd dated her a time or two, and she swarmed all over him just about the time he was drawing back from you. I expect he was flattered by her attention and being invited into that highbrow social set that shut out his mother after she was disinherited because she married his father. The local society women just turned their backs on her. She was never invited anywhere ever again. Jordan felt it keenly, that some of his playmates weren't allowed to invite him to their houses."

"I didn't know it was so hard on him. He's only told me bits and pieces about his upbringing."

"He doesn't advertise it," he added. "She gave up everything to marry his father. She worked as a house-keeper in one of the motels owned by her father's best friend. It was a rough upbringing for Jordan."

"I can imagine." She sighed, unable to prevent her heart from thawing.

* * *

Shea's was filled to capacity on Saturday evening. Cash Grier got a lot of attention because he brought Tippy with him. She looked good despite her ordeals, except for the small indications of healing cuts on her lovely face. She was weak and still not totally recovered and it showed. Nevertheless, she was still the most beautiful woman in the room. But she had eyes only for Cash and that showed, too.

When they got on the dance floor together, Libby was embarrassed to find herself staring wistfully at them. Tippy melted into Cash's tall body as if she'd found heaven. He looked that way, as well. They clung together to the sound of an old love song. And when she looked up at him, he actually stopped dancing and just stared at her.

"They make a nice couple," Jordan said from behind her.

She glanced up at him. He looked odd. His dark eyes were quiet, intent on her uplifted face.

"Yes, they do," she replied. "They seem to fit together very well."

He nodded. "Dance with me," he said in a deep voice, and drew her into his arms.

She hesitated, but only for a few seconds. She'd built dreams on those kisses they'd shared and she thought it was all over. But the way he was holding her made her knees weak. His big hand covered hers against his chest and pressed it hard into the warm muscle.

"I've been an idiot," he said at her ear.

"What do you mean?" she wondered aloud, drugged by his closeness.

"I shouldn't have backed off," he replied quietly. "I got cold feet at the very worst time."

"Jordan…"

"…mind if I cut in?" Hayes Carson asked with a grin.

Jordan stopped, his mind still in limbo. "We were talking," he began.

"Plenty of time for that later. Shall we, Libby?" he asked, and moved right in front of Jordan. He danced Libby away before she had a chance to stop him.

"Now that's what I call a jealous man," Hayes murmured dryly, glancing over her shoulder at Jordan. "No need to ask about the lay of the land."

"Jordan doesn't feel that way about me," Libby protested.

"He doesn't?"

She averted her eyes to the crowded dance floor. "He isn't a marrying man."

"Uh-huh."

She glanced up at Hayes, who was still grinning.

She flushed at the look in his eyes.

Across the room, Jordan Powell saw that flush and had to restrain himself from going over there and tearing Libby out of Hayes's embrace.

"What the devil are you doing here?" Calhoun Ballenger asked abruptly.

Jordan glanced at him wryly. "Not much," he murmured. "But I came to ask if you needed another willing ally. I've, uh, changed camps."

Calhoun's eyebrows went up almost to his blond hairline.

"I do like to be on the winning side," Jordan drawled.

Calhoun burst out laughing. "Well, you're not a bad diplomat, I guess," he confessed, holding out his hand. "Welcome aboard."

"My pleasure."

Jordan contrived to drive Libby and Curt home, but he was careful to let Curt go into the ranch house before he cut off the engine and turned to Libby.

"There's been some news," he said carefully.

"About Janet?" she exclaimed.

"About Julie," he corrected. He toyed with a strand of her hair in the dim light of the car interior. "One of Grier's men saw her with a known drug dealer earlier today. She's put her neck in a noose and she doesn't even know it."

"She uses, doesn't she?" she asked.

He shrugged. "Her behavior is erratic. She must."

"I'm sorry. You liked her…"

He bent and kissed her hungrily, pulling her across his lap to wrap her up in his warm, strong arms. "I like you," he whispered against her mouth. "More than I ever dreamed I could!"

She wanted to ask questions, but she couldn't kiss him and breathe at the same time. She gave up and ran her arms up around his neck. She relaxed into his close embrace and kissed him back until her mouth grew sore and swollen.

He sighed into her throat as he held her and rocked her in his arms in the warm darkness.

"Libby, I think we should start going out together."

She blinked. "You and me?"

He nodded. "You and me." He drew back and looked down at her possessively. "I could give up liver and onions, if I had to. But I can't give you up."

"Listen, I don't have affairs…"

He kissed her into silence. "Neither do I. So I guess maybe we won't sleep together after all."

"But if we go out together…" she said worriedly.

He grinned. "You have enough self-restraint for

both of us, I'm sure," he drawled. "You can keep me honest."

She drew back a little and noted the position of his big lean hands under her blouse. She looked at him intently.

He cleared his throat and drew his hands out from under the blouse. "Every man is entitled to one little slip. Right?" His eyes were twinkling.

She laughed. "Okay."

He touched her mouth with his one last time. "In that case, you'd better rush inside before I forget to be honest."

"Thanks for bringing us home."

"My pleasure. Lock the doors," he added seriously. "And I'm only a phone call away if you need me. You call me," he emphasized. "Not Hayes Carson. Got that?"

"And since when did I become your personal property?" she asked haughtily.

"Since the minute you let me put my hands under your blouse," he shot right back, laughing. "Think about it."

She got out of the vehicle, dizzy and with her head swimming. In one night, everything had changed.

"Don't worry," he added gently, leaning out the window. "I have enough restraint for both of us!"

Before she could answer him, he gunned the engine and took off down the road.

Chapter Ten

For the next few days, Jordan was at Libby's house more than at his own. He smoothed over hard feelings with her brother and became a household fixture. Libby and Curt filed the insurance claim, paid off the mortgage, and started repurchasing cattle for the small ranch.

Janet was found a couple of days later at a motel just outside San Antonio, with a man. He turned out to be the so-called attorney who'd phoned and tried to get Libby and Curt out of their home. She was arrested and charged with murder in the death of Violet's father. There was DNA evidence taken from the dead man's clothing and the motel room that was directly linked to Janet. It placed her at the motel the night Mr. Hardy died. When she realized the trouble she was in, she tried to make a deal for a reduced sentence. She agreed to confess to the murder in return for a life sentence without hope of parole. But she denied having a gas can. She swore that she never had plans to burn down Riddle Collins's house with his children in it. Nobody paid her much attention. She'd told so many lies.

It was a different story for Julie Merrill. She continued to make trouble, and not only for Calhoun Ballenger. She was determined that Jordan wasn't going to desert her for little Libby Collins. She had a plan. Two days before the hearing to decide the fate of the police officers who'd arrested her father— Saturday, she put it into practice.

She phoned Libby at work and apologized profusely for all the trouble she'd caused.

"I never meant to be such a pain in the neck," she assured Libby. "I want to make it up to you. You get off at one on Saturdays, don't you? Suppose you come over here for lunch?"

"To your house?" Libby replied warily.

"Yes. I've had our cook make something special," she purred. "And I can tell you my side of the story. Will you?"

Dubious, Libby hesitated.

"Surely you aren't afraid of me?" Julie drawled. "I mean, what could I do to you, even if I had something terrible in mind?"

"You don't need to feed me," Libby replied cautiously. "I don't hold grudges."

"You'll come, then," Julie persisted. "Today at one. Will you?"

It was against her better judgment. But it wasn't a bad idea to keep a feud going, especially now that Jordan seemed really interested in her.

"Okay," Libby said finally. "I'll be there at one."

"Thanks!" Julie said huskily. "You don't know how much I appreciate it! Uh, I don't guess you'd like to bring your brother, too?" she added suddenly.

Libby frowned. "Curt's driving a cattle truck for Duke Wright up to San Antonio today."

"Well, then, another time, perhaps! I'll see you at one." Julie hung up, with a bright and happy note in her voice.

Libby frowned. Was she stupid to go to the woman's home? But why would Julie risk harming her now, with the primary election so close? It was the following Tuesday.

She phoned Jordan. "Guess what just happened?" she asked.

"You've realized how irresistible I am and you're

rushing over to seduce me?" he teased. "Shall I turn down the covers on my bed?"

"Stop that," she muttered. "I'm serious."

"So am I!"

"Jordan," she laughed. "Julie just called to apologize. She invited me to lunch."

"Did she?" he asked. "Are you going?"

"I thought I might." She hesitated. "Don't you think it's a good idea, to mend fences, I mean?"

"I don't know, Libby," he replied seriously. "She's been erratic and out of control lately. I don't think it's a good idea. I'd rather you didn't."

"Are you afraid she might tell me something about you that I don't know?" she returned, suspicious.

He sighed. "No. It's not that. She wasn't happy when I broke off with her. I don't trust her."

"What can she do to me in broad daylight?" she laughed. "Shoot me?"

"Of course not," he scoffed.

"Then stop worrying. She only wants to apologize."

"You be careful," he returned. "And phone me when you get home. Okay?"

"Okay."

"How about a movie tonight?" he added. "There's

a new mystery at the theater. You can even have popcorn."

"That sounds nice," she said, feeling warm and secure.

"I'll pick you up about six."

"I'll be ready. See you then."

She hung up and pondered over his misgivings. Surely he was overreacting. He was probably afraid Julie might make up a convincing lie about how intimate they'd been. Or perhaps she might be telling the truth. She only knew that she had to find out why Julie wanted to see her in person. She was going.

But something niggled at the back of her mind when she drove toward Julie's palatial home on the Jacobs River. Julie might have wanted to invite Libby over to apologize, but why would she want Curt to come, too? She didn't even know Curt.

Libby's foot lifted off the accelerator. Her home was next door to Jordan's. Julie was furious that Jordan had broken off with her. If the house was gone, Libby and Curt would have to move away again, as they had before…!

Libby turned the truck around in the middle of the road and sped toward her house. She wished she had a cell phone. There was no way to call for help. But she was absolutely certain what was about to happen. And she knew immediately that her stepmother hadn't been responsible for that gas can on the porch.

The question was, who had Julie convinced to set that fire for her? Or would she be crazy enough to try and do it herself?

Libby sped faster down the road. If only there had been state police, a sheriff's deputy, a policeman watching. She was speeding. It was the only time in her life she'd ever wanted to be caught!

But there were no flashing lights, no sirens. She was going to have to try and stop the perpetrator all by herself. She wasn't a big woman. She had no illusions about being able to tackle a grown man. She didn't even have a weapon. Wait. There was a tire tool in the boot! At least, she could threaten with it.

She turned into the road that led to the house. There was no smoke visible anywhere and no sign of any traffic. For the first time, she realized that she could be chasing make-believe villains. Why would she think that Julie Merrill would try to burn her house down? Maybe the strain of the past weeks was making her hysterical after all.

She pulled up in front of the house and got out, grabbing the tire tool out of the back. It wouldn't hurt to look around, now that she was here.

She moved around the side of the house, her heart beating wildly. Her palms were so sweaty that she had to get a better grip on the tire tool. She walked past the chimney, to the corner, and peered around. Her heart stopped.

There was a man there. A young, dark man. He had a can of gasoline. He was muttering to himself as he sloshed it on the back porch and the steps.

Libby closed her eyes and prayed for strength. There was nobody to help her. She had to do this alone.

She walked around the corner with the tire tool raised. "That's enough, you varmint! You're trespassing on private property and you're going to jail. The police are right behind me!"

Startled, the man dropped the gas can and stared wild-eyed at Libby.

Sensing an advantage, she started to run toward him, yelling at the top of her lungs.

To her amazement, he started running down a path behind the house, with Libby right on his heels, still yelling.

Then something happened that was utterly in the realm of fantasy. She heard an engine behind her. An accomplice, she wondered, almost panicking.

Jordan Powell pulled up right beside her in his

truck and threw open the passenger door. "Get in!" he called.

She didn't need prompting. She jumped right in beside him, tire tool and all, and slammed the door. "He was dousing the back porch with gas!" she panted. "Don't let him get away!"

"I don't intend to." His face was grim as he stood down on the accelerator and the truck shot forward on the pasture road, which was no more than tracks through tall grass.

The attempted arsonist was tiring. He was pretty thick in the middle and had short legs. He was almost to a beat-up old car sitting out of sight of the house near the barn when Jordan came alongside him on the driver's side.

"Hold it in the ruts!" he called to Libby.

Just as she grabbed the wheel, he threw open the door and leaped out on the startled, breathless young man, pinning him to the ground.

By the time Libby had the truck stopped, Jordan had the man by his shirt collar and was holding him there.

"Pick up the phone and call Hayes," he called to Libby.

Her hands were shaking, but she managed to dial 911 and give the dispatcher an abbreviated account of what had just happened. She was told that they contacted a deputy who was barely a mile away and he was starting toward the Collins place at that moment.

Libby thanked her nicely and cut off the phone.

"Who put you up to this?" Jordan demanded of the man. "Tell me, or so help me, I'll make sure you don't get out of prison until you're an old man!"

"It was Miss Julie," the young man sobbed. "I never done nothing like this in my life. My daddy works for her and he took some things out of her house. She said she'd turn him over to the police if I didn't do this for her."

"She'd have turned him over anyway, you fool," Jordan said coldly. "She was using you. Do you have any idea what the penalty is for arson?"

He was still sobbing. "I was scared, Mr. Powell."

Jordan relented, but only a little. He looked up as the sound of a siren was heard coming closer.

Libby opened the door of the truck and got out, just as a sheriff's car came flying down the track and stopped just behind the truck.

The deputy was Sammy Tibbs. They both knew him. He'd been in Libby's class in high school.

"What have you got, Jordan?" Sammy asked.

"A would-be arsonist," Jordan told him. "He'll confess if you ask him."

"I caught him pouring gas on my back porch and I chased him with my tire tool. I almost had him when Jordan came along," Libby said with a shy grin.

"Whew," Sammy whistled. "I hope I don't ever run afoul of you," he told her.

"That makes two of us," Jordan said, with a gentle smile for her.

"I assume you'll be pressing charges?" Sammy asked Libby as he handcuffed the young man, who was still out of breath.

"You can bet real money on it," Libby agreed. "And you'll need to pick up Julie Merrill as well, because this man said she told him to do it."

Sammy's hands froze on the handcuffs. "Julie Merrill? The state senator's daughter?"

"That's exactly who I mean," Libby replied. "She called and invited me over to lunch. Since she doesn't like me, I got suspicious and came home instead, just in time to catch this weasel in the act."

"Is this true?" the deputy asked the man.

"Mirandize him first," Jordan suggested. "Just so there won't be any loopholes."

"Good idea," Sammy agreed, and read the suspect his rights.

"Now, tell him," Libby prodded, glaring at the man who'd been within a hair of burning her house down.

The young man sighed as if the weight of the world was sitting on his shoulders. "Miss Merrill had something on my daddy, who works for her. She said if I'd set a fire on Miss Collins's back steps, she'd forget all about it. She just wanted to scare Miss Collins is all. She didn't tell me to burn the whole place down."

"Arson is arson," Sammy replied. "Don't touch anything," he told Libby. "I'll send our investigator back out there and call the state fire marshal. Arson is hard to prove, but this one's going to be a walk in the park."

"Thanks, Sammy," Libby said.

He grinned. "What for? You caught him!"

He put the scared suspect in the back of his car and sped off with a wave of his hand.

"That was too damned close," Jordan said, looking down at Libby with tormented eyes. "I couldn't believe it when I saw you chasing him through the field with a tire iron! What if he'd been armed?"

"He wasn't," she said. "Besides, he ran the minute I chased him, just like a black snake."

He pulled her into his arms and wrapped her up tight. There was a faint tremor in those strong arms.

"You brave idiot," he murmured into her neck. "Thank God he didn't get the fire started first. I can see you running inside to grab all the sentimental items and save them. You'd have been burned alive."

She grimaced, because he was absolutely right. She'd have tried to save her mementos of her father and mother, at any cost.

"Libby, I think we'd better get engaged," he said suddenly.

She was hallucinating. She said so.

He pulled back from her, his eyes solemn. "You're not hallucinating. If Julie realizes how serious this is between us, she'll back off."

"She's going to be in jail shortly, she'll have to," she pointed out.

"They can afford bail until her hearing, even so," he replied. "She'll be out for blood. But if she hears about the engagement, it might be enough to make her think twice."

"I'm not afraid of her," she said, although she really was.

"Humor me," he coaxed, bending to kiss her gently.

She smiled under the warm, comforting feel of his hard mouth on her lips. "Well…"

He nibbled her upper lip. "I'll get you a ring," he whispered.

"What sort?"

"What do you want?"

"I like emeralds," she whispered, standing on tiptoe to coax his mouth down again.

"An emerald, then."

"Nobody would know?"

He chuckled as he kissed her. "We might have to tell a few hundred people, just to make it believable. And we might actually have to get married, but that's okay, isn't it?"

She blinked. "Get...married?"

"That's what the ring's for, Libby," he said against her warm mouth. "Advance notice."

"But...you've always said you never wanted to get married."

"I always said there's the one woman a man can't walk away from," he added. He lifted his head and looked down at her, all the teasing gone. "I can't walk away from you. The past few weeks have been pure hell."

Her eyes widened with unexpected delight.

He traced her eyebrows with his forefinger. "I missed you," he whispered. "It was like being cut apart."

"You wanted Julie," she accused.

He grimaced. "I wanted you to think about what was happening. You've been sheltered your whole life. Duke Wright's wife was just like you. Then she married and had a child and got career-minded. That poor

devil lives in hell because she didn't know what she
wanted until it was too late!"

She searched his face quietly. "You think I'd want a
career."

"I don't know, Libby," he bit off. He looked an-
guished. "I'm an all-or-nothing kind of man. I can't just
stick my toe in to test the water. I jump in headfirst."

He...loved her. She was stunned. She couldn't believe
she hadn't noticed, in all this time. Curt had seen it
long before this. He'd tried to tell her. But she hadn't
believed that a man like Jordan could be serious about
someone like her.

Her lips fell apart with a husky sigh. She was on
fire. She'd never dreamed that life could be so sweet.
"I don't want a career," she said slowly.

"What if you do, someday?" he persisted.

She reached up and traced his firm, jutting chin with
her fingertips. "I'm twenty-four years old, Jordan," she
said. "If I don't know my own mind by now, I never
will."

He still looked undecided.

She put both hands flat on his shirt. Under it, she
could feel the muted thunder of his heartbeat. "Why
don't we go to a movie?" she asked.

He seemed to relax. He smiled. "We could grab a ham-
burger for lunch and talk about it," he prompted.

"Okay."

"Then we'll go by the sheriff's department and you can write out a statement," he added.

She grimaced. "I guess I'll have to."

He nodded. "So will I." His eyes narrowed. "I wish I could see the look on Julie's face when the deputy sheriff pulls up in her driveway."

"I imagine she'll be surprised," Libby replied.

Surprised was an understatement. Julie Merrill gaped at the young man in the deputy sheriff's uniform.

"You're joking," she said haughtily. "I…I had nothing to do with any attempted arson!"

"We have a man in custody who'll swear to it," he replied. "You can come peacefully or you can go out the door in handcuffs," he added, still pleasant and respectful. "Your choice, Miss Merrill."

She let out a harsh breath. "This is outrageous!"

"What's going on out here?" Her father, the state senator, came into the hall, weaving a little, and blinked when he saw the deputy. "What's he doing here?" he murmured.

"Your daughter is under arrest, senator," he was told as the deputy suddenly turned Julie around and cuffed her with professional dexterity. "For conspiracy to commit arson."

"Arson?" The senator blinked. "Julie?"

"She sent a man to burn down the Collins place," he was told. "We have two eyewitnesses, as well."

The senator gaped at his daughter. "I told you to leave that woman alone," he said, shaking his finger at her. "I told you Jordan would get involved if you didn't! You've cost me the election! Everybody around here will go to the polls Tuesday and vote for Calhoun Ballenger! You've ruined me!"

"Oh, no, sir, she hasn't," the deputy assured him with a grin. "Your nephew, the mayor, did that, by persecuting two police officers who were just doing their jobs." The smile faded. "You're going to see Monday night just how much hot water you've jumped into. That disciplinary hearing is going to be remembered for the next century in Jacobsville."

"Where are you taking my daughter?" the senator snorted.

"To jail, to be booked. You can call your attorney and arrange for a bail hearing whenever you like," the deputy added, with a speaking glance at the older man's condition. "If you're able."

"I'll call my own attorney," Julie said hotly. "Then I'll sue you for false arrest!"

"You're welcome to try," the deputy said. "Come along, Miss Merrill."

"Daddy, do try to sober up!" Julie said scathingly.

"What would be the point?" the senator replied. "Life was so good when I didn't know all about you, Julie. When I thought you were a sweet, kind, innocent woman like your mother..." He closed his eyes. "You killed that girl!"

"I did not! Think what you're saying!" Julie yelled at him.

Tears poured down his cheeks. "She died in my arms..."

"Let's go," the deputy said, tugging Julie Merrill out the door. He closed it on the sobbing politician.

Julie Merrill was lodged in the county jail until her bail hearing the following Monday morning. Meanwhile, Jordan and Libby had given their statements and the would-be arsonist was singing like a canary bird.

The disciplinary hearing for Chief Grier's two police officers was Monday night at the city council meeting.

It didn't take long. Within thirty minutes, the council had finished its usual business, Grier's officers were cleared of any misconduct, and the surprise guests at the hearing had Jacobsville buzzing for weeks afterward.

Chapter Eleven

Jordan drove Libby to his house in a warm silence. He led her into the big, elegant living room and closed the door behind them.

"Want something to drink?" he asked, moving to a pitcher of iced tea that Amie had apparently left for them, along with a plate of homemade cake, covered with foil. "And a piece of pound cake?"

"I'd love that," she agreed.

He poured tea into two glasses and handed them to her, along with doilies to protect the coffee table from spots. He put cake onto two plates, with forks, and brought them along. But as he bent over the coffee table, he obscured Libby's plate. When he sat down beside her, there was a beautiful emerald solitaire, set in gold, lying on her piece of cake.

"Look at that," he exclaimed with twinkling dark eyes. "Why, it's an engagement ring! I wonder who could have put it there?" he drawled.

She picked it up, breathless. "It's beautiful."

"Isn't it?" he mused. "Why don't you try it on? If it fits," he added slyly, "you might turn into a fairy princess and get your own true prince as a prize!"

She smiled through her breathless delight. "Think so?"

"Darlin', I can almost guarantee it," he replied tenderly. "Want to give it a shot?"

He seemed to hold his breath while he waited for her reply. She had to fight tears. It was the most poignant moment of her entire life.

"Why don't you put it on for me?" she asked finally, watching him lift the ring and slide it onto her ring finger with something like relief.

"How about that?" he murmured dryly. "It's a perfect fit. Almost as if it were made just for you," he added.

She looked up at him and all the humor went out of his face. He held her small hand in his big one and searched her eyes.

"You love emeralds. I bought this months ago and stuck it in a drawer while I tried to decide whether or not it would be suicide to propose to you. Duke Wright's situation made me uncertain. I was afraid you hadn't seen enough of the world, or life, to be able to settle down here in Jacobsville. I was afraid to take a chance."

She moved a step closer. "But you finally did."

He cupped her face in his big, warm hands. "Yes. When I realized that I was spending time with Julie just to keep you at bay. If she'd been a better sort of person, it would have been a low thing to do. I was flattered at her interest and the company I got to keep. But I felt like a traitor when she started insulting you in public. I was too wrapped up in my own uncertainties to do what I should have done."

"Which was what?" she asked softly.

He bent to her soft mouth. "I should have realized that if you really love someone, everything works out." He kissed her tenderly. "I should have told you how I felt and given you a chance to spread your wings if you wanted to. I could have waited while you decided what sort of future you wanted."

She still couldn't believe that he didn't know how she felt. "I was crazy about you," she whispered huskily. "Everybody knew it except you." She reached up and linked her arms around his neck. "Duke's wife wasn't like me, Jordan," she added, searching his dark eyes.

"She lived with a domineering father and a deeply religious mother. They taught her that a woman's role in life was to marry and obey her husband. She'd always done what they told her to do. But after she married Duke, she ran wild, probably giving vent to all those feelings of suffocated restriction she'd endured all her life. Getting pregnant on her wedding night was a big mistake for both of them, because then she really felt trapped." She took a deep breath. "If Duke hadn't rushed her into it, she'd have gone off and found her career and come back to him when she knew what she really wanted. It was a tragedy in the making from the very beginning."

"She didn't love him enough," he murmured.

"He didn't love her enough," she countered. "He got her pregnant, thinking it would hold her."

He sighed. "I want children," he said softly. "But not right away. We need time to get to know each other before we start a family, don't we?"

She smiled. "See? You ask me about things. You don't order me around. Duke was exactly the opposite." She traced his mouth with her fingertips. "That's why I stopped going out with him. He never asked me what I wanted to do, even what I wanted to eat when we went out together. He actually ordered meals for me before I could say what I liked." She glowered. "He ordered me liver and onions and I never went out with him again."

He lifted an eyebrow and grinned. "Darlin', I swear on my horse that I will never order you liver and onions." He crossed his heart.

He was so handsome when he grinned like that. Her heart expanded like a balloon with pure happiness. "Actually," she whispered, lifting up to him. "I'd even eat liver and onions for you."

"The real test of love," he agreed, gathering her up hungrily. "And I'd eat squash for you," he offered.

She smiled under the slow, sweet pressure of his mouth. Amie said he'd actually dumped a squash casserole in the middle of the living room carpet to make the point that he never wanted it again.

"This is nice," he murmured, lifting her completely off the floor. "But I can do better."

"Can you really?" she whispered, biting softly at his full lower lip. "Show me!"

He laughed, even though his body was making emphatic statements about how little time there was left for teasing. He was burning.

He put her down on the sofa and crushed her into it with the warm, hard length of his body.

"Jordan," she whispered breathlessly when he eased between her long legs.

"Don't panic," he said against her lips. "Amie's a scream away. Lift up."

She did, and he unfastened the bra and pushed it out of the way under her blouse. He deepened the kiss slowly, seductively, while his lean hands discovered the soft warmth of her bare breasts in a heated silence.

Her head began to spin. He was going to be her husband. She could lie in his arms all night long. They could have children together. After the tragedy of the past few months, it was like a trip to paradise.

She moaned and wrapped her long legs around his hips, urging him even closer. She felt the power and heat of him intimately. Her mouth opened, inviting the quick, hard thrust of his tongue.

"Oh, yes," she groaned into his hard mouth. Her hips lifted into his rhythmically, her breath gasping out at his ear as she clung to him. "Yes. That feels...good!"

A tortured sound worked out of his throat as he pressed her down hard into the soft cushions of the sofa, his hands already reaching for the zipper in the front of her slacks, so far gone that he was mindless.

The sound of footsteps outside the door finally penetrated the fog of passion that lay between them. Jordan lifted his head. Libby looked up at him, dazed and only half-aware of the sound.

"Amie," Jordan groaned, taking a steadying breath. "We have to stop."

"Tell her to go away," she whispered, laughing breathlessly.

"You tell her," he teased as he got to his feet. "She gets even in the kitchen. She can make squash look just like a corn casserole."

"Amie's Revenge?"

He nodded. "Amie's Revenge." Jordan paused. "I want to marry you," he said quietly. "I want it with all my heart."

She had to fight down tears to answer him. "I want it, too."

He drew her close, over his lap, and when he kissed her, it was with such breathless tenderness that she felt tears threatening again.

She slid her arms around his neck and kissed him back with fervent ardor. But he put her gently away.

"You don't want to ravish me?" she exclaimed. "You said once that you could do me justice in thirty minutes!"

"I lied," he said, chuckling. "I'd need two hours. And Amie's skulking out in the hall, waiting for an opportunity to congratulate us," he added in a whisper. "We can't possibly shock her so soon before the wedding."

She hesitated. "So soon…?"

"I want to get married as quickly as possible," he informed her. "All we need is the blood tests, a license, and I've already got us a minister. Unless you want a formal wedding in a big church with hundreds of guests," he added worriedly.

"No need, since you've already got us a minister," she teased.

He relaxed. "Thank God! The idea of a morning coat and hundreds of people…"

She was kissing him, so he stopped talking.

Just as things were getting interesting, there was an impatient knock at the door. "Well?" Amie called through it.

"She said yes!" Jordan called back.

The door opened and Amie rushed in, grinning from ear to ear.

"She hates squash," he said in a mock whisper.

"I won't ever make it again," Amie promised.

He hugged her. After a minute, Libby joined them. She hugged the housekeeper, too.

"Welcome to the family!" Amie laughed.

And that was the end of any heated interludes for the rest of the evening.

The next few days went by in a blur of activity. When the votes were counted on Tuesday at the primary election, Senator Merrill lost the Democratic candidacy by a ten-to-one margin. A recall of the city fathers was announced, along with news of a special election to follow. Councilman Culver and the mayor were both implicated in drug trafficking, along with Julie Merrill. Julie had managed to get bail the day before the primary, but she hadn't been seen since. She was also still in trouble for the arson conspiracy. Her father had given an impressive concession speech, in front of the news media, and congratulated Calhoun Ballenger with sincerity. It began to be noticed that he improved when his daughter's sins came to light. Apparently he'd been duty-bound to try and protect her, and it had almost killed his conscience. He'd started drinking heavily, and then realized that he was likely to lose his state senate seat for it. He'd panicked, gone to the mayor, and tried to get the charges dropped.

One irresponsible act had cost Senator Merrill everything. But, he told Calhoun, he still had his house and his health. He'd stand by his daughter, of course, and do what he could for her. Perhaps retirement wouldn't be such a bad thing. His daughter could not be reached for comment. She was now being hunted by every law enforcement officer in Texas and government agents on the drug charges, which were formidable. Other unsavory facts were still coming to light about her doings.

Jordan finally understood why Libby had tried so hard to keep him out of Julie's company and he apologized profusely for refusing to listen to her. Duke Wright's plight had made him somber and afraid, especially when he realized how much he loved Libby. He was afraid to take a chance on her. He had plenty of regrets.

Libby accepted his apology and threw herself into politics as one of Calhoun's speechwriters, a job she loved. But, she told Jordan, she had no desire to do it for a profession. She was quite happy to work for Mr. Kemp and raise a family in Jacobsville.

On the morning of Libby's marriage to Jordan, she was almost floating with delight. "I can't believe the things that have happened in two weeks," Libby told her brother at the church door as they waited for the music to go down the aisle together. "It's just amazing!"

"For a small town, it certainly is," he agreed. He grinned. "Happy?"

"Too happy," she confessed, blushing. "I never dreamed I'd be marrying Jordan."

"I did. He's been crazy about you for years, but Duke

Wright's bad luck really got to him. Fortunately, he did see the light in time."

She took a deep breath as the first strains of the wedding march were heard. "I'm glad it's just us and not a crowd," she murmured.

He didn't speak. His eyes twinkled as he opened the door.

Inside, all the prominent citizens of Jacobsville were sitting in their pews, waiting for the bride to be given away by her brother. Cash Grier was there with Tippy. So were Calhoun Ballenger and Abby, Justin Ballenger and Shelby Jacobs Ballenger. And the Hart brothers, all five of them including the attorney general, with their wives. The Tremaynes. Mr. Kemp, with Violet! The Drs. Coltrain and Dr. Morris and Dr. Steele and their wives. Eb Scott and his wife. Cy Parks and his wife. It was a veritable who's who of the city.

"Surprise," Curt whispered in her ear, and tugged her along down the aisle. She was adorned in a simple white satin gown with colorful embroidery on the bodice and puffy sleeves, a delicate veil covering her face and shoulders. She carried a bouquet of lily of the valley and pink roses.

Jordan Powell, in a soft gray morning coat and all the trappings, was waiting for her at the altar with the minister. He looked handsome and welcoming and he was smiling from ear to ear.

Libby thought back over the past few agonizing weeks and realized all the hardships and heartache she'd endured made her truly appreciate all the sweet blessings that had come into her life. She smiled through her tears and stopped at Jordan's side, her small hand searching blindly for his as she waited to speak her vows. She'd never felt more loved or happier than she was at that moment. She only wished her parents had lived to see her married.

Just after the wedding, there was a reception at the church fellowship hall, catered by Barbara's Café. The wedding cake was beautiful, with a colorful motif that exactly matched the embroidery on Libby's wedding gown.

She and Jordan were photographed together cutting the cake and then interacting with all their unexpected guests. The only sticky moment was when handsome Hayes Carson bent to kiss Libby.

"Careful, Hayes," Jordan said from right beside him. "I'm watching you!"

"Great idea," Hayes replied imperturbably and grinned. "You could use a few lessons."

And he kissed Libby enthusiastically while Jordan fumed.

When they were finally alone, hours later in Galveston, Jordan was still fuming about that kiss.

"You know Hayes was teasing," she said, coaxing him into her arms. "But I'm not. I've waited twenty-four years for this," she added with a wry smile. "I have great expectations."

He drew her close with a worldly look. "And I expect to satisfy them fully!"

"I'm not going to be very good at this, at first," she said breathlessly, when he began to undress her. "Is it all right?"

He smiled tenderly. "You're going to be great at it," he countered. "The only real requirement is love. We're rich in that."

She relaxed a little, watching his dark eyes glow as he uncovered the soft, petal-pink smoothness of her bare skin. She was a little nervous. Nobody had seen her undressed since she was a little girl.

Jordan realized that and it made him even more gentle. He'd never been with an innocent, but he knew enough about women that it wasn't going to be a problem. She loved him. He wanted nothing more than to please her.

When she was standing in just her briefs, he bent and smoothed his warm mouth over the curve of her breasts. She smelled of roses. There was a faint moisture under his lips, which he rightly attributed to fear.

He lifted his head and looked down into her wide, uncertain eyes. "Women have been doing this since the dawn of time," he whispered. "If it wasn't fun, nobody would want to do it. Right?"

She laughed nervously. "Right."

He smiled tenderly. "So just relax and let me drive. It's going to be a journey you'll never forget."

Her hands went to his tie. "Okay. But I get to make suggestions," she told him impishly, and worked to unfasten the tie and then his white shirt. She opened it over a bronzed chest thick with dark, soft hair. He felt furry. But under the hair was hard, warm muscle. She liked the way he felt.

He kissed her softly while he coaxed her hands to his belt. She hesitated.

"Don't agonize over it," he teased, moving her hands aside to unfasten it himself. "We'll go slow."

"I'm not really a coward," she whispered unsteadily.

"It's just uncharted territory. I've never even looked at pictures…"

He could imagine what sort of pictures she was talking about. He only smiled. "Next time, you'll be a veteran and it won't intimidate you."

"Are you sure?" she asked.

He bent to her mouth again. "I'm sure."

His warm lips moved down her throat to her breasts, but this time they weren't gently teasing. They were invasive and insistent as they opened on the hard little nubs his caresses had already produced. When his hands moved her hips lazily against the hard thrust of his powerful body, she began to feel drugged.

She'd thought it would be embarrassing and uncomfortable to make love in the light. But Jordan was slow and thorough, easing her into an intimacy beyond anything she'd ever dreamed. He cradled her against him on the big bed, arousing her to such a fever pitch that when he removed the last bit of her clothing, it was a relief to feel the coolness of the room against her hot skin. And by the time he removed his own clothes, she was too hungry to be embarrassed. In fact, she was as aggressive as he was, starving for him in the tempestuous minutes that followed.

She remembered the first kiss they'd shared, beside her pickup truck at his fence. She'd known then that she'd do anything he wanted her to do. But this was far from the vague dreams of fulfillment she'd had when she was alone. She hadn't known that passion was like a fever that nothing could quench, that desire brought intense desperation. She hadn't known that lovemaking was blind, deaf, mute slavery to a man's touch.

"I would die for you," Jordan whispered huskily at her ear as he moved slowly into total possession with her trembling body.

"Will it…hurt?" she managed in a stranger's voice as she hesitated just momentarily at the enormity of what was happening to her.

He laughed sensuously as he began to move lazily against her. "Are you kidding?" he murmured. And with a sharp, deft movement, he produced a sensation that lifted her clear of the bed and against him with an unearthly little cry of pleasure.

From there, it was a descent into total madness. She shivered with every powerful thrust of his body. She clung to him with her arms, her legs, her soul. She moaned helplessly as sensation built on sensation, until she was almost screaming from the urgent need for satisfaction.

She heard her own voice pleading with him, but she couldn't understand her own words. She drove for fulfillment, her body demanding, feverishly moving with his as they climbed the spiral of passion together.

She felt suddenly as if she'd been dropped from a great height into a hot, throbbing wave of pleasure that began and never seemed to end. She clung to him, terrified that he might stop, that he might draw back, that he might pull away.

"Shh," he whispered tenderly. "I won't stop. It's all right. It's all right, honey. I love you...so much!"

"I love you, too!" she gasped.

Then he began to shudder, even as she felt herself move from one plane of ecstasy to another, and another, and another, each one deeper and more satisfying than the one before. At one point she thought she might actually die from the force of it. Her eyes closed and she let the waves wash over her in succession, glorying in the unbelievably sweet aftermath.

Above her, Jordan was just reaching his own culmination. He groaned harshly at her ear and shuddered one last time before he collapsed in her arms, dead weight on her damp, shivering body.

"And you were afraid," he chided in a tender whisper, kissing her eyes, her cheeks, her throat.

She laughed. "So that's how it feels," she said drowsily. "And now I'm sleepy."

He laughed with her. "So am I."

"Will you be here when I wake up?" she teased.

He kissed her swollen mouth gently. "For the rest of my life, honey. Until the very end."

Her arms curved around him and she curled into his powerful body, feeling closer to him than she'd ever felt to another human being. It was poignant. She was a whole woman. She was loved.

"Until the very end, my darling," she repeated, her voice trailing away in the silence of the room.

She slept in his arms. It was the best night of her life. But it was only the beginning for both of them.

* * * * *